PRAISE FOR *THE BUTTERFLY GIRL*

"Denfeld summons the lives of abandoned girls in frank, matter-of-fact detail, never glossing over the filth or violence or the myriad ways in which society lets them down. But ultimately *The Butterfly Girl* is a crime novel with a murderer on the loose. In the final pages, Denfeld speeds up the narrative, creating a propulsive denouement."

—*New York Times*

"Denfeld reminds us that storytelling remains one of the most powerful means we have of confronting our darkest human impulses, and sometimes overcoming them."

—*Washington Post*

"In the hands of Denfeld, *The Butterfly Girl* is a crime thriller built upon redemption. A survivor of trauma who was herself homeless as a young girl in Portland, Oregon, Denfeld knows the harsh truths of her book's world. . . . Amid a steady supply of darkness, *The Butterfly Girl* still has room for light."

—*Los Angeles Times*

"Denfeld tells her twinned stories with a remarkable sense of calm and forbearance in prose that is close to lyrical."

—*Toronto Star*

"*The Butterfly Girl* is edge-of-your-seat taut, balanced with impossibly tender insights. Denfeld's prose is like water: smooth, cool, fluid. While the story itself is painful, it's also brimming with hope and healing. In Denfeld's world, no matter the suffering, there is always love."

—*Guernica* magazine

"Society so often tries to frame homeless people as hopeless victims of their own 'poor' choices. Of course, readers of *The Butterfly Girl* know that this is far from the truth. While [Denfeld] certainly [doesn't] sugarcoat the pain and hardships of a life lived on the streets, each of [her] characters hold on to their own version of hope."

—*The Rumpus*

"[M]arvelously done, and Denfeld's characters . . . are human in the best sense of the word — humorous, loving, scared, and easily rooted for."

—*San Francisco Chronicle Datebook*

"Sharp, often lyrical prose. . . . Ultimately, it's an intense page-turner that leaves the pulse racing. Like a butterfly emerging from a chrysalis, the story unfurls in surprising ways."

—*Oregonian*

"Denfeld depicts the bleak lives of street kids in heart-wrenching detail; the realities of homelessness are rendered in stark language. . . . Denfeld emphasizes throughout that even where there is horror, there is still hope, a theme borne out in the bittersweet conclusion. Readers will be enthralled."

—*Publishers Weekly*

"A heartbreaking, finger-gnawing, and yet ultimately hopeful novel by the amazing Rene Denfeld."

—Margaret Atwood via Twitter

"Equal parts chilling, tragic and hopeful, Rene Denfeld's new novel combines her haunting, lyrical prose with a page-turning and harrowing mystery, putting *The Butterfly Girl* into a league of its own. Fans of *The Child Finder* will devour this."

—Mary Kubica, *New York Times* bestselling author of *The Good Girl*

"*The Butterfly Girl* is a beautiful and very moving novel about lost souls. This heart-stopping thriller left me breathless."

—Shari Lapena, bestselling author of *The Couple Next Door*

THE BUTTERFLY GIRL

THE
BUTTERFLY
GIRL

A NOVEL

RENE DENFELD

HARPER PERENNIAL

NEW YORK • LONDON • TORONTO • SYDNEY • NEW DELHI • AUCKLAND

HARPER ● PERENNIAL

A hardcover edition of this book was published in 2019 by HarperCollins Publishers.

FIRST HARPER PERENNIAL EDITION PUBLISHED 2020.

Designed by Leah Carlson-Stanisic

Art by Mrs. Opossum/Shutterstock, Inc.

Library of Congress Cataloging-in-Publication Data has been applied for.

ISBN 978-0-06-269817-9 (pbk.)

20 21 22 23 24   LSC   10 9 8 7 6 5 4 3 2 1

For Luppi, Tony, Markel, and Tamira.

Loving you gives me flight.

THE BUTTERFLY GIRL

ONE

—

CATERPILLAR

Celia knew a bad place when she saw it.

The abandoned-looking house was in the industrial area next to skid row, where loading docks glistened with moisture and train tracks crossed the broken streets. The windows were covered with boards. What looked like blankets peeked out from under the slats. The front door was heavy and covered with locks.

Celia had been hunting for returnable bottles when she noticed the place. The few houses left in this area were usually empty. Not this one.

She balled her hands in the pockets of her jean jacket and studied the house. Her hair, dirty and musty, but still with a copper sheen, was cut short into wayward curls. She may have only been twelve, but she knew more than most. Or so she told herself. But deep inside her was the fear that she didn't know enough.

A shadow seemed to move behind the boarded-up basement window. Celia froze, then made herself breathe. Someone was looking at her through a tiny pane of glass. She could feel the heat of their gaze. For a second, it seemed that their eyes locked.

Celia disappeared inside herself. She was used to doing that. She could make herself vanish even as she stood there, just another street urchin with no future in sight.

Celia, who believed in nothing but herself and the butterflies, knew that the worst fears of the streets were always real. You can find this out the hard way, or you can be watchful. She backed away, and then ran back to skid row. But she could still feel those eyes in the window, burning into her with something that could have been anger—or might have been hope.

Naomi awoke, and for one brief moment, she thought she was back there. In the place. She heard her sister's voice, calling through the years: *Come back and find me. I'm twenty-five now. The water drips we once felt are gone, and the chariot has flown away.*

Naomi opened her eyes to find herself in her friend Diane's sunny guest room, curled with her husband, Jerome, in a bed once reserved for her alone during her rare visits. She breathed out in relief that the dream was over but still felt the anxious echo of the call.

I'm getting closer, she thought. This was why she was here in the city with Jerome. After almost a year of searching for her long-lost sister, their investigation had brought them here.

Her nose twitched. She could smell fried ham and coffee. The room was filled with sunshine, and Jerome was next to her, the cap of his shoulder rising against the sheet. In a moment she would get up and make her way down the narrow stairs to eat breakfast with her friend.

Diane served the ham with redeye gravy and scrambled eggs flecked with chives. Naomi poured cream in her coffee. She knew Jerome was probably awake upstairs but giving her these few minutes alone with Diane—she appreciated that.

Diane drank her own coffee black, wincing at the taste. She looked at Naomi's cream like it might spite her. "To be young," she said.

"You never worried before," Naomi said cheerfully, adding sugar to her cup.

Diane had aged in the last year. Silver laced her abundant red hair, and lines crossed her face. Her usual warm demeanor had quieted, and Naomi could see the loneliness in the slack skin under her jaw. And in her eyes.

"Staying long?" Diane said hopefully.

"Probably not," Naomi responded, cutting into her ham and tucking a piece into her mouth. "Thanks for letting Jerome come along."

"Of course. He's your husband." Diane said this mildly, but Naomi caught a whiff of disapproval. Disappointment with Naomi? The last time she had seen Diane was a year ago, at their wedding, right here in Diane's living room. Both Naomi and Jerome were thirty. It was their first serious—and for Naomi only—relationship.

She let it go, there among the matching breakfast plates with flowers on the rims, the linen-colored cups, the cream pitcher. Outside the birds were calling, and Naomi heard a crow silence them. She had been raised in the country and could identify a dozen birds by their sound. Yet she could not find her sister.

Diane's hand reached for hers. "You think she might be here," she said, softly.

"We heard about some missing girls," Naomi said, cautiously.

"One might be your sister?"

Diane knew that Naomi had escaped captivity as a child. For most of Naomi's life her only early childhood memory had been running through a strawberry field at night after escaping from a rotten trapdoor in the woods, deep in the Oregon farm valley. A group of migrants had found her and driven her to Opal, a small town an entire day away. Naomi had grown up there, with a loving foster mother named Mrs. Cottle. She was nine when she was found, but no matter how hard she tried, she could remember nothing more of her past. Terror had wiped her memory clean. Naomi had grown up to become an investigator, dedicated to finding missing children. She thought she wanted to find children like herself—but the real truth was that she wanted to find the little sister she had left behind.

Naomi shook her head. "I don't think so. They're too young. But I wanted to check it out. They were dumped in the river here. Those who have been found, at least."

Diane frowned, letting go of her hand. "I hadn't heard about that."

Naomi blinked at her plate. "The Green River Killer murdered at least seventy-five women. Dozens before anyone even noticed."

Diane looked sympathetically at Naomi. She knew how hard it must be to stay inside the center of the storm. "Were these prostitutes, too?" Diane asked.

"Street kids. Does it matter?"

"You know me," her friend said tartly. "Of course it doesn't."

Behind them, she could hear Jerome's soft descent from their guest bedroom upstairs. The man who had once been her foster brother, now her lover, friend, and more.

Diane reached for her coffee, sat back. She didn't know Jerome well.

Naomi looked up, smiled briefly. "Jerome. You explain."

The narrow form of her husband took a chair. He smiled at Diane, dark eyes on her, a hank of black hair falling. The shoulder cap of his missing arm—taken in the war—twitched. "We were visiting the task force in Salem when we heard street girls are going missing here. They're all Jane Does—even their street friends don't know their real names. Some have been murdered; their bodies have turned up in the river. Naomi wants to talk to her detective friend, visit the medical examiner, put up some flyers about her sister—rule out that she might have been one of the girls." He paused. "And maybe use her expertise to do something for these girls."

"I hope this all works out," Diane said quietly, blowing on the hot, bitter coffee.

Jerome reached with his one arm, found the cream pitcher with his long slender fingers, and, without asking, poured a rich stream into her cup. His eyes told Diane he understood what it was like to love Naomi. Diane found solace in his glance.

"Hope is enough," he said.

A heavyset man with a mashed face was watching Celia. He wore a blue jacket zipped up to his reddened neck, the kind of jacket worn by guys who work in automotive shops, only this one didn't have an I AM PETE name tag stitched on the front pocket.

He could be anyone. That was the truth of the streets: If there was danger, anyone could hold it. No one could be trusted, not in the end.

Celia believed this.

The beefy man, his eyes like tiny periscopes on her, could be *him*. The man prowling the downtown streets, making her friends disappear. Some turned up as corpses, floating in the river. Others just vanished. Not that such things didn't happen anyhow, but lately—in this heady spring of rain showers and streets that ran blood dark with freshets—it was happening more and more. Like all the time.

She stole another glance at him. His mashed face, pinched through the nose and eyes, was still watching her. Under his damp silvery hair, two funny-shaped ears protruded like little cabbages. His mouth was torn with scars.

Celia was down on skid row as dusk fell, the last of the business-people rushing, briefcases against their hips, like horses spurring themselves home. Oil puddles, sheened with water, made rainbows under the streetlights, and the night sky rushed away, reminding her the universe was vast. The gay bars were lighting up, the first of the cross-dressers coming out after dark when the night lights were kinder to their coarse faces, the stubble that the razors never quite got. Some had fake eyelashes so long they poked you when they came in for a hug. Which they liked to do, plenty.

She told herself she had nothing to fear. She had her friends for protection: Stoner and Rich, the two boys she hung around, street kids like her. Numbers in safety, Rich once joked. The boys were on the corner now, panhandling, their cold palms damp and empty. "Spare some cash?" they asked the suits whirling by. "I'm hungry, mister." Celia watched as the flood of commuters rushed down the street. Soon all that would be left would be the street people because the night was made for them.

She looked back over at the scar-faced man, but he was leaving. She saw his back and wet shoulders as he walked down the street. The brick wall where he had stood was empty. There was a dry shadow where he had been, like the outline of a shape from an atomic war.

Rich waved to her, a bill held triumphantly in his fist. "Some fool gave me a twenty," he bragged as she came closer. "Let's get some food."

Sometimes Celia thought she was a bird, flying over these

streets. Sometimes she felt more like a slip of air that could disappear, like the tendrils of mist rising from the gutters. But mostly, in her secret heart, she was a butterfly, with magic wings beating hard for escape.

*   *   *

That night Celia called her mom.

The other street kids didn't know she had a mom. None of them talked about that stuff anyways—it was too raw. Some of the kids said they were orphans, but Celia thought probably they were not. Orphans of the heart, maybe.

Celia borrowed a cell phone from another girl and tapped in the newest numbers written on the damp scrap of paper from her jacket pocket, fully expecting this number, too, would be out of service.

But the number was still alive. Maybe, too, the voice on the other end.

"Who is this?" her mom asked softly.

"It's me. Celia," she said, turning away from her friends. She remembered the first time she had heard the term *opioid addiction* and realized they were talking about her mom.

"My baby." In the background Celia could hear the television blaring. She strained to hear any sound of her sister, Alyssa. Now six, the same age Celia had been when her sister was born. The voice lowered. "I miss you."

"How is Alyssa?" Celia asked.

She could hear the airy high in her mother's voice. "She's fine."

When Celia talked to her mom her very pores cried with

sadness, and in just moments she became heady with despair, dizzy enough she had to reach for something to hold on to, which turned out to be the brick wall where she so often stood.

"You coming home?"

"You know I can't, Mom."

There was silence. She could hear her mother's slow breathing. Celia wished she understood this world, the things it did to you.

The other girl wanted her phone back—she poked Celia in her back with a broken nail. "I got to go, Mom. I was just saying hi."

Her mother yawned. "Celia. Is that you?"

Celia ended the call. A life can now be extinguished with the swipe of a finger. Then she went and sat on the curb, the car lights scoping the dark. The men in these cars, like her stepdad, were part of her. Her very cells had tasted them. Her blood coursed with them. But this was her life now, and she had to make something out of it.

*   *   *

Oh, the butterflies. They soften the edges of this hard world. Caught up so high in the sky, they fall to earth like meteorites, their iridescent wings trailing red thunder and liquid gold and the kind of purple only nature can provide.

Celia felt her back scrunch against her denim jacket, then relax. Sometimes she thought she had wings, bare nubs under the skin, and if others said these were her shoulder blades, she would say, Naw, that is where my wings are hiding. She could imagine the other kids along the row having wings, too, folded tight against their backs, wet and pulsating, opening now to feathered wonder. Bright green that flashed, the kind of silver that became light, white that became gold.

There could be legions of us, she thought, flying into the night sky. If all the street kids suddenly took flight, why, the night sky would glow with gold currents. Or maybe, she thought, it would just be her.

With a deep exhale, she flew.

Naomi understood that in investigations, the ground matters.

She had worked dozens of missing child cases, and each search began on the ground. It might be soft and dappled, with fir needles, as in one case of a Boy Scout who stepped off the trail. Or frosted and covered with snow, as in the case of a child gone missing in the Pacific Northwest woods. Or it might be rutted with concrete, a spill of black asphalt steaming on a city street.

The ground mattered because it led her someplace, always. She would find her sister on this earth because of the steps Naomi took on the ground. The thought filled her with impatience to begin.

Naomi knew to go to the darkest streets first. She went looking for the street people.

The place was called Sisters of Mercy, and it existed on a street known for winos and junkies. As night fell, Naomi passed crowds of street nomads, dusty in black leather, and skid row alcoholics with faces like bruised cherries. She saw a skinny old woman with tufts of hair on her balding dome digging through the loam of a gutter, cackling. There was a troubling number of families—mother, father, one or two kids, all with the tired, tense faces of poverty but not much else to say they were homeless but this: the long line.

It snaked around the corner, with the orderly discipline of the hungry. Having worked many missing cases involving the poor—they were usually the ones who needed her the most—Naomi had found they were the most orderly of all. Desperation was a profound governing force.

Cutting past the line, Naomi walked in the front door with scarcely a murmur behind her. That, too, was being poor. They were afraid of not being served, of going hungry. The empty café was filled with tables and rickety chairs, like any other restaurant. Only this one had a nun behind the counter, and her tired, warm eyes caught Naomi's.

"It's not time yet. Back of the line."

In the open kitchen, volunteers were busy cooking: giant vats of what smelled like beans and vast industrial sheets of cornbread coming out of the oven. At a table nearby stood self-serve jugs of water with paper cups. On the wall was a blackboard menu: *Rice, beans, and cornbread, pay what you can. Or work for your meal.*

"I bet you get a lot of dishwashers," Naomi said, stepping close to the counter. She pulled her investigator's license out, expecting the suspicion. "I'm not a cop," she said. "I'm looking for someone. My sister, actually."

The tired eyes met hers. There was a permanent wimple crease in the woman's forehead. "We don't talk about our customers."

"That's nice, that you say 'customers.'" Naomi smiled. "Usually I hear 'client,' like they are here on sufferance, or a boulder around our necks."

This nun apparently was not ready to be charmed. Naomi could feel the body across the counter, under the cloth: the exhaustion, the heavy-boned fight against injustice. "Look. I don't want to make trouble," Naomi said. "Do you have a community bulletin board where I could leave a message?"

There was a terse nod. Then the nun looked over Naomi's shoulder, and now she was genuinely smiling, because it was time. One by one the families and winos and street people filed in, and the nun's voice met each of them with a personal greeting, a name, or a question that sounded like love.

The bulletin board was in the annex of the soup kitchen, where Naomi also found a row of mailboxes so the homeless could get mail, as well as a message board plastered with notes. *Tony, brother, please call me*, read one. *Looking for my birth mom*, with details. Notices for AA meetings. Help for veterans. PTSD support groups.

And the posters for the missing street girls. Naomi read these with a chill in her heart. Most of the missing girls didn't even have real names—they went by street names like Mercedes and Diamond. Rich objects, dream worlds a life away. With relief, Naomi saw a name she trusted on the older posters: *Please call Det. Winfield, state police.* But underneath them were the crime stopper flyers for those found murdered, and these listed the number for the local FBI. Naomi frowned.

Naomi took a flyer from her messenger bag, the text circled in bright yellow so it would get attention. She pinned it in the center of the board.

I am looking for my sister. She is about twenty-five, the flyer said. Naomi had added the few details she could remember: the Oregon farm valley where they had been held captive, the bunker underground where a man had kept them, the year of her escape. She didn't know her own sister's name, so she couldn't add that. And then: *If you know her, tell her I am sorry and I miss her.*

Naomi stepped back.

An old man, querulous with alcohol or other shakes, had come up behind her, as silent as a whisper. Naomi could smell his gummy breath. He blinked, reading her flyer. "There's a lot of girls in this world," he said, grinning at her with horsey teeth.

"I know," Naomi said, huskily.

"What does she look like?" the old man asked, friendly.

"I don't know," Naomi had to admit.

"You ain't got a picture?"

"No."

"What kind of sister are you, to not even have a picture?"

Outside now the line was gone, the sidewalk empty. Behind her, through the dusty window, the tables were all full, the customers eating piles of the delicious-looking beans and the cornbread, cut in slabs and drizzled with honey at the table. A little girl with lank blond hair looked up at her. The mother touched her head, and the child's eyes returned to her plate.

Naomi felt tinny with despair. Night had fallen and she wanted to fall with it. She moved down the street, approaching every makeshift shelter and human sleeping in a doorway. "I'm looking for my sister," she began, each time, but at the end of the block she stopped, suddenly flooded with hopelessness.

This wasn't like her other cases. The fact those other missing children were not her family had allowed her to face the possibility they were never going to be found. Naomi understood now the panic of the parents, how they told her they couldn't breathe as long as their child was missing. Even in her sleep she was searching. If there was any chance her sister was connected to the missing street girls, she would find out. She knew from experience that those on the streets watched out for each other. They might help her.

She passed RVs crowned with tarps, a drunk retching on the curb. Tent camps that appeared overnight in parking lots, the wet sounds of sex in an alley. The lights of bars were ahead of her, the smell of exhaust, the sound of car doors opening and shutting. The red-light district. Naomi could see shapes of what looked like children, begging in the half dark. Begging and maybe something worse.

She moved towards them.

Celia was standing on the corner, the car lights white eyes in the dark. She hated the men in the cars, hated them and their reaching hands, their spongy needs, even as sometimes she, too, got in.

It was better than dying.

That was when she saw the woman coming down the street. The woman was medium-sized, not skinny and not fat. She looked strong. She had long silky brown hair that fell over her shoulders, and she pushed it back, impatient. Celia caught the wink of a ring on her hand. Her skin glowed in the night.

The woman clearly did not belong here, not in these days of sea creatures washed up onshore. What happened in the night was meant to stay secret—like what had happened with her stepdad, Teddy. Celia had made the mistake of telling. She had found out that the people of the day don't want to know what happened in the night.

This woman was a day person. Celia could see it at a glance, and her lip curled.

"Check her out," Celia said to Rich. The big boy looked down at his little friend, eager to see what sparked such scorn. Usually Celia was soft. Not now.

"Probably one of those church types," Rich said.

Celia's eyes were hard and green. "She should go home, then," she said.

The two watched the woman make her way down the sidewalk, talking with the other street kids. The cross-dressers were gone, blown away to the bars like so many drifting feathers from their boas. As the night got later, the people got smaller and harder, until the night whittled them away to nothing. Then it was time to run.

The woman walked into the street to talk to a kid. He was in the middle of what you might call a transaction, hanging in an open car window. The kid turned towards her, shocked at the intrusion, and behind the wheel Celia could see the astonished O of the john's mouth.

"What the fuck is she doing?" Celia asked.

"Maybe she's trying to find her good friend Jesus. He needs his nails redone," Rich cracked, and then looked disappointed that the sick joke had gone right over Celia's head.

Celia felt hot jealousy. She hated the woman instantly. To be so beautifully bold in the night—to walk and ask questions with her shoulders thrown back like she had the *right*. To act like she mattered.

Behind them their friend Stoner emerged from a car, all arms and legs, uncoiling until you could see his skinny height. His long limbs reminded Celia of how butterflies had six jointed legs so they could escape predators. It wasn't working for Stoner. He wiped his mouth, and no one said anything about where he had been, what he had done. He would feel the stain enough on his own.

"Let's go," Rich said, shifting his backpack. They left as the woman turned, the moon lighting her face into something beautiful.

The street kids crossed the river on the creaking footbridge, smelling the muddy water that ran thick below them. The cars on the bridge above them thudded by. Celia thought about the way life was lived overhead: the tall buildings, the big sedans, the groomed drivers. On the other side of the river rose the freeways, and under them a network of nests. The biggest was called the Caves. The homeless had tunneled underneath the concrete overpass, creating a labyrinth of caves. The Caves were ruled by rape, and the street kids stayed far away. Other overpasses were also viciously fought over, sometimes to the point of death: a crumpled body would roll off the freeway incline, only to be picked up the next day with a shrug by the city trucks.

Celia and her friends had no power and got no mercy from the others. They took what was left, the table scraps. But sometimes they found treasures, including a forgotten freeway ramp behind a closed paint factory, the entrance hidden by bushes. They called this place Nowhere. It was code, a way to keep this sleeping place hidden: *Where are you guys crashing tonight? Nowhere.*

The kids darted across the emptying freeways, between the whistling cars, until they came to the paint factory, then slipped under the torn cyclone fence around its parking lot. From there they climbed a steep hill to the overpass above, blackberry bushes tearing their hands. Where the rising freeway ramp met the dirt was a hollow the size of a small room. The ceiling was just high enough for anyone inside to stand up straight.

As they parted the bushes, Celia and her friends smelled old sweat and dust and urine. In the darkness they crouched, pulling food from their backpacks, gulping and tearing in their eagerness to be fed. They forced the food down in soft chunks, afraid even of the sound of their own swallowing. When they were done, they collapsed, simply falling over. But sleep didn't come, not for a long time. The boys lay wide-eyed listening to the cars passing overhead, and as night paled to dawn, these sounds became the metronome of their insomnia and fears. Every rustle of the wind in the bushes outside their cave was a night prowler.

Stoner put his long hand over his eyes and wept in the dark.

Celia lay awake, too. The air around her was blacker than darkness. She thought of the woman they had seen. She felt the jealousy return. The woman was going to sleep someplace, and it was not a dirt hollow under a highway, with spiders biting in the night. It would be a place with a bed that was safe. Not like her—or her sister, Alyssa.

Celia thought of Alyssa. She saw her stepdad, and her eyes glossed with tears. She made herself breathe deep. Butterflies never sleep, she remembered. They rest with their eyes open. This helped her calm down. She focused until she could see them in her mind, flying towards her, surrounding her with gentle flutters. Their wings cupped her ears, soft velvet on her cheeks, their tendrils tracing her closing lids, murmuring reassurance. More of them flew under the overpass, flying in great soft clouds until she was completely covered. They landed on her jeans, her tired feet, her empty middle. They drank her tears. They turned her into a cap of radiant color, and only when she was fully covered did Celia finally feel safe.

"You don't want me coming with you?" Jerome asked Naomi.

It was morning, and they were standing on Diane's porch. The charming Victorian was painted bright colors. Their guest bedroom overlooked the street—Diane had the master in the back, above the quiet gardens. Naomi had met Diane when they both were testifying in a case. They became fast friends, perhaps because Diane accepted the way Naomi moved in and out of her life as she traveled the country for her cases. She had even let her store her case files in the empty attic.

But now Naomi and Jerome were broke. The past year had burned through what little savings they had been able to put aside. Naomi had refused to take on any other cases until she found her sister, and the travel meant Jerome couldn't find work either.

"We need some money, honey," Naomi said with a smile.

"I'm trying," he joked, flexing the one arm. The missing arm spoke for itself: You try finding work with one arm.

Jerome, who had been both a soldier and a sheriff, knew he was an excellent officer and investigator in his own right. But that didn't mean he was going to get hired into a local law enforcement agency, and he didn't know if they would stay in the city anyhow. He'd much rather live out in the country. But that conversation was waiting until they found Naomi's sister. If they didn't find her . . . well, he didn't want to think about that.

The one option he could think of was to become a private investigator like his wife. He wasn't exactly sure what Naomi would think of that. The failures of the past year had left them uncertain with each other. For the first time since she had come into his life, Jerome was hesitant to speak his mind with Naomi.

Jerome wished that someone had taught him how a marriage worked. Without a mother or a father, all he had known growing up was their foster mother, Mrs. Cottle, who, bless her soul, had been widowed. He wanted to be a good husband to Naomi.

She came closer, in for a hug. Surprised, he put his one arm around her, remembered the first time they had made love. Her face under him. "It's going to be okay," he told her, wishing he felt better about himself.

* * *

In Jerome's earliest memories of Naomi, she was a new child in their home, first scared but then full of bravado that slowly stilled into courage. Running along the rock ridges outside Opal, finding the miracle stones left by the petrification of time: quartz and jasper, shiny agates they polished with their shirts, and the ever-present opal. Spit and it will shine.

Their other favorite thing to do was search for old Native American artifacts. Parts of his heritage, like pieces of his own bones picked from the ground. Sometimes they found arrowheads—or what they pretended were arrowheads but were probably just triangular pieces of rock. A few times they found what appeared to be ancient campsites in the woods, with unusually large clearings where the plank houses might have stood. In such places were piles of rocks that did bring treasures, which Jerome was sad he had not kept. Horn spoons and rotting skin bags that fell apart at a touch.

Sometimes in the woods the fir trees gathered in a certain way, and Jerome could see on Naomi's face that there were things she was remembering even if the rest of her had to forget. At these times he took her hand and led her away. He distracted her by telling her about what he had read of his people—information that he would discover was true only some of the time—like how when his ancestors died, their families would tie their belongings in trees.

He and Naomi would walk back to the farmhouse, looking on the underside of every tree, hoping to see a relic from his ancestors. It didn't matter that they never found anything. He was with her, and that was what counted.

* * *

"If it isn't the child finder!"

Detective Lucius Winfield rose from his desk, one large hand held out, the office lights glistening in his short natural hair. Naomi smiled right back. She always felt comfortable in his presence. She took the leather chair, moving restlessly. Naomi could feel the clock ticking.

"What's up?" the detective asked. Winfield had known Naomi for almost a decade—they went back to her earliest missing child cases, some of which had been his cases. Parents often hired Naomi when police cases stalled. Winfield didn't mind sharing, if it got the job done.

"Still trying to find my sister," Naomi told him. She explained all they had done the past year, based on the slim handle of her memory. She told the detective how she and Jerome had combed old farm censuses, visiting dozens of strawberry fields in the Oregon farm valley. They had gone to Arizona and California to inquire after the makers of underground bunkers, seeing if there was a list of buyers. They had interviewed dozens of men imprisoned for stealing children. Her DNA had been swabbed and entered into databases to see if there was a match with unidentified bodies. They had even looked into international child trafficking. Nothing. She couldn't even find out who *she* was. It was as if she had been born the day she escaped, rising from the earth.

But then one day she and Jerome had stopped at a gas station on a country road deep in the valley. A truck of migrant farm workers had pulled up. The women and children were in the back, dark and swaying from the sun. They had pulled out empty plastic jugs to fill with water from the hose. It was Jerome, polished in Spanish, who struck up the conversation. An old woman, crossing herself, said yes, she remembered such a place. It had been an evil place, near a town called Elk Crossing.

"From there it was a race," Naomi told the detective. She and Jerome had finally found the fields, and the bunker in the forests nearby. But the rotten trapdoor was broken, the underground rooms empty. Her sister was long gone. Their captor, Naomi figured, had taken her sister away after Naomi's escape.

"I'm sorry," Winfield said, his voice full of sympathy. "It must have been awful for you to go down there."

Naomi nodded, swallowing the pain. "So we went back to the task force offices, and that's when I heard you got some missing street girls here. Some have turned up murder victims."

Detective Winfield leaned back in his chair, put his hand on his desk. "I should have known that would bring you to town."

"Five girls, all stabbed and found in the river," Naomi said. "At least a dozen other street girls have gone missing according to their friends. You could have another Green River Killer on your hands."

"I know," Winfield said. "We're drowning out there." He waved his worn hand at the city outside his office walls. "You've seen what it's like. Homeless all over the place. And all the ways the vulnerable get preyed upon. Trafficking. Crime. Disease. Murder. I'm up to my neck in cases."

Naomi frowned. "What about social workers and community agencies?"

"They're drowning, too."

"That why you gave the case to the local FBI?"

"I didn't give—they took." His voice was sharp. She saw a flash of anger. "You want to help, be my guest." His voice softened. "Look, we all care. I know you do, and so do I. But I can only do so much. I got over fifty open cases right now. How many you got?"

Stung, Naomi said nothing. She had exactly zero cases if she didn't include her sister. It was easy for her to judge. She felt bad and said so. "I'm sorry."

"Forgiven. If you find anything, if you need my help, you just say so," Winfield said, looking at his watch. "Now, I gotta go. You should go pay the Feds a visit. I think you might be surprised."

"At what?"

"You'll see."

Celia woke to a dome covered with the hieroglyphics of their times. Graffiti saying, *Sweet sickness. Dope. Death was here. Suicide?*

Stoner was at the lip of the overpass, pissing into the bushes. The sun filtering in the thick foliage looked bright. Celia had no idea what time it was. She wore no watch—watches were things of the past—and she couldn't afford a phone.

Her pockets were as empty as her eyes this morning, staring blankly out at the shimmering leaves, tipped with white shadows. Behind her Rich was still asleep, his arm thrown over his face, belly sloping against the dirt.

"Come on." Stoner came and kicked Rich in the leg.

Rich opened his eyes. "I was dreaming," he said.

"Don't tell me."

"Pancakes. A big stack of them, with butter and syrup. And orange juice."

"Fuck you, Rich," Stoner said. Rich rose slowly, groaning from sleeping on the hard ground. Celia shook out her dirty jeans and stomped the dust off her sneakers. Her denim jacket was as filthy as the rest of her. Sometimes she liked being dirty. It felt like she was part of the pavement, part of the city. Or nestled inside a cocoon, waiting for a brilliant birth.

She went to the corner of the cavern and lowered her jeans, pissing in the dirt. "I'm glad I'm not a girl," Stoner said, watching her.

"You're not?" Celia looked up, shaking her rump before pulling on her jeans.

"Ha." He tightened his belt.

Rich took his backpack and turned it upside down, showering the ground with crumbs. "I could swear there were pancakes in here," he said, and strapped it on his back.

Celia and Stoner picked up their empty backpacks. Celia felt her belly clench with hunger. Her stomach didn't even bother making noise anymore. It had learned silence like the rest of her. "Anyone got money?" she asked.

The boys looked away. No one wanted to say what they thought, which was Celia was a bit of a mooch. She was always begging and borrowing off the other street kids, and hardly turning any tricks or panhandling herself. Rich thought she used her tiny size as a charm. Anyhow, everyone was getting tired of it. "Maybe we should be asking *you*, Celia."

Stoner was the first one through the bushes, sending a white ray of sunlight back, piercing their night-shadowed eyes. Rich followed, and finally Celia, nursing her shame.

It always felt longer and hotter to walk back downtown in the daytime.

The street kids had to wait an eternity at the busy freeway, finally darting through the bawling cars. They walked back over the footbridge, the river below now pregnant with reflected light, the swells thick and hung with green particles of life. The smell was cold and fertile, like nature was waiting to give birth.

Nearby, in the industrial area, Celia could see the ancient docks reaching into the river. The waterfront there was muddy, torn up by cars. Johns went down there to park. Creeps, too. Celia tried to avoid it now, after seeing that scary house.

Skid row was chastened by day, empty bottles like holiday streamers in the gutter. The shelter doors were locked. They walked down to Sisters of Mercy, where it was almost time for lunch.

Celia had a powerful prayer for lunch. She wanted it to be served.

They were sweaty and tired by the time they reached the end of the line. Celia felt the hot sun melt the top of her head. It was an unusually warm spring day. Dark clouds lay in a sticky line on the horizon, promising a storm later. The air tasted like a copper penny, and Celia relished this, rolling the electric taste in her mouth.

The line moved slowly. None of the kids said anything. They shuffled. Somewhere behind them, two drunks started arguing and a man threatened to cut them if they didn't shut the fuck up. They did.

Shuffle. Move. Celia could feel the rough sidewalk through the thin soles of her shoes. She could feel each toe pressing down, holding her to the earth. Her mouth felt dusty. Even her ears felt closed, the canals thick. She was inside herself, a contented place to be, buzzing. Butterflies, she knew, live in a world of silence. They do not have to talk.

Rich touched her arm. Celia opened her eyes. He smiled at her, eagerly. She closed her eyes, ignoring him. She wasn't ready to be friends again yet.

Finally it was their turn. Given a plate each, heaped with the beans and cornbread and rice. They took the last table and sat with something like relief. Within moments the food was gone, and Celia stared at her empty plate.

"Are we gonna stay and help clean up?" Stoner asked. His voice sounded tired, like he was talking from the bottom of a deep well.

"Count me out," Celia said, scraping her plate to see if a stray bean might materialize.

"We said we would," Rich said. But when the boys got up, they found there was a ready line of dishwashers working off their meal.

"Come back tonight, to help with dinner," the nun said to the boys.

Celia wandered back into the annex. Her eyes were drawn to the message board and the posters for the missing and murdered girls, some of whom she had known. There in the middle, surrounded by yellow marker, was a brand-new flyer. She stepped closer, lured to it. Another missing girl, this time years ago. Celia shuddered when she read they had been held in captivity. *I am looking for my sister. Tell her I am sorry and I miss her.*

At the bottom was a name and number. Naomi, investigator.

"'Tell her I am sorry and I miss her.'" Celia tried the words out, saying them out loud.

They sounded funny—not ha-ha funny, but sad funny, like that was the last thing she expected anyone ever to admit in public.

* * *

In Celia's own memory she was six and her mother was pregnant. A girl, her mother announced, after a rare visit to the county health office. Celia was old enough to remember a time when her mother was a different person, the kind who went to doctors and even took Celia to the dentist, though they couldn't afford it. Somewhere, in her misty recall, was the feeling of her mom reading to her, the warm softness of her arm.

But then came Teddy. One of Celia's earliest memories was getting up late at night to pee and finding her mother on the couch with her white arm extended. Teddy, crouched as if he were proposing marriage, was sticking a needle in her mother's arm. Her mother had looked up, her eyes thick with sleepiness and guilt. She had been too high to even really notice her daughter.

But Teddy did, later.

He became the proud owner of a swollen drum of a belly he patted, lasciviously. And then it seemed like the day turned over and her baby sister was born. The infant lay in the hospital, wrapped in blankets. She had a dimple between her legs just like Celia, a confusing place of lies and secrets. From next to the hospital bed her stepdad had watched her, a warning on his mouth.

But Celia didn't want to tell, not then. What she wanted was to hold her baby sister, love her, protect her as she had not been protected. She had looked into her sister's sleeping face and promised, in her heart, that she would be her mother.

On the day they left the hospital, no one looked twice at the deflated mother, her eyes closed, sweat of withdrawals on her brow, the tall, lanky man next to her, his face grizzled with a red beard, or the little girl walking alongside, holding no one's hands but her own. Celia often walked that way, hands entwined in front of her like a monk on a stroll, and adults commented, chuckling, how it made her seem old and wise. They didn't know Celia clenched her hands like that to keep her limbs from flying off in fear.

Walking next to her mother and baby sister, Celia felt then, as she often did later, that she moved in and out of buildings and schools, waiting rooms and stores, and no one ever saw her. She was invisible, someone to be erased.

But her sister would be seen. Her sister, she promised herself, would be loved.

That night, on the row, Celia turned a trick. It was just her mouth, she told herself. You can always spit it out.

Her friends watched her climb back out of the car. The look in Rich's eyes was something like sadness. Celia strode up to him, holding out the money. "What I owe you," she said, voice hoarse.

"You can keep it," he said, face turning scarlet in the night. Behind them, loud in the dark, they heard sirens. Sirens all night, sometimes, until it seemed the streets turned into a puddle of flashing lights, spilled blood and mercy.

Some nights seemed made for magic, and this was one. It caught Celia unaware, like the hard breeze off the river, like the clouds rushing overhead. One moment she was standing on the sidewalk, rocking in her thin shoes, eyes half closed to the world, and the next a warm feeling swept through her body until her eyes blazed open.

Like she wasn't really a twelve-year-old street kid, ears closed against the crack of thunder. Like her mouth wasn't open to the pure cleansing rain.

The next morning, crossing the bridge, they watched the men on the patrol boat pull a body out of the river. It was a naked girl, as pale as a fish. The street kids stood at the railing and watched. A group of day people gathered on the esplanade nearby, and they, too, watched as if death were interesting to them, and not a little bit scary. One of them was the woman with the glossy hair. She had her arms folded as if she was enraged.

As the men on the boat hooked the body, Rich asked, "Do we know her?"

Stoner shrugged. "I think she was called Destiny."

The officers were touching the girl's body with more tenderness than she probably ever had felt.

Stoner was watching Celia with his sleepy eyes.

"We'll keep you safe, Celia," Rich promised, but Celia didn't say anything because she didn't think that was possible. It was one of those nice thoughts that had no power. The three of them walked slowly with their heads down away from the river as the boat churned water.

The FBI satellite offices downtown looked designed by someone with a degree in '70s kitsch: glossy mirrors, silver everywhere, burnt orange rugs. The modern desks and the high-tech computers reeked of money, and the receptionist looked like she was trying to fit in. Her silver eyes matched her hair.

"I'm here for Special Agent Richardson," Naomi said, sliding her license across the desk.

"Winfield said you would come," the agent said moments later, coming out into the waiting room, where Naomi was contemplating a recipe for stewed chicken in a cooking magazine. She wondered if there would ever be a day when she owned a kitchen and Jerome would come home to find she had stewed a chicken. Something made her doubt this.

Sean Richardson had glossy black hair that went with his title. He wore the classic Fed suit: pinstripe, with a neat little tie that suggested he was one tight asshole. Naomi disliked him instantly but had expected that: she and the Feds never got along. Unlike detectives like Winfield, they resented her for cracking cases they had spent years on.

He signaled at the chair. Naomi stayed standing. She looked out his window, at the river. "You were the one that solved the Nick Floyd case," Richardson said. He was annoyed at also having to stand, since he didn't want to sit if she wasn't about to.

Naomi glanced over. "I was glad to help," she said, gently.

"I read what you said about our office."

Naomi smiled, to herself. She didn't feel bad. Men like this were nothing. All she trusted in life was love, and none of it was here.

"I told the press that you are a bunch of bumblers who would make a beat cop look like a genius, and the only reason you get away with such ineptitude is the public has a bizarre and inexplicable belief in the FBI. I'm pretty sure they quoted most of that."

"All except the 'bizarre' part. No one likes to question the public."

Naomi turned. She saw the ghost of a smile on the man's face. Well. Maybe this was a new breed of special agent.

He came to the window. Both of them studied the river. "That's six now," he said, quietly.

He turned towards her. She saw his eyes were brown, and his eyebrows unruly. He had freckles on his cheeks. Another human. "I've got a good man on it, undercover," he said. "He's trying to break it from inside."

Naomi thought of the Floyd case. Nick Floyd was a generic-looking man who had led a generic-looking life, only he had kidnapped and murdered over twenty children. The previous FBI agent had fumbled the case badly, first releasing confidential information, then targeting a false subject for no other reason than that he was black and mumbled when he talked. By the time that poor man had finally been let out of jail, the trail had gone cold, and since the media had moved on, the FBI had tried to ignore the whole mess.

Naomi had been hired by the parents of one of the boys. It turned out the evidence had been under the agents' noses the entire time: a wet, almost indecipherable receipt from a feed store stuck in the bottom of the boy's backpack. The family owned no livestock. The receipt had led to a common point of intersection for all the children: the Floyd Family Feed Store, where kids were welcome to pet the baby chickens.

Naomi knew it wasn't callousness or indifference. The Feds just didn't have the right experience. They wanted to think men like Nick Floyd were smarter, more brilliant and cunning and unique than themselves. They didn't want to accept that the reason so many crimes against women and children went unsolved was not because a handful of brilliant sociopaths were outwitting the police at every turn. It was because people let such crimes happen.

It puzzled Naomi because she knew from experience that most people were good, or wanted to be good. They just couldn't see that fellow people were capable of being monsters, their own family and friends included. So they had to pretend such men were different, and in pretending they took away their own greatest power to stop them.

For Naomi, the men—and occasional woman—who took children were not her concern. The only thing that mattered was how they got away with it. They were doors to walk through to find the children. She refused to romanticize them by pretending they were extraordinary. This, she told herself, would include her own captor. If she found him—and finding her sister would probably mean finding him—she would look at him and know there was nothing special about him at all. She hoped.

"I still don't think you guys are right for it," she said. "Winfield knows more. Hell, I know more. Go back to busting PTA moms stealing the bingo money and claim it was first-degree embezzlement."

Sean Richardson surprised her by laughing. His brown eyes were on her, and he seemed delighted. Naomi suddenly felt mysteriously close to him. Maybe love was in these offices, too.

"Do you have a daughter?" she asked.

"No." He swung his hand towards the river, the city. "The world is my child. Funny, I know. But I feel that way. That's how I came to this work."

"I like you," Naomi said.

"Then you are going to leave well enough alone?"

"No."

* * *

For years Naomi had no memory of her captivity except for running through that strawberry field at night, her naked heels striking the black dirt. Running in terror to escape, only to turn back, horror filling her, not knowing why. Until one morning she had woken from sleep screaming a single word.

Sister.

After realizing she had left her sister behind, Naomi had expected that more memories would come—an avalanche of them, burying her in fear and regret. But that hadn't happened. What Naomi had willed herself to forget as a child had stayed forgotten. Maybe that part of her mind had erased the experiences, tossing them away like spoiled food. Or maybe the memories were waiting for when she was strong enough to access them.

Only one detail had come back. She was with her sister, deep underground, while the ceiling dripped. It was dark in the bunker, and a lamp cast yellow shadows. Her little sister was looking up, trust in her face, hazel eyes like her own.

Naomi was singing to her sister, softly. The lamplight flicked over them.

"Swing slow, sweet chariot," she had whisper-sung, "coming for to carry me home."

The song had a meaning that now filled Naomi with remorse. *If you get there before I do, tell all my friends I'm coming, too.*

It was a sin, Naomi knew, to forget. People stop existing once you forget them. Naomi had committed an unpardonable sin, and it didn't matter how many times others made excuses for her, like saying she had been a child or she had lived in terror. She had forgotten the one who mattered the most, and there would be no life, no future, until she found her. When she found her sister, she would beg forgiveness.

Naomi spent the rest of the day exploring downtown, hanging flyers in businesses and talking to people. Not just in the growing skid row district, where the street kids would prostitute themselves later. She walked all of it. The shopping malls, the delis and cafés tucked in the alcoves of buildings. She saw where the drug dealers hung out, and the addicts, and the women leaving department stores, wrangling large shopping bags and chattering like magpies.

Naomi thought about what it would be like to be one of the homeless kids she had seen. She wondered what it was like to live on the streets, where every doorway was a different hiding place, every tall man a knife.

On a deserted street back on the edge of skid row, she went into a corner market and got a drink. Outside she tried calling Jerome. His phone didn't pick up. She hoped it meant he was finding work. Maybe it was unfair to ask him to work, but the thought of not looking for her sister made Naomi feel sick at heart.

Dusk was falling, and a cold fog was rolling up the emptying streets. Walking along the street, Naomi found the downtown public library. The stone facade was lovely, damp with the mist.

Public libraries were often places where street people hung out.

She would talk to the librarians and post some of her flyers.

Celia was in the library. It was her favorite place to be, besides her own imagination.

She perched, sneakers swinging, in one of the wood chairs. The hard chair didn't bother her. Nothing bothered her in the library. Her head floated up to the clouds, the ornate ceiling above, and when her hand touched the burnished rails of the marble staircase, she became part of the world.

The best part of the library was becoming one with the butterflies.

She carefully turned a page. She was reading her favorite book on butterflies, the one with the dull blue cover that gave no hint to the treasures inside. The edges were grayed to the point of silver. Like the dust of butterfly wings, Celia thought. The elderly librarian kept this book behind the counter just for Celia. It was a secret they shared—a good kind of secret. Once, when she was in third grade, a neighbor had invited Celia to her house for soup. The librarian reminded Celia of that neighbor. It helped her remember there were nice people in the world. She didn't blame them for what happened. They were too busy taking care of each other.

Celia could spend hours inside the book. She touched the color plates with her dirty fingers. The butterfly colors leapt off the page: a skyrocket of red, the brightest blue you ever saw, the gold of a perfect sunset. On pieces of scrap paper nearby she drew pictures of the butterflies, some fantastical, some real. When she was done, she tucked these inside the book, like treasures.

"Celia?" It was Rich, in a hoarse whisper. Rich hated the library. He said the library made him smell like piss. Of course that wasn't really true; it was just the warm, dry, close air that made it obvious. Celia didn't tell him this.

"You can go. I'll come later," she told Rich, who put down his comic book.

"It's almost dark—" he began.

"I'll catch up to you. You know where." Celia was lost in the butterflies.

Rich left. It was getting wet and cold outside, moisture dripping from the building eaves. The last of the day people were leaving their offices, hurrying through the darkening mist. Overhead a giant black clock ticked. Seven o'clock.

In the room above him, Celia was swinging her feet, smiling and reading. She pulled a piece of paper forward to draw another butterfly.

Outside the man with the mashed face and cauliflower ears was waiting. He saw Rich leave. The girl was alone, inside.

* * *

What is it you want?

When the butterflies talked to Celia, it was like the sweetest notes of music. She could hear them coming from afar. She could see them now, covering the misty library windows. They were above the fantastic chandeliers, flying all around, as thick as fabric flowers above the bowed heads of readers. She named them as they passed: painted lady, swallowtail, viceroy, brush-footed, gossamer. The original brimstone. Metalmarks, hairstreaks, nymphs, and skippers.

There was no creature at all like the butterfly—they were unique animals unlike any other. It wasn't just their wings, covered in thousands of tiny reflecting scales. It was the truth of their complex bodies, their all-seeing eyes, their feelers. They landed on the table and smiled at her, tapping with musical feet. She smiled, drawing a wing.

Sometimes the butterflies sang to *her*, Celia, and their songs were like bits of music, the sound of a piano maybe. A single finger on a key, the note hanging in the air, too pretty to fall. Celia's eyes filled with tears as the butterflies gave voice to her own wonder.

I want to be okay, she answered the butterflies. And the butterflies said yes, of course. They had promised this, from the time before she was born. They had made her mother promise this, too, before it was too late and the darkness overtook her.

One, two, three. Look!

The library lights flickered on and off above her, and the butterflies startled, rising in thick clouds. It was time to go. Celia slid her drawing into the book, gave it a kiss, and rose. Like the others with nowhere to go, she went down the stairs.

* * *

Having a baby sister had changed everything in Celia's world.

Before, she became a wooden tree left in the bed where Teddy came on nights when her mom passed out on the couch. He put his thing into the hollow of the tree trunk, then held its lifeless branches until he groaned. But then her sister was born. During those long days when her mother slept, or sweated and moaned, waiting for her fix, it was Celia who rocked the baby, changed her diapers, learned how to mix the formula, and later, standing on a stool at the stove, boiled the carrots she mashed, testing with her own tongue to see if they were cool enough for the baby to eat. It was Celia who learned to read so she could understand the words in the Dr. Spock book she had found on the living room book-shelf. It was Celia who called the ambulance one night because she misunderstood the thermometer and thought her baby sister was dying of fever. Her mother, she explained to the ambulance driver, had the flu. That was why she slept through the entire incident.

It was because of her sister that Celia discovered time. Before she knew it, her infant sister was kicking in the dirty high chair, sucking on a pork-chop bone. Then she was two, and three, play-ing with pots and pans on the floor while Celia stood on a stool at the stove, cooking dinner. Celia, too, grew in these years, but she never stopped being a tree.

It had happened when Alyssa was five and Celia was eleven. She watched her sister change from being a baby to having a shape around her mouth, to having legs that lengthened and arms that took on a honeyed hue in the sun. She had the same copper hair as

Celia, only lighter. She's a pretty girl, strangers started saying, and deep in Celia the alarm sounded.

Make it me, Celia prayed. I will be the tree.

One day Celia took Alyssa out in their backyard to look for butterflies. The backyard had not been mowed for years. Celia liked it this way. There were little garter snakes in the grass, and baby toads, and sometimes the most precious of all, butterflies. "Butterflies are magic," she told her sister as they hunted carefully in the tall grass, Celia whispering the names when they saw the ones she could identify.

A shadow fell over them. It was Teddy, come home from work. Teddy worked construction, and it was his money that bought the dope her mother now needed. Her mom was as captive to Teddy as Celia was captive to being a tree. He was standing behind them, a fresh beer in one hand, scratching his belly with the other. His blue eyes were on Alyssa. And in that moment, Celia saw how her stepdad was looking at her baby, the speculation in his glance. The planning. *No*, her heart cried, I will not let this happen.

The next day she went into the nurse's office at school and reported what was going on at home. She knew exactly what she was doing; she was telling on Teddy to save her sister. She was going to save all of them.

It was the greatest mistake of her life.

Naomi was climbing the steps to the library when a teenage boy came out. He had the unwashed look of a street kid, and his furtive glance, his eyes widening slightly, told her she was on the mark. She reached out, but the boy lowered his head and hurried off. The evening was getting cold, more rain clouds coming.

It was then she saw the man. He looked like a former boxer, his eyebrows broken with scars, his lips thick with keloids. He wore a blue repairman jacket, zipped up, old trousers, worn shoes. Silvery hair hung down to his chin. Not quite down-and-out, the look said. Dangerous. The man felt dangerous to her.

The man looked back at Naomi indifferently. His thick lips smiled, but it was a cold smile. He was standing under a small alcove sheltering him from the misty rain. Like he was waiting for someone.

Naomi went inside.

"We're closing," the librarian said as soon as she entered, not even looking up from her desk. She was absorbed in a worn paperback copy of *The Shell Seekers*, by Rosamunde Pilcher. Naomi smiled. It was one of her favorite comfort books, too.

"I have some flyers," Naomi said, coming closer. "And a few questions, if you don't mind." She showed her detective license. The librarian put down her book, sliding a homemade crochet bookmark in place, and then put on the sparkly glasses hanging on her neck, leaning over.

A girl was coming down the marble stairs, holding a thick book. She was small and slender, wearing a dirty jean jacket. She had a heart-shaped face under a mop of messy hair, and her green eyes seemed to view the world with trepidation. She was absolutely filthy. Naomi saw a stain of dirt on her cheek as she came closer.

A part of Naomi pinged. She remembered only too well thinking they wouldn't notice you hiding behind the dirt. But it never worked that way.

The girl glanced at Naomi, then quickly looked down. She slid the book back over the desk. Naomi caught a glimpse of the title, something about butterflies, and saw how the pages were stuffed with pieces of scrap paper. She thought of her own fascination with the wilderness after escaping captivity. The outdoors represented more than nature. It represented freedom.

The librarian smiled gently at the girl. "Thank you, Celia. See you tomorrow?" The girl nodded shyly. The librarian reached under the desk and, with a conspiratorial wink, passed the girl a small jar of nuts. Blushing with pleasure, the girl took it.

The girl cast a green-eyed glance in Naomi's direction that was hard to read, and then hurried for the big black doors. The librarian watched her leave. She sighed. "I wish I could take her home," she said. "I wish I could take them all home."

Naomi remembered the man on the steps. "Excuse me," she told the librarian, leaving the flyer on the desk to go after the girl.

Outside the mist was catching the streetlights, flickering with reflected colors. Shadows marched up and down the empty streets like the legs of monsters. The girl was at the bottom step, moving fast, with the energy of youth.

The scar-faced man had left the stoop. He was trailing her.

*　*　*

Celia, unable to contain the excitement of a world that brought butterflies and rain, almost danced in her movement. She raced towards a group of pigeons, waving her arms and sending them to flight: gray and magenta, tipped with a green so brilliant she couldn't help but smile. The pigeons made a sound like the best of mothers, cooing, and in Celia's mind they were cooing at her.

The man behind her melted into the shadows so easily that even Naomi, an expert tracker in her own right, was impressed. Impressed and more than a little scared. Not for herself but for the girl.

Naomi was aware of how empty the streets were here. A child could be grabbed, easily, and hustled into a dozen hiding places. The girl was about a block away, the man still trailing her. At any moment they might turn a corner and disappear.

Naomi began to run.

At the very last moment the man heard Naomi and spun around, light flashing on his scarred knuckles. The expression registering on his broad, pebbled face was one of consternation. His mouth opened, but then closed. Backing up quickly, he moved with surprising grace and ducked into an alley. He was gone.

Breathing heavily, Naomi stopped. The girl had whipped around, too, backing up a couple of steps while taking everything in. She quickly covered her fear with a protective sneer. The streets were silent.

"Your name is Celia, isn't it?" Naomi asked.

"How did you know?"

"The librarian. She said, 'Thank you, Celia.'"

"I remember you from the row," the girl said. "The church lady."

"What makes you think I'm a church lady?" Naomi asked, catching her breath. She smiled now, at ease.

"I saw you down there. You don't belong."

"Belong here, or there?"

"Anywhere."

Taken aback, Naomi thought: She's like a messenger. A messenger from my past, speaking my own sins, my fears. The girl was staring at Naomi with the kind of hate that comes from envy. Just for a moment Naomi saw it: she wants to be like me, but she's afraid she never will be. The night had come up behind the girl, darkening her ears, catching the copper of her hair. Soon it would be pitch black, and a girl like this—well, she could disappear.

"I was worried for you, with that scary man following you," Naomi said. "I'm an investigator. I specialize in finding missing children."

A blink. No response. Naomi was close enough to see the lines of dirt on her grimy neck. She wondered when this kid last had a bath.

"How old are you?" she asked. "What's—"

The street boy Naomi had seen earlier had reappeared down the street. The little girl turned and saw him, and her whole face collapsed in relief. She's afraid, Naomi thought. She doesn't know who to trust. I don't blame her.

I know what her life has been like.

I'm glad I came back for you," Rich said to Celia.

They were on the row, in the circus of lights. A bunch of frat boys were downtown, and the air was sharp with them. Celia preferred old men, for the times she had to. Old men were soft and called her "darling" and "little baby." They wanted to pretend she was their daughter. It was gross, but something Celia told herself she knew.

Young men—they were made of blades. They liked to hurt, and skid row turned into a bloodbath when they were downtown.

"Thank you." Celia came forward and leaned her face against his chest. Rich froze. In his wildest dreams Celia was doing exactly this. He lifted up his arms, slowly, to capture her, but she moved away. The moment was gone, stolen by the night. It was almost like it had never happened. Rich felt sick with despair. Nothing in this life was made for him.

"Hey, ya fat fag," a frat boy called out of a car, as if to prove the point. The other frat boys hung out of the windows, faces wet with drink. Rich imagined scythes cutting close to the car, taking them all off at the waist, their bodies falling with a clunk, lips and blinking eyes able to say no more.

"You're not gay, are you, Rich?" Celia asked, curious.

No, he shook his head, and his very soul ached with loneliness.

That night it was like a party on the streets. Rich and Stoner were there, of course, but so was everyone else and more. Bags filled with glue, to be huffed in the dark alley shadows. Someone carrying a gas can up a street clogged with cars. A junkie falling in a fit, drunks with wet groins, one of the frat boys vomiting against the wall while his friends, all in polo shirts, pitched bets and urged more.

Sometimes Celia hated life. She hated it even as it unfolded, even when it seemed so wondrous. The night sparkled and showed her more:

A man saying "Touch this" and "You get a dollar, my sweet," and looking down to see the bulge of his groin, hearing his manic giggle. Dancers swaying with arms around trannies and slim-hipped boys in the night. Wondering what was in her drink, the soda someone—was it a friend?—had passed her. Black cherry cream, her favorite.

Sometimes the streets felt like acid. You didn't need to drop it to know this. You could crawl in the gutter, taste the same dank butts as anyone else, marvel at the view. You could stand below strip club lights, seeing the whirl of a dozen lovely girls—and hear the catcalls of the men outside. Their voices were rich with want, heady with sweat and something she could not name but hoped was love. That's all she wanted.

She felt hands grabbing her, pushing her towards the entrance, saw the security man at the door, smirking. He was large and had a greasy smile like Teddy, and this set off alarm bells in her. Celia jerked back, trying to get away. The men outside, drunk on lust, swung her around, catching her in their tangled arms and rude laughing faces, ugly teeth yellow and crooked, until suddenly she felt a hand on her and—

Everything stopped.

"I got you." It was a small man in a tidy suit. In her befuddled state Celia saw only a slim dart of a being, with blue eyes flashing behind round glasses. He had bright silver hair, cut short at the sides, and looked far too elegant for the streets.

"Hey." It was Rich, and he was reaching for the sodden Celia, and the nice man handed her over, smiling tightly. Celia crouched at the gutter, vomiting.

"I think someone spiked her drink," the man told her friends. "She ought to be careful of what she drinks on the streets."

"What happened?" Celia asked what felt like hours later, wiping the wet from her chin, aching all over. The sun was coming up.

"Let's go sleep," Stoner said, circles of exhaustion around his eyes.

Which was how Celia woke up to the concrete dome of the overpass above her. She was lying on her back in the dirt, the smell of urine around her, and above, the thud of passing cars counted out the time. When she felt this sick, it was hard for the butterflies to come, and this alone was reason not to do drugs or drink. The butterflies might abandon her forever, just as they had her mother.

* * *

One butterfly.

She was in a courtroom, shaking. The victim advocate—a booming woman who kept saying everything would be all right—had told her just to take the stand. Tell the truth, they all said, but how can you tell the truth when the lie is right in front of you?

Teddy.

Two butterflies.

It took most of a year even to get there. Can you imagine? A year of her mother crying, listening to Teddy on the jail phone saying he had done nothing, she would know if he had, wouldn't she? And her mother finally saying yes. The addiction not going away but getting worse, fed by the money Teddy sent. Two candles her mother put on the mantel. "We are going to light these every night Teddy is in jail," her mother said, as the candles flickered, and the look she gave Celia was haunted, like she had made a choice she had since forgotten.

Three butterflies.

Celia losing herself in the maze of lies, questioning her own reality, watching her mother talk to social workers, telling them it couldn't possibly be true. Celia knew her mother couldn't tell anyone about the syringes under the couch, about how the drugs had taken over her own life. She might go to jail, too. Celia in the bathtub with a strainer in her hand, watching the water pour through the holes. Who was telling the truth?

All Celia had to do was look at her sister to know she was.

Alyssa, her beloved. Taken by child services because of the allegations of sexual abuse in the home. Why did they leave Celia then? Not enough foster homes, especially for older kids, she was told. Teddy was in jail, they said. Celia was safe. They didn't know her mother, how strong her addiction was, how open her veins were to Teddy's lies.

Four butterflies.

Alyssa finally coming home. Different. Smelling of laundry soap from another home. Having learned to wipe her mouth as she ate, all dainty like. Flossing her teeth every night, which Celia never did, and she felt guilty and angry she wasn't the one who had taught her. Talking about her foster family like they were the ones who really loved her, saying they had wanted to adopt her and she hadn't wanted to come home.

"Light a candle for your father, dears. The one *Celia* put in jail."

Five butterflies.

That final day in court. Led to the witness chair by the victim advocate, her hand imprisoning Celia's wrist. Celia sitting down, quaking, seeing Teddy there, in a suit next to his public defender. The lawyer had stood, smoothing out his jacket.

"Miss Celia . . ." The attorney had stepped forward, victory already in his eyes. "What does your family call you?"

She had felt the roof of her mouth with her tongue. Looked over the people in the pews, all looking back at her. The judge was a black vulture at her back. In the midst of all this was her mother. She sat with her head bowed. She wore a pretty new dress, long sleeves over the marks. Her eyes looked up, full of guilt that ran to the bones.

Six butterflies. As old as the sister you will lose.

"They call me Celia the liar," she had said, and was surprised at how clear it came out.

Naomi had put up flyers, visited her detective friend, paid her call to the Feds. Seen some street kids, asked around about shelters.

It was nothing, she told Diane in her mind, driving to her house in the puttering Datsun. By the time she got in the door the echoes of her mind were no longer soft and listening, but hard and frustrated.

"I'm not doing anything on this case!" she barked to Jerome and Diane, both in the kitchen, looking up from the homemade pizza they were taking out of the oven. Jerome's eyebrows rose, and Diane's merely arched. Her entire being said, Don't even.

"You mean your sister or the street girls?" Diane said, wiping her floury hands on a towel. Jerome glanced from where he was testing the pizza.

"Both." Naomi pulled out a chair hard.

"Mind your manners."

"I'm not five."

"You're acting like it." That was Jerome.

Naomi whipped on him. "Maybe you should get a job."

Dead silence followed that. The whole kitchen took on a polar chill. Naomi felt the tick of shame in her belly, the rising fear. She wanted to apologize, but Jerome turned and left to go upstairs. She had never seen the look he had on his face before. It wasn't even anger.

It was distance.

"Naomi. Honey." Diane was coming to her, moving her hands toward her head. Naomi leaned in, unwilling. "I'm sorry," she murmured, against Diane's hair, once so silky, now brittle. Naomi could feel something, deep in her friend, something that felt like sadness, but in her own distress she let it slip away.

"It can only take a minute to ruin a lifetime, my dear." Diane's voice was firm against her. Her arms held Naomi tight. "Just like your cases. It only takes a minute to ruin a life."

Naomi collapsed. The anger ran out of her. She fell into the chair, crying helplessly into her hands. "I keep trying," she kept saying.

Diane lowered herself carefully and held Naomi's knees. "Trying to do what, my dear?"

"To remember."

"And you think you need to?"

"I don't know."

"You think you failed because you haven't found the one you think matters the most. But Naomi. My dear. Your sister isn't the one who matters the most."

Naomi lowered her hands. Her face was wet with tears and hard with fear. "Who does, then?"

"He's upstairs right now. The future."

Naomi stood up so hard the chair knocked over. She left the house.

They didn't talk for two days. Them—once foster siblings, running in meadows, fashioning whistles out of split grass, teaching each other how to skip stones play leapfrog jump rope double dutch fly-fish do algebra drive a tractor look in my eyes now Naomi. Two children who once couldn't go ten minutes without a serious smile or giggle, who fell asleep telling each other stories—now silent.

At one time, not long after their marriage, when as adults they had realized the truth of their love, Naomi had woken up thinking she had swallowed Jerome's missing arm and was going to make it for him, like a paper wasp spits a nest, and when she told him this, he had merely smiled, and looked at the empty space his arm would take, and said, "I can see it already."

I wanted to be your future, she thought.

You are making me the past, he thought.

Diane's thoughts whirled in her room, trying to figure out a way to make things right between Naomi and Jerome. But she knew better. The silence in the house was two young people stuck in a sea of stubbornness. Like so many of their era, and maybe like people of all times, they had no role models.

Naomi's entire body was filled with self-loathing when she and Jerome were not talking. Naomi, too, remembered the hunts for artifacts that she now suspected were more about love than arrowheads or bundles in trees. In Jerome's own child face she had seen the hunger for a place to call home. He didn't know how deep her own longing ran, or the terror. For Naomi, home could be a prison.

But it had happened anyway. One day—whether looking into trees for treasures tied in the branches or picking up agates on the ridges—she had fallen in love with him, and it had taken her most of her life to admit it.

Not knowing what else to do, she made a list:

Jane Doe bodies, morgue
Psychiatric hospital? Maybe she was committed.
Stop in/visit every homeless shelter

And last but not least:

Who is that man? The one with the scars.

Riding the bus made Celia sleepy. She closed her eyes, putting her cheek against the soothing chill of the window glass. She folded her hands inside her thighs and dozed off. She was aware of the warm bus, the smell of other poor people around her, someone playing loud music through their ear pods.

She was on her way to visit her mother.

At stops she heard the accordion hiss, felt the bus lower. She was counting the stops as she dozed, feeling back in time as the distance between stops got longer and glimpses of yards furred with weeds and grass, gnarled apple trees, and gutters rusted with moss ran through her mind. In her dreams she was running beside the bus, feeling the wind in her lungs. Then she was tired and rode back inside her body. The butterflies, floating against the window, were tapping. Celia, they said. You are no liar. You never were. Remember that.

"Mom?" She stood on the dime-sized concrete porch, peeking in the broken screen door. Inside was a haze of stale cigarette smoke and the din of the television. "Mom?" This time louder, a little squeak in her voice.

"That you, Celia?"

Her mother's voice was hoarse with sleep and sickness. Celia could tell in that moment her mother was on the same afghan-covered sofa. It felt like Celia's heart broke and fell to the ground in pieces, so much she had to crouch to scoop them up and shove them back in her chest.

"Yeah. It's me." She saw her hand reach out, slowly. She heard the creak of the screen door, paused. "Teddy isn't here, is he?"

Silence. A quiet no.

An hour later, Celia stood at the sink, washing dishes. She had picked up the floor, swept cigarette butts, cleaned the foul mess of the litter box. One of the cats was nowhere to be seen, and her mother, slipping in and out of her nod, couldn't seem to remember when it went missing. Celia hoped it hadn't been hit by a car. Maybe a nice neighbor had taken it.

Her mother lay on the couch, a dried-out washcloth over her face. Celia took it, wringing it out with fresh cold water and putting it back. Her mother sighed. Celia picked up ashtrays and the dirty clamshell takeout containers with petrified fried rice.

"That you, Celia?" her mother asked again.

Celia stood and looked at her. She didn't know why she kept coming back. Nothing changed. She remembered a junkie on the street telling her that his brain felt like a fuse, burned out and dry. Maybe her mom had lost her memory, too.

"It's me, Mom, remember?"

"Oh." Her mother turned her head. "Can't you come home, Celia?"

"We've talked about that, Mom. You know I can't."

"Teddy would forgive you."

"I didn't lie." It took all of Celia to say it. Her mother's disbelief was like a stone in her throat. Her whole stomach felt filled with the sickness of it. Her mother's mouth moved, but no words came. After a moment, they did.

"That's not what the jury said," her mom whispered.

Celia went into the tiny, messy bathroom. Using her mother's scissors, she hacked at her hair until it was short again. She liked looking more like a boy—it was safer on the streets. She went back to cleaning the kitchen and left when she was done.

The pavement behind the school was broken with time, sprouting grass from the cracks like whiskers on an old man's chin. The metal bars of the jungle gym, glossed by decades of dirty hands, cast long shadows.

Celia was hungry. She should have tried to find something to eat at her mom's house. She thought of the always dirty, crowded fridge, the bags of old meat leaking brown juices. The last thing she was able to teach Alyssa was to make sure and ask the lunch lady if she could help for extra food.

She saw her sister coming out in a group of other girls. Celia was always too dirty, too ashamed, for friends. And once she had reported, everyone knew. *Fuck bag*, some of the boys called her, and tried to stick their fingers up her shorts. *You already did it, so what's the big deal?* Celia hadn't worn shorts since.

Her sister saw her. An uncertain smile. Celia, filthy in her street clothes, aware now that she smelled. Maybe she was her mother after all. Just dirty in another way.

"Hi, Alyssa," Celia said. The other little girls tittered nervously. Alyssa stared up at her sister, and her friends left to find their parents. Celia and Alyssa were alone on the blacktop.

"You look nice," Celia said.

Alyssa was wearing a decent shirt and cleanish pants. Celia could imagine her, closed into their bathroom, trying to stay clean. She had been brushing her hair, but had missed a big spot in the back, and there was a knot. Celia reached for it, but Alyssa jerked away.

Why not you? Celia wanted to cry out. She had done everything to save her sister, yet her sister hadn't needed to be saved. Was there something wrong with Celia? Had it all been for nothing?

Acquitted, the victim advocate had told Celia after the verdict. She had to explain what the word meant. "You mean he is coming home?" Celia had asked, terror grabbing her throat.

The very next day he did, and Celia couldn't go to school for a week for the beating that followed his return. Celia didn't wait for the next beating. Or rape. That was the only good thing she got out of the entire trial—she learned the right words for what Teddy had done. That night she had taken her backpack, some clothes that were soon stolen, and ridden the bus downtown. She had been lucky enough to meet Rich while she was wandering the streets, trying to look tough when really she was so scared.

All for nothing. Because now, as her sister stood before her, Celia didn't think Teddy had ever touched her. Not in that way, at least. Alyssa was looking up at Celia with something like suspicion. No doubt she was thinking what everyone else said: that Celia had made it up. The jury had said so.

But it was true, Celia wanted to say. I told to save you.

All the way back downtown—walk, buses, walk—Celia engaged in her favorite pastime, which was to daydream. "Dream by day," her teacher Mrs. Wilkerson once told her. "Dream by night. Your imagination can save you, Celia." Reality is whatever you chose to see: the face of a gnome in the grass, a construction team of elves on an anthill, the way tree leaves lace together to make messages only you can read.

And yes, the butterflies. They cascaded around her now, tickled her tired feet, lifted her shoes all the way back to the bus stop. They rode next to her through the bus window. As she got off downtown, one grabbed hold of a strand of her hair. Celia laughed. She could remember being a little girl in a sun-splashed meadow with her mother. She could feel her wings open.

What are you doing, Celia?

Flying, she told the imaginary person in her mind.

Arms out now, running through the downtown streets, seeing the shocked faces of the day people as she passed. Celia the butterfly, brilliant green, blue, red like a star. Celia the truth.

Rich looked up to see his friend running down the middle of skid row, her arms stretched out, a glorious look on her face. It was funny—he could almost see the shine of her wings. People stood back, watching her fly.

Celia. Just Celia.

The city morgue had, at one time, been set near a community center, and across from a bookstore selling used library books. Naomi had visited the facility on other missing child cases that brought her to the city. She had found it a friendly place, with attendants bustling in their greasy plastic aprons, a pot of coffee stewed to sharp bitterness on the counter, and a plate of cookies no one wanted to eat. The old place had been associated with all sorts of scandals, including an attendant caught taking dried blood home to fertilize his roses.

The new building had been built out in the suburbs, possibly to clean that stain. It sprawled, all pale stone, and yet the refrigerator chill was more obvious. There were no more strange cookies in the waiting area. There was only a fan circulating the muddy air.

The medical examiner was a quiet man named Mike Morton whose hobby was making model airplanes. One for every case that haunted him, he had once told Naomi—now he sat behind a desk so crowded with flying machines it might take off with him. Maybe that's what he wanted, Naomi thought.

"Child finder," Mike said, rising quickly to shake a hand.

Naomi smiled at her nickname and sat down. Mike Morton was a small man, made smaller by his work. His skin was the same gray color of the bodies he worked on.

"I'm looking for my sister," Naomi said, and explained.

"If you've entered your DNA into the system, I don't have anything new for you," Mike said. Naomi felt some relief, but not much. In her heart she was convinced her sister was alive.

"I had assumed you were here about the murdered street girls," Mike said.

Naomi hesitated. No one had hired her officially on the case, but no one was stopping her either. Now that she had met some of the street kids—Celia especially—she felt responsible. She told herself it wasn't hurting to work that case while searching for her sister.

"I thought you might have some ideas how to identify them," Mike said.

Naomi remembered her foster mother, Mrs. Cottle, and how hard she had fought to get Naomi a legal identity. Like so many children who ended up in foster care, Naomi didn't have a birth certificate. If she had run away or been kidnapped before Mrs. Cottle managed to get her a social security number, there would have been no way of tracking her, just like there was no way of tracking her sister.

"I'd check with child welfare," she told him. "Maybe those girls were in foster care before they became homeless. That could be why you're coming up empty."

His eyes widened. "What a good idea. Thank you. Would you be willing to look at them, tell me what you think?"

Naomi hated looking at corpses. They left a lingering shadow on her, a mark. And now she couldn't go back to Jerome and decompress. But she knew it would be impossible for her to say no, not if it helped a child find her way home, dead or alive. She followed Mike back into the chilly morgue. Soon he was pulling open body drawers, citing the Tanner stages—the ages of sexual development—of the girls as he went. Most were Tanner stage four: about thirteen or fourteen. One was barely pubescent. Her narrow, undeveloped body reminded Naomi of the street girl she had confronted outside the library. Celia, she remembered.

Part of her licensing as an investigator was in examining remains, but Naomi's greatest knowledge came from her past. She put the last foot back down on the table. For a long moment she stood motionless. She was remembering how after running in escape, her feet had hurt for weeks. The ground had been too tender to touch, so Naomi had wrapped her feet in Mrs. Cottle's flowered dishcloths and hobbled around until her soles toughened.

Once free, Naomi couldn't stop moving. Mrs. Cottle had understood. It was a puzzle because Naomi had never asked Mrs. Cottle *how* she knew, and now it was too late. Naomi had run away, as usual. She had an excuse—she was working a missing child case at the time—but she had missed saying good-bye to the only mother she had ever known.

"They weren't in the river very long, but I bet you knew that. A day or two at most," Naomi said. "What needs to be investigated is what happened before the murders."

Mike stepped closer. "What do you mean, what happened before?"

Naomi lifted the white foot. "Look at these feet. No calluses. None of them have any signs of wear or activity on their feet. It's one of the first signs you see in cases of captivity."

"Jerome?"

He was sitting in Diane's living room, ensconced in her velvet sofa. The room had the scent of incense and the leftover pizza he had heated for lunch.

He looked up, his face cautious.

"I'm sorry." She went to him, sat down, held on. She felt his hair against her cheek. She had always loved his hair. Naomi knew that might not be the right way to see it—Jerome was Kalapuya, an Oregon native—but those childhood memories, of magic, held on. For her, at least.

"I'm tired of moving, Naomi." She saw his firm mouth, the tender chin. "I'm tired of being second best."

"You're not—"

"Yes, I am. Either we make this a partnership or it doesn't work."

Naomi felt fear. It was a fear as vast as an empty tomorrow. "What does that mean?" she asked.

"We need to put down roots. Make a home, someplace. It doesn't have to be forever, but it needs to be now."

"I need to find my sister."

"I know." His voice was gentle.

That broke her. She wept against him, just as she had cried against Diane, and he put his arm around her. It wasn't just fear of not finding her sister, Naomi realized. It was fear she would not be strong enough to stay once she did.

* * *

When Jerome was little, a woman came for him. She came picking her way over a yard littered with dog turds, swollen black garbage bags, a knocked-over hibachi with a vacant grill. The woman had the look of a farmhouse wife, the kind of grandma you see in books. She wore a checkered or flowered dress—now he wasn't sure—stout shoes, the kind of thick pantyhose you wear for varicose veins. Her hair was silver and piled on her head, and her eyes were a kind, bright, merry blue that said Christmas and cookies rolled into one.

Angrily, his last foster family shoved his belongings—another black garbage bag, this one full of torn shirts and a broken frame photo of his mom, who had died when he was an infant—out the door. Later, back on the farmhouse porch, Mrs. Cottle carefully took everything out and even folded the garbage bag into a tiny square. "When you have lost everything, everything matters," she had said, in her gentle voice. "I will keep this for you."

But before that, she had called him out of the weeds at the edge of that other yard, a skinny little boy with arms covered with painful deerfly bites. Mrs. Cottle had taken him by the hand and led him to her truck. They had driven away, forever. Jerome had looked up at her, riding tall behind the wheel, and she had looked down at him and smiled.

"You're going to be okay," she had said, with the sure conviction of any mother. "I'll see to that."

And she had.

Mrs. Cottle had said the exact same thing to Naomi, too, when she arrived. Jerome wondered if Naomi even remembered it. She acted like she had forgotten what it was like to be found. Jerome, who had found refuge in family, did not understand why Naomi kept running. She had found safety before, and had it now. But still—she ran.

Celia had been on the street, what now, six, seven months? She counted, dispirited, the butterfly book blurry in front of her.

Nine months. It had been nine months.

She would turn thirteen soon. A birthday on the streets—she had seen those. Street kids trying to pretend that going into the soup kitchen and trying to find a candle to stick in a pile of beans was okay. No. Not for her. It would be better to spend her birthdays in the library, drawing as rain ran down the windows, and the afternoons passed into nights, and the seasons passed into years, and one day soon she would find her feet on the stone stairs outside, years older.

She had no future. She knew that.

"You can become an electrician." The street kids were playing the game of what-if. "I saw an ad about that once. All you need is your diploma."

"I'm going to be an airline pilot."

"Naw! That's fucking bullshit, man."

"Really."

"You need like eight thousand degrees. My mom dated this guy once, he was a pilot—"

"Your mom sucked cock down here with the rest, Stoner."

The voices faded out. Celia was sitting on the curb with the others. She was aware night was coming. The sunset had lit the sky above them into tatters of orange and blood red, streaks of lavender and a bruised purple like a kiss. The city buildings rose like giant smiles, and in each window Celia saw an eye. The figures moving inside, turning off lights and lowering shades, reassured her.

Rich plopped down next to her. His broad, sweaty face looked at her with concern. "You've been quiet lately." He suddenly sounded much older, and Celia could see him as a boyfriend, a man, to some future woman.

"I'm turning thirteen soon," she said, reaching forward and capturing her toes. They were starting to poke through her canvas shoes.

"Really? That's cool." But Rich knew. His measured glance told her.

"You really think you're ever getting off the streets, Rich?" she asked.

She saw the crumbs in his eyes, the dirt on his forehead, the curly hair starting under his chin. The beginnings of a mustache. The pink line of his lips, the uncertain eyes, and for the first time she wondered about his past. What had made Rich? He was as gentle as a butterfly.

"Sometimes I think I'll get off the streets, get a job," he said. He picked a bottle cap out of the gutter. "But I don't think they make jobs for people like us. I mean, me. What would I tell them?" His voice was forlorn.

Celia had no answer. She looked at the sky, unfurling like glorious banners. All through the world people shared this sky. They didn't know she deserved a piece, too.

* * *

Oh, the butterflies. It was like a chant. Once Celia had passed a shop up in a tony highbrow neighborhood called Pearl or something equally stupid. What had her mom once said? "It doesn't matter what color you paint a turd, it's still a turd." The shop had said MAGIC in the window, and SPELLS, and Celia had been intrigued. But when she went inside and tried to smell the incense that cost ten dollars or look at the glass balls that turned out to be plastic, the woman clerk had made an expression that told Celia she was the painted turd and should leave.

Celia had stood outside for a long time, then, thinking about magic and spells, just as she was now, getting ever more lost inside herself, only it wasn't lost; she was *finding* herself, someplace deep in this warren of memories. She was tracing her steps *back*. To the beginning.

It was her most precious memory. She was very young, maybe three. She was with her mother in a sunny meadow. It was the time of sweetness, before Teddy. Her mother had her hands clasped over Celia's eyes. Counting, each breath like a measured, small bell. One, two.

Three.

"Look, Celia!"

She had opened her eyes, let the bright in. Focus.

Oh.

They were bright as discs of color, circling like the spots of sun. A blue brighter than the sky, a sunshine yellow tipped with gold coming closer.

"Butterflies!"

The butterflies would always be there, Celia thought now, feeling her bottom against the curb, the faint voices of the other street kids, the gassy smell of exhaust growing distant. Walking hand in hand with her mother through the meadow, she saw one land on a purple flower.

"What's this one, Momma?"

"A great spangled fritillary."

Her mother had picked a dandelion and rubbed it under Celia's chin, laughing, but the yellow petals were no match for the yellow of the golden butterflies. The white of an eye could not be whiter than the butterfly whites, and no sky was a match for their iridescent blues. Celia, like her mother, was in a swoon.

Tiny feckless feet on burred limbs. Kind eyes that rotated, seeing all. Even Celia. Celia was not a monster that day.

"Where you going, Momma?"

"Time to go, sweetie."

Celia had wanted her mother to stay—she had grabbed her hand. Now, sitting on the curb, her face slack with memory, Celia was unaware that her own hand was wide open and reaching out.

Her mother's eyes had softened. She had smiled.

"Okay. Let me tell you a story, then, about the most magical place of all. It's called the butterfly museum."

*　*　*

The scar-faced man. He had begun to haunt Celia's life. She saw him on the corners, melting into the crowd. He was in the corner market, picking through the sandwiches as she and her friends reached for the marked-down cartons of milk, the ones they had to sniff carefully before drinking. Once at the river, he was watching the bridge as she and the boys crossed—that really freaked her out. "Did you see him? Did you see him?" she kept asking the others.

Now he was staring at her from down the street. He frowned at her, the scars on his lips wriggling like little worms. Celia pointed him out to the others.

"He's a perp." Stoner laughed, and Celia knew then that the boys really weren't going to keep her safe. They had no idea what it was like to be a girl.

"I think he's trying to kill me," Celia said, with fearful simplicity.

"Float you in the river with so many holes you might drown?" said another street girl who came up to Celia, her hair a bright orange flood in the dusk.

"Would you want that?" Celia asked her, a girl she had never seen before. Kids came and went: trains, buses, hitchhiking. Many ended up captives, pure and simple, kept like dogs in dirty hotel rooms.

The girl shrugged. She had pimples on her chin, small fleshy eyes, earlobes like globes of fat. She smiled at Celia, showing a line of mercury teeth. "Anything is better than this," the girl said, sashaying away, her hips pounding a beat only Celia could hear.

And then there was the woman. The one with the glossy tail of hair. Galloping up and down the street, sticking her flyers on telephone poles. Celia saw her and sighed. The woman took whatever fun there was out of the night.

The women's shelter was called Aspire. The sign was bolted on the side of a building that had seen better days. Pigeons, roosting, had left the brick sides a smeary Jackson Pollock painting of bird droppings. Inside was a familiar sad smell: sweat, sorrow, grief. Naomi passed a large dorm room, empty and waiting for nightfall, the cots tucked hard with green army blankets. A sign-up clipboard for available bunks hung to the side of the door. The last bunk for the night had been claimed by a woman named Laverne.

In the dayroom Naomi found a table of women playing cards. Whist, from the look of it. One was the skinny bald woman she had seen before, digging through the gutter. She seemed to be in a much better place today, sitting upright, dealing a card. A heavy-set woman was at the head of the game, wearing an Aspire shirt. "Game's full, honey."

Naomi showed her license, explaining her cause.

"I seen your flyers around," the woman said, dealing another card. "Would have called you if I knew, but there's not much there. Twenty-five, white? It could be anyone."

The other women nodded, sagely. All looked to be in their forties or older and hard-bitten. Naomi told them her story, emphasizing how she was checking to see if her sister had ended up in the city.

"I don't know anyone who talked a story like that," the woman said, taking a drag on a cigarette and putting it down in an overflowing ashtray. "You say you were held in some bunker out in the woods?"

"I've heard shit like that, even worse," the older bald woman said, serenely.

"Really?" Naomi turned to her. "Like what?"

"Yeah, what?" another woman asked.

"Right here, in this town. Shit you wouldn't believe. Maybe you would, stay on the streets long enough."

"Amen right there, sure enough," one of the women said, reaching for a card.

The bald woman looked at her hand. "I heard some creep is taking those girls. Keeps them in some house, cuts them to pieces."

Naomi felt her heart pound. "How do you know that?"

"Men talk. Maybe they smell it on each other. Dogs."

"Yeah, uh-huh," another woman agreed, picking up the communal cigarette and adding her own lipstick stain.

"Do you know where this house is?"

"Hell no. You think I want to get my ass anywhere near such craziness? I got enough troubles as it is. Besides, I'm too old for him to take. Thank the Lord."

None of the women seemed fazed. One shook her head, passing a card.

"Who might know more?" Naomi asked.

"Maybe those little kids he's taking." Another drag on the smoke. "Poor babies."

Naomi pulled up a chair. "Help me," she said, smiling.

The women exchanged looks, laughed. They talked with Naomi until the shelter manager stubbed out her final smoke and said the fun was over, it was time to turn down the beds. Turning down the beds, Naomi found out, meant checking in the long line of women who had appeared outside. No weapons, no pets, no drugs. There was a line of battered lockers for locking up the knives, sharpened screwdrivers, and other self-defense tools the women carried.

Naomi followed, helping as best she could. "I'm curious about a man I've seen around," she said, describing the scar-faced man.

"Oh, I've seen him," the manager said, pulling a stack of the olive green army blankets out of a locker and handing it to a short woman behind her, beaten by time.

"You have?" Naomi asked.

"Sure. Major creep if you ask me. Seen him loitering around. There's not much we can do about the pimps and rapists hanging outside. Scratch that. There's *nothing* we can do."

In the dorm room women were milling around and sitting on the edges of their beds. One of the volunteers who had been playing cards circulated with tiny paper cups of juice and packets of donated cookies. Baskets of high-demand items—sanitary napkins and face wipes—sat on tables at the edges of the room. *One per day*, handwritten signs said. The women seemed relaxed, as if the stress of the streets was rising off their shoulders.

"You come back, in the morning," the manager said, shutting the locker. "We unlock the doors then and the women leave. Ten dollars you'll see some pimp in a car, thinking he can grab the woman he was beating and get her back in the fold. Or you go outside right now, when the women line up. It's like open season out there." There was bitterness and hurt in her voice. "That's why we lock the doors every night. To keep us safe. Lord help me, though, sometimes I want to go out there and give them payback. But then I'd be the one in jail. I got a friend doing life for killing her pimp."

Naomi thought of the river, wide and deep. She thought of the girl she had seen pulled out by the bridge. "If there was a place close by where someone wanted to throw a body in the river and not be seen, where would it be?" she asked.

"The industrial area, at the old docks," the woman answered immediately. She smiled at Naomi. "I grew up here. I was an honor student, back in my day." The smile vanished. "Then one of those pimps caught me. Made me feel loved for the first time, and it was all a lie."

"One more question—"

"Time for me to lock the doors, honey." Behind them in the dorm the women were laughing. One had put a pillowcase on her shoulders as some sort of cape and was telling a story.

"There are children out there. Aren't there any shelters for them?" Naomi's voice was pleading.

The manager stopped. She shook her head.

"Why not?" Naomi asked.

"I think it's a legal thing," the woman answered. "The city would be responsible. There's some shelters for older youth. But not for the younger ones. Little kids, why, they leave the shelter and get killed or raped, the city's got a lawsuit on their hands. Easier to just pretend they don't exist." She paused. "Maybe we're afraid to admit they're there. What that says about us."

"I appreciate what you do," Naomi said, somberly.

The woman looked surprised. "I appreciate you, too, honey."

Naomi stepped outside, hearing the door close for the night behind her. In the distance she heard a bird. Finch, she thought automatically. Even here. It made her long for the clean crispness of a farm field at dawn, or the trail through the woods you know will loop and return to safety. But she could smell the river, and was struck for the first time that the city, too, had its own beauty.

Down the street, a group of street kids had gathered in the dusk. The little girl Naomi had run to save by the library was sitting among them, the big boy next to her.

H ere she comes," Rich said, and one of the other kids picked it up into song: "Miss America . . ."

"Her tits ain't big enough," Stoner said.

"Ha! Caught you looking," Rich answered.

"She's better-looking than that creepy guy Celia keeps seeing, the one with the scars."

The kids fell silent as the woman approached. To Celia, sitting at the curb, Naomi looked tall enough to touch the stars. Her shiny head was Orion, sparkling in the sky. At least she had made the scar-faced man disappear. He had vanished from the corner.

"Well, hello!" She smiled at everyone.

Celia looked at her nice shoes. They were leather and laced up the front, with low walking soles. Thick. Comfortable-looking. Celia spit on the sidewalk, close enough to those shoes to make a point.

"Fuck, Celia, that's harsh," Rich said. He stood up, smiling at the pretty woman. "That's no way to treat someone." Celia turned away. "I'm sorry for my friend here," Rich said.

Celia made a small noise of contempt. Her face felt hot with embarrassment. All the other kids were looking at her like she was an asshole.

"I'm looking for my sister," Naomi was telling the others.

"We saw the flyers," Stoner offered.

Celia's eyes secretly traveled up the trousers, past the sturdy middle, saw the underside of her soft chin, the planes of her face. So this was the woman who had written the flyer in the annex of Sisters of Mercy. *Tell her I am sorry*, the flyer had said. *I miss her.*

The street kids looked at one another, shrugged. No one knew anything.

"Don't know a thing. I'd tell you if I did," Rich offered, gallantly. "No one should lose their sister."

Celia got up, walked away.

Celia walked until she found herself at the church at the top of downtown. The evening bells were ringing. The streets looked clean, swept by the rain brooms of God. Celia had been to no kind of church, ever, except for the one that mattered, and that was the church of the butterflies.

They flew around her, even now. Butterflies are emissaries of God, her mother had said, that fateful day before the flood of darkness came over them both. Every country has butterflies, she had said. There is no place you can go without butterflies.

"Not even the deserts, Momma?"

"Not even. The sagebrush checkerspot lives there."

"You know a lot about butterflies, Momma."

"I wanted to be a lepidopterist, when I was young."

"What happened, Momma?"

No answer, the words taken by time. But Celia could swear that she had learned about butterflies deep within her mother's womb. Her mother had fed them to Celia with her own blood, and when she was born, the sack was pulsating with them, so the doctor stood back, astounded as she erupted, covered with wings.

Those butterflies had flown away, but Celia knew. They were emissaries of God.

She climbed the steps of the church, and a man stood at the top, smiling at her. He handed her a pamphlet, though Celia probably stank. Inside most of the pews were empty. At the booths on the side, Celia was told, she could confess. But Celia didn't want God to forgive her. She wanted life to forgive her, and she didn't even know why. She walked deeper into the church and smelled the old incense, the warm cloth of people. Their skins, their hopes, their sins. She looked up to the altar and asked the white figure on the cross, Did God bring butterflies to you, too? Did your mother hold her hands over your eyes, and count, and whisper?

When Celia got back, Naomi was gone. No one talked about her. It was as if she didn't exist. The day people were like that. If this was hell, they were in heaven, and they peeked around the clouds to look down at the others, then flew away like unconcerned angels.

She found Stoner and Rich in the dumpster behind the Greek restaurant. The tall girl with the phone told her where to look. The owner of the Greek restaurant refused to spray his dumpster with

Raid or pour bleach on the food. The business association was trying to make him, but the old man said no, his people knew what it was to go hungry.

Unfortunately, everyone else knew about the dumpster, so usually it was picked over. But tonight, Stoner had found a foil tray of crusty moussaka, and this he was eating by the palmful. Rich nuzzled from an empty yogurt container. He had been licking it, and there was now white yogurt under his chin. Celia didn't say what it looked like. The world was gross, sometimes.

"Hey, let me," Celia bossed, and Stoner passed her the tray. Celia scooped a piece out with her dirty fingers, ate. It tasted really good. She bet it would taste even better heated up. Once a month at school lunch, they'd had international day, and the food had tasted this good.

In the alley entryway a bum appeared, shambling like a scarecrow. The street kids gave him the eye. He gave them the finger in return but left. First come, first served was street law. The street people were hungry for rules, thought Celia, maybe because the rest of their lives were so lawless. Sometimes the older kids formed hard-edged street families with laws of their own. Celia stayed away. She'd had enough law to last her a lifetime.

The streetlights flickered. It was getting too dark to see. Their shifting feet made crunching sounds in the alley. Stoner and Rich and Celia ate the moussaka until it was all gone and their bellies hurt. It made Celia think of how caterpillars can eat two hundred times their own weight. That was Celia, eating until her thorax expanded.

Celia had once heard a story of a girl who escaped the streets and gained so much weight she couldn't move. Celia thought maybe that was one of those made-up stories. But it made sense to her. If she had all the food in the world, she might eat it, too. But unlike that girl she would eventually stop, put her arms over her own face, curl into a ball, and rest until spring, when she could be born anew.

Naomi, having barely made up with Jerome, felt she was sliding on an ice cap that ended at his shoulder. She woke in the same bed with him, but though they lay close together, there was a distance that had never been there before.

Rising quietly so as to not awaken him, she considered her conviction that her sister was alive. But how could she know that if she couldn't even remember her name? Her mind skittered uncomfortably away from this thought.

It was very early. Outside, the birds were quiet. The dark sky lay over the city like a silent blanket. Naomi wondered where Celia and the other street kids slept at night.

* * *

Naomi met Sean Richardson from the Feds in a café on the first floor of his building. He had called asking to see her. From their table Naomi watched the businesspeople pass, always in a hurry.

She thought of the homeless on skid row, only blocks away and yet in a completely different world.

"Are you always so quiet?" Richardson asked, sipping his coffee. "I had always heard you were super friendly. Big smile and all."

"The past year took it out of me," Naomi admitted.

Richardson noted the ring on her finger, didn't say anything. His own hand was as lonely as his heart. Some people didn't know how lucky they were. "I got a call from the medical examiner," he said. "He told me in a few minutes of examination you were able to pick up something neither he nor my team noticed."

Naomi took another sip of her coffee.

"Their feet were soft," she explained. "Even children show wear on their feet from daily use. Corns, calluses, broken nails. None of those girls had walked for weeks."

His brown eyes looked pained. "Anything else?"

Naomi paused for only a moment. She decided to take a risk. "I heard about a house where the girls might be kept before they are killed. I don't know where it is—yet."

Outside the crowds were dwindling. Everyone had scurried inside the buildings where they worked, which Naomi now imagined as giant hives, the workers nesting bees.

"And you?" Naomi asked. "Has your man on the ground found anything?"

He shook his head. "I'm thinking of hiring one of those profilers."

"You guys really don't learn, do you?"

He flushed. His brown eyes were on her. "Do you think this has something to do with your sister? All this time?"

Naomi was staring at him, as if he were a grim reaper.

"Breakfast?" Naomi stuck her head in Winfield's door.

They went to his favorite deli at the top of downtown. The food was crap, but the waitresses comped Winfield's meals. Naomi noticed a group of street kids in one booth—Celia was not among them—and wondered how long such kids had been in plain sight and she had not noticed them. Winfield ordered a Denver omelet while Naomi asked for a tofu scramble.

His eyebrows went up at that. "Didn't know you for a tofu gal."

"I'm trying something new, spark my appetite."

Winfield added three sugars to his coffee, looked over his cup. The Naomi he had known had the appetite of a truck driver.

"This city is a hell of a mess," Naomi said after the food arrived and she took a small, curious bite. They were in Winfield's favorite booth, the window shielded, easy access to both the front and back doors. Winfield was safety conscious like that. When he walked with her down the street, he ambled at her side like a bear. She thought it was silly. What could he protect her from?

Winfield shook hot sauce over his omelet. "You must be hanging out on skid row."

"It isn't a row anymore, it's a mile," Naomi said. She explained what the woman at Aspire had said about the lack of shelters for children. Her eyes kept glancing at the street kids as she spoke.

"That what you want to talk about?" Winfield said, scooping

food into his mouth and quickly wiping. The Naomi he knew also didn't waste time on what she couldn't fix. She kept her eye on the prize. Naomi reminded Winfield of the parable of the starfish: A man, out on the beach one day, stopped to find a boy throwing starfish back into the sea. There were hundreds of starfish washed up on the beach, and the man explained to the boy he couldn't save them all. "I can save one," the boy replied.

"I want to know if my sister is in the state mental hospital," Naomi said. "It would explain why I can't find her."

Winfield wanted to point out that maybe Naomi couldn't find her sister because she didn't even know her name. But Winfield knew this was how investigations were solved, one small step at a time. "I can call down there for you, ask," he said.

"I'd rather visit in person. Can you get me clearance? It takes longer if I try."

"Sure." Like a lot of cops, Winfield ate like there was a timer in the room. Naomi once used to beat him to the bell, but not anymore. She pushed her plate aside.

"Not good?"

"Just not very hungry lately."

Yes, something was wrong with Naomi. The waitress came to take their plates. She smiled. Winfield put down some dollar bills for a tip.

"Something else bothering you, child finder?" he asked, rising heavily.

"Just the usual," Naomi replied sardonically. Her sister was missing. Wasn't that enough?

"The world is full of heartache," the detective said. Naomi could see the sadness he bore, too. "You got to carve out some happiness for yourself. Otherwise it will take you down."

Naomi nodded, looking away.

"Saw your husband the other day," Winfield added as they headed out. He held the heavy door open for her, eyes scanning the street.

"Where?"

"Down at the licensing agency. He was asking after being an investigator, like you."

He saw her face. She hadn't known.

Naomi found a note from Jerome on the kitchen counter. Raised in the country without cell service, they had the habit of leaving notes for each other instead of sending text messages.

Gone to the firing range, the note said. Jerome's truck—adapted for driving with one arm—was gone from outside, and the house was empty. Walking heavily up the narrow stairs to their guest room, she saw his holster was no longer over the chair.

Carrying a gun never worked for Naomi. Whenever she wore one, her leads dried up, and witnesses refused to talk. She could swear people could smell it on her. For her a gun was a small object that fired wildly, threatened fewer than it should, silenced the good witnesses and emboldened the bad. She preferred to use her hands. She had extensive self-defense training and stayed in good shape. She had had some close calls, but so far it had worked.

Sitting at the end of the bed, Naomi looked around the room. She remembered the times over the years she had shown up here, exhausted from travel, and Diane had taken her in, let her spend a night or two, and hugged her wordlessly when she left. Here was where Naomi had left her heart. The walls were covered with cards sent by the families of children she had saved. Thank-you notes and *How are you doing, child finder?* Concern in their voices for her. The kids could always tell. She remembered the soft touch of one girl, looking up at her and *knowing*.

"I hope you don't get lost," the girl had said.

Lost. You can be lost even when you've been found. You can make the wrong turn in life even if you're surrounded by people who love you. That was what suicide was, Naomi figured. It was choosing the final exit instead of another path. Not because you wanted to hurt anyone, but because you feel too hopeless to find your way home. There was more than one kind of suicide, too, more than one kind of leaving. How many people spend their entire lives not even knowing that they have already left?

She leaned over, sighing. Diane and Jerome were right. The past year she had stopped even thinking about anyone else. All she had cared about was finding her sister. When Jerome came back, they would talk about their future. She would tell him she thought it was a good idea for him to get his investigator license. He could help her, and still make some money on his own cases.

And they would talk about her stopping running, at least for the time.

* * *

Diane spent her days saying good-bye to the past. She figured this was what lonely people did, and since she had done everything in her life with gusto—from being a short-order cook to put herself through college to running a treatment center for emotionally disturbed teenagers—she had decided to do lonely well, too.

She went to the train station with the clock tower and ordered a cosmopolitan in the adjoining jazz lounge, which looked unchanged since the '40s. That was in memory of her dear mother, who had once nurtured a dream of being a jazz singer but instead became a pediatrician. She went to the Chinese gardens where she had met her first and only love, a woman named Marsha. Then she drove into the west hills to visit the Japanese gardens, where they had watched the koi on the day when Marsha told her that she was going to die. That had been over twenty years before, she reflected now. On the way down she stopped at the high concrete aqueduct known as the suicide bridge, the site of one of her greatest regrets. There a teenage patient named Daniel had swan-dived to his death.

But getting back in her car Diane realized she was being silly. This wasn't how she wanted to spend her final years—being alone. There would be enough loneliness after death, she figured. She would go home and tell Naomi that she wanted her, and Jerome, to stay. They could make a family. It wouldn't be the most ordinary family, but it was something.

Diane turned her key in the door. Jerome and Naomi sat close together on the couch, waiting for her. Naomi was trembling, ever so slightly. Diane could see it in the hand holding the teapot.

A cup was waiting for her.

❥

"That wasn't what I expected," Diane told her evening mirror, later. She could see the fine crepe under her eyes. She picked up the hairbrush on the vanity. She seldom used it: it had been her mother's. She inspected a strand of silver hair in it, wondering if it was hers.

She remembered the last days of Marsha's death from liver cancer, when she had become delirious, breaking vases, trying to attack Diane. The hospice nurses had to wrap her hands in thick mittens to keep her from clawing out her own eyes. Marsha had died right here, in this house, in a hospital cot set up in the living room. Diane had never regretted it. It was a precious thing, to say an intimate good-bye.

"We want to stay here, with you, if you will have us," Naomi had said, and Diane had seen the flutter in her throat, and how Jerome had turned to look at his wife as if a miracle had happened.

The librarian kept stacks of scrap paper—soft pink, yellow, plain white—in a small wood box on her desk next to a cup of stubby pencils. Celia took a handful of the paper, looking at the librarian to see if it was too much, but the woman only smiled. Celia carried the paper and pencil and her favorite book to her favorite chair, upstairs in the big room, where the light came in the windows no matter how hard it rained.

Most of the time she drew butterflies—long, magical butterflies, with trailing wings and otherwordly eyes. But other times she drew her sister, tracing her face as if to remember it always. When Celia drew her sister, or anyone she loved, she added butterflies: all over their shoulders, sprouting from their eyebrows. Even the tiny dot inside the eye became a single, precious beast. In this way the butterflies were the people she loved and the people she loved were free.

When she was done with the drawings, Celia slid them into her favorite book. It was the only safe place she knew to keep them. They would get wet under the overpass and lost on the streets.

Celia knew it was hard to find safe places. The most unsafe places were the cars and the beds of any man. Alleys and dark tunnels. Any place where she could be trapped. The secret to survival was a map inside her mind, where Celia was always trying, like a butterfly, to find the right place to land. But there seemed to be no such place.

It was cold under the overpass when Celia awoke the next morning, and she felt a stinging sensation on her leg. She lifted her jeans to see a large, raised red spider bite. She knew it was a spider because the insect had gotten squished against the cloth. Probably she had rolled on it when it bit her.

"Is this a black widow?" Celia asked, pulling the jean cloth inside out.

"Looks like a black smear to me," Stoner said. Rich peered closer. All of them had seen street kids with bad wounds from infected rat and insect bites. Celia vividly remembered one girl who got a cockroach stuck in her ear while sleeping in an abandoned house. Her screaming carried for blocks.

"I hear you can bathe in bleach and it kills germs," Stoner said.

"You say that all the time," Celia said.

"Well, it's true. You just have to dilute it."

"I don't have a bathtub."

"I guess you could do it in the river."

Celia and Rich looked at Stoner like he was insane. He blushed. He bit his thick lips, looked away, hoped they would drop it. They did. Celia limped to standing. Maybe if she walked it off the pain would go away.

"I'll go with you to the free clinic," Rich offered.

The free clinic was at the top of skid row, along the park blocks where the city police were always tearing down the tents the homeless families put up. Celia and Rich sat on the slashed seats for hours, waiting to be seen. The doctors there were nice, but did it matter?

Her stomach felt like a cave, and she was dizzy from hunger when she finally got called back to the exam room. For some reason she kept thinking of peanuts, and the salty taste flooded her mouth at the thought of one. If she had a peanut, she would suck on it for like an hour.

Celia had been in the free clinic before. That had been for an STD check. Celia didn't want to get pregnant or get STDs. She was worried about her period starting because then it would mean she could have a baby, and she already had one—her sister. She had told the doctor all this while filling her pockets with the free condoms, not understanding why his face looked so sad.

Day people.

The doctor was a tall, skinny man with black curly hair, like Stoner grown up, only with a small round potbelly under his white jacket, which already had smears and stains from other patients. He smelled like Juicy Fruit gum. He looked at Celia's leg, at the red raised circle around the spider bite and the hole in the middle. She showed him the dead squished spider. "I left it there so you could see it," she said proudly.

She read his name tag as he leaned over. DR. ALEX LOPEZ, it said, and she thought of the scar-faced man and his nameless blue jacket.

"Well, I don't think it's a recluse or widow," he said doubtfully, looking at the squished bug. He cleaned the bite and wrapped it with a clean bandage that would be filthy or lost within a day. He shook his head as she left, knowing he would make the mandated report call, and the recording about yet another homeless child on the streets would enter whatever endless system stored them, for a caseworker to find next week or next month. Even when they picked the kids up, they had nowhere to take them. The doctor had heard about kids sleeping in child welfare offices, on the floor.

Outside, the rain had started again. Rich was waiting for her, so hungry, too, that he felt faint. Together they walked down to skid row, looking for food and their friends. Celia wondered if butterflies savor time more because they know they will die soon. Then again, Celia knew she might die soon, too, and that didn't make her enjoy life more.

"I saw a doctor who looked like you," Celia told Stoner, importantly. Rich had panhandled enough money to buy them both sandwiches from the corner market, and Celia had finished hers. She kept the crumpled paper in her pocket, touching it for reassurance that she had eaten.

"Yeah?" Stoner wasn't paying attention. He was panhandling on the corner, almost coming out of his skin with worry. Anxiety, Celia guessed. ADH-motherfucking-D. Jostling, dancing, his long legs so skinny they never met.

"Except he had like a beer belly."

Stoner snorted. "I'll never have one of those."

"I bet you're related."

"Why?" She had his attention now. His dreamy eyes, thick with lashes, met hers. Stoner was a pretty boy. The men in the cars said that all the time. But he was pretty in a way that wasn't just for perverts. He had those beautiful eyes, curly black hair, and golden skin. Stoner was part Puerto Rican. Puerto Ricans, he said, cross the street for each other.

"His name was Lopez. What's your name?"

Stoner was staring at her. "Don't be an idiot, Celia," he said.

"Why not?" she persisted.

"We're not all related, okay?"

"Fine." Celia stared at the cars. Another old man gestured at her, twinkling his fingers like a fucking creep. Ignoring him, she tried to panhandle, but no one wanted to give her any money. It was always that way trying to beg as a girl. The men in suits hurried away like they were afraid to be seen talking to the merchandise. The women walked faster when she approached, like she was a disease they might carry home to their daughters. You'd think the day people would give more to the street girls, but it didn't happen that way.

* * *

Every Friday in school, Celia was pulled out of class early. She held a ruler out and whacked the lockers as she passed. The kids weren't allowed to use the lockers anymore. It wasn't safe, the principal said.

She would sit in the waiting chairs with the others. There were always three or so of them. Kids on lice check. The nurse was a rude lady named Sally who blew out her nasty breath in frustration whenever she checked Celia. First she checked Celia's head for lice, then her arms for the ringworm that kept growing in circular patches, and, finally, her wrists and legs for the angry, scratched red trails of scabies.

Your child has _____, the form note said, and the nurse would fill in the bug of the month for Celia to carry home. *Please treat your child before returning him/her to school.*

"Just give me the medicine," Celia started telling the nurse, who refused. Finally it was Mrs. Wilkerson who did, sneaking it to Celia like it was some sort of contraband. She locked herself in their bathroom at home while her mom slept on the couch and rubbed the foul pink pesticides all over her naked body and scalp until she was covered in the sticky mess. She waited, head down, shivering, not thinking while the medicine worked, and then she stepped into the dirty tub and rinsed off with the old yogurt container left at the side.

Sometimes, when Celia was hungry, she would eat the plaster chunks that fell from her bedroom wall. They tasted sweet. The paint from the windowsills also tasted sweet, but Mrs. Wilkerson had told the kids not to eat the paint in their homes because it had lead in it.

Celia often dreamed of the day her mother would stop using. She would walk into the house. Her mother would look up, her face clear and bright. She would smile, and her eyes would be determined. *We're leaving Teddy,* she would say happily. *Tell your sister.*

* * *

Munch, munch, like the sky ate the moon every night, until only a sliver remained. Like Stoner standing at the edge of the street, searching for every tablet and drop, talking about liquid acid you put in your eyes, or sticky stuff to melt into the brown liquid that made your soul flow down the streets. All that begging and hustling only to get some fix he would forget tomorrow.

Only Celia and Rich remained clean, sitting on the corner while the night spiraled out of control around them. It wasn't out of some snotty judgment or anything like that, but more a matter of laziness or fear. If someone had come up to Celia and said, *Here*, she might have, despite all her promises to herself. At some point the night would be right. Then she would be like one of the junkies on the streets whose veins had all collapsed into dry little threads.

It made Celia think of how butterflies turn poison into protection. The monarch eats milkweed plants and turns them into honest-to-God cyanide, so any predator that eats it will die. Celia liked that. She wished she was capable of killing men for just a taste. She imagined what the streets would look like then. But the poison comes with a cost, she thought. The butterfly, eaten, still dies.

Naomi drove into the industrial area the Aspire manager had mentioned, finding the deserted waterfront that ran next to skid row. She parked her car and walked to the edge of the decaying docks. From here she could look downriver and see the city.

It would be easy to throw a body into the river here, unseen. It would take a day or so for it to resurface, down by the bridge. It lined up.

Naomi stepped tentatively onto one of the docks. The wood was splintered, the creosote-soaked pilings mired deep in the muddy water. Feeling each board carefully, Naomi made her way out to the pier. The water sloshed over the edges of the rotting wood. She could feel how deep the river ran underneath. The channel was big and dark ahead of her.

She walked to the end of the dock and peered down into murky depths. Tangles of old rebar, sprouting like lethal rusted spears, rose from the unseen bottom. Anyone who fell over the side here was courting death, or at least a trip to the emergency room and a tetanus shot.

Naomi imagined a man carrying a body. She saw him coming out here in the dark, with only the moonlight for illumination. He carried the body to the dock and dumped it off the edge, certain the river would erase any evidence from the corpse and the current would carry it far enough away no one would know where it had been dumped.

Getting down on her hands and knees on the wet boards, Naomi examined both sides of the dock. She took her time, crawling, peering at the underboards, studying the oily pilings. More nests of the rebar rose from the gloomy depths below, like lazy venomous snakes. She assumed the rebar was from the shipping industry that once made this city—coils of shipping cables and reinforcement for pilings that had since rotted away.

She froze. There was a pale reddish glint on the end of one of the spears. It was about a foot beneath the surface, waving like the softest filaments, or mermaid floss. Pushing up her sleeve, Naomi lay down flat on the wet boards. The shockingly cold water wet her arm. She reached down for the floss, brought it to the surface with her fingers.

It was a hank of human hair.

Back on the relief of dry land, Naomi stood in the rutted dirt and pulled out her phone, ignoring the cold water running down her sleeve.

"Sean Richardson?" she asked. "You need to bring a team down to the old docks. Yes. In the industrial area adjacent to downtown.

A dredge team, with divers experienced with river hazards. You are going to find more missing girls here. They're snagged."

She stayed only long enough to see the cars and dark vans arrive. The search and rescue boat came down the river, the divers holding on to the sides. A news copter drew a bead in the distance, but Naomi left before anyone tried to talk to her.

If Jerome had the firing range, Naomi had the boxing gym. The best was when she had real people to spar with—it seemed every town offered up at least a few curious longshoremen, teenage martial arts hopefuls, or retired prizefighters willing to go a few rounds. If she ever did settle in one place, Naomi figured, she might take a few girls under her arm to train.

She found the local gym on the east side of town, near a set of train tracks and a disreputable strip of car lots. The smell was intoxicating: sweat, old leather, and the musky scent of fear. To Naomi, new fear smelled bright and hard, but fear already spent smelled entirely different, like an animal resting.

The young men—and more women, she noticed—had faces lacquered with Vaseline. The only language was the hiss of breath and the smack of the bags, and gloves hitting flesh. Naomi spoke to the woman in charge, a retired female fighter, one of the first, of pink shorts and a bannered name. Now she was just smiling, ruddy faced, a team of kids around her.

Naomi changed in a tiny bathroom where the sink was stained with spit blood, and carried her boxing bag back out by the ring that dominated the room. She warmed up, shadowboxing and hitting the heavy bags while the others snuck glances, curious about her. Then she wrapped her hands, asked the trainer to help lace her sparring gloves, and found a willing partner.

He was a young man, supremely confident at sparring with a woman. He spoke to Naomi through his mouth guard as they climbed in the ring. "You ever fought before?"

"Yes," Naomi said, tucking in her own mouth guard with a gloved fist. "You better cross yourself."

He thought it was a joke.

"Where did you learn to fight like that?" the woman trainer asked, after a wrung-out but satisfied Naomi climbed through the ropes several rounds later. Two hectic patches had appeared on her cheeks, but otherwise she was mostly untouched. Her eyes were clear.

"A retired fighter down in Mexico," she answered as the trainer slipped off her gloves. "He specializes in dirty fighting."

"I can tell. You wouldn't last two minutes in front of the judges in this state. Poor Mikal there is going to piss blood for a week from those kidney punches."

"He could have said stop," Naomi said, feeling chagrined.

"Men." The woman grinned. Her grin faded. "You looked like you were holding back, too."

"I was." Naomi saw images of crushed bones, smashed fingers, gouged eyes.

The trainer turned to two teenage boys behind her. "Roberto and Jason, get in the ring." The slender boys slid through the ropes, smacking playfully at each other. "No horseplay," she chided.

Naomi unwrapped her hands, checked all her fingers. The cotton wraps were well-worn and stained with blood. At least it wasn't her blood. That was the rule, she thought, watching the boys lark around the ring, looking more like best friends than opponents. Mikal came and joined her, holding a cold wet towel to his bruised face. "Can you teach me some of those moves?" he asked her under his breath, during a break in the action. "Maybe another time," Naomi answered.

One of the boys split the lip of his friend, and the two instantly stopped sparring, the hurt one leaning through the ropes. Naomi watched as the trainer reached into her fanny pack and pulled out a piece of cold metal, pressing it tight against the cut. Holding the boy's head with firm hands, she pinched the wound shut, hard. He closed his eyes.

"I'm looking for a man," Naomi began, and told her about the scar-faced man. Naomi described him in detail.

The trainer got a faraway look in her eyes. "Except for the blue jacket, that sounds a lot like Ray, our custodian. He's not much of a custodian, actually. He pushes a broom here for free membership. He's punchy." She said this as if in apology, like it was her fault.

"What kind of punchy?" Naomi asked. She knew that there were brain-damaged boxers who were docile while others were violent, even criminally insane.

"Uhhh . . ." The trainer seemed disinclined to answer.

"Where can I find this Ray fellow?" Naomi asked, her heart beating stealthily.

"You're not going to do him like you just did poor Mikal, are you?" The woman had a glint of mischief in her eyes, but also concern. The hurt boy lowered his head towards his coach, his skin stretched white where her fingers were holding the wound shut. A trickle of blood was on her thumb.

"Only if he deserves it," Naomi said, almost idly. She was watching the boy, the wound, the woman. "If I had wanted to take Mikal down, I would have hit him in the body more," she added, and caught the trainer's knowing glance.

"Ray comes in early Monday mornings. So you've got a few days. And no, I don't know where he lives. It could be behind a dumpster, for how he smells some mornings. If you're looking for scars, he's your man."

The woman slowly removed her fingers. The wound had closed. "We do a lot now to prevent that kind of scarring, but you know—skin tears."

"I know," Naomi said, collecting her bag. "Hearts do, too."

Back at Diane's she found Jerome, his head bowed over *Oregon Revised Statutes: Criminal Procedure, Crimes*. He was sitting at the kitchen table, a plate next to him with hard pretzels, bread and butter pickles, mustards, and slices of sharp cheddar cheese. Naomi ate a piece of the cheese, looked over his shoulder. "Studying for your license?" she asked.

He looked up, saw her rosy cheeks, sweat-dampened hair.

"Work out?" he asked, closing the book.

"I found the boxing gym," she said.

Jerome's dark eyes caught her, warmed her. Usually after fighting, the first thing Naomi wanted was to go to bed. Love and war. Once Jerome had teased her about this, but it had not gone over well. So he stayed quiet. Their lovemaking was something neither of them discussed. He knew that for Naomi it was a sacred thing, but scary. Jerome had been her only lover outside of whatever had happened in her youth, and that was not love. What had happened to her as a child wasn't even sex, he thought. It was grotesque and something he kept far from his mind. Making love to Naomi, he found it easy to forget what had happened to her, because in that moment she was purely herself, smiling, loving him. He had never known anyone else like her and knew he never would. She was his heart.

But their love was like a deep trench, and the vulnerability of it always threatened to pull Naomi down. So she danced with him, close and then far. He was trying to accept this. There might never be a magic moment with Naomi, a time when he could relax and feel all was well. She might always be like this, looking over his shoulder, her eyes cautious.

"I beat up this guy. I feel kinda bad about it."

"He could have said stop."

"That's what I said!"

She took another chair, grinned at him. He grinned back, and they both laughed. It wasn't all better, but it sure was closer than before. "You hungry?" he asked, thinking of the bed upstairs, pushing the plate of pretzels closer to her.

"Actually, I am," she said.

Celia was sitting outside Sisters of Mercy, scratching the bloody bandage around her leg. She had rolled up her jeans so anyone walking by could see the bandage, the blood. She knew what she was doing. She was trying to get attention. See, she wanted to say, I am hurt. Someone care.

But no one did. They walked on by, not even looking at her.

Except for Naomi. She came down the sidewalk, arms swinging, face like a lamp. It was big news on the streets, how the FBI was pulling bodies out of the river down at the old docks. Some of the street people had gone down to watch, but not Celia. She guessed next to dead bodies her spider bite wasn't much news.

Naomi had worry on her brow, but it wasn't the expression Celia knew would be there if any of the girls dragged out of the river were old enough to be her sister. That some would turn out to be girls Celia knew probably didn't even occur to Naomi.

"You're hurt!" Naomi said, crouching near Celia. She reached out, and Celia made a show of pulling away until she saw Naomi's hands. Naomi's hands were rough. She had scars on her knuckles—fights, somewhere along the way—and the nails were clipped short. They were hands that had known life, and this comforted Celia. She let Naomi touch her.

"I'm always hurt," Celia said, hearing how foolish that made her sound.

"Did you get cut?" Naomi asked.

"Spider bite."

"That's not good. That can get infected."

Naomi quickly and professionally unrolled the bandage, peeking at the wound. The edges were raised, the hole angry and red. Celia could smell Naomi's hair, leaning over, and the smell was like apples. Celia closed her eyes, drank in the smell. It made her think of Alyssa. Washing Alyssa's hair with the shampoo from the dollar store, soaping it slowly, rinsing her clean with the old yogurt container at the side of the tub.

"I went to the free clinic," Celia told her.

Naomi stopped. The concern went out of her face. She stopped paying attention to the bite, or to Celia. "I should go there," she said. "I didn't even think of that! The doctor might know something. I'll put up a flyer, talk to them."

Her hand had left Celia's leg. Her face was empty, and it gave Celia one of her shivers. Celia could see that Naomi was thinking about her sister, but there was nothing there to remember. Naomi was missing a ghost.

"I saved the dead spider, here, on my pants," Celia said, quickly, trying to recapture Naomi's attention. She began unfolding the dirty cuff to show her.

But Naomi was rising. "You should keep that bandage clean," she said, as if Celia were another adult. "Who is the doctor up there?"

"I think it's Lopez," Celia replied, turning away. Shutting off.

Celia was puzzled. If Naomi cared so much about children, why did she keep walking by?

Celia watched Naomi walk away. Naomi didn't know it, but she was covered with butterflies. They swarmed all over her, attaching to her new clothes, making them as old as time. She would carry them inside the free clinic, and the tall skinny doctor who looked like Stoner, all grown up with a belly, would not see them either. But they would be there, waiting to comfort her when Naomi heard the doctor say he knew nothing, nothing, nothing.

That was the thing about the butterflies. They could be kind when Celia felt bitter. They could encompass all the beauty of this world even when the skies smarted gray and the old men pulled up at the curb, their dicks already in their hands. Celia closed her mind against the men and went to find the other kids. See ya, Celia, the butterflies said. Celia lifted her small hand and waved good-bye.

Stoner had found a piece of cardboard and written *Homeless please help* on it with a black marker pen he borrowed from the woman who ran Aspire. Stoner had wanted to get a red pen and make it look like he had written in blood. "That'll get them," he had said, but Rich and Celia told him that was stupid; it would just scare the day people.

That had started a truth-telling session where all the street kids started talking about chicken hawks and creeps who had invited them home, and all the weird shit they wanted—the girl with the phone talked about a guy who insisted she fuck him up the ass with his electric toothbrush. That got everyone laughing so hard they fell off the sidewalk. Celia laughed until her stomach hurt. Stoner held up one finger and made a *buzz-buzz* sound, and that cracked them up all over again.

Then Celia saw Naomi walking back along the other side of the street. She looked sad.

Celia must have been staring at her because Stoner said something. "Got the hots for her?" Stoner asked, teasing.

"No." Celia glowered at him.

"Celia's got the hots for the church lady."

"She's not a church lady."

"Oh—what is she then?"

Celia looked at the pavement while the other kids laughed. Rich looked at her, concerned. But Stoner frowned. "Hey, you're not thinking she's *the one*, are you?"

Celia stared down, blushing furiously. She could feel the blood pouring to her cheeks. Rich looked on the verge of saying something, but then pulled back.

"Come on, Celia, you know better than that," Stoner said. "No one down here is going to be your *mommy*."

"I—" Celia didn't know what to say. She looked helplessly at her feet.

"Just don't even think it," Stoner emphasized.

"You're not, are you?" asked the girl with the phone. "I've been on the streets a long time, since I was ten. No one is coming to save you. You better get rid of that shitty thinking fast."

"That's enough," Rich interrupted. "She got the point."

"I hope so!" the girl said. She gave Celia a kinder look. "You're only twelve, right? You got time. Make a plan, like me."

"What's your plan?" Celia's voice was muted.

"I'm going to survive until I'm sixteen. Then I'm going to hitch to Alaska and work the canneries there. You can get a work permit at sixteen. I got it all figured out." She spoke with authority.

"If you're so smart, help me with this sign," Stoner said, and the conversation resumed. Celia snuck a glance up the street. Naomi was gone.

Naomi was driving to the state mental hospital. Jerome was at home, studying for his license test. Naomi liked the idea of each of them doing their own thing. Maybe the last year had brought a little too much togetherness.

The radio was playing the top news story of the day: the FBI had retrieved the bodies of four girls from the dock area. Special Agent Richardson, the man on public radio said, was being close-mouthed about details, but a reporter had heard the girls were all prostitutes. The newscaster said this like it was a relief.

Naomi reached for the dial, turned it off.

The old Datsun was without air-conditioning, but she liked the wind rolling in the window, blowing her hair. Once, Jerome had asked why she never wore her hair up. Reflecting, Naomi had realized that she liked her hair being down because it felt like she was moving even when she was standing still.

The bucket seats were comfy, and the car smelled of long trips. For many years it had been her house on wheels. For almost ten years, in fact. She had kept everything she needed in the trunk, moving from case to case, never staying in one place for long. She had become an expert at finding cheap hotels, eating on the road, and doing her laundry at massive truck stops that always seemed to be playing Steely Dan.

Ahead of her, a turn off the freeway. What was once a horrendous big pink building was now a sweet calm gray, and the rest of the new mental hospital unfolded across manicured lawns and pleasant open walking areas. It was still a prison, and there were still barbed curls of razor wire on the fences and armed guards inside. But the state mental hospital was vastly improved since the days it had inspired movies like *One Flew Over the Cuckoo's Nest*.

She parked in a lot where families left cars, the newer visitors carrying cards, the more experienced with bags of change for the vending machines.

The prune-voiced lead psychiatrist was talking to Naomi. "Oregon statute allows the commitment of anyone posing a threat," he intoned. I know that, Naomi thought with annoyance, trotting after him, but she didn't say anything. She wanted his cooperation. They passed the visiting room, and Naomi dodged tables to follow his rapid, frenetic pace. The families were entering, saying hellos to the men and women at the tables.

She followed his back into their main office, thankfully cooled by a fan. The psychiatrist had a receding high hairline, a rind of colorless hair, a humorless mouth. Astonishing in all this were some of the most caring eyes she had ever seen. The eyes changed his face, made it mobile, human. "Most of our patients were convicted of crimes," he said. "But most of those are minor offenses, like public urination or disturbing the peace. It's a shame they have to get arrested to get treatment."

Naomi sat down heavily in the chair across from his desk. She felt her anxiety run out of her. "I'm looking for my sister," she began, and went on to explain the little she knew.

To her deep surprise, in a few minutes he frowned and said, "She might be here."

Later it was like a dream in slow motion. Naomi had walked into a dayroom to find a young woman looking bewildered at being abruptly summoned from her room. She wore the blue smock and pants of the patients, her yellowish hair cut to her shoulders. Her clean skin spoke of decent living, but her eyes were dull. They fixated on Naomi with a question in them, and the question was one for a stranger.

Naomi found the back of a chair with her hand. "We call her Deirdre," the psychiatrist had said, "because it means 'the sorrowful one.'"

She was in her twenties and fit all the descriptors. Deirdre had been found wandering around a lake in the mountains not far from where Naomi had been found. She had twigs in her hair, a fearful expression on her face, and her mouth was stained with blackberries. From the softness of her body, investigators believed she had been fed, and kept. But where she had come from, no one could figure.

Initially they assumed Deirdre was suffering from selective mutism, the result of severe trauma. It was only after a series of neurological exams that they realized that Deirdre had brain damage. At some point Deirdre had almost died from drowning. Her body worked. Her mind did not. She remembered people and had mastered rudimentary sign language. But she could not say where she had been.

Interviews of everyone who lived near the lake had found no one willing to take responsibility for the young woman, and eventually the police decided she had been dumped. She could have been driven from anywhere. A civil commitment judge had sent her to the state hospital. Her favorite thing to do was play with the cards others used for games. Her favorite thing to drink was chocolate milk.

Naomi held on to the chair as her legs buckled, and looked into the wide face. Are you my sister? she wanted to ask.

The psychiatrist watched, consumed with a professional interest. Once he had helped twins reunite after being separated their entire lives. The men had known it instantly, crying and hugging. Nothing like this encounter.

"Deirdre, this woman thinks she might be your sister," the doctor said, making the sign for sister off his chin.

Deirdre looked at Naomi and frowned.

"Is there anything you want to ask her?" the psychiatrist asked Naomi.

"I want to know if she remembers . . . being underground," Naomi said, taking a deep breath. Her cheeks pinked. Her eyes teared up, looking at the floor. "I want to know if she remembers me singing about the sweet chariot."

A hand touched her. It was soft and impersonal. Deirdre was looking right at her, into her. No, she shook her head.

"Thank you," Naomi whispered, her voice strangled. The psychiatrist smiled at Deirdre. He looked at Naomi with sympathy. "I'm sorry for all you went through," he said. "The both of you—wherever she is, too."

Naomi left, running for her car. She saved the tears for the drive home.

* * *

Once, when Naomi was in community college, studying criminal law, a woman who had survived a terrible flood came to talk. She talked about the waters coming over their lands when she was a child, and how she climbed to the roof of their barn, hoping to survive. Days later, rescue workers found her blistered with sun. The waters had receded, revealing the tops of the trees in their yard, and tangled in the branches of those trees were large pillows.

Only they weren't pillows. She realized years later those were her parents.

The other students had questioned the woman, the fear obvious on their own faces. What if we are all capable of lying to ourselves? But the story didn't bother Naomi. Instead it reassured her, confirming that the stories we tell ourselves have more meaning than the facts. That doesn't make them lies. Seeded with every myth was the emotional truth.

"Can you come home?"

It was Alyssa whispering over a nighttime phone. Celia stood straight, felt the fear rush right up her back to the sky.

She was on the row with the others, watching the cars circle like so many metal vultures. The girl with the phone had brought it to her. Celia, breathless with anxiety, thought it was her mom, calling the last number back. "Yeah?"

But it was Alyssa, of the soft little voice. She was sobbing, quietly, that swallowed kind of crying that Celia knew too well, that broken-voiced whisper that reminded her of bed slats and the cry of the wind late at night.

"Please come."

Teddy was in the background, yelling for her to give over the fucking phone. Celia could remember the sounds of Teddy's rage carrying out the open windows. She remembered the slammed windows of other houses, the waiting for the dialing for help, the police cars and the heavy knock on the door. Her mother, wiping her cheeks with her hands, giving fearful glances to Teddy, and Teddy opening the door to the police with a regretful smile on his face. All was well here, sir. Never mind the girl hiding in the corner, and the woman sitting on the couch, scratching her arms to ragged sores with desperation and fear.

"Did he hurt you?" Celia asked, and this was the thousand-dollar question.

"Yes—I," her sister answered, and Celia closed her eyes. She saw herself bounding there on huge dragon feet, smashing the house with her claw hand and reaching in to rescue her sister.

"I have to take the bus," she promised Alyssa. "I'll be there."

It was midnight when the last bus finally crawled down their street, and Celia got off, knowing she was stuck out here for the night. She ran up the street, seeing how dark the house was now, the hulking shape of Teddy's truck parked outside, the teamster sticker in the back window. The wind moved through the long grass of the yard, and from inside she heard . . . nothing. A tick of silence. Far away an owl called.

Creeping through the long grass, Celia slid up alongside her sister's bedroom window. It was the bedroom that once belonged to Celia. The same bed, even, filled with sickness. Sometimes Celia thought the mattress was forever wet with the pollution he left. Teddy.

She scratched at the window. Nothing. Pulling her hands along the aluminum seams, Celia felt for the metal runners. She was an expert now at popping cheap windows out of their metal frames.

Her sister unlatched the window, slid it open a bare inch.

"Celia?" It was a whisper, and relieved, Celia collapsed against the side of the house.

"Alyssa? You okay?" she breathed.

"I'm okay." The whisper was calmer now. "You should leave."

"I came all this way."

"I know." Both of them breathed in the night. Celia could smell the inside of the room through the open window, and her nose prickled at the aroma. No.

"He's doing it to you," she said, her heart breaking inside.

A sniffle, and a wipe of the nose. "You should go. He's going to hear you."

"Where's Mom?"

"You know." The image of a couch hung between them.

"You don't have to stay."

"Where would I go?" Her sister's voice was so young. "The teachers say I'm smart. I don't want to live on the streets. Like you."

I was smart, too, Celia thought. But not smart enough. The familiar smell coming from inside the room was stronger now, and Celia's heart dissolved in pain. The smell of sadness and fear and what a man did because of all that. The juice of hate.

"You can tell someone," she whispered, closing her eyes, knowing that was crazy; no one would believe Alyssa, especially now. They would say Celia had talked her into it. She reached out, stroked the rough siding like it was her sister, there on the other side of the—

A sound in the grass behind her and suddenly he was *there*, taller than the night and angrier than the sky, his head above her, and he was swinging at her as she howled in pain. "Caught you, you bitch!" Teddy yelled, and Celia burst into tears as Alyssa did, too, in sympathy. Celia was being shaken by her stepdad, smelling his angry fish breath, seeing how much he wanted to bite her—it was one of her biggest fears, being bitten, and she remembered afresh how he would play those ugly teeth against her childhood nipples and threaten to do just that. "You'd like that, you'd like that," he would say—

He swung her hard against the side of the house. The air escaped her lungs when her head cracked against the wood. She fell to her knees into the grass, dimly aware that the spider bite on her leg was bleeding.

A neighbor's back porch light flashed on. "Don't make me call the cops on you, fucking creep!" someone yelled, and Teddy's arm stopped above her, raised like a sword.

Instead he flipped her over, falling down on his knees, too, and Celia felt him, hard against her like a dog. No, not right here, she thought, and felt that long arm reach around and pin her stomach against her spine so she couldn't breathe. His voice was coarse in her ear. "You'd like that, wouldn't you, ugly little bitch."

Celia tried to breathe. He wouldn't. He would. His other hand came around, to grab her throat, and all of the horror of the world stole over her. The sky was turning black. He was whispering, talking to her, telling her all sorts of secrets. On the other side of the wall Alyssa was sobbing, and Celia was making her promise in her mind to not listen. Go someplace else, Alyssa, she thought. Think of the butterflies.

He stopped. Other lights were turning on. Celia came to, slowly, hearing the tap of his breath, becoming aware of her own limbs.

She wasn't dead after all. She wormed out of his hold and stood up, feeling his grossness all over her body, imprinted through her clothes. He stood, too, looking strangely shamed in the night. On the other side of the wall Celia could hear Alyssa sobbing. She was pleading, under her breath, saying, "Don't hurt my sister, I will do anything."

Celia breathed into the night. Her throat burned. She felt herself coming back, heard the murmur of voices, the secrets he had told. Suddenly she knew. Bending over, swept with nausea, she spoke:

"I wasn't the first," she said. "You hurt other girls. You made my mom an addict, just so you could have me. It wasn't the first time either, you fucking disease."

"You don't know shit, Celia." He wiped his mouth.

"I do know! You raped me! Now you're raping my sister! *You are a fucking rapist.*" The last came as a shout, and around the neighborhood a silence fell. All the murderous rage of Celia's life was coming out now, she was boiling and she didn't care, she was going to run, run, from this horrible man and this terrible life.

"*I am not a liar,*" Celia screamed into the night.

TWO

—

CHRYSALIS

It was early Monday morning, and that meant Naomi arrived at the boxing gym before it opened. She snuck up to the broad glass to make sure it was empty, and then retreated to her car to watch for the mysterious Ray. If he was the same scar-faced man she had seen downtown, she wanted to keep her distance. To start.

She drank the coffee resting in her console, ate a granola bar without tasting it.

Ten minutes before the place was due to open, a group of teenagers showed up and sat politely outside on a piece of concrete barrier. One rose, looked in the dark window, gestured down the street at a Jack in the Box. The others rose to follow him.

A hulking figure walked across the street, towards the gym. From the angle Naomi couldn't see his face. He wore a baseball cap, pulled tight over his temples, and had his collar turned up. His walk was sloping, almost jerking. Nerve damage, Naomi thought. She put down the granola bar, reached for the door handle.

The man walked to the gym door, pulled out a mess of keys,

tried to find the right one with his shaking hand, finally unlocked the door.

Naomi slipped from her car, softly closed the door, and moved swiftly across the street. In moments she was behind him, following his back as he entered the gym, the door still open. Her leather shoes made no sound.

The door shut behind them.

The door jangled.

Ray turned.

He was an older man with a small face, perched like a dried apple on his oversized neck. The small mouth had a strange beauty: pummeled so much it had taken on the appearance of a purpled fig, radiating lines to his still mercifully full cheeks. His friendly eyes were so cut with scars, they looked like he'd had a date with a hedge trimmer. And under his hat, perched like two little Brussels sprouts, were a pair of cauliflower ears. His face reminded her of the hors d'oeuvres that Mrs. Cottle had made for church socials, with vegetable crudités stuck with toothpicks on a cabbage, the inside hollowed out for dip. Mrs. Cottle called these "horse dubbers."

He took a step back, startled. Naomi raised her own hands with caution, turning them to show her palms.

"I don't have no money, miss," Ray said.

"It's okay," she said. "Mistaken identity. I'm sorry to startle you."

"You come to box?"

"No." Naomi shook her head, and then reconsidered. As long as she was here. Her bag was in the back of her car.

"Thank you for coming in," Mike Morton told a still sweaty Naomi, who had rushed to the morgue after his call. She was aware she needed a shower. She pressed her armpits closed.

Mike reached for a model plane and held it in his hands. "I followed your advice and paid a visit down in the capital." Naomi waited, looking at him across his desk, his gray skin a silver color next to his scrubs. She didn't think that was why he had called her. She assumed he wanted her to look at the new bodies they had found.

"I found a researcher. She ran what we know about all the girls we've found—age, physical specs—through their databases. You were right. Some of the girls had been in foster care before they were on the streets. She's confirming their identities right now."

Naomi smiled. It was a vestige of her usual smile, but she was glad to help.

Mike took a deep breath, steadied himself. "There's more. When I was down there, I was looking at these old photos of the state orphanage outside Elk Crossing, on their office walls."

Naomi felt a sense of foreboding.

"There was this photo with a line of girls outside, dressed in winter parkas. There was snow on the ground. In the middle of the group stood a little girl who looked a lot like you. She was maybe three or four and holding the hand of her baby sister. I asked the researcher about it. She told me a story how over twenty years ago, two sisters went missing from that orphanage."

"Who do I talk to?" Naomi barely managed to find the words.

He pushed a number at her. "This is the woman who used to run the orphanage."

Once called Claremont, then Fairfield, the state girls' home was a place of sour ghosts. You could feel it, stepping inside. Like in all institutions, only bad things had happened here.

Naomi had driven a few hours to get there, noting as she passed the small towns along the freeway how she was retracing a path back to her captivity. The orphanage wasn't far from the woods where she and her sister had been held underground. She passed thick forests that would have seemed beautiful to others but sent a shiver of fear through her. Something about the tangled underbrush, the manzanita and sword fern among the chaos of the trees, said *here* to her. And in the woods of her imagination she ran and ran.

Naomi stood in the decayed main hall and tried to remember. Did she hear the sound of running feet, the hushed whispers of little girls? The wet sweep of a mop, the taste of corned beef and cabbage? She could feel the memories in the background of her mind.

"I'm pleased you could come." The retired woman held out spring-cold hands. Naomi could see rims of dirt in her broad nails; she liked gardening. She stared deeply into Naomi's eyes. "I didn't think it could be true . . . You *are* her. The older Bolen sister."

Naomi closed her eyes. She now had a last name. She was someone, not just a nameless girl born from the dirt. A shiver began in her feet and moved up through her legs, making her feel faint. Bolen. My name is Bolen.

"Are you all right?"

"Yes." Naomi's eyes were closed.

She now had a past. A mother. This woman was going to tell

her about herself. The long-sought past was rushing up to her, a voice crashing through the woods behind her. It might pull her all the way back down the trapdoor, down the metal rungs she now felt with her hands. Into a room where she had whisper-sung to her little sister.

But she had to.

"I'm sorry. It must be hard."

"Life is always hard," Naomi said, her own voice tough. She opened her eyes, brought back the smile. "Tell me about myself."

They walked the grounds, the beds of soil loamy and turned over for spring. A set of gardeners were at work, shoveling compost. Inside, down cavernous halls where girls once lined up for dinner, were various parts of machines, broken down. The dining hall was empty, only the shadows of the tables on the floor. A desolate industrial-sized kitchen in the back where men were tearing the wiring out from the walls.

"You came just in time," the silver-haired woman said. "The building sold a few months ago. They're making a lodge out of it, one of those fancy hotels." She gave a skeptical laugh. "Lord knows the nightmares the guests will have, the ghosts that haunt this place."

Upstairs, climbing stairwells worn by hundreds of small feet, they reached a narrow hall, with bedrooms off each side. Without thinking, Naomi marched directly down the hall and turned into a bedroom. Peeling wallpaper covered the walls—dogs and puppies. Naomi looked at the wallpaper, then out the window, to where the gardeners were working below. To the east, not far at all, was the town of Elk Crossing and the woods. She hadn't thought to come here because there had been no reports that even mentioned the orphanage.

"You knew this was your room," the woman said behind her, in wonder. "You and your sister. We tried to keep siblings together. It's never good to keep children in orphanages, but . . . we did our best."

"Do you remember me?"

"Yes."

Naomi felt the pulse in her neck. She had come without Jerome yet again. But she had told him why. She needed to be alone for this, her genesis. This was where it had started.

"We had a hundred and sixty girls living here, and dozens of staff working. Some of the staff stayed nights. I was one of the ones who came and went, from my house nearby."

Naomi wondered why the woman was telling her all this. Guilt, probably.

"Staff—we called them counselors—did head counts every morning. One morning they did a head count, and two girls were missing from this room. Naomi and Sarah Bolen."

Sarah, Naomi marveled.

"At first we thought maybe you had escaped, to run back home. But I knew that wasn't likely."

"Why not?" Naomi asked, but part of her knew.

"You were orphans. Your mother died giving birth to Sarah. That's why you came into care. You had no surviving relatives. You were all alone in the world."

"Except for each other," Naomi said in a husky voice. She lifted the back of a hand and wiped her eyes. "Did you check all the staff?"

"You're smart. I'm not surprised you went into this line of work."

Naomi waited.

The woman sighed. "All accounted for. There were no clues, no leads. It was as if both of you had just vanished in the night."

"What happened then?" Naomi's voice was low.

"Nothing."

The two women squared off in the room, with its decaying wallpaper, the marks where the teeth of multiple beds had dug into the floor. "We called the courthouse in Elk Crossing, but nothing seemed to happen." Naomi frowned. She didn't recall seeing any reports of missing sisters from that town. "Eventually everyone moved on. Of course we didn't forget. I never forgot. But everyone else did. Life just moved on. I moved on. I am sorry."

"I need my records." Naomi swallowed.

An hour later Naomi left, tires crunching down the long drive. A slim file lay in her passenger seat. She silently talked to it as she drove. Sarah. Now I know your name, too. Sarah Bolen. We are sisters. I was barely four and you were only two when we were taken. That's why I can't remember anything before captivity.

And I don't want to remember what happened during it.

The file said more: Names of her mother and her father, who had died in a factory fire not long before Sarah's birth. Relatives, all deceased. Hometown. Birth dates. Naomi now had a birthday—until now she simply celebrated it in the spring, the time of birth. "My forever child," Mrs. Cottle had called her, encouraging her to see every day as her awakening to life. Blood types, medical histories. Each word was a clue, a treasure.

From this Naomi could find her own story. Their mother and father were dead, but she had a past. A lineage. Someplace out there, there would be other Bolens, and she could find them and say, I know you. You are family.

But first she had to find Sarah. And the way to do that was to find the man who had stolen them both.

Driving back, all she could think was, Jerome. I need you, she thought. I hope you are there.

It took most of a night and a morning for Celia to get downtown because she didn't have any bus fare and had to walk all the way. By the time she finally got back—to a big hug from Stoner and Rich—her feet and legs hurt. At least the spider bite had stopped bleeding.

She sat outside the Aspire shelter with a few other kids. Rich had taken off as he sometimes did. Celia thought he had probably gone home, like she did, to check on people who didn't want him. A reporter had come by, asking the street kids if they knew who was killing the girls. "If we knew, wouldn't we tell someone?" the kids asked.

Celia was outside the shelter because of the popsicles. Every week the popsicle man showed up. He was a skinny old hippie who reeked of pot and body odor, and he brought downtown a big cardboard box filled with half-melted popsicles. Over time the kids had figured out the popsicle man was okay. No one had died from eating one of his popsicles, and to their knowledge he had never skeeved on any of them either. Of course no one was letting his dirty fingers anywhere near them anyhow.

He came now, and the street kids gave a little ironic cheer. They gathered round and he opened his box, handing out the purple, red, orange, and green, Celia's favorite. The heavyset woman who ran the shelter came to the gated door, wearing her blue Aspire shirt. She watched them, sympathy in her face.

Shaking her head, she hung the sign for the coming night: FULL.

* * *

"I can tell you like lime."

It was Naomi again. Naomi was on skid row so much it was like she was part of the streets, and even Celia, she had to admit, was looking forward to seeing her, even if it was a mistake, as the other kids said.

Celia had finished sucking the popsicle stick so dry barely even a stain of green remained. That remained on her tongue, which she had been showing to the other kids. They had been sticking their tongues out at one another, making rainbows of purple, red, orange, and green. Sometimes street life could be fun.

"It's okay," Celia muttered, to the ground.

"I'm still looking for my sister," Naomi said. Then she smiled. "But I'm learning more. I've learned her name is Sarah."

"Have you ever had a shower?" Celia asked, suddenly.

Naomi looked puzzled. "Yes."

"Once, when I was little, we went to stay in this scummy hotel. It was because our landlord kicked us out of our house for not paying the rent. The hotel was for poor people—they call it section eight."

Naomi, listening, nodded. She understood.

"I never had a shower before. I didn't understand the curtain goes on the inside. I left it outside."

"Did the water flood?"

Celia's chin trembled. "It poured all over the floor."

"What happened then, Celia?"

Celia looked away. Her face was blank. Naomi waited a long moment, but the girl never answered. "Maybe," Naomi said softly, "you forgot."

Celia's eyes turned towards her. "I never forget."

Celia had been thinking of that day, the pour of golden water down the shower curtain. She had seen it. Oh yes, she had. She had felt the delicious way the water poured over her body, and she had raised her face to the pelting warm rain of it.

Then she had noticed the way the water streamed down the inside of the curtain. She had knelt, hair pouring, and traced her small fingers down the rivulets. She had seen the way they meandered, like creeks in the woods. Some wandered away, thin and delicate and yet brave for doing so, but even they changed course and came back and joined the strong ones. And then all of them ran together, a race, faster and faster, down the plastic curtain, to make brand-new exciting puddles and lakes on the bathroom floor.

For at least an hour the water had pounded down, until it went from hot to cool to cold, and her shoulders thrashed with it, until she felt she was swimming in the iciest lake or ocean—Celia had never swum, but she could imagine it—and the water turned from golden warm to refreshing cold blue. She was now a waterborne creature, swimming in the deep. She was a new kind of chrysalis, rising from the shore. She was a pupa. She had wings; she was a golden butterfly flying over open water. She was tired. Her wings were wet.

She had suddenly come to and realized the bathroom floor was covered with water. Not just covered. Flooded. Celia was naked, kneeling in the tub, red with cold, and she saw her hand, shaking, reach out to turn off the tap. Drip. Drip. The last of the cold water ran down the drain. But the floor of the bathroom was still covered. Inches of it, sloshing around the rusted coffee can they used for trash. Soaked through the stack of stiff towels on the floor. Ruining the toilet paper left by the cracked porcelain bowl.

Moaning, she had stepped out. She heard shouts of fury from the hotel room below her. The stampede of feet from outside. Teddy, awoken from his nap in front of the television, buried in beer cans.

That was when Celia did stop remembering, so what she had told Naomi was kind of a lie. She did remember, only she chose to forget. But that was a different kind of pretend.

*   *   *

Rich got off the last bus to a late-night street sparkling with dew. The buildings were slick with moisture, a fog billowing down the streets. The dead hours, he thought, before dawn. When the world might rise again. But only if Mother Nature allowed it.

He was a boy of many thoughts, all carefully hidden. All through school, even before his dad was sent to prison, before his mother turned into the laughingstock of not just their town but the entire world, he had kept his thoughts to himself. He didn't want anyone to laugh at him, too.

The video of his mother still pained him. He wondered if any of the millions who watched it ever thought she was a real person, dancing on that roof, smashing a beer can against her head. Rich remembered the video in colors of red and veins of black, taken by a laughing stranger with a phone camera.

Child Protective Services had come a few days after the video went viral. They had put Rich in the social worker's car. They had left the fetid house, the piles of empty bottles, left his mother. They had punished her for being human, for making the same mistakes others did off camera.

He walked quickly, hurrying through the dark, empty streets. He had waited too long to catch the bus. He figured Celia and Stoner had already gone to the overpass. But to get to the overpass, he had to go through the waterfront park, and that, even more so than most of their world, was a dangerous place. It was a place without lights, where wilding packs of jocks roamed at night.

Moving as quietly as he could, Rich crossed into the waterfront park, trying to move under the deepest shadows so he wouldn't be seen.

The last time Rich had seen his mother was the day they took him. No, that wasn't really true. He had seen her once more, at a visit in the child welfare offices. Her drinking had gotten worse, it was clear. He didn't blame her. His dad had been sent to prison for doing nothing—literally, his dad had been arrested for loitering— and his mom had been working two jobs ever since and still couldn't afford their rent. That was how she started. She was so stressed all the time.

His mom had needed a friend. That was what she had needed and never got. Just one good friend, someone who would come to the house and clean up the bottles and encourage her to take a shower and sit with her until she got herself right.

Not the kids who spray-painted *LOSER* on the side of their house. Or the boss who fired his mom after the video went viral. Or the teachers who looked at Rich and then looked away. Or the group home where he was sent.

There was something behind him.

Rich froze. His thighs prickled with fear, and his stomach somersaulted. Slowly he turned around.

They were right down the path, stalking him. He could see them moving under the cherry blossom trees, coming into view. They came out into the path, and he felt his bowels loosen in terror.

High school jocks. They formed a line across the path.

For a terrible moment he didn't know what to do. The skid row was behind him, all the shelter doors locked for the night. The footbridge was ahead of him. He could dash there, but they could follow. There was no place to run.

He turned and began running for the bridge as fast as he could, knowing it wouldn't be fast enough. All the memories of gym classes and sports events, the efforts of his mom to get him to do something besides play video games when she was at work.

"Hey! Catch the—"

He could hear them gaining behind him, their voices mad with joy and the excitement of pursuit. Rich felt his feet pick up, his legs churn in terror. His mouth was open, gulping air that could not reach his lungs, already burning.

"Fucking fag!"

Rich wished he could close his eyes, melt to the ground in sorrow. The footbridge was ahead of him, but he wasn't going to make it. He could hear them right behind him.

He whipped around before they could tackle him. There were six of them, all in new clothes, windbreakers, sneakers that probably cost hundreds of dollars. Their hair was cut short, their faces strangely plastic, honed to sharpness by razors and cruelty.

"What do you want?" he asked, backing up. He immediately wished he hadn't said anything. His voice cracked with fear.

"Whatcha running for?" the leader asked. He was a muscular boy with bright yellow hair, dyed. He had a diamond in one ear. Rich remembered some old bum telling him that once upon a time that meant you were gay, only now it didn't, but that didn't change anything, did it?

"I'm talking to you. You fucking loser."

The leader was puffing up, his arms turning into deadly triangles. His eyes were like dead fish. He reminded Rich of the body they had seen in the river. Maybe the boy had come from the river, too. Maybe they all had. Maybe they were all already dead, and that was why they played this game.

Rich felt the fear widen, encompass him. *Please*, he wanted to tell the world. Don't do this to me. Again.

"Fucking street trash."

The leader was winding up, relishing. A light dancing, athletic. One of the other boys held up his phone, recording. Another video, Rich thought, as the first fist swung. Taking out the trash, as they called it. By the next night it might hit a million views, and everyone would be laughing at him, too.

Rich felt the first blow against the side of his head. It was like the stars, and the moon, yes, exploding into pain, and he could feel himself dropping, trying to catch his hands on the pavement, thinking dimly maybe they wouldn't want to bloody their new shoes by kicking him. But that didn't work either.

This time Naomi asked Jerome to come with her. It was a bit like the past year of travel: increasingly long silences broken by spontaneous laughter and warmth. Jerome recognized his people's home country as they crossed the valley: long-neglected oak savannas, fertile farmland crested with dark fir mountains.

ELK CROSSING, the bullet-punched sign outside of town said, leaning over a ditch frenzied with spring growth. POPULATION: 740.

Naomi felt her body tense driving into the empty town. A spider was in the back of her skull, hissing danger. This was strawberry country. This was terror.

Naomi and Jerome had come through here before, after finding the bunker nearby. But they had come up empty. Now they had a name. They had a story to follow.

The town of Elk Crossing looked abandoned, the shop windows soaped. They drove past the funeral home, low and squat and pink, with dried shrubs outside the walls like freckles, and a boarded-up high school. The fields were still planted. But the family farms had been eaten up by the corporations that now combed the fields. Few people lived here anymore. It was a place managed, not occupied.

The solitary bar was still open. Naomi watched a man with a face like burlap stagger down the street to his truck.

She parked at one of the forgotten meters.

"What are we looking for?" Jerome asked. Their efforts to find anything online about how Naomi and her sister went missing from the orphanage had been fruitless.

"I don't know yet," she answered.

Naomi was surprised to find the small courthouse was still open. Inside the front entry was a solitary clerk. She looked up, lines of surprise in her face.

"I need to see your records," Naomi said, showing her license. Jerome, next to her, stood, wearing his Purple Heart pin on a white shirt with the sleeve neatly pinned up over the cap of scar tissue from his missing arm. That's all it took. Glancing reverentially at Jerome while completely ignoring Naomi, the clerk hustled. "Right this way," she said, leading them down a hallway floor lined with mop streaks. Naomi rolled her eyes. "Hero," she whispered to Jerome.

Naomi looked around as they walked, at the crumbling walls, the circles of water damage on the ceiling. They passed the solitary courtroom, the heavy doors now latched. The bench outside was polished down by generations of bottoms. Above the bench was a painting of an older man labeled with a brass plaque.

The clerk unlocked a door to a long narrow room lined with shelves. In the middle was an oak table. Naomi walked down the row of brown file boxes, checking dates. All the town records were here: police, court, and land.

"Here," she said, pulling down a box for the months that she and her sister had gone missing. She carried it to the table, surprised at how light it was.

The clerk, her face curious, hung in the doorway. Behind her the pure light of farm-valley Oregon poured into the room. "We're okay," Naomi said so the woman would go away. Naomi shut the door behind her.

The box, as it turned out, was almost empty. They found traffic tickets and divorce decrees, a few deeds. No missing child reports. Jerome and Naomi went through box after box and found the same paucity. There was no sign that the kidnapping had ever been reported, let alone investigated. It was as if she and her sister had never existed.

Jerome set down a land deed. "This doesn't make sense," he said, frowning. "There's no such thing as a town without crime." Naomi leaned over, looked at the signature at the bottom. *Judge Thurman*, it said. She looked at the other records. They all had the same name.

Naomi stood below the painting down the hall. THE HONORABLE RALPH THURMAN, the plaque said. The judge had been a heavy-jowled man with crinkled grandfatherly eyes. She checked out the dates below. He had died not long after she went missing.

"The migrants who found me nearby didn't want to come here," Naomi said under her breath. The clerk was hovering nearby, inquisitive. "They drove me all the way to Opal. There was a reason why."

Jerome stood behind her, waiting.

Naomi turned to the clerk. "Where's the local graveyard?"

The Elk Crossing graveyard had the shy, quiet look of all abandoned places. Naomi and Jerome walked the rows of headstones, passing under tall firs. A mossy statue of Mary reached out her consoling hand, a sparrow nest in her pitted palm. Jerome looked over the grassy oak savannas that were once populated by his people, only to be stolen and now neglected.

In the back, crowded against a falling-down stone wall, they found the baby nursery. Baby nurseries, also called baby graveyards, were a Northwest tradition that went back to pioneer times. Naomi didn't know if other places had the same practice of burying children in a separate graveyard, or if it was just an Oregon peculiarity.

The baby nursery was surrounded with a row of overgrown hedges, almost swallowing an arching cast-iron entryway. Inside was a maze of tiny headstones sunken into the grassy soil. The dates went back to the 1800s. Many, she could tell, were stillbirths. Naomi stopped to read one. *Baby Agnes, Nov. 2, 1901, born already with our Lord.*

Other graves were of children well into their teens. You could almost track epidemics and flus, Naomi thought, walking past the clusters of graves. "This is sad," Jerome said, pointing to a row of five children, all from the same family. Their names told the story, starting with Hope and moving on to Faith and finally the last one, Perseverance. "I wonder if they kept trying," he said.

Naomi didn't respond. She told herself she was used to death, used to being buried alive.

The sun, passing through the trees, caught on Jerome's black hair.

"What do the Kalapuya believe about death, again?" Naomi asked, curious.

Jerome knelt and swept dirt off an ancient headstone with his one hand. "My people believe that no one really dies. When it is time for us to leave this world, one of our loved ones comes to walk us on. They take us to the other country."

"Where is this other country?"

"No one knows. You have to die to find out."

"Well, no thanks."

He rose, brushing dirt off his jeans. "Remember how we used to hunt for their belongings in the trees, Naomi?"

"I do." It sounded like a promise. Naomi gazed in adoration at Jerome.

Her shoe had hit a line of newer graves. This section of the child graveyard was crowded, and Naomi instantly recognized another graveyard tradition: the pauper graves. She was looking down at a cheap metal plate from decades past. She followed down a line of graves. There were over a dozen of them, ending around the time she had gone missing. Each contained a child with an estimated age of five to ten.

Jerome stood next to her. The wind sloughed through the trees. Each of the plates said the same thing: *Child Doe*.

"Something terrible happened here," Naomi said.

"Stop here."

Unaccustomed to Jerome speaking so abruptly, Naomi pulled over. They had just left the town and were passing by another set of strawberry fields. The green crowns were just now budding with white flowers. An old farmhouse stood on a hill, as empty as the sky. A torn scrap of fabric flew out a dormer window. In the pasture was a single majestic white oak tree, its tightly budded arms reaching for the sky.

Jerome got out. Naomi followed.

Finding the rusted pasture gate, Jerome walked into the field. The unruly grass came to his waist. The air was heavy with the rich scent of cottonwoods, the fences draped with the long white blooms. Jerome walked until he came to the spreading, majestic oak.

He stood underneath the tree and lifted his one hand and squinted. Naomi, curious, looked up, too.

Tied high up in one of the branches was what appeared to be an old blanket, wrapped tightly around bulky objects. The bundle was securely tied to the tree with ancient rope. The rope was so old the tree limb had overgrown part of it, swallowing it. The blanket was tufted from birds and rotten in places, dried hard by the sun in others.

"Well, after all this time, I think we found one of the relics we were looking for as kids," Jerome said, smiling at Naomi.

"Do we climb up there, take it down?" Naomi asked.

Jerome shook his head. "I should get an elder from the tribe. If it is an ancestor's belongings, I don't want to be disrespectful. It's been there for years. It can wait a few days."

In the distance the farmhouse, empty windows for eyes, seemed to smile. The breeze lifted Jerome's hair, and the skin of his arm looked dark under the tree. All around the cottonwoods bloomed, the soft down catching on the wind.

On the way back to the city it began raining.

Heading back downtown from the overpass was miserable when it was raining.

Celia and the boys had waited for what felt like hours hoping the cloudburst would stop, crouched in their overpass cave. The heavy rains soaked under the bushes, running in wet muddy fingers up to their feet.

Finally, too hungry to bear it any longer, they slid down the hill, getting covered in mud, and ran, squelching in sopping-wet shoes, to the freeway, where the cars, wipers on full tilt, didn't even slow down for them. Celia could see the faces of the drivers huddled over the wheels. She wondered if she would ever learn to drive. Her mother had lost her license for driving while high. Celia understood that was punishment, but she didn't think the judge understood that meant her mom couldn't work anymore and that meant Teddy owned them and Celia was trapped forever.

Finally a break in the traffic came, and the street kids ran, their jeans black with water. Rich kept his head down, his swollen lids almost closed with bruises. They crossed the footbridge, the river below them a wild torrent. Celia could see the back of Stoner's neck where the rain had parted his hair, the twin tendons as delicate as musical instruments.

The street kids went to the deli at the top of downtown. The booths were made of a sticky fake leather that made squishing noises when they sat down. The waitress put the water glasses down, stared at Rich and his swollen, bruised face. "Someone beat you up, honey?" she asked with concern.

No, he shook his head, miserable.

"Let me guess," she addressed them. "Biscuits and gravy."

"I want pie. Pecan, à la mode," Stoner said, and a rivulet of water poured down his neck. Celia stared at him. That was a stupid thing to buy. Pie was more expensive and didn't last as long. Biscuits and gravy was big and cheap.

The plates came, heavy and white. On the plate in front of Celia, thick white goo was ladled over two stale biscuits with dry crumbs on the sides. Celia stuck a fork in one, twanged it. She pulled the fork out. Most of the gluey biscuit came with it, tiny pieces of gray mystery meat in the pasty white gravy. She put the chunk on her tongue. It tasted like salt and nothing else. She was hungry. She ate it.

Rich had come back late the night before, crawling into their cave, whimpering. Celia had woken just enough to smell the blood. She had lain against him until he stopped shivering, putting her arms around his cold middle. Waking, she had seen he had been beaten. With the others she had counted his teeth, made him lift his shirt so they could see that his ribs, though bruised, were not broken. His breath had whistled in and out okay, and his eyes, though bloodied, could see. A beating was ordinary and deeply sad. But ordinary. Or so she told herself, once again.

Celia thought about the apartments and trailer courts they had lived in when she was little, with names like Pine Top Estates and Chantilly Arms. The grosser the place, the nicer the name. It almost felt like a personal insult.

Stoner ate his pie in three bites. Then he waited to see if anyone wasn't going to finish their food, his lowered eyes checking, then coming back again.

Rich ate, head down, fork moving rapidly from plate to mouth. You could tell it hurt Rich to eat, but he did it all the same. They all kept their arms cocked around their plates, like someone might steal them.

Celia looked out the window. Sometimes she wanted bad things to happen just to relieve the moments like this. Like the way her feet itched in her wet socks, or the way her soaked jeans clung to her icy thighs, getting colder by the second. The feeling of needing to go to the bathroom.

The food was gone. They pulled out wet pennies and linty nickels, counting their change onto the wet table. Stoner licked his plate. The waitress watched from behind the counter, then went into the kitchen.

In a moment the waitress came back, bearing another white plate. Biscuits and gravy for Stoner. She put down the plate with a smile. "Manners," she reminded him.

"Thank you," he mumbled.

"You looked hungry," she said, looking relieved.

When they left, she waved at them, and Celia turned around, waving back.

There was one good thing about a heavy rain:

It got rid of the creeps. The pimps, the freaks, and the johns.

The only people on skid row when it was raining were the street people and the nuns and the volunteers trying to help. Those people were real. They didn't tell lies like *go to the police if anyone touches you* or *it will all be okay.*

One of the nuns came down the wet sidewalk now as the homeless huddled under the gusts of rain and wind. Families protected their children under their coats. The nun handed out clear white plastic rain ponchos, knowing the street people liked these best—you could see through them to make sure another was not holding a weapon—and they kept the water off better than any jacket.

Grateful, the street people donned the ponchos, and Celia and her friends became one in a line of white plastic gleaming objects. "Like a row of condoms," Stoner joked, his mouth wet with rain, but Celia thought more like pictures she had seen of jellyfish, bobbing along in a gray pavement sea.

In the late afternoon the sky cleared and became a hard metallic blue. The sun shone, and the mist evaporated off all the buildings, twining like snakes off the turrets. It got so hot that the metal trash cans were warm under their touch as Celia and Rich dug into them, looking for returnable bottles others had missed. It was then that Celia noticed the ponchos littering the street. The families had returned to holding their kids in front of their jackets, and it was like everyone had forgotten the rain.

With the heat came danger.

Stoner, living up to his name, got into something wicked. Only instead of smoothing him out, relaxing his always tense face, it turned his mouth into a black cavern full of teeth, and Celia, like the others, ducked and ran from his swinging-wide fists.

"Slow down, Stoner, slow down," Rich kept saying, getting chased in a circle in the hot street, the sun pounding down. The bums, lying on their sides in the heat, panted and watched the show. Stoner spun and spun, and Celia and the other street kids stood under the ASPIRE sign and watched, heads cocked for—

There. The sound of sirens. The cops only came when there were fights. Or bodies on the streets. No one ever knew who called the cops since skid row was all street people. Maybe it was the re-covering alkies sulking in the dirty rooms above, sent there by the agencies to test the dry among their friends.

The cops came to a halt, sirens muted by the day, the sun striking off the domed lights. They got out of the car. One walked towards Stoner, talking to him. Another stood to the side, watching, hand on his gun. Celia was watching, too, her head tilted. She became cautious, times like this. She became an eye in the sky.

Were the cops going to kill Stoner? That was the worry in her mouth, and the cynical fear in the eyes of the bums. But the cop talking to Stoner soon had him cornered, and he had his hands up. Profanity was pouring out of his mouth. "Fucking cocksuckers,"

Celia heard. "Clit fuckers." My friend is high, she wanted to tell the cops.

But the cops seemed to know. They pushed Stoner into the back of the car, cuffed. In a moment they were driving off, Stoner's curly hair visible through the window. The kids could hear him yelling from inside the car.

"Where do you think he's going?" Celia asked Rich after coming down from the clouds. She realized several minutes had passed. Rich had been watching her, curiously.

"Juvie, I bet," Rich said. "Maybe he'll get some help now."

Celia looked at him, sideways. It had never occurred to her that Stoner needed help. Or that any of them might get it.

Celia awoke under the overpass, her mind as smooth as stone. Only the butterflies were there, caressing her awake just as they had carried her to sleep.

She had never told anyone about the butterflies. She knew people would shake their heads, like she was being stupid. Girls like her were damaged, broken, not worthy of the butterflies. Even the victim advocate in court had acted like Celia was slime you could wipe up, but the stain would remain. When the victim advocate had said Celia could move on to a good life, the lie on her mouth never reached her eyes.

But Naomi—she was different. Naomi wasn't afraid of what had happened to Celia. She acted like Celia wasn't broken at all. Which was funny, because when Celia was around Naomi, she didn't feel broken either.

Celia turned over. Rich lay next to her. He opened his eyes, and the two of them just looked at each other, for the longest time.

* * *

In the butterfly museum, Celia knew, nothing dead is allowed. Inside the museum is the soft velvet of plants, the smell of moisture and the lick of leaves. The rooms there hum with spirits, and they are like a movement you can feel but not hear. There is the soft crunching of leaves, the spiraling crawl of the caterpillars, and the soft dusky noises of the instars inside their shells.

In the butterfly museum the butterflies flit from plant to plant, moving their majestic wings in absolute, pure peace. There are no predators there. You can go in, and the butterflies will accept you. You can stand in the middle of the rooms, among all the basking plants, the fruitful air, and you will be one of them. If you hold very still, they will come to you. They will land on your arms, and your head, and, yes, even your cheeks, and they will touch you like you are the most tender piece of fruit or the sweetest pollen of any flower.

You will know then. All their life they have been waiting for you.

I might have found something," Jerome told his friend Ed Ashtree.

Jerome had driven down to see him. It was only a few hours out of the city but a world apart, in the chilly coastal ranges. He had found Ed chopping wood at his house, an unfriendly-looking manufactured home in a gully, damp with stunted trees, festooned with moss. "This is a bad country," Jerome remembered a chief had said of this inhospitable land over a century before, after his people had been forced to march here. "It is cold and sickly. There is no game on the hills and the people are dying."

Ed, sixty-two years old with a seamed face, had befriended Jerome on his first trip to the reservation a few years before. Standing in the tiny library, Jerome had looked lost. Ed, recognizing a fellow Kalapuya from his features, offered greetings.

"What?" Ed asked, yanking the axe out of the stump. The wood was so rotten it split at a touch. The damp got in everything here.

Jerome explained the bundle tied in the tree. "It's in a white oak tree, in what used to be our people's country."

Jerome felt comfortable with Ed, in a way he had never felt before with anyone else. That first day, wandering around the reservation, Jerome had realized he was seeing other natives. It was a feeling he didn't try to explain to Naomi, who was used to looking like she belonged, even if she felt different inside.

"Our people used to burn those fields, to preserve the white oak savannas," Ed said. "We were among the first to practice wildfire control that way. For the acorns, the huckleberries, the deer." A thin spire of wood smoke from the house punctuated his words.

Ed, like Jerome, was one of only a few thousand Kalapuya left, from a mighty nation that once ruled the valleys. After being almost eradicated by epidemics, the few survivors of their people had been forced to this sickly land. A civilization that had flourished since the ending of the Ice Age, almost wiped out in less than a few hundred years.

"Do you want to go check it out with me?" Jerome asked.

Ed gave Jerome a puzzled look. Jerome was so clearly hungry to know his people, and yet he acted as if he didn't matter. Maybe it was growing up in foster care. Jerome had bought into the lie that some histories matter more than others, and this angered and grieved Ed.

Ed thought Jerome played second fiddle to Naomi, even though he was a decorated soldier, a war hero. "Of course I want to check it out," he replied testily, and then softened. "Stay the night here. We'll go back in the morning."

"Naomi will miss me. I'll meet you there."

"Naomi can take care of herself," Ed said, picking up the rotting split wood and adding it to the stack.

Jerome thought of all the times Naomi woke shaking from nightmares and he held her. Since they had started looking for her sister, he often awoke to find Naomi pacing the floor, restlessly, fast asleep but ready to search. "I'll meet you there," he said.

Jerome realized he had the better part of a day—a few hours to sunset—before he needed to head back to the city. The ocean beckoned, over the rest of the scrubby mountains. Manzanita and bent pines, hills that rode back from the winds and trees that remained, stubby reminders of faith and perseverance.

He drove into a tiny, ramshackle fishing town. On a sand dune covered with bladelike sea grass, he stood watching the fishing boats ride the waves directly onto the shore, sparkling with the last of the sun. The cold sand was empty except for one lone woman walking with a tea cozy hat on her ample gray hair and a long coat.

Jerome wondered what he had wanted to find out here besides memories of the long years between Naomi leaving their foster home and them getting married. They were lost years, and not even the scurry into war had helped him feel like he had a cause in this world besides loving her. He kept this hidden from her because he was terrified of how helpless it made him feel. He knew some would say he loved too much, too deeply, but he asked himself what else on the earth were we here for.

He got into his truck and drove back to the only home he knew, which was her.

Naomi was standing outside the Aspire shelter. The smeary brick, the narrow streets, the shapes huddled in the doorways—all felt familiar to her now. She had crossed the threshold. The world of the missing had become her own world. She knew the regulars, the bruised-cherry alcoholics, the families on nodding acquaintance, the street kids like Celia.

And the scar-faced man.

He was at the corner. He turned to see her and their eyes met. Naomi moved towards him, quickly, at a trot, dodging through the street people.

But when she got to the corner, he was gone. She blew her breath out in exasperation.

A small, fussy-looking man in round glasses was standing nearby. He had been studying one of her flyers, taped to a telephone pole. His face was as round as his glasses, with a narrow, upturned nose. He wore a suit, even in the warmth of the day. His neat little bow tie reminded her instantly of Sean Richardson, and she remembered his talk of an undercover agent. This man's shorn silver hair was a dead giveaway he was a cop.

"Do you know who that man is?" Naomi asked him.

"I have been wondering that myself," the man replied in a soft, cultured voice. The sun flashed off his glasses. She noted his shiny black dress shoes. Not even trying to fit in, she thought. She lost even more respect for the Feds.

"Have we met before?" Naomi asked, politely. "Maybe at a training?" She was thinking of all the law enforcement classes she had taken where the FBI showed up, acting dark and aloof in the back rows. He tilted his barbered head at her.

"I'm sure we have," he said.

Naomi was moving up the library stairs, feeling the dense air. The air of a thousand books, hanging serenely over the heads at the tables.

She was on her way to the third floor to look at old microfiche for the town of Elk Crossing. She had a lot to learn. Exactly what she wasn't yet sure. Libraries had been the saving grace of many of her cases. Old phone directories, ancient city maps, blueprints, self-published biographies—you never knew what you might find. She cracked one missing child case because a corner store grocer had written a diatribe against the Piggly Wiggly chain and, unbeknownst to himself, given away the location of his disappeared son.

She was passing the fiction room, and there, perched like an urchin in one of the wood chairs, reading as if all alone in a magical universe, was Celia.

Naomi slid into the chair across from Celia, making sure to cough first. She didn't want to startle the girl. Celia looked up, her expression cold—probably expecting a pervert—and then her face changed with surprise. She looked possibly even happy to see Naomi.

Naomi smiled at the stack of books around the girl, along with scraps of paper. Butterflies and more butterflies and, perhaps to mix things up, a few novels. About butterflies. FLIGHT BEHAVIOR, read the thick spine of one. Barbara Kingsolver. That's a serious book, Naomi was on the verge of saying, but stopped herself. It might sound insulting to the bright girl.

Celia looked over Naomi's head as if she saw something there.

Naomi looked around, saw nothing but the ornate ceiling. The girl had been drawing something, but she hid it with one hand, pulling the paper closer to her.

"I'm doing research about my sister," Naomi said. Her hands were relaxed on the table.

Celia looked interested. "What kind of research?"

"Oh, you'd be surprised at what you can find in the library." Naomi paused and then said, directly, "It's hard to keep secrets. Sooner or later they come out."

Celia looked slightly sick. Her soft hand hid the drawing. "Sometimes people don't believe you even when you do tell," she said.

Naomi could feel the silence around them. She had suspected it, but now knew it to be true. People act as if reporting childhood sexual abuse solved the problem, but Naomi knew that most cases don't end in conviction. What no one talked about was what life was like for the victims after acquittal.

"I did everything right," Celia said.

"I'm sure you did," Naomi answered.

Celia glanced again above Naomi, as if she were seeing something there. Her green eyes were clear and bright. "No one cares," she said. "It's all bullshit."

Naomi felt a twisting. "I care. Same with Jerome, my husband, and lots of others you don't know. There's even an FBI undercover man trying to find out what is happening to the missing girls. People do care, Celia."

"Try to talk yourself into that—huh." Celia picked her book

back up. She held it in front of her so Naomi couldn't see the tears in her eyes. After a while, she heard the chair squeak. She felt rather than saw Naomi leave the room.

Celia looked down at the sketch she had been working on.

Up the steps into the periodicals room. Naomi knew she was wronging Celia but was not sure how. *Oh yes, you do*, her mind said.

She unspooled ancient periodicals into the reader. The long-defunct *Elk Crossing Gazette*. Ads for tomato soup and a short-lived beer garden. She combed the obituaries carefully. Warm eulogy for Mrs. Blankenship, who made a mean mince pie. No one liked to cook strawberries in strawberry country, Naomi knew. They were sick as fermented jam of them.

She came to the week she and her sister had been stolen. The most exciting event reported was a log-rolling contest. You'd think nothing bad had ever happened in the town of Elk Crossing. There were no articles about missing children, or the dead and unidentified Child Does buried in the local graveyard. She read until her eyes grew blurry.

She stopped, like her hand was on a Ouija board. *Locals spruce up state orphanage*, read the caption under the photo. Naomi enlarged it. There were no names, no identities. Just a group of men in the orphanage yard decades before, pitching brush into a trailer. One man had turned towards the camera, a hat shading his eyes. Naomi put her face close to the reader, trying to discern features. They were too far away to make out their faces.

Stopping, rubbing her mouth, Naomi was unaware that her eyes had gathered into a dead-set stare. She got up and found the Census of Agriculture. Most people knew that the census counted humans. They didn't know the government also counted every sheep and cow. Returning to her reader, Naomi was again immersed. Thickets of lines and numbers. Dewberries and goats, cows right down to the weight.

Naomi got to the page showing the number of migrant farm workers hired, which got her thinking. She remembered the migrants wrapping her in an old serape the night she escaped, keeping her by their fire. In the morning they had driven her away from Elk Crossing. They had saved her life.

Her fingers following the numbers, she noticed a dwindling workforce. Fewer migrant workers had been willing to work the Elk Crossing strawberry fields as the years passed. It wasn't wages, Naomi could tell. Other towns reported increasing numbers of laborers. She remembered the children buried in the graveyard. If their parents were undocumented migrants, it would explain why others would be unwilling to work the fields. They had known something was very wrong in the town of Elk Crossing.

She stood up, stretched, was surprised to see the sun was setting. Hours had passed. The main room was empty. Celia could have been sitting outside the door in the hall, back against the wall, her special book in hand, waiting, and Naomi would not have known.

Naomi opened the online card catalog, cross-checking names. Elk Crossing newspapers, check. Elk Crossing courthouse, done.

Elk Crossing and strawberries. Now look at this. An old listing for the Thurman Family Strawberry Farm.

Owned by none other than the judge himself, Ralph Thurman.

The lights flickered above her. It was time to go.

Floors below her, Celia had decided to leave, but her warmth was still in the rooms, haunting Naomi with her longing.

ook." Rich spoke with fear as ripe as the bruises on his face.

He and Celia were at the edge of an industrial area, looking for cans. It was just the two of them now. Word had filtered back, as it sometimes did on the streets, that Stoner was in lockdown treatment. He liked it there, they had heard. They had food.

Celia had thought about telling Rich about the scary house she had seen some weeks before, with the eyes behind the basement window. But Rich might want to go look, and Celia wanted to stay the hell away from it.

The street was cold and empty. The sky was the color of smoke, with a magenta sun, and Celia marveled at how the dumpsters filled up despite how desolate the streets were. She had just pulled out what looked like a completely uneaten and unfucked-with McDonald's burger when Rich spoke. She opened the bun, checking for broken glass. People did mean shit in life.

She froze. Down the street a group of jocks had gathered, climbing on a dumpster. Larking, their faces said. All the old-fashioned words for the hunt, Celia thought, when it stops being play and starts turning wild.

But this wasn't play, unless Rich and Celia were the prey.

"Are they the same ones?" she asked, putting the burger back in the trash.

Run, the butterflies warned, suddenly. They masked the falling sun with their fury.

Rich slowly backed away. "Let's go," he said.

The jocks turned. The leader had yellow hair.

"*Fuck*," Rich said.

For real, the butterflies added. Run, Celia!

Celia ran. She felt as unreal as the coming night sky. Her thin-soled shoes, hitting the rough road. Her legs, lifting the sun-dried jeans. Her mouth, breathing the dusky, red-tinged air. None of this was real, a voice in her said, and that was why she might end up a junkie strung to the last hope of life, or a phantasm that went in and out of the cars, nothing but a hollow shell that performed as the men wanted. A doll. A toy. Never was here.

The last fury, the butterflies told her, flying in great clouds now, up by the falling sun, was if Celia was to believe her cells had hope. If she was to claim her body was as real as the blood that might jet from her veins, as real as the cars and the roads and everything else that mattered down here, everywhere. If Celia could only think she was alive.

That would be the most radical act, the butterflies said, coating the sun. If only Celia could think she deserved to live.

"They're getting closer." Rich's mouth was a choo-choo train, collecting breath, his cheeks florid. The two darted around corners, running faster, faster. Through a narrow street, closing in towards downtown, the last stretch of vacant road, littered with the empty warehouses that posted security guards so the homeless could not camp. FOR SALE FOR DEVELOPMENT, read the graffitied signs as the two street kids ran, the pack of jocks chasing them, their own faces blurring.

Part of Celia wanted to dart off to the side and run straight at the river, to her own doom. Or to turn around and walk slowly towards them, her arms out, her eyes closed. A sacrifice.

But her body was saying live, and the butterflies were, too, and she and Rich ran.

* * *

"I brought you a book," Naomi said, smiling wide.

Celia was sitting on the curb on skid row, arms wrapped around her legs, deeply ashamed of herself, because in running, she had pissed her pants, and now she didn't know what to do. She could feel the scalding piss on her inner thighs, feel the damp circle in her jeans. If she stood up, the whole world would know.

The butterflies, flitting around, consoled her. They traced her tender skin with their antennae, delighting at her beauty.

Flashes of memory, of all the times she had pissed herself. Sometimes she had pissed on purpose to keep Teddy away, but it never worked. She got spanked instead, and the single wet pair of torn sheets were stripped off the naked mattress, and she had to go back and lie on the cold damp circle. Then there were all the times she had pissed without even knowing it, going home with yet another note in her hand. *Celia smells like piss*, the other kids started saying, which is why Celia never teased Rich for the same. The kids couldn't find a name that rhymed with both *piss* and *Celia*, so they finally settled on calling her "Pee-lia."

Now Naomi was standing above her, pride reeking from every shiny pore, sturdy leather shoes on the filthy pavement, beautiful trouser legs, and holding out in her hand was a brand-new book.

BUTTERFLIES OF THE PACIFIC NORTHWEST, it said.

"It's for you," Naomi added. She sounded like she was all of twelve herself.

Fuck you, Celia wanted to say. She was filled with a sudden rage. I'm sure that book will taste good for *dinner*. Thank you for *nothing*. She turned away. She didn't want to speak because the anger might come out, and she didn't want Naomi to see or hear it. But it was there, settling cold and hard in Celia's chest, rising to her throat, choking her.

"You don't want it?" Naomi's voice, teasing, still light, but now with an edge of concern. The book stayed held out.

Celia shook her head, still looking away, her lips pressed together. Rich, down the row, looked at her. A car horn honked—a john picking up a kid was holding up the line. Naomi turned around, saw the cars, and the realization of exactly what Celia did down here struck her like a cold slap. Moving slowly, she set the book down on the sidewalk, near the girl. "I'll leave it here for you," she said, softly.

Then she walked away, head bowed.

Rich came down the row, sat next to Celia. He took the book.

He leaned over quick and kissed Celia on the cheek. That was an excuse to whisper in her ear without others seeing. "What do you need?" he asked.

"A pair of pants," she whispered. His nose wrinkling, Rich knew why. But he didn't say anything. He simply rose, tucked the book into Celia's backpack, and zipped it up. Then he took off at a trot to the Goodwill trucks, to see if there were any garbage bags of free clothes.

A half hour later he returned, and Celia was still there, reeking. But night had fallen and in the dark he and the other street kids circled Celia so the men in the cars would not see her change. They covered her with their bodies while she stripped and put on the pants Rich had found. They sang silly songs to her to make her feel better. Celia threw the wet jeans into the gutter, where they lay for the rest of the night.

* * *

"I'm going to do something," Celia said to her sister.

Alyssa squinted at her suspiciously, and for the first time Celia saw herself. The two were behind the school. This time they were hiding behind the cafeteria dumpster, in case either Teddy or Mom showed up.

It smelled bad, back here, by the dumpster. Their whole lives smelled bad.

"Here, I brought this for you," Celia said, and handed her sister the book Naomi had given her. Alyssa turned it over, looking bored. Butterflies. "Try it," Celia said, like she was asking her sister to try mashed peas or carrots.

"Why bother?" Alyssa asked, her voice low.

She sounded so much like Celia in that moment that Celia was scared. She couldn't let Alyssa give up hope. Maybe Alyssa blamed her. Just a month ago Alyssa was walking across this blacktop, as pure as the tops of flowers. Now she was hurt, and in some mysterious way this seemed like Celia's fault.

"I just wanted to be a good girl," Celia heard herself say, and Alyssa looked up in shock. "That's all I ever wanted."

"Me, too," Alyssa whispered.

Jerome met Ed at the pasture with the white oak. The piece of fabric still hung from the farmhouse dormer, blowing lightly in the wind. The front door was open. Jerome took that as an invitation for what the two men were about to do.

Ed lifted a stepladder from his truck. He and Jerome carried it under the majestic tree. Ed climbed the ladder and cut the frayed rope with a sharp knife, and the blanket bundle loosened from the tree limb. He passed it down to Jerome, who took it carefully with his one hand, bending slightly with awkwardness.

"A few more weeks, the leaves coming in, you never would have seen it," Ed said, climbing down the ladder.

"I was lucky," Jerome said.

The two men carried the bundle to a soft place under the tree. The rope was tightly embedded in the fabric, so Ed carefully cut it open. "Might as well find out now," he said.

They pulled open the blanket.

There, coiled in years of dark, spotted with the passing rains and dried by the sun, was a collection of artifacts. Jerome knew no other way to describe it. Several nightgowns, tightly coiled. A faded dress. A pair of worn brogans. A rusted brooch. A favorite teacup. Set on top of all this was a photograph of a woman.

Jerome gently lifted the bordered photo. It was a Kalapuya woman standing outside the farmhouse above them. She was wearing a simple farm dress, tight at the waist. Her hair was swept off her neck, and her face was beautiful, with serious eyes and wide cheeks. There was resolve in the full mouth.

Jerome turned the photo over. A note was written on the back, in spidery pen: *Tasmin, remember I kept you safe*.

"That sounds ominous," Ed said.

Jerome looked back at the empty farmhouse. "This whole area is bad. It almost makes me believe in evil spirits."

"People don't need spirits to make them evil," Ed said, surprising Jerome.

"Can I keep ahold of all this?" Jerome asked. "Just for the time being."

"Sure," Ed said, after a moment's hesitation. He wrapped it back up, loosely. "If you don't find her family, I'd like it all. There is so little of us left."

Jerome stretched. He wondered what kind of life the woman had led, living in this farmhouse outside of Elk Crossing. Had her people come from afar, to help her walk on in the traditional way, once her time had come? Maybe more importantly, what had she known about the graveyard, with its row of child graves?

Naomi had been thinking about graves, too. Those bodies hadn't just tumbled themselves into their coffins, she thought, morbidly.

After dropping Jerome at the pasture, she had headed to the Elk Crossing funeral home, named the Crossing Home. It was still open, no doubt until the final population of the town was put to rest. Naomi let herself in the pink building, hearing the chimes ring. She stood in the waiting room, taking in the way the Oregon light poured in the windows. She rang the bell on the counter, sharply. After a time, the funeral director hobbled out, tucking in his shirt with one hand, balancing on his cane with the other.

He was a short, round man who looked to be in his eighties, with a large head and wobbly blue eyes. He had the unkempt look of sin, his cheeks peppered with old beard. His large eyes looked at her, accusingly. His face said nap.

Naomi gave her best country smile and extended her hand. He ignored it, shuffling out with his cane and lowering his wide bottom into a waiting room chair.

"I heard about you," he sniffed after she introduced herself. He was of the generation that looked to the side of young women, as if they were contemptible. "Missus Horn at the courthouse said a lady and a soldier come, inquiring after records. You asked after the graveyard." He gave another self-important sniff.

Outside the windows the white cottonwood blooms drifted, catching on the bushes. "I lived down in Opal," Naomi said. "Used to be cattle country, but nothing left now. There's no place like home, is there?" She added the last with a touch of menace.

His blue eyes caught her. They were cold, filmed inside like a dead baby bird in its shell. Naomi dropped the pretense.

"Have you been the director here for long?" she asked, knowing the answer.

"Fifty years," he croaked, his neck wobbling.

"That's a lot of dead to bury," she said.

He grunted.

"What do you do when you get unidentified bodies?"

The hands on the cane changed somehow. "You mean the Does in the graveyard."

So much for sneaking up to it. "Yes," Naomi said, leaning forward to let him know she was serious.

He didn't answer straightaway. Most people didn't. "I take care of the cemetery. Well, me and Missus Horn. No one left to mow or trim, and that's gotten beyond us. I really shouldn't be taking care of the dead either, to tell the truth." He held up a weak hand. "It's hard work. Physical." He sounded petulant, like a child.

Naomi waited.

"The judge used to call us on those." He took a sudden interest in the floor, rubbing at the old tiles with the bottom of his cane.

"Judge Thurman?"

No answer.

"Judge Thurman is dead and gone," Naomi said. "There is nothing to be afraid of."

His opaque eyes told her otherwise. "There's no statute of limitations for murder, is there?" His voice was as soft as the gossamer strings of white blossoms outside, blowing across the empty parking lot.

"Was it you, or were you an accessory?"

His eyes closed, and Naomi saw sweat appear high on his nose.

It might have been the first sweat of years for him, glossing his cheeks now, too. Maybe those were tears. He put his face against his white hands on the cane. "I stay away from those graves. Sometimes I think they are haunting me. Haunting all of us. Those of us left, anyhow.

"Maybe I should get an attorney," he added.

"I'm not a cop. Invoking counsel won't make me go away."

He glanced at her, terrified.

Naomi suddenly changed tack. "I saw an article about locals who volunteered at the orphanage."

His eyes widened.

"I bet you remember hearing about two little sisters that went missing from that orphanage. Maybe you thought the judge would be calling you about them, too."

There was a deadly silence. He looked dead already, and Naomi had a vision of him on one of his rubber tables. She leaned close enough to feel her cheek warm his unwilling face. She spoke directly to the ghosts in front of him. "One of those girls was me."

"Oh my." His chest began moving, and his hand scrabbled over his cane. His mouth blubbered open, a wet hinge.

"Look at me."

He shook his head. He had hearing aids in his ears, she noticed. Just another human.

"*Look at me.*" Naomi's voice was soft and gentle, and yet so hard. "You can't hide anymore. I'm going to stand on your grave and shout it to the world."

"Please."

"You're old," Naomi said, and the monster was now in her voice.

"You're going to die soon. You will rest with them. The children."
She saw him give a shudder.

"There is no absolution," he croaked.

"I know."

He shook his head, rapidly, as if denying that after all this time
a truth teller had finally arrived.

"It was the judge," he said. "The judge and . . . his son."

Naomi closed her eyes then. A feeling like the darkest relief
swept her. "What was his son's name?" she asked.

Fever. Naomi had the name. Like the malaria and measles, Jerome
thought, that once swept the villages of his people, shaking them
like acorns from the trees. Like the fire that burns the heart with
true love, Ed thought, watching both of them at the table.

They met in the Country Kitten Diner in nearby Murky Grove
before heading their separate ways home. The tablecloths were
greasy red-and-white-checkered and the special on the blackboard
said *Sad Susie*. Jerome ordered it around without knowing what it
was, wanting Naomi to stay in the reverie, knowing that was what
she needed right now. If you take a burrowing animal and deny it
anything but a glass cage, it will break its own claws in the madness to escape. Naomi, who once had no escape, had created one
with her mind.

Wesley. Her lips, soundless, formed the word, tried it on, cautiously. It felt okay. *Wesley*, she tried again, her face contorting. Jerome watched, his eyes kind. Ed watched, thinking he was seeing
a transmogrification.

Naomi looked up as the waitress was putting down plates. Sad

Susie, Sad Susie, same. It was just stewed vegetables, cooked until limp. "Wesley Thurman," Naomi said clearly, looking brightly around the restaurant as if the world had just awoken and given her a gift. "The man who stole me and my sister is named Wesley Thurman. He kept us in that bunker. He's still alive. He left town after I escaped. But I'm going to find him because he has my sister."

Then, neatly, she began eating, only it was as if she couldn't stop. Jerome wanted to reach, to still her hand, but knew better. They finished their plates and went out to another Oregon spring day. It was the same one that had opened the sky that morning, Jerome knew, only it would always be different. It would get better now, for Naomi.

* * *

Sometimes Naomi thought she had a mother. It was a mother she had never met, maybe the one she had always known in her heart had died giving birth to her sister, as the orphanage director had told her. This mother was like an angel. She was out there, floating around, watching Naomi. She was watching Naomi tell Jerome how the funeral director said her sister was not buried in one of the pauper graves. Those were all migrant children. So that meant, Naomi said, that her sister could still be alive.

The ghost of Naomi's mom—maybe—watched as Jerome and Naomi sat in his truck and made a flurry of phone calls, looking for addresses, utility records, credit histories, but it was all smoke and mirrors because Wesley had gone underground. Naomi knew how easy it was to disappear yourself, because this is a big country, full of dark and light. Both she and Jerome had cases where people had created new identities. Naomi had one where a child kidnapper had made a new identity from a Costco card he found on the ground. He had stayed hidden for years that way—until she found him.

There was a part of her that wished she could be one of those people who could read books or watch movies about murder and not even know it was real. But the ghost of her mother knew better.

Naomi knew Wesley was probably good at hiding. But she was better at finding.

It was field trip day. Celia *hated* field trip day. All of downtown was clogged with yellow buses and kids streaming off them, laughing like they owned the fucking world.

Even down in skid row, where she and the other street kids now clustered, the students walked through in groups, their teacher tour guides pointing out the architecture. Celia sat with Rich at the curb, watching. Both of them had the same curdled look on their faces. It was envy and desire at the same time.

"That could be us, Rich," Celia said.

"Well, it's not." His face looked like a bruised pumpkin.

"How old were you when you left school?" she asked.

He turned towards her. "I didn't *leave* school. I was kicked out."

"Why?"

He scratched a leg. "There were some kids. Picking on me." He hesitated, as if he wanted to say more. "I put a firecracker in one of their lockers. You'd have thought I tried to burn down the White House. I got expelled."

"I thought there was some sort of law where they have to educate you. Or something like that."

"Yeah, well, what good have laws done you?"

Celia thought of the jury, their eyes on her.

"So here I am."

Celia decided she had missed part of the story. She watched a group of kids across the street. They looked her age. But they were different. It wasn't just their clothes. It was the way they carried themselves, the way the girls laughed with each other and preened. Everything she questioned they took for granted.

"Did your parents kick you out?" she asked, cautiously.

"You don't understand me. I left."

She made a face at him, appalled. The idea anyone would be on the streets without being forced out made no sense to her.

"I didn't live with my mom," Rich explained. "I was in foster care. My mom lost her parental rights to me. But there aren't enough foster homes, so I had to go to a group home. It was more like a prison. I ran away, and here I am."

"Oh." Across the street, as the kids milled around, their teacher pointed to the turrets above, touching the sky. Celia gazed upwards, too. She was listening to the teacher, following along, pretending to be one of them.

* * *

Once, in fifth grade, Celia had done her class project on butterflies. She had stapled together paper and colored in her own drawings with pencils. She had taken her time and followed the details from the books perfectly. Red admiral, painted lady, peacock. Viceroy.

She had even stolen nail polish from the drugstore to get the metallic sheen just right.

"These are all red butterflies, Celia," said her teacher at the time, Mr. Calhoun. Celia was scared of male teachers. To cover her fear she acted bold.

"Yeah," she told him, and then added sarcastically, "I like the color red. It's bloody."

He had glanced up at her. "Is that a joke?"

"No." Muted now, but the specialness of her book was soiled, touched by his gross fingers. He turned the pages. "You have talent," he had said, with surprise. The next day in class he called on Jessica first—Jessica of the blond hair, the clean neck with a gold necklace around it. Twenty-four carat, Jessica was always boasting. Celia hated her. Then Jessica stood in her white pants and everyone had seen: Celia was not the only red one.

The others had laughed as Jessica bolted from the class, but Celia felt sorry for her. She had followed Jessica to the girls' bathroom, where she was crying. Celia had taken brown paper towels and folded them into long rectangles. "This is what I do," Celia told her. She showed Jessica how to put the homemade liners in her panties.

"Can't you afford pads?" Jessica had asked, and Celia had shaken her head, confused. "That's for when you get your period," Celia had replied. Celia could hear the water dripping in the bathroom sink before Jessica answered: "If you don't have your period yet, why are you bleeding?"

Red butterflies, Celia had thought. Up on the gray ceilings, drinking from the rust-stained sink. Flying in soft red crescents. Landing softer than silk on her arms, stroking the secret softness of her upper arms. Jessica had put the paper towels in her panties. Then the nurse Sally had come, and Jessica got to go home.

Celia had returned to class, to the titter that was now saved for her. Like she had caught the blood. "Do you want to share your project?" Mr. Calhoun had asked in a kind voice, and Celia shook her head, no.

The next day he gave her project back. He had written a big *A* on every single page, ruining it. Celia threw it in a ditch on the way home.

* * *

The scar-faced man hadn't been around for a couple days. Celia hadn't seen Naomi either. The last time she had seen her was the evening Celia pissed her pants and Naomi gave her the book. Celia wanted to talk to Naomi but didn't know how. She thought maybe Naomi could tell her what to do about her sister. She didn't want to leave her sister with Teddy. There was one risk Celia could take, but it might mean losing her sister forever.

Without the scar-faced man around, the streets felt safer. Not that they really were. Celia guessed that was proven true when the next day they pulled another corpse out of the river. It was the girl with the orange hair, and Celia, like all the others, hadn't even noticed she was missing.

The only thing worse than a street birthday, Celia decided, was a street funeral.

It was pathetic, really. All of Celia fought back against the spectacle: a little gathering of the street people outside Sisters of Mercy, a small pile of candles and flowers—which Celia knew would be stolen by morning—on the corner where the girl had often hung out.

"What was her name?" the others asked one another, and someone said she was called Ginger or maybe it was Josie. One boy said she was from Madras, but no one believed him because he was a liar, and the girl with the cell phone offered that once the orange-haired girl said she came from the mountains. Which mountains? No one knew.

Suddenly everyone had been her best friend, and then she was forgotten. This happened in the space of twenty minutes. If Celia died, no one would remember her either.

She sat down next to the candles, scraping wax off the sidewalk with her nails. Rich came and crouched next to her. "Did you know her?" he asked, damp bangs against his forehead.

"Not really," Celia answered, stealing a look at him. "I mean, do any of us know each other?"

"I know you."

"You don't know the worst about me." Celia turned away.

"No. I know the best."

He reached with a cold damp hand. Celia took it.

"Come on," he said, "let's have some fun."

Rich took her on the bus to the outskirts of town, to an area that first looked industrial and then fascinated her when it switched to marshy ditches and ponds. She even saw a man fishing. Finally Rich signaled it was time to get off.

"I don't like surprises," Celia said, like every other abused kid on the planet.

"It's a good surprise," he said, and they stepped off the bus to a warm, curious smell. It took her a moment to realize what it was. Hay. There was something else, too. Celia couldn't place it, but it reminded her of circuses coming to town. Manure, she realized. They walked an empty service road, and then, turning the corner, Celia was astonished to see corrals. Barns. And horses.

"This is the back of the horse track," Rich said, and sure enough, in the distance, Celia could see the corrugated steel of the stands.

For the next dream of a few hours, she got to pet the horses, brush them and touch their velvet noses, see their amazing teeth, giggle at their pendulous bellies. The old Mexican man who worked the stables seemed to know Rich. "I was riding the buses one day, just to stay warm, and saw the track," Rich explained. "I come here to help out when I can."

"You should get a job here," Celia announced, and the old man nodded yes, yes, but Rich shook his head. "I don't even have a diploma," he said, when what he was really thinking was he didn't want to leave Celia all alone on the streets.

"No one needs a diploma to ride a horse," Celia announced, though she never had.

That changed when the old man helped her sit on a stable pony, used to guide the racehorses to the track. The pony felt huge to

Celia, broad-backed and sweet. She sat on his back and closed her eyes and felt the rough hair, the saddle between her legs. Her hands tangled in the mane.

"Celia?" Rich asked after a while.

This, she agreed, was fun.

Naomi put the autopsy photo, given to her by the medical examiner, facedown on the kitchen table. It was out of respect for the sad girl with orange hair and blackened eyes. Once alive, but no longer.

"Didn't the Feds put up surveillance on the docks?" Jerome asked.

"It's been all over the news," Naomi said. "I'm sure he knows better than to return there. He just found someplace else to dump her." She paused. "Her feet show signs of recent use. He's not keeping them as long."

"Do you think it's Wesley taking the street girls?" Jerome asked. It was the first time either of them had voiced the possibility out loud.

Naomi took a deep breath, picked up the cold cup of coffee left on the table. She carried it to the kitchen window overlooking Diane's garden. She thought of all the nonwindows of her captivity.

How she had made windows out of dirt. She thought of Celia and her butterflies.

"The pattern is the same," she said, taking a drink of the bitter coffee. "Children of the forgotten, harvested like the berries of the field."

Jerome winced behind her. He let his face smooth out before she turned.

"I wonder," Naomi said, "what Celia is doing right now."

With Naomi gone from the house, Jerome made a work area on the kitchen table. Diane was out, running errands. Since hearing Naomi and Jerome wanted to stay, she had been a flurry of activity, sewing curtains, finding her old knitting needles. Jerome viewed the knitting with suspicion. He sure hoped Diane didn't expect—

He turned his attention to the photograph from the bundle.

Mary Tarseed. He found her easily enough in the online census. The Tarseed family had been the rare natives who had been allowed to stay when soldiers had forced them off their rich ancestral lands. From what Jerome could gather, Mary's grandfather had been the Elk Crossing town blacksmith, which might have explained why their family was not forced out.

Jerome turned the photo over. *Tasmin, remember I kept you safe.*

One of the census listings showed Mary Tarseed had a toddler daughter, Tasmin. If she was alive, she would now be thirty— his and Naomi's age. But in the next town census—ten years later—Tasmin was not listed. Jerome hoped it was not what he feared.

* * *

Celia was lying on the grass of the waterfront. The girl was motionless, eyes open but unseeing. The clouds passed through the cherry blossom trees above her and speckled her face with shadows.

Naomi sat down under a tree nearby and waited.

Rich, who had led Naomi here, stood behind her, awkwardly. "I can keep an eye on her," Naomi told him, and he shambled away. Naomi could feel the humiliation that followed the boy. To be so alone at such an age.

Celia had taken off her jean jacket. She was wearing a faded blue T-shirt underneath. Her arms were slender, her chest flat. Her hands lay open, relaxed in the grass. Her eyes were unfocused, her cheek against a patch of tiny daisies in the clover. Naomi wondered what Celia was thinking or feeling. Maybe it was just a moment of respite in the middle of the terror. She could see now that Celia was trapped. The streets were a kind of captivity, too.

Celia sat up, and in her eyes Naomi could see the clouds, passing.

Moving slowly, wanting to talk to the girl while she was still in her dreamlike state, Naomi walked over to where Celia sat, her hands soft in the grass.

Lowering herself carefully nearby, Naomi joined her.

"What are you thinking about, Celia?" she asked, her voice gentle.

"The butterfly museum."

Naomi felt her strong thighs press against the velvet of the grass. The world transmitted through her legs reaffirmed her life force. "Tell me about it."

Celia's eyes filled with wonder. "It is a building, out in the country, where there are green hills. It is big, with tall walls and many windows. At the top are skylights, and they keep them polished clean. My mother told me about it."

"Of course," Naomi said.

There was a long pause. Celia was looking away, over the river. Naomi saw the tender heartbeat of her temple. The air seemed to lift around the girl.

"It's a con—conservatory. A living museum. There are full-sized trees in pots, and all sorts of plants. Every room is filled with flowers. There is every kind of plant a butterfly might need for nectar there, and food for the caterpillars, too. There's even humidifiers. To make the air soft."

"For moisture."

"Yes! That's it." Celia's dreamy eyes found Naomi. "You can go room to room there, and each room is filled with butterflies. Sometimes they all take flight, and you can look up to see them flying all together and swirling around the skylights above you. There are more butterflies than you can imagine there. In the butterfly museum."

Naomi could feel her heart aching in her chest.

"Do you want to go there, Celia?"

"Yes. Someday I will go there. I'm going to stand in the middle of the butterflies. I will know then."

"What will you know?"

Celia did not answer. The two sat for a long time. Naomi could see Celia slowly coming back to herself, saw the aching pain in the girl as she woke back to the reality of her life.

Celia blinked. She thought of the dark house she had seen in the industrial area, the boarded-up windows. She felt the eyes behind the window. She wondered if she should tell Naomi about it. But what if Naomi thought Celia was a liar, too? Celia couldn't bear that.

Celia glanced at Naomi. She seemed like she would listen. Celia opened her mouth, but Naomi was standing up, shaking out her legs. Her eyes were on the falling sun.

"I need to go, Celia," Naomi said. "I promise I'll come back, and find you, soon. Will you try and be safe for me?"

Celia nodded.

Rushing through the waterfront back to her car, Naomi saw the small man in round glasses, wearing his fussy suit. He looked like he had been watching her and Celia talk. She felt frustration. Once again the Feds were piddling around when they should be working. The small man watched her hurry past. He smiled at her, as if he were the one judging her.

Naomi walked in to dinner on the table. A lamb chop was sticking up off a plate, a bowl of Jerome's succotash. Diane turned and smiled over a salad she was carrying to the table, and Jerome was at the counter, pouring fresh cider. It was a scene of domesticity that reminded Naomi, sharply, of her years with Mrs. Cottle. The pungent smell of canning spices, the bulbous pickles in the brine on the back porch. A wind swept through the kitchen of her mind, reminding her of all she had lost.

Run, Naomi, said her mind. Run now while you have the time.

Shut up, mind, she responded.

"You're just in time," Diane said, smiling. She looked years younger. Jerome was smiling to himself, as if pleased to see Diane so happy. "Did you have a busy day, dear?"

"I did," Naomi said, taking a seat.

Naomi woke in the middle of the night. Usually this would be from a nightmare, but this time there was nothing. She turned her head to look out the window. Outside a fog hung above the street, sparkling the trees with a thick mist. The moon shadowed behind the clouds. Each of the little branches, Naomi thought, was a hand waving hello.

How had she survived? She knew someplace in her mind was a story. It might be like Celia's butterflies, rich in color, like a children's book. Maybe she had pretended to be someone else, as the woman in the shelter did, making a cape from a pillowcase. She knew she had sung to her sister—she had that knowledge—but the rest of it was gone. Whatever escape hatch Naomi had used had disappeared behind her, and for this she was sad. She would never know how she had survived. The miracle of her own mind was lost to her.

But not for Celia. The girl reminded Naomi of children she had rescued. The ones who survived captivity were the children who had learned to escape into make-believe worlds. Sometimes, later, their parents wanted them to forget these imaginary worlds. They thought that would be a sign of healing—to leave it all behind. Naomi tried to caution such parents. What the children needed, she told them, was to hear they were loved. Not loved despite what happened to them. Loved including it.

That's what we all want, Naomi thought, yawning. She felt the warmth of Jerome next to her and felt herself slide back towards sleep. I must remember to tell my sister that, when I find her.

Celia waited, for the longest time, in the waterfront grass. She had heard Naomi say she would come back.

Dusk fell and night came, and the lawns filled with more street people. Schools of drunks like fish, gasping mouths open as they slumbered, passed out in the grass. A junkie took out his kit right there, in front of Celia. He couldn't hit his arm, so he did his neck, his black bullet eyes on her the whole time he injected the dirty shit.

Still she waited.

Rich came. He was eating an old hoagie sandwich, the kind the corner market sold way past the pull date. A slice of bologna hung out the end like a flap, and Celia could see how the inside was green. His face was at the yellowish point of healing, like a sick banana.

"We should go, this place sucks," Rich said, which was his way of saying it wasn't safe.

Celia didn't want to go. Naomi had said she was coming back.

The junkie had fallen over, the needle still in his neck. Celia wondered if he was dead. Rich ate his sandwich, folding the end of bologna in his mouth. He stood over Celia, watching as the night deepened and the bars closed, ejecting drunks like spawn, and the cars drove by on the ramps above them like Christmas lights, blinking for a party they were not invited to.

"Come on, Celia," Rich said, worried.

From down the waterfront came the sound of hooting, and Rich jumped. Celia could almost smell alcohol on the wind. The jocks might come back. They would come find the junkie. They would find Celia. There were no lights down here. Celia could get beat up like Rich had been. Or worse.

"I don't want to leave," Celia said. "Naomi said she would come back."

She turned her head, peering in the dark, hoping that at any moment Naomi would materialize from the dark, walking with that calm, open look in her eyes.

It didn't happen.

"I want to get the fuck out of here," Rich said, nervously.

Slowly, Celia rose. Her legs had stiffened in the grass. Looking up from the waterfront, they could see groups of young men. Were they friendly? There was no way to know.

Her heart pounding, Celia looked around desperately.

"*Please*, Celia." Rich had his hand out, ready to drag her away.

* * *

"Do you remember telling me about the butterfly museum, Momma?"

It was the next day, and Celia's mother was sitting on the edge of the couch. She was in the place between coming down and needing her next fix, the desperate, sweaty time that would soon drive her to distraction. There really was no good time to talk to an addict, Celia had discovered. They were either high or in withdrawal. Either way they forgot what you said.

"What?" Her mother looked confused. She rubbed a shaking hand over a pale forehead.

"It's not too late," Celia said.

The eyes startled, looked up. Celia could see the fear.

"Not too late for what?" her mother asked, reluctantly.

Celia noticed her hand had left a mark, as though her mom was shrinking inside.

"Too late"—Celia took a deep breath—"to get rid of Teddy. To get clean. Remember how you said you wanted to be a lep—a lepi—lepidopterist?"

Her mother's eyes were on her. They were panicked. The addiction was talking to her, saying, Run away, hide. Cover your tracks. "I never said that."

"Yes, you did!"

"You were too young to remember that."

Celia felt helpless fury. Her mom had just admitted saying it. "Just because you gave up doesn't mean I need to!"

Her mother's eyes teared up. "You're just saying that."

"Teddy hurt me, Mom."

"That's not true. Teddy said—"

"No more, Mom. No more lies. I'm not the liar. Teddy is. The jury was wrong. You were wrong. I told the truth."

Her mother's face looked up at her, white with shock at being told so firmly. Celia could see the guilt rising, all the questions belief would bring. Her own failures as a mother. The face that would stare back in the morning mirror, asking, What did you do? The black call of heroin, not just to soothe the need but to wash away the truth.

"You can still stop, Mom. It's not too late."

"Maybe it is," her mom whispered, looking at the floor.

Celia turned and walked away. She knew she was never coming back.

The inside of the school was the same. The chairs in the front office where she'd sat for lice check were still there. The hallways were empty. Celia had made sure to arrive as school was letting out. Alyssa would be going home, to find their mother more than likely stoned on the couch.

Mrs. Wilkerson looked up from her desk when Celia entered. She no longer looked incredibly old to Celia. She was more like maybe sixty.

"Celia!" Mrs. Wilkerson stopped organizing the papers she had been stacking.

"I'm here for Alyssa," Celia said, unsure.

Mrs. Wilkerson had a broad backside and a reassuring, firm waddle. "She's gone home, sweetie."

"I'm not here to talk to her."

"What is it then?"

"I want to file a report," Celia said.

It felt like the room stopped. *It didn't work before*, the walls said, and almost the same words came from the teacher. Her voice was incredibly kind. "I believe there's a thing called double jeopardy, Celia. You can't try a man twice for the same crime. Even if he was guilty."

Celia closed her eyes. Someone *had* believed her.

"The report isn't for me. It's for my sister."

Mrs. Wilkerson moved quickly around her desk, her hand touching Celia lightly, and then she returned to her chair. "Sit down," she said. She pulled forward a notepad. "How about you start with everything you know."

"Can she go to the same foster home?"

"I can't say, Celia. Child Protective Services makes the decision, but if they think she is in danger, they will remove her. Usually they ask the last foster family if they are willing to take the child back." There was something in her voice that told Celia that Mrs. Wilkerson knew more about the situation than she was allowed to tell. Since she was Alyssa's teacher, she would have met the foster parents when Alyssa was in their home. Celia felt reassured. If Mrs. Wilkerson felt Alyssa would be safe, then Celia would, too.

"Okay," Celia said, breathing deep. She knew that if the family wanted to adopt Alyssa, they could change her name and refuse to let Celia see her. The family could move across the country if they wanted. Celia might lose her sister. Forever.

It was worth it. She began. "She told me."

Celia waited for that night to pass, and another day. Finally she found the girl with the cell phone and offered her the package of

Ding Dongs she was eating as a trade. On the corner, she noticed with a sinking sensation, the scar-faced man was back.

"Mom," Celia said when her mother answered the phone, almost before the first ring was over.

Celia could hear the tears in her voice. "They took her! They came and had her pack a bag and the police were here, too, just in case we tried anything. They arrested Teddy again." Her mother burst into loud sobs.

"What did Alyssa tell them?" Celia asked, calmly, holding the phone and looking at the ebony sky. Little stars out, watching over her sister right now.

"Alyssa asked if they could make her come home, just like you did after the trial, and the officer said no, not after all this. And then Alyssa said Teddy had been raping her, and now I lost both my daughters and *you are never coming back*."

The wind, coming down the street, ruffled Celia's hair and touched her skin, reminding her that right now Alyssa was being tucked into a safe bed, looking out a window, seeing the same stars. The foster family would keep her, and everything Celia had lost would be okay because she had saved the person she loved more than anyone in the world.

Tell her I love her, she wanted to tell those foster parents. Tell her I miss her.

Her mother was crying over the phone. Celia closed her eyes, felt her own tears. Finally her mother stopped. Celia listened to the clicking sound of her mother's ragged breath and remembered so long ago, walking through the meadow. The hands over her eyes, lifting. One, two.

"I'm sorry, Mom," she said, and hung up.

"Why are you saying sorry?" the tall girl asked.

"I don't know," Celia said. "I just am."

The next day Celia fetched her favorite book from the librarian, its pages bulging with drawings. She took one of the stubby pencils from the wood box on the desk and a slip of scrap paper from the stack nearby. Sitting at the table, she closed her eyes to contemplate what she wanted to draw.

She took her time. She paused, her mind tracing the streets. She saw the dark house, remembered the path there. Maybe it meant something. Maybe it meant nothing at all.

After finishing her drawing, she tucked the paper into the middle of the book, between two of her favorite butterfly pictures. She didn't feel relief. The drawing was for herself. No one was coming for her. Long after Celia was gone, floating in a nameless river called time, this paper would be here. A child of the future would open the book and find . . . her.

Find me, she thought.

There's something bothering you."

Naomi was with Diane, fixing up the bedroom. Diane had made new curtains and gotten a lighter bedspread out of storage in the attic, for the coming summer. It was soft and fresh, with embroidered flowers.

"It's this girl," Naomi confessed, and told her all about Celia.

Diane blinked. "You've been keeping all that to yourself?"

Naomi blushed. She kept a lot inside. It wasn't because she wanted to keep secrets. It just didn't occur to her to share.

"How old is she?" Diane asked, hanging the curtains and stroking them smooth with her hands.

"Twelve, I think." Naomi sounded unsure.

"Parents?"

"I don't know."

Diane's eyes slid away. Her expression said that while Naomi had been trying to find one child, she had abandoned another. Naomi lowered her head.

Diane reached out, patted her arm. "You seem to care about this girl."

"I do."

"Well, help her find her way home."

Naomi turned. Jerome was standing in the doorway, truck keys already in his hand. "I found Tasmin," he said, to Naomi's blank look. "The daughter of Mary, the woman in the tree."

"Now that sounds like a story." Diane chuckled.

*   *   *

"My mother wanted to keep me safe," Tasmin Tarseed said.

Jerome and Naomi were sitting with her, in front of a campfire. In the distance were rows of rusted boxcars, used as housing for the migrant workers. Clotheslines were strung between the metal boxcars, and from a cracked green hose trickled the only clean water supply. The evening camp held the pure silence of exhaustion. Their work in the berry fields done, the families gathered around the fires, and even usually frisky children sat slack-jawed at the flames.

Tasmin, wearing an orange vest that marked her as an outreach worker, sat politely away from the families. She added another stick to the fire. Her face was ruddy with sun, the smile lines baked in, making her look older than her age, which was thirty. Her black hair was sun-streaked, and she had a restless air about her. Naomi sat comfortably, radiant in the safety of smoke.

"Will you tell us?" Jerome asked, his voice as low as song.

In the distance an owl hooted. Barn, not horned, Naomi thought.

Tasmin nodded. "My mother was concerned. Panicked, more like it. My earliest memory was her coming back from the graveyard, knocking over things in the kitchen—and she was a gentle, careful person. She was muttering something about the children."

She reached for a stick, rubbing moss from it. "I didn't piece it together until later, and by then it was too late. I was too young, you see. Only five. I do remember the tension in town. This one time I went shopping with my mom, and a white man pushed her and called her a drunk Indian. My mother didn't drink, and this puzzled me. Other kids began teasing me, saying my mother was crazy."

Naomi hugged her legs to her chest, wrapping herself in her arms. Jerome looked over at her. "Go on," he told Tasmin.

"It was hard because my mom *was* acting crazy," Tasmin said, guiltily. "What could be crazier than saying you had seen the beloved town judge in the woods, carrying a bound child in his arms?"

Naomi's eyes were wide. She was drinking the truth.

"Did anyone believe her?" Jerome asked, quietly.

"I don't know. I was a little kid. The judge ran the town. It was his berry fields that brought in the money. And it wasn't the local kids dying. Just the odd migrant kid turning up in ditches or the woods. It was easy to blame that on accidents. I remember one they said had drowned. My mom said no one drowns with strangulation marks around their neck."

She put the rubbed stick into the fire. They all watched the flames.

"But then something happened," Tasmin said. "It had to do with the nearby orphanage."

Naomi jerked fully alert, her eyes piercing through the smoke. She stared at Tasmin as the woman went on. "My mother confronted the judge and his son. She got in their faces, said she was going to get a ride to the city—my mother didn't drive, she had never learned—and tell the authorities."

Tasmin took a deep breath. From one of the nearby fires a migrant boy looked over at her. "The Greyhound used to stop in Elk Crossing once a week. One day my mother packed up a suitcase with my clothes. She pinned a note to my shirt. It said my name, and where I was going, which was to my older cousin on the reservation. She sent me away, and I never saw her again. A few days later she died. My cousin said she went back to find out what happened. The judge claimed it was suicide. My mother had been cut ear to ear."

The fire crackled.

Tasmin looked across the campfire. "I went back one summer. The farmhouse was empty, looted by those antique hunters, I guess. Her stuff was gone from her bedroom, too."

Jerome reached into his bag and took out the photograph. Tasmin looked at the picture, turned it over, and read the note in the firelight. She was quiet for a long time.

"I found it in a bundle, tied in the oak tree," Jerome said.

"She wanted me to be the one to find it," Tasmin said. "Will you leave me, now?" she asked, and they did.

He wants to stay hidden, Naomi thought, as nameless as his victims.

She was in her own dream state, standing in the living room. In the kitchen Jerome—frustrated, from the sounds of it—was cleaning her dishes. Naomi reminded herself she had better start picking up more. This wasn't a hotel.

The judge was dead, but Wesley was still alive, and he was here. Naomi could feel it. But Wesley was faceless, just as he wanted to be. Men like him liked to hide. It made them feel bigger to stand in the shadows.

Well, pull him out.

I will, Naomi thought, taking out her phone. Investigations, she thought, were like a ball of yarn. You pulled on one string after another until the whole ball unraveled. And inside, always, was a lost child, arms raised, crying for help.

"Elk Crossing school district," she asked, dreamy. "I know they're closed. I need archives."

Outside birds called. Naomi counted their voices while she waited. Scrub jay. House sparrow. The *tee-yee* of the lesser goldfinch. She began to see the virtue of waking up to the same sounds every morning. It reminded her of her interlude in Opal—because that was what it had always felt like, an interlude between captivity and work, from age nine to eighteen—and how the sweet rhythms of farm life had allowed her and Jerome to grow close. Naomi had learned love and trust. It was astonishing, she reflected, how quickly Mrs. Cottle had taught her just by embodying both herself. And now Diane was trying to do the same.

The phone clicked. She was being transferred. Records were always somewhere. People had a drive to immortalize their past. Even the evil stuff, like Abu Ghraib or the Holocaust. They liked to take pictures, keep journals. Because they believed in what they were doing. No one, Naomi had learned, did evil without believing it was right at the time. Maybe this was why it was nearly impossible to talk them out of it.

Finally the phone connected to the school district offices in Murky Grove, and there she could imagine a woman in a flowered smock—her name was Patty—making her way into a cold basement filled with files. Getting a call from a real-life investigator was about as much excitement as she could stand, Patty said. Naomi reminded herself to send Patty a box of chocolates later. People liked to be thanked like that.

"Thank you, Patty," Naomi said warmly, and hung up.

Jerome was behind her, holding a dishcloth in his one hand. Naomi turned, saw his handsome face. "Sorry about the mess," she said. "We're getting the Elk Crossing yearbook, express mail. We're going to find out what Wesley looks like."

But in her heart she thought she knew.

Later Naomi sat with Jerome on the front porch. It was a cold night, and she wondered again where Celia and the others slept. Behind them the house was dark with silence. Diane usually went to bed early.

Jerome put his arm around her. They always sat like this so Naomi was on his good side—his left—to hold hands or let him touch her. It had already become instinct.

"Tomorrow?" he asked.

"Back downtown," she answered, and she told him Celia's story about the butterfly museum.

"Do you think it's real?" he asked, his voice soft.

"I hope it is, for her sake."

"She'll find something else to believe in if it isn't," he replied. "People with hope are like that."

"I know." She sighed. "I just hope she doesn't have to."

He kissed the top of her head. "Come to bed?"

She leaned against his cheek, felt his warm breath. "Yes."

You didn't come back!"

This, Naomi thought, was not what she had been expecting. Celia, instead of being grateful, was spitting mad. All the rage of her young life was pouring out.

"Well, I'm here now," Naomi said, her back bristling a bit.

They were down on the waterfront, in front of the river. Naomi had found Celia and Rich crossing the footbridge—the other street kids said they usually came that way late mornings after sleeping under an overpass. Naomi felt bad Celia was sleeping in the dirt, and this made her feel guilty, and that made her mad. That along with waiting for hours, from morning until noon, until she finally saw the two figures nonchalantly crossing the bridge. Her relief, like that of a parent who catches her kid playing in the street, was mingled with frustration.

Celia stopped. "Oh. You," she said, sarcastically.

Then they were off. Rich backed away, eyes wide, at the sight of the two of them fighting. Catfight, he knew others would joke. But he could see the pain radiating off both of them. So much disappointment in the world.

"Long time no *see*," Celia said, her eyes mirroring the river.

Naomi knew she should have stopped there, be the adult to the child, but something in her flared, too. "Sorry, I was too busy trying to save you."

"You're not trying to save me or anyone else! All you care about is your sister, and that isn't even about her!"

All the air in the world could not help Naomi then. Her breath froze in her chest.

"You don't even want to save her! You just want to stop feeling guilty, and guess what?" The poison was leaving Celia now, collapsing her into tears. "You can't! She's dead! She probably fucking died or died fucking, years ago, I bet in that house, and you didn't care because *you are too late*."

Naomi tried to breathe.

"No one can save me now." Celia had fallen to her knees, her cheeks red, her face shiny with mucus and tears. "No one can save anyone." Her voice came out dead and remote.

Rich went to lift his friend. He used his loose shirt to wipe her face. The look he gave Naomi was one of reproach. You should have come back, it said.

I'm sorry, Naomi wanted to say, but didn't. Her backbone felt like fire. Rich was walking Celia away, and pretty soon they disappeared up to skid row. Skin row, Naomi remembered a cop calling it once. Like it was funny.

* * *

Celia had escaped to the place before time. Lemon yellow, an ocher like the reddest of hearts. More of them coming now. Sapphire blue, silver tipped. Eyes gazing in astonishment from the backs of wings. Zephyr. Swallow. Long-tails. Creatures longer than history, before the Stone Age. There are fossils of butterflies.

Rich was shaking her, saying, "Hey, Celia." And others were saying "What the fuck" and "Why doesn't she snap out of it." But Celia wasn't there. She could feel the grainy curb outside Sisters of Mercy under her bottom; she could see her limp hands at her side. That didn't matter. She was floating someplace above them all, her arms as light as the wings surrounding her.

Rich led her to the dumpster behind the Greek restaurant, but it was locked, a bright new padlock on it. Rich leaned against it, putting his face on the metal lid and closing his eyes in despair. Celia just stood there. It figured, she thought. It just did.

"Come on," Rich said, leading her by the hand like she was a little child. They went back to the row, and Rich carried her a plate of beans from Sisters of Mercy.

Later Celia climbed tiredly up the hill to the overpass. She lay down in the dirt hollow that knew her body. She hadn't spoken since seeing Naomi that morning.

She felt rather than heard Rich moving in the dark. Slowly, with tenderness, he moved his big body until he was close to her. He reached out, touched her side, felt for her hand. She gave it to him. Rich cradled her hand like it was the most precious gift he had ever been given, and she could hear his breathing in the night.

Closing her eyes, Celia felt the butterflies. Come live, they said, flying all around her. Say you are sorry.

A sweet chariot, swinging low, flickering out of the light. A wide-open feeling. Her sister laughing, toddling across an orphanage yard. A forgotten memory, returning.

Naomi woke. She untangled from Jerome, his naked skin silky against hers. When she had come back yesterday, he had consoled her, and later they had made love under the quilt and Naomi cried afterwards.

Rising quietly, Naomi slipped into her pair of soft cotton pants and a shirt. Going downstairs, she thought of a big breakfast. Bacon, eggs, toast. A pot of coffee strong enough to make your hair curl, laced with plenty of cream and sugar.

Today she had an appointment with Sean Richardson. Then she was going to find Celia. She didn't want anything to happen to the girl.

* * *

Jerome spent some time cleaning up after Naomi left—she had made an effort this time, but boy, she had a long way to go—and called Ed Ashtree, arranging to visit him. Then he went online for a while, fruitlessly searching for any information about Wesley. It appeared the man had dropped off the face of the earth. There was nothing.

The mail slot banged open, and a thick manila envelope dropped through the slot. It landed in the basket Diane used for mail. *Elk Crossing School District, Archives*, the return address said. Patty had added a smiley face to the front.

Setting it down on the kitchen table, Jerome slipped a sharp knife under the flap. The faded red yearbook slid out. ELK CROSS-ING HIGH, the front said, in crooked gilt lettering.

Jerome sat down, broke the spine, flipped open the yearbook, and began turning the pages.

There. A thumbnail photo. Wesley Thurman. He frowned, remembering what Naomi had told him.

"There's something we'd like to share with you," Agent Richardson said.

Naomi walked into his office. There, sitting in the chair she had once refused, was the scar-faced man. He was wearing a suit.

He rose, holding out a thick hand. His broad face smiled, the scarred seams of his lips moving. "Specialist McConnell," he introduced himself, in a thick, warm brogue.

"Shit," Naomi said.

Specialist McConnell, as he told her, was a field agent from New York. Hearing about these cases, he had offered to come out—he had a sensitivity for work involving street kids, he said. He had been on and off the streets himself when he was growing up. He understood the culture.

The scars? Naomi asked. "I started boxing when I joined the Marines," he said, folding his legs. "Obviously I didn't stop in time. Truth to tell, the scars help in the undercover work. No one believes someone who looks like me is FBI."

"You were following Celia outside the library because you were worried about her?" Naomi asked, swinging her arms restlessly with anger. Not at him. At the sense of dread creeping on.

"I've been worried about her. All of the girls." He paused. "I didn't know who you were, so I thought it best to vamoose when you came running up behind me. Then Agent Richardson told me, and I haven't wanted you to blow my cover."

"Have you found anything out?"

"I've been posing as a john. A creep. Asking around," he explained. "I know all the code, the language. Asking for 'sweet treats.'" He made a disgusted expression with his mouth. "I've gotten a break. Rumors. There is a house where a man takes the girls."

"But no one knows where it is."

He looked over at Richardson. "You were right about her." He turned back to Naomi. "He's hiding in plain sight."

Naomi felt a wave of sickness coming. A generic-looking man who had led a generic-looking life, she remembered having thought scornfully. "Oh no." Naomi almost doubled over with the pain. Her phone pinged, and she reached for it.

It was a message from Jerome, with a picture of the yearbook photo of Wesley Thurman attached. Naomi looked down.

Even as a young man he had looked the same: small and fussy, with round glasses, and shorn hair.

It was Celia's birthday.

After eating, she said good-bye to Rich and then jumped the fence for the Goodwill truck, rummaging through the black plastic bags left by others. She found a fresh pair of boys' jeans, a newish top, and a stained white sweatshirt that said DANCE. She even found new socks, soft and white and pink.

She lugged these treasures up the steps to the library. The scar-faced man was not around, and Celia felt relief. Inside, the elderly librarian said hello.

In the family washroom Celia locked the door, then filled the sink with hot water and hand soap. She stripped, shoving her dirty clothes into the trash can. She washed her pits with their soft beginnings of hair, her tummy, her cloven buttocks, and, last, the place between her legs. She dried off the best she could with the rough paper towels. Finally she doused her head in the now grayish sink, scrubbing her scalp with her nails, and vigorously washed her face.

Drying off with more paper towels, she leaned forward at her reflection.

Her eyes, staring back in the clean mirror, were large and luminous. Her skin, relieved of dirt, was soft and pale, with honey-colored freckles on her cheeks. She touched the thin skin under her eyes, saw the eyebrows, the soft pink of her lips.

She smiled defiantly. Fuck you, Teddy. I am pretty.

She put on the new clothes, enjoying them against her skin. Finally she slipped on her worn shoes, unlocked the door, and ran up the marble stairs, her hand barely touching the rails. Below her the librarian smiled.

The library had a new book about butterflies. Celia was immersed in it, aware of the sun passing over the windows. She was in her favorite chair, where the sun traveled the corner of the building, catching like fire on the tables. Celia felt her breathing slow, turning the pages. She was lost inside the book, seeing herself in a different world—among the butterflies.

"Hello, miss."

She looked up, annoyed. This was the cost of getting clean: every creep would want to talk to her. Instead she was surprised to see a small man with round glasses. It took her a moment to place him. He was the one who had helped her that night someone spiked her drink.

"Hey," she replied with cold caution.

"Mind if I sit?" He flashed a smile at her and signaled at the chair opposite her. Between them the table gleamed.

Celia shrugged. She could always get up and move if he bothered her.

He had a book and soon opened it, reading across from her. Celia snuck a glance, her own concentration broken. It was something about police work. She saw his silver hair, cut short on the sides, just like a cop. A flash of understanding came to her. This was the undercover man Naomi had mentioned! Relieved, she returned to her own book, wiggling a little in her chair, pleased she had figured it out.

The clock ticked. The sun was behind clouds. Celia kept sneaking glances at the man, but he seemed immersed in his book. For some reason, he looked mildly put out, and this caught at her. Gave her a tug.

"Are you . . . studying?" she asked.

He gave her a curt nod and turned a page.

She yawned and put her book down. Getting clean made her sleepy. She wished there was a place she could lie down for a nap.

"Tired?" the man asked. It was hard to see his eyes behind his glasses.

"It's not a big deal," Celia bragged.

"What are you up to today?" he asked indifferently, as if it didn't matter.

"It's my birthday," Celia said, proudly, and then added, "I'm going to find my friend Naomi later. I bet you know her."

"I bet I do."

"I'm going to help her."

"Help her what?"

"Find her sister."

"And how are you going to do that?"

"I think I know where her sister might be."

"Oh." The small man put down the book. Now she could see his blue eyes behind the glasses. They were grave and—what was it? Worried. No, Celia told herself. Not worried. It was respect, for her. "And where would her sister be?" he asked.

"I saw this house. In the industrial area."

Now the face was still. The blue eyes were on her, watching.

"I saw it a while ago," Celia said. "There was someone inside, watching me. I think it might be the man who is taking the girls. I bet he took Naomi's sister, too. That's where she's at, and I'm going to help Naomi get her."

The small man spoke slowly, carefully, like her answer mattered. "Did you tell Naomi where this house was?"

She saw an edge of his narrow teeth—she was surprised they weren't nicer. "No." She shook her head, embarrassed. "I was going to, only . . ." She trailed off.

She didn't think the undercover man would understand what it was like to be told your entire life you were a liar. How after a while you started believing no one would ever believe you, and maybe you even stopped believing yourself.

But he was smiling. It was okay after all.

"You can show me," he offered.

◀

They walked down the wide marble stairs, and below them the librarian looked up to see Celia leaving with an older man in a suit. The man looked professional, but all the same, the librarian frowned. She swallowed her instinct to say something, to call out. She wasn't sure why.

Above them the sky was a clear blue, with fluffy white clouds.

"It's pretty, isn't it?" He smiled. "Just like you."

"How long have you known Naomi?" Celia asked and, just for a second, caught a passing look of surprise on his face.

"Oh, I've known her . . . forever." He smiled to himself.

"Really?"

He asked, slyly, "Do you know what I do?"

"You're undercover," Celia answered, proudly. In the blocks below them was skid row. Her friends would be there, and the strip clubs, the gay bars. But the streets were empty here, and besides passing the corner market, they would stay empty until she showed him the boarded-up house. Celia felt a small sense of disquiet at that, but she told herself he was okay; he was like Naomi: a good guy.

"See that store up there?" he asked, pointing at the corner market.

Celia nodded.

"I'll buy you a soda. You can drink it on the way. You like black cherry cream, right?"

"How do you know that?" she asked, slowing.

"That night we met, remember? That's what you were drinking."

"Oh."

Celia really didn't want the soda. She wanted to show the man the scary house so Naomi would be impressed. She would find out Celia was a nice girl after all.

"I thought I told you, you ought to be careful what you drink on the streets."

Celia remembered him handing her the soda outside the store, the top already opened. Watching her, carefully, as she drank it.

They were outside the house. The blank boarded-up eyes of the windows, tufted with blankets, stared back with horror at her. Her limbs felt numb. Celia watched one eye become five become nothing. She was whirling. She saw his teeth: narrow, edged in dark. She was falling.

"I got you," he said.

* * *

Naomi came sprinting down to skid row. "Have you seen Celia?" She stopped, leaning over, panting, asking Rich.

Rich was on the corner, panhandling. "She said she was going to the library," he said.

"I was just there," Naomi said. The librarian said Celia had left with a man in a suit. Naomi had shown her the picture of a younger Wesley on her phone, and the librarian said yes, that was him.

Naomi felt pure, unadulterated panic. Nothing in her recent life had felt like this. Rich, his own thighs tingling with fear, was unable to speak.

"You looking for Celia?" It was the girl with the phone. "I saw her a little bit ago. She was in the corner market."

"Was she with anyone?"

"Some dude in glasses." The girl shrugged, chewed a hangnail.

Naomi ran to the corner market. Inside, the clerk shrugged. Outside, Naomi spun around in a circle.

Celia was gone.

THREE

—

BUTTERFLY

In the basement of every house there was an urn. It was the bowl of water he gave her to wash her face. It was the toilet that had to be flushed with the waiting buckets. It was something more: love in the night.

Sarah liked the basement because she could catch a glimpse of the world outside the barricaded windows. Sometimes she touched the boards nailed over the window—lightly, because Wesley had told her he could see and hear everything she did. Sometimes she thought Wesley crawled inside her skin and saw through her eyes. But no. That was too scary to be true.

In the basement Sarah could talk to Little Self. Little Self lived under Sarah's armpit. She hid under the skin between her rib and her rushing heart, where Wesley could not see or hear her. When Sarah was alone, Little Self came out, scampered down her arm, and Sarah opened her hand so Little could perch in her palm and they could talk.

The dirt floor of the basement was spotted with blood. Wesley did that. He said he would do it to Sarah, but she didn't think so, though she didn't know for sure.

He has the girl I saw outside, Sarah told Little Self. He put her in the room, Sarah said, her lips moving silently.

Little Self shook her tiny head. This was bad. This was worse than bad.

Sarah had seen the girl outside through the window before. She had short curly hair and was just standing there, staring at the house. Sarah had wanted to yell, Run away! Run now! Before he catches you! But now it was too late.

You need to leave now, Little Self said. She often told Sarah to escape. But the last time Sarah had tried, Wesley had hurt her real bad. It had taken her forever to mend, and now one of her ankles was twisted forever. If she tried to run, she would not get far.

I'm waiting for Big Sister, Sarah mouthed.

You can't wait anymore, Little Self announced.

Big Sister said she would come back for me, Sarah replied stubbornly.

Sarah wanted Big Sister to come back. She was scared. She had no idea what that world out there might be like. It might be full of worse men than Wesley. There might be giant monsters out there who would eat her, tear her skin from her bones.

You need to—

There was a sound on the wooden basement steps behind her, and all the spit in Sarah's mouth dried up. She closed her hand, and Little Self scampered up her arm, ran under her armpit, and burrowed into her skin next to the noisy blood of her heart. There she curled into a tight ball so she wouldn't have to hear or look at Wesley.

Sarah heard his rough voice behind her. No matter how long it had been, just the sound of Wesley's voice was enough to make Sarah's legs watery with fear. She closed her eyes and, turning around, forced herself to see him in the only way she could.

* * *

Celia didn't open her eyes at first. A smell came over her, like a formaldehyde she had never known. Dried liquid, crystalline on her cheeks. Dim memories of a forgotten place before it all. Can you dream what you don't know?

Celia's eyes opened.

* * *

Wesley was sitting, hunched, at the kitchen table, eating. There was only one chair, and Wesley was the only one allowed to use it. His short silver hair shone in the lamplight. Inside one of the hall closets he kept the suits and shoes he wore when he went out. When he returned he took his street costume off, put on old pants and a dirty shirt. Like a boogeyman.

Baked beans were the only thing on the plate in front of him.

He scraped the plate with his fork and ate. He looked at Sarah standing in the corner. She made sure he could look through her, and that her hands were hanging like bags of meat at her side.

Wesley had brought Sarah to this house when she was small. He put something over her head and put her in the back of something that bumped, and she threw up inside the cloth. When she had gotten bigger, Wesley had started leaving and finding others. He didn't keep them very long, and lately he didn't keep them hardly at all.

He would have gotten rid of Sarah, too, if he weren't trying to punish her sister for leaving. He did that by keeping Sarah alive.

Then the beans were gone. He stood up, dunked the plate and fork in the plastic bin full of cold gray water. "Wash this," he ordered her before going back upstairs.

Sarah was back in the kitchen. Put crackers on a plate, Wesley had told her.

Wesley didn't know Sarah had thoughts. He thought she was dumb. That's what he said. Dumb as a post. Not like her big sister, who was the only one smart enough to escape. Sarah could tell Wesley hated that—he talked about her sister with hate—and yet he seemed to respect her, too.

Wesley didn't know about Little Self, or that at night she peeked out, looked around to check all was safe, and climbed carefully onto Sarah's chest to protect her. Now, in the kitchen, Sarah held her arm straight out and watched Little Self slide down to land, triumphantly, in her open palm.

Look, Little Self told her.

Sarah looked around. The counters were covered with cans and boxes, kerosene for the lamps, big jugs of water that glimmered in the dark, and a hot plate for Wesley to heat his food. There was nothing sharp in the kitchen. The only metal was dull butter knives and forks. On the edge of the counter was a small locked box. That was where Wesley kept his gun.

No, not that, Little said.

Sarah looked around again, saw a box of rat poison in the back of the mess. Wesley put the little pellets around the house and Sarah found the rat bodies later, dried up and tiny at the waist. Sarah shook her head. So many times she had wanted to die but not here. She wanted to die on the outside. She wanted to die feeling free.

Sarah looked at her soft feet on the dirty floor. The toes looked boneless. The twisted ankle hurt. She looked back at Little, perched in her palm. Little had hard feet that could run. Little had legs that could stretch. Not Sarah.

I'm afraid, Sarah told her.

Little Self shook her head. You need to leave *soon*.

She climbed up Sarah's arm and burrowed back into her armpit. When Sarah put the crackers on the plate, she heard crying.

In the courthouse downtown Naomi and Jerome found records of the trial against Celia's stepdad. They located Alyssa's foster parents, unraveled the rotten core of Celia's story until Jerome landed outside Teddy's jail cell, where he was again awaiting trial, this time for raping Alyssa.

Teddy, greasy in his jail jumpsuit, had no answers. The defense attorney sat nearby, in the plastic chair. He was there to make sure Jerome didn't ask Teddy about his crimes. That was their deal. Jerome could only ask if Teddy knew where Celia might be, or knew anything about the man who had taken her. As if pedophiles had a secret grapevine. Jerome thought of the games he used to play with Naomi as kids, making phones with two orange juice cans and string, talking from room to room.

Teddy didn't know anything. "Sorry I can't help you, brother," he said, as if they were kin, and Jerome wanted to spit in his face.

* * *

After long hours of searching, Naomi fell apart, sobbing on a street corner. "We have to find her," she kept saying, and Jerome noticed that for all of Naomi's determination to find her sister, it was this homeless child that had sparked the terror.

Jerome held her with his one arm, wishing he had two.

Do you have any idea where she might be?

No, said Mrs. Wilkerson, tears in her eyes as she passed them an old school photograph of Celia. Naomi had filed a missing persons report and was making flyers.

No, said Alyssa, trembling between her foster parents, each holding one of her hands in their laps.

No, said Rich and the others. No, said the nuns at Sisters of Mercy. No, said the manager at Aspire, turning her head into the locker to weep. No, said everyone they asked on skid row, until at long last Naomi turned a corner a week after Celia went missing, and a junkie scratching his neck said he had never heard of the girl.

Even now, more than ever, the butterflies came. They blanketed Celia in the darkest night. They filled the foulness and beat back the air. The ceiling was not a ceiling; the room had no doors. The butterflies kept Celia from asking the wrong kinds of questions, the questions that would unlock the scream of panic from her throat. They told her, *It's nothing*, and *Let's focus on that window*. They told her, *Shhhh*, and they covered her face with their glowing beauty when the pain got too much. Nothing, not even he, could penetrate her glory.

But sometimes the predators come no matter how hard you try. They want to pin you down. They want to kill you. Celia knew that's what he planned to do. *Shhhh*, said the butterflies, filling the room. Think only of your escape.

When she got ahold of herself, Celia let the butterflies carry her gently back down to earth—and she watched the young woman who came with the food.

The young woman was ageless, her face like plastic stretched to some unseemly point. She had eyes that turned inwards. She came in twice a day, first turning the deadbolts from the outside. She brought crackers on a plate. *I am looking for my sister*, the flyer had said. *She is about twenty-five.*

The young woman handed her a dirty towel, her face mute. Celia wiped blood off her chin. The towel smelled impossibly bad, like it had never been washed. Someplace in this horrible house, Wesley breathed. Celia could feel his dragon breath from afar.

Her name is Sarah, Naomi had said.

This, Celia thought, is Naomi's sister. They even looked alike.

Looking over her shoulder, Sarah held her left arm out. She opened her palm. Rising from her corner, Celia carefully, painfully, hobbled close. Celia opened her mouth to speak, but Sarah shook her head. Wesley might hear them. So instead Celia tilted her own head, in question. Is there something there I should see?

Sarah nodded, eagerly.

Celia looked into the empty palm.

Tell her I miss her. Celia remembered the flyer. *Tell her I am sorry.*

Celia opened her mouth and stopped. Be careful, something inside warned her. She might not be ready.

Together they peered into the palm. Sarah's lips moved. She was talking to whatever was there. Celia closed her eyes in relief. She knows she is in hell, she thought, and if she knows that, she wants to escape.

At nights Wesley locked Sarah in the closet. Little Self liked it there. She climbed the metal rod above Sarah, swinging upside down above her. Sometimes she sang the same songs Sarah's big sister had sung so long ago. The best one was about a sweet chariot. Sarah didn't know what that meant except her sister was coming back. It was taking a long time.

The girl reminds you of Big Sister, doesn't she? Little said.

Yes! Sarah breathed, sleep filling her. She does.

Stay awake, Sarah. You have to think.

Think about what? Sarah asked, fearful.

How to escape, Little said. You have to take the girl with you. She can show you the outside. Ask for her help. You can find your sister out there.

He said he will keep me forever, Sarah's lips murmured.

No. It is time. Before he—

Yes, Sarah breathed out, her eyes closing.

* * *

After about a week, Celia had, miraculously, found a way to talk to Sarah. She did it without making any sound. Sarah was remarkably good at reading lips. Sarah had learned to read lips from watching Wesley. It was easier, and better, than looking in his eyes.

The cracker plate was on the dirty floor between them. Wesley was somewhere in the house. It was enough to make a breath drop with fear.

Sarah smiled at Celia, showing a line of teeth pebbled from neglect. Celia felt sorry for her, seeing those teeth, feeling this house. What a tender heart Sarah must have—as scared as any street kid. Sarah looked over her shoulder, held her left arm out again, and opened the palm. Celia stepped closer and carefully put her arm around Sarah's waist. The flesh was soft, and at first stiffened in fear and surprise. Then it softened.

Little Self wants us to leave, Sarah's lips moved.

I will help you, Celia answered, her heart rising with hope.

One window in the basement, Sarah said. That's where I saw you.

That was you! Celia was astonished. I thought—

Don't say his name.

But how can we get out? He is always watching.

Sarah frowned, thinking.

I have an idea, Little Self said from Sarah's palm.

You left me, her sister was saying, whispering down an empty street. *You left me and you left her.*

Naomi woke with a start. The night was wet outside her window. The foul hours of dawn, she remembered a fellow survivor saying. The time when those in pain remember. The knowledge that tomorrow has brought yesterday back.

Her mind was grainy with lack of sleep. Next to her Jerome was in the deep, soundless slumber of the exhausted. His gun holster was slung over the armchair. Naomi remembered Diane laughing when they first met, outside the courtroom where they were both testifying.

Her sister had been about to say something else in the dream. Naomi turned to the window. No, it was Celia. Naomi winced as she remembered that last, explosive talk, the child's cheeks lathered with tears. Celia had been saying something Naomi hadn't wanted to hear. But she did now.

"You can't! She's dead!" Celia had yelled. "She probably fucking died or died fucking, years ago, I bet in that house, and you didn't care because you are too late."

I bet in that house.

Oh my God, Naomi thought, sitting straight up.

"Celia knew where the house was," Naomi told the gathered men.

They were sitting around Winfield's desk. Sean Richardson was there, and so was Specialist McConnell. It was very early morning, and they all looked sleep deprived. A row of takeout coffee cups circled the desk. Naomi had bitten hers.

"The question"—Winfield cleared his voice—"is how we find out what Celia knew."

"We've talked to all her friends," Jerome said. "None of them know anything. That boy Rich is beside himself with worry."

"What did she tell you again, Naomi? *That house.*" Specialist McConnell spoke in his warm brogue. "Nothing more?"

Naomi shook her head, sick with herself for not asking when Celia had told her.

"What about her mom?" Sean Richardson asked.

Everyone had read the court transcripts. The trial had been a travesty. "Celia the liar." That the judge had allowed the jury to hear this still inflamed Naomi. Of course Teddy was going to call her a liar—she was speaking the truth.

Jerome had done an interview with Celia's mother because Naomi didn't think she could handle it. "She's in a treatment center. She says that losing both Celia and Alyssa made her get clean. I don't know what to think. But she doesn't know anything."

"It seems like Celia didn't tell anyone where this house was," Richardson said.

"She told someone," Naomi replied obstinately.

"How do you know that?" Richardson asked, respectfully.

"It's like the fairy tales," Naomi said, remembering her other missing child cases. "Celia was trapped and lost, alone in the wilderness. She will have left a trail of crumbs somewhere. All children do."

"Then let's find the trail," Winfield said, ending the meeting.

Jerome stood outside next to his truck with Naomi. He wanted to drive down to the reservation. If there was the smallest chance the cousin who had raised Tasmin Tarseed knew anything about Wesley, he wanted to find it. "Will you be okay?" he asked, as if he were leaving for a week and not just a day.

Naomi didn't say anything. Instead she pushed at him with her mind: *Go, help me find her.*

Jerome found Ed in the reservation library, small and overly warm, in a clapboard building. The parking lot outside was almost empty.

"You still got that bundle?" Ed asked, sorting books.

"I gave the photo to Tasmin Tarseed. That's the daughter of the woman whose picture it was. She lived in that farmhouse. Her older cousin still lives here."

"Mrs. Tarseed? Tell her she's got fines." He chuckled.

"Naomi's little friend is missing. A street girl by the name of Celia."

Ed's entire demeanor changed. The two men walked out of the

building. Moss hung off the stunted trees, and mist coiled around their feet. Ed poured strong coffee from his thermos, which once said OREGON DUCKS on it, most of the letters worn off. He passed Jerome the lid cup, and he took a swallow. The coffee was strong and sweet, and tasted like birdsong.

"I'm here to see if there is anything her cousin might know, about where Wesley Thurman went," Jerome explained. "My heart is breaking watching my wife right now. She thinks it's her fault that Celia has gone missing."

"Does she know it isn't?"

"I don't think that matters to her." Jerome handed back the cup, and Ed finished the coffee, screwing the cup back on the thermos. Jerome dug in his jacket pocket, the empty sleeve brushing against Ed. "Pardon my sleeve," he said. He pulled a slip of paper out of his pocket, and Ed smiled. Notes. "This is the address I found." He showed it to Ed, and Ed gave him quick directions. Once in the mountains, Jerome knew, his GPS would chirp off.

His truck bouncing up spring-washed roads, Jerome found the house. It was low and ramshackle, a series of rooflines like the sky. In a pen was a shaggy pony, its hooves split from neglect. At the door was an older woman, curious and waiting. Jerome turned to her as though he had known her his entire life.

*   *   *

Spring rains lashed the windows. Cousin Tarseed made a living by collecting wild salal to sell to florists. It was hard work, she said, showing her leathery hands. The beds of her nails were stained an eerie fluorescent green. "Looks like I got moss for hands, doesn't it?" she asked, and then grew serious. "I was a bookkeeper once. But the economy went south, so now I live in the mountains and cut salal."

The blanket was open, the tender belongings of Mary Tarseed spread across the table. The cousin thought she would like to keep the teacup for herself, give the rest to the tribe. "I liked Mary," she said. "She was hardheaded. That doesn't do for a woman, most of the time." She sat in her chair, primly, green hands folded in her soft lap. "She shouldn't have taken on that judge."

"So you heard about all that?" Jerome asked, brushing his hair from his eyes.

"Of course! I practically raised Tasmin. It was all she could talk about for ages. But then she stopped. Once she got big enough, she went away to university. She comes home on occasion—works for one of those migrant labor outfitters." She gave a brief laugh that faltered. "I ought to get her into the salal business. They sure work us hard."

"I'm wondering if there is anything you ever heard—anything at all—having to do with the judge's son, and where he might have ended up."

Her eyes met his. She waved a green hand. "All I know is what I heard. I will repeat it for you."

"Okay," Jerome said, and she began.

It was the judge who had gotten the praise, Mrs. Tarseed said. Owner of the Thurman Family Strawberry Farm, big and bluff with those grandfatherly eyes. Imposing on the bench—she had seen him once, while visiting her cousin before she died, and he had been kind to her, waiving a speeding ticket she had gotten out of town. No one had paid much attention to Wesley, small and priggish. He had a sniveling way about him that would have led to teasing had he not been the judge's son. As he got older, he was the one who fixed the problems with the reluctant migrant workers, cajoling and threatening in turn. If a child's body turned up every now and then, it was easy to chalk it up to field accidents. Especially when the son of the judge also began to make a name for himself doing good works. Like volunteering at the orphanage.

The year her cousin died, there had been a restlessness in the town. The people were starting to suspect. They could *feel* it, Cousin Tarseed said. But they went on with their town parade, a festive march of children on Main Street, pulling their Radio Flyer wagons decorated with flowers. It was the height of strawberry season, and the air was filled with their rotting scent. That was the last time she had been in town, trying to recover her cousin's remains, hoping their ancestors had walked her home.

Around that time, Mrs. Tarseed said, there was talk of two sisters gone missing from the orphanage. That got the town's attention. The evil was moving closer to home; it was crawling up their doorsteps in the middle of the night. There were now hushed conversations on sidewalks, quiet as the judge and his son walked up. The judge was aging, and maybe in their secret hearts the townspeople thought whatever was happening would die with him. Instead they now had Wesley and his stove-dial eyes.

The judge passed away and was duly cremated. The bodies stopped appearing in the fields. Maybe because Wesley kept what his father had thrown away. The town swallowed their fears of the missing sisters. They didn't want to think about the graves or the memory of the judge, so complacent in his chair. The last Mrs. Tarseed had heard, Wesley had left town himself. By then most of the people around had either died or moved away.

"What about a mother?" Jerome asked as the story concluded. The rain had stopped. "Didn't Wesley have a mother?"

"Oh, her," Mrs. Tarseed answered. Her green hands suddenly clenched in her lap, as if grabbing a bough. "The story was she left the judge, long ago. Divorced and went to the city and died there. They say she lived in some awful house."

It was then that Jerome knew just what to do.

"What was her maiden name?" he asked.

Rushing back to the city, Jerome saw the coming night sky as he parked by the downtown courthouse, moments before closing. The sheriff deputies frowned at him, hurrying through the metal detectors, until he mentioned their boss by name. Darting up the stairs, proud that he could balance so well even after missing an arm, Jerome bounded up all the flights and sprinted down the echoing hallway of the top floor until he came to the door at the back.

PROBATE, it said.

He ran in to find a lonesome clerk, ready to close for the night. "I need a copy of a will," Jerome breathed, and gave them the mother's name. "It is going to have an address I need."

Wesley was at the kitchen table of what was once his mother's house, eating baked beans again, this time with a tuna sandwich.

After Naomi had escaped when she was nine, he had brought Sarah here. It had been easier to disappear than he would have assumed, just as it had been easy to take children. He had survived on the proceeds of selling his father's strawberry fields and the family home, and when he needed a last name to use, he used his mother's maiden name. He lived a subterranean life, surprised at how quickly time passed even when you didn't have much of anything to do besides dream in the vast expanse between murder and hate.

It had been twenty years since Naomi's escape, he had realized when he saw the flyers around skid row. A woman looking for her sister. The details were clear. Naomi had not only tracked him to the city; she had, in the interlude, become an investigator specializing in finding children like herself.

Yet he hadn't worried. He didn't worry for the same reason he didn't worry about all the girls he had taken over the years. No one had ever stopped him. Or his father.

In his earliest memory he was playing with his father's gavel on the bench, wondering why it was called a bench and not a desk. In the chambers nearby—which looked like just a plain office to him—the door was closed, and his dad was doing something in there to a child around his own age. The gavel was warm and smooth and had heft in his own hand. He remembered holding it, seeing the way the light came in the windows, and had the sudden realization that he might never figure himself out. From the other room came sounds he did not want to hear.

Soon after that, his mother left and his father began building something deep in the woods behind the strawberry fields. No one was allowed to go back there, and young Wesley wasn't sure they would have been able to find it, anyhow. One day he had followed his dad without his dad knowing it. But his father, dressed in the worn trousers and baggy shirt he wore away from the bench, had acted like it was okay. *"You will come to like it,"* he had said.

Now Wesley looked at Sarah, moony-eyed in the kitchen corner. There was something about her that was different. A beacon of light shone from the top of her head and pierced all the floors and the roof above, shooting straight into the sky.

He shook his head, scraped the plate. When he looked in the mirror in the hallway closet and put on his courtroom suit, there was no reflection he could discern. That was the most terrifying idea of all: that it had all been for nothing.

"These taste too sweet," he complained. He looked at the bag of sugar on the counter. "Did you put something in them when I went to piss?"

Sarah looked at him, her eyes blank.

"Stupid." He shook his head again, finished the meal.

The cramps started a few minutes later.

The deadbolts turned. Sarah gestured at Celia. It was time to go.

Wesley was crawling across the kitchen, trying to reach the water. Foam covered his lips. His fingers were wet from making himself vomit, and Celia saw the trail of regurgitated food he was sliding through. They didn't have much time.

Passing, Sarah stepped in his waste, felt it against her toes. He looked up, gasping. She limped past, cringing with fear. His hands grabbed at her twisted ankle as she hobbled by. She reached beyond the empty rat poison box hidden behind the cold gray dishwater tub and found a butter knife.

Hurry, said the butterflies. Celia ran down the basement stairs and Sarah limped, following. Celia tried pulling off the board with her bare fingers. It was too tight. Celia turned to Sarah, her face a white blotch of terror.

Above them, in the kitchen, they could hear Wesley. A gushing sound like water pouring. More vomiting. A crash of metal on the floor. The gun box.

Sarah passed her the dull knife. Celia put it between the board and window and pulled as hard as she could, crying with effort. The wood complained as the nails began to lift. One nail, two, three—

Then a sound on the steps behind them.

Wesley was coming.

Naomi was in the library. She could feel Celia in every room. The marble staircase, without her eager steps racing to the bookshelves. The reading room, where the empty chair mocked Naomi.

"She talked about a house," Naomi told the elderly librarian. Behind her was a new flyer, this one for Celia. Naomi had added the school photo she and Jerome had gotten from Mrs. Wilkerson. Celia looked impossibly young in the picture.

The librarian frowned. Naomi felt she was forgetting something.

"She didn't say anything to me," the librarian said. "I only ever talked to her about books."

"You were kind to her."

"Well, why not?" The voice was peevish, full of guilt. The feeling was stronger. Yes, Naomi was forgetting something.

"It can't be your fault," Naomi told her.

"Why shouldn't it be? Why can't it be all our faults?"

Naomi turned, ready to leave. She looked up at the marble staircase and remembered her first glimpse of Celia, coming down the stairs, holding a thick book in her hand. The cover was dull blue, the edges of the pages silvered. It was a place Celia hid inside. A place where she confided her secrets. A place she filled with sketches.

She turned back.

"Do you still have Celia's favorite book back there?"

The librarian reached under the counter and handed it over.

Sitting down at one of the tables, Naomi opened the book. Scraps of paper fluttered out. Naomi saw drawings of butterflies but also faces and places. She opened one and saw herself. She was smiling in the sketch, her head surrounded with butterflies.

Tucked in the middle of the book was a piece of paper folded tight and tucked between two color plates. Naomi unfolded it. Thick pencil had been applied carefully.

It was a map.

Downtown, the careful script read, and at the heart of the map was the industrial area near skid row. In the middle was a house, with *X*s over the windows and a gate over the door. Under the house Celia had written *Here*.

Celia had oriented it with the one landmark anyone would understand: *River*.

Naomi spun the map. North, you are here. South, you are leaving now. Grabbing the paper, running out the door, panic under your once soft feet, healed and now strong.

She didn't bother going for her car. She ran.

The empty streets became the fields Naomi ran once in escape, now in pursuit. She was turning around in the past, running backwards to what she had feared and lost. She felt the air fill her chest. She felt the strength in her legs.

Deep in the industrial district, Naomi knew she was getting close. She had not seen anyone for blocks. She paused, opened the map, and oriented herself.

The house rose out of the gray landscape like a foul toadstool. The sky above was slate, the sun frightened behind darkening clouds. The windows were all boarded-up, and the door covered with locks. The only window that looked even faintly breachable was at the basement level. A sliver of light showed at the side of the boards. The light was warm and golden. Naomi instinctually recognized the lamplight of her captivity. No electricity, she thought.

From inside, a dim scream. Naomi knew that voice.

Celia.

Without hesitating, Naomi ran up next to the house and, rolling down on the dank soil, in one smooth motion drew her knees back and kicked hard. Glass shattered, a board crumpled, and chunks flew as her feet busted in.

She heard a cry of alarm, and then she was flipping on her belly and dropping in, sightless, before she could even see the ground, before anyone had time to react. She could feel the cool air around, felt her eyes open and her feet willing to find the floor.

She went in with only what she knew: her hands, her heart, her wild fists.

Landing on the dirt floor, Naomi saw, instantly, Celia, shrinking with terror. A defunct oil heater. Sour dirt and the deep, hopeless smell of death.

Wesley Thurman, his silver hair somehow dimmer inside, was holding a gun. He was wearing dirty trousers and an untucked shirt, soaking wet at the chest. He looked completely different from the man she had seen in the fussy suit, as if he had shed a skin and become his own truth. Naomi recognized this Wesley. He looked at her with the vicious temperament of a dog that has only learned to bite. All the hollowness of evil. The sadness.

Cowering in front of Wesley was a young woman. She had brown hair, like Naomi. A wide face, unmarked with time. The sun had never shone on it. The moon only knew it in eclipse. Two wide hazel eyes.

Her sister. This was Sarah. Her sister was in front of her. Naomi saw her bare toes in the bloodstained dirt. She saw a bent ankle.

Sarah tilted her head and stared at Naomi.

Naomi suddenly saw the two of them in a room with the puppy wallpaper. Naomi tucking her baby sister into a crib as the branches traced the window. Singing her the lullabies their mother had sung, songs only a big sister could know. The creak of a step behind them, and a young man coming into the room holding a cloth in his hand.

Wesley pointed the gun at Naomi.

Celia opened her mouth to give warning. Her hands rose, as if to protect Naomi.

But Naomi stood frozen. She saw herself running, forever running, across a night field, the sickness in her that she was leaving her sister behind, that her life had grown so terrible she could knowingly make this sacrifice.

She had known. She had known all along.

"I am so sorry," Naomi said, gutted with pain.

Celia cried in alarm as Wesley shot Naomi.

* * *

Celia yelled. It was a guttural cry, a howl of a childhood lost. Naomi was still standing, a look of white surprise in her face, her hand holding her hip, looking down at a bloom of blood.

Wesley held the gun, hot in his hand. It had been so long since he had fired it. The feeling brought back memories better left unexamined. His dad, looking up from the freshly built trapdoor, the smile on his face as hollow as a fly landing on a sill. He remembered all the times he could have chosen a different path, ended up different—and yet he didn't.

A person came flying at him. He was expecting Celia and could have easily batted her away. But what stunned him was that it was Naomi. She simply ran towards him, bloody hand coming off her hip. In a split second she had reached for the gun with both hands, pried it hard from his fingers. She yanked the gun away as if he were the child, and she swung back and struck him with it quickly, with force, across his eyes. It was hard enough to break his nose and split his forehead, blinding him with blood, and she followed with an immediate punch to his stomach. It felt like her hard fist had touched the inside of his spine, and he doubled over in pain. A dim part of him registered that this was the first time in his life anyone had ever struck *him*. Naomi knew body blows could take a man down. It was more painful than he could have imagined.

It was all happening too quickly. It wasn't supposed to be this way. Wesley fell to his knees, tried to get back up, only to receive a heart-stopping kick under the ribs that sent him sprawling in the soiled dirt. Another hard kick rocked his head back so far he felt his jaw break. With a decisive stomp Naomi landed on his right wrist, breaking it and causing him to scream in pain.

In agony Wesley rolled over, clutching his broken wrist, and he was looking through skeins of blood at the child he had once stolen. Naomi looked down at him. She lifted the gun. She was shaking, not from fear but from rage. The desire to hurt him came from a place so deep she felt it in her teeth. It was the healthiest thing she had ever felt.

"Naomi?" It was Celia.

From above came new noises. The front door was being battered in. The future entered the room.

Jerome dropped in the broken basement window, and in moments was gently taking the gun from Naomi, sliding on the safety, examining the wound at her hip. Winfield came rushing down the stairs to cuff Wesley, who was clutching his wrist in agony. Others were arriving, wrapping Celia in an insulated blanket.

Naomi was left alone, staring at her sister. The men pulled back.

Sarah was trying to make her mouth work, but it had been too long. Instead long sounds came out, as twisted as old cloth.

"You're going to be okay," Naomi told her sister, tears filling her mouth. All of her felt like one big cry. "I'll see to that."

I don't believe in revenge. But maybe I already had it."

This is what Naomi told Diane, who asked Naomi what she did believe in, only to be told prevention. Yet she knew that she had to go into the courtroom and speak the truth.

She walked through the polished courtroom doors, following the deputy. At tables were the district attorney—his forehead cried for mercy under the glare of lights—and a tired-looking public defender, willing to defend even this, his worst nightmare of a client, and Naomi understood that, too. We all deserve to know there is an outside. Even Wesley, sitting next to his public defender, a cast on his wrist.

Naomi strode to the front, and the deputy held the swinging gate to the witness box. The judge kept his eyes averted from the defendant, lest his contempt influence the jury.

Naomi met the jurors' eyes as she took the stand. She sat, tucked her one and only court skirt under her with her palms, straightened her back, and looked them right in the eye. Middle-aged school-teacher, she guessed. Mechanic. That one, with the nicotine hands? Retired. The angry-looking young man would be the hard one.

The oath. Naomi raised her hand. Her eyes were on the court clerk, but her warmth was for the jury. This parcel of humanity would decide what would happen to Wesley. The media would soon move on, but what was left behind had been so profound. The murdered street girls had all been identified. The unidentified migrant children in the graveyard had been exhumed, and a task force was at work locating their long-ago families. Teddy had been convicted for the sexual assault of Alyssa and was now serving time in prison. Alyssa was being adopted by her foster family—they had promised that Celia could visit as often as she wanted. Celia's mother . . . well, that was a longer story, and one that was not going to end soon.

And Celia? Naomi and Jerome were her new foster parents, and Celia lived in a room they had made for her in the attic. The walls were covered with her butterfly drawings. It had not been easy. Celia, left on her own so long, had almost feral characteristics. She hoarded food; she came and went as she pleased. The one way Naomi had discovered to get her to mind was the promise of a trip to the boxing gym. The fighters there called her Lil' Diablo.

But there was a lot of good all the same. Jerome had never smiled as much as when he saw Naomi and Celia together, walking home from the neighborhood library. Naomi had signed Celia up for the local school, where she was slowly making friends. Her favorite class was art, and at home she liked cooking with Diane.

Naomi had gone back to working missing child cases, and Jerome was building his own caseload—he was on the trail of a horrifying number of missing native women.

Even Rich had a home. He had gone to live at the horse track, where he had a little room above the stables. He was being trained by the Mexican man to work with the horses. He seemed happy, Celia had told Naomi.

Sometimes at night Naomi woke from sleep thinking, *We could have stopped it.* She hoped it was true, cordoned in the witness box, giving her small, careful answers to the jury. Yes, I was held captive by Wesley Thurman. Yes, I became an investigator to find missing children like myself.

And Celia.

Of all the events in her life this reverberated more than any. The green eyes, the willingness to fight. The courage. The joy in butterflies.

"Excuse me?" Just for a moment, she had faltered, and the district attorney repeated the question.

"I asked you, when you entered that home, who else did you find, held captive all these years?"

Naomi turned to the jury and let them see the pain in her eyes. "It was my sister."

* * *

Now Naomi was one of the people parking outside the state hospital, carrying a small plastic bag of quarters. As long as it takes, she had told the civil commitment board in a courthouse meeting. Her sister deserved the chance to heal. To discover her own reality, the path of a life that is chosen.

Perhaps for a magical reason, Sarah always waited at the same table. Naomi helped her feed quarters into the machine to get her a package of soft ginger cookies—Sarah loved sweets and couldn't get enough. After much dental surgery her mouth was healing, as was her ankle, broken and reset. Her mind would take longer. Holding an arm out, Naomi led Sarah outside. Sarah could now handle up to an hour of fresh air. She no longer cried out in pain from the touch of grass or the kiss of rain.

PTSD, the doctor had said. Dissociative disorder. Names like pillows trapped in trees. All Naomi saw was Sarah. Beloved, beautiful Sarah.

Sometimes Celia came with her. The psychiatrist said this would be healing to both of them. Naomi had her doubts. She didn't like the intimate looks they exchanged, as if sharing a secret past. Maybe it was jealousy. Naomi's own memories had stopped coming back. She was coming to terms with the fact they might never return, and that was okay. She didn't need to remember, Diane kept telling her.

Naomi led her sister to a plastic chair on a small patio outside. Sarah carefully lowered herself into the chair, turning around several times to make sure she got it right. Chairs were new to her. So was television. People. The sky. And noise from airplanes— the entire world seemed one earth-splitting scream—and tastes and smells. The smells of the world nauseated and delighted her in turn. She slept a lot. Sometimes the nurses found her in the hall closet, nestled under the coatrack.

Sarah smiled at Naomi. This was one reality she could trust. Big Sister had come back to her, just like she had promised. She had brought all their friends.

They sat in silence. They even sat the same way, legs open, shoulders back. Overhead fall clouds passed. The same trees that had budded were now shedding their leaves, getting ready for sleep. Rest here, Sarah. When you wake, you will be better.

Sarah's face was shifting, eyes awake and then vacant. "Whatever you want to tell me," Naomi had told her, "I will listen. There is nothing you can say that is wrong. I love you."

Sarah held her left arm out and opened her palm. She often did this when Naomi visited. Their eyes met, and Naomi smiled at her. Sarah turned to her own palm and her lips moved. She was telling her, or it, something, and this time Naomi could read a bit of her lips.

Sister, she was saying. Back.

* * *

The train rocked as it crossed the green hills, crowned with gold where the sun touched. To the north was a great river, and to the west even greater forests. This entire land was as old as time and as new as the dawn. Celia looked out the train window. In her mind her hands were pressed to the glass, like the child she once was but never had been.

"It's okay," Naomi had told her. "Grieve. Be all of you at once."

Naomi rode next to her, her body gently rocking with the train, her eyes closed. A peace had come over her. Celia could feel it.

Jerome knew it. Everyone who was around her felt it, even the nice detective who had come to Celia's welcome-home party.

A distant bell, a hooting. This was the world, too.

Naomi opened her eyes. The train slowed, and Celia and Naomi got off at a small, deserted station. They walked over a green hill to where a tall building stood alone, its windows recessed against the light.

Naomi stopped at the door, but Celia rushed forward.

She ran into the middle of a large room that rose to skylights of polished glass. The air was thick and warm with plants, with a smell that said forever.

All around her were the butterflies. Real butterflies! She spun, delighted. The soft, brilliant blue of a forester. A bright yellow of a cloudless sulfur, a white clearer than an eye, a green that trembled with life. Spicebush, tiger! The friendly eyes of a common wood nymph, a hotshot of a brassy red admiral. And who could forget the blue of a pipevine that runs east to west?

That was the sky.

From the doorway Naomi stood, smiling.

Celia raised her arms, and the laughter poured out. She clapped her hands in joy, and all around her the butterflies rose, fluttering against her skin, turning her silver with their dust. She lifted her head. For the first time in her life, she was unafraid.

She turned to Naomi, mouth open in delight.

Walking slowly, Naomi stepped into the room. The butterflies landed on her, too, caressing her skin. She felt them on her hair, her arms, her hands, which she raised to look at, covered with blurs of moving color.

The butterflies took flight, and they circled around her head: once, twice, three times. Like the rotation of the sun, they said thank you.

Reaching, Celia felt for Naomi's hand. She smiled at her.

"Now I know," she said.

"What?"

"Who I am."

ACKNOWLEDGMENTS

This book was raised by libraries and love. I wouldn't be a writer today if not for the public libraries of my difficult childhood, and the books that saved me with story. I will never forget the librarians of the downtown Portland, Oregon, library who expressed care for me when I, too, was a homeless kid. Thank you for showing me a path through the pain, and the beauty in the darkness.

Thank you to Luppi, Tony, Markel, Tamira, and to the other children I have been blessed to care for as a foster and adoptive mom. I am so lucky to be part of your journey. I love you beyond measure.

Thank you to my clients in my day job as a public defense investigator, including the trafficking victims, homeless, refugees, immigrants, veterans, and others who have filled my life. You have shared your pain with me, and I am honored to help you seek justice.

Thank you to my dear friends. This list is only partial: Stephanie, Sara, Alice, Andrea, Cheryl, Lidia, Karen, Julie, Mary, Laura,

Acknowledgments

Eric, Jen, Ellen, Samantha, Liz, Jane, Rhonda, Diana, Michele, Kelly, Monica, Kristi, Wendy, Nayomi, Dianah, Cece, DeAnn, Maggie, Sheila, Bette, Ronni, Mary, Pam, Rod, Monica, Sia, Jane, Angela, Leah, Jo, Scott, Anna, Kristina, Jenny, Joe, Gayle, Jackie, Bill, Susan, Marilyn, BJ, Skip, Shannon, Zoe, Cathy, Katie, Christopher, Cate, Bill, Kate, and all the fine folk at the Metropolitan Public Defender's Office. Thank you to Marty and Bill.

Thank you to my amazing team at HarperCollins: Gail, Doug, Tina, Rachel, Emily, Katie, Falon, John, Mary, and everyone else in Editorial, Production, Marketing, and Publicity. Thank you to Richard Pine, Eliza, Lyndsey, Nathaniel, and the wonderful folk at Inkwell. Thank you Kirsty and Lettice for your valuable input, and Nicole Dewey for all the hard work.

And thank you, dear readers. Life is a story we tell ourselves and one another—we can make the story full of justice, kindness, and redemption. It's up to us.

ABOUT THE AUTHOR

RENE DENFELD is an internationally bestselling author, journalist, and licensed public defense investigator. She has written for the *New York Times Magazine*, the *Oregonian*, and the *Philadelphia Inquirer*, and is the author of the novels *The Child Finder* and *The Enchanted*. She lives in Portland, Oregon, with her children from foster care.

www.renedenfeld.com

ALSO BY RENE DENFELD

THE ENCHANTED
A NOVEL

"A wondrous book that finds transcendence in the most unlikely of places."

— Erin Morgenstern, author of *The Night Circus* and *The Starless Sea*

A luminous novel about redemption and survival told from the point of view of a convict whose magical interpretations of prison life allow him to find joy while isolated from the rest of humanity, and a female investigator who experiences her own personal salvation in her work as a death penalty investigator.

THE CHILD FINDER
A NOVEL

"Loaded with suspense, its resonance comes from its surprising tilt towards storytelling restraint, a rarity in this typical crackling genre. Elegiac, informative and disquieting… The novel gallops to a suitably heart-racing finish."

—*New York Times Book Review*

A haunting, richly atmospheric, and deeply suspenseful novel about an investigator who must use her unique insights to find a missing little girl.

Extraordinary Praise for

Hunting Shadows

and the Inspector Ian Rutledge Mysteries

"Tricky plotting and rich atmospherics distinguish bestseller Todd's sixteenth novel featuring Scotland Yard's Insp. Ian Rutledge. . . . Todd (the pen name of a mother-son writing team) has rarely been better." —*Publishers Weekly* (starred review) on *Hunting Shadows*

"Another well-written, well-plotted entry in this always engaging mystery series." —*Booklist* on *Hunting Shadows*

"Another winner. . . . Strong atmosphere and a complicated mystery make this book one that readers won't be able to put down." —*Romantic Times* 4½ stars on *Hunting Shadows*

"As always, the North Carolina–based mother and son who write under the pseudonym Charles Todd do a beautiful job with the period detail, making these books a nostalgic outing to England between the world wars." —*The News & Observer* on *Hunting Shadows*

"Readers who stick with the chase, though, should be enthralled, as Rutledge sorts through a fascinating portrait gallery of witnesses and suspects, most of whom aren't telling him the whole truth." —*Wilmington News Journal* on *Hunting Shadows*

"Of all the places where Inspector Ian Rutledge's Scotland Yard assignments have taken him, the desolate Fen country must surely be the eeriest. [This is an] excellent historical series." —*New York Times Book Review* on *Hunting Shadows*

"Elusive clues, suspense and excellent writing make for reading pleasure."
—*The Oklahoman* on *Hunting Shadows*

"You're going to love Todd."
—Stephen King, *Entertainment Weekly* on *A Question of Honor*

"As with any good mystery, the tension ramps up as the story progresses, pulling more and more characters into the fray, weaving three murders flawlessly into a tight tale. Mr. Todd's characterization is his strength."
—NewYorkJournalofBooks.com on *The Confession*

"Another excellent Inspector Ian Rutledge mystery. . . . You follow a twisting road when you read this book. You won't soon forget your trip to Furnham and the people who may not be who they seem to be."
—*Suspense Magazine* on *The Confession*

"A gripping whodunit."
—*Publishers Weekly* on *Proof of Guilt*

"[A]nother dark and gripping saga."
—*Washington Times* on *Proof of Guilt*

"With its typically intricate plotting, detailed characterizations, and red herrings, this is a compelling addition to the popular Ian Rutledge series."
—*Library Journal* on *A Duty to the Dead*

"[A] complex British-style police procedural that explores the intersection of justice and vengeance served up cold. It's especially recommended for readers who relish P.D. James's Adam Dalgliesh mysteries."
—*Boston Globe* on *A Matter of Justice*

HUNTING SHADOWS

Also by Charles Todd

The Ian Rutledge Mysteries

A Test of Wills

Wings of Fire

Search the Dark

Legacy of the Dead

Watchers of Time

A Fearsome Doubt

A Cold Treachery

A Long Shadow

A False Mirror

A Pale Horse

A Matter of Justice

The Red Door

A Lonely Death

The Confession

Proof of Guilt

The Bess Crawford Mysteries

A Duty to the Dead

An Impartial Witness

A Bitter Truth

An Unmarked Grave

A Question of Honor

Other Fiction

The Murder Stone

The Walnut Tree

HUNTING
SHADOWS

An Inspector Ian Rutledge Mystery

Charles Todd

wm WILLIAM MORROW

An Imprint of HarperCollins*Publishers*

P.S.™ is a trademark of HarperCollins Publishers.

HUNTING SHADOWS. Copyright © 2014 by Charles Todd. All rights reserved. Printed in the United States of America. No part of this book may be used or reproduced in any manner whatsoever without written permission except in the case of brief quotations embodied in critical articles and reviews. For information address HarperCollins Publishers, 195 Broadway, New York, NY 10007.

HarperCollins books may be purchased for educational, business, or sales promotional use. For information please e-mail the Special Markets Department at SPsales@harpercollins.com.

A hardcover edition of this book was published in 2014 by William Morrow, an imprint of HarperCollins Publishers.

FIRST WILLIAM MORROW PAPERBACK EDITION PUBLISHED 2015.

Library of Congress Cataloging-in-Publication Data has been applied for.

ISBN 978-0-06-223710-1

17 18 19   OV/RRD   10 9 8 7 6 5

For Robin Hathaway, author of the Dr. Fenimore series, the Dr. Jo Banks series, and countless short stories.

Robin was a voracious reader, had an eclectic library that filled three houses, and possessed one of the most creative minds we've ever come across. She had plots and stories yet untold, and a love of the written word that was deep and abiding. And she was a good friend, something that was very precious to a great many people, including us. . . . What she didn't have was Time.

Here's to the Chrysler Building, Robin. And all that it stood for.

Chapter 1

The Fen Country, Cambridgeshire, August 1920

He read the telegram with dismay, and a second time with a heavy sense of loss.

Major Clayton was dead. He'd been in hospital outside London since the closing days of the war, fighting a different battle. Sometimes winning. More often than not losing. They had kept in touch until three months before, when Clayton had been too ill to write, and his sister had been too distressed to write for him.

Dropping the telegram on the table, he gazed out his window. Clayton would be brought back to the Fen country for burial. Services would be held at two o'clock Friday next in the Church of St. Mary's, Burwell. Only a few miles away.

He intended to be there.

He'd tried hard to put the war behind him. Avoiding weddings and funerals alike, refusing even to deliver the eulogies for men he'd known well. It would bring back too many memories, and he wanted them to stay buried, along with the dead left behind in the torn earth of Flanders Fields. Unable to explain, he'd simply cited ill health as his reason for declining. Burying himself here, he had shut out as much of the rest of the world as he could. He had even stopped reading obituaries. They were too sharp a reminder of the fact that he had survived when so many had not. For the dying had not stopped with the Armistice.

The service for Major Clayton was different. Clayton had saved his life, and in doing so nearly lost his own. The leg had never healed correctly, and in the end it had become the source of the gangrene that overtook first his foot, then his knee, his leg, and finally his body. Dying by inches, he'd called it.

For Major Clayton, he would have to make an exception. He hadn't been asked by Clayton's sister to deliver the eulogy, even though he knew the man better than anyone living. And he was just as glad.

Instead the sister had invited a Colonel from London to do that honor. He wondered what Clayton would have made of that, given his feelings for HQ and the generals who had given orders they themselves would never have to carry out. Decisions that sent men to their deaths, maimed them, made them numbers on interminable lists, names and ranks and dates but never the faces or shortened lives that should have reminded the generals that they were dealing in flesh and blood.

Of course St. Mary's would be full for the service. He reminded himself that he would have to stay well back, where he wouldn't be noticed.

Only for Clayton, he thought on the Friday as he shaved and then dressed himself with more than his usual care. The Major had been a stickler for appearances; he'd said often enough that if a man respected his uniform, he would respect himself. It would not do to be less than parade perfect even in civilian clothes.

At half past one, he set out for Burwell, planning his journey to arrive shortly before the mourners went inside to take their places. He had no desire to greet anyone, exchange pleasantries or memories. Or to offer condolences to the sister. He barely knew her, and his brief words of sympathy would not lessen her grief.

As it was, by the time he'd reached Burwell and walked on to St. Mary's by a roundabout way, ending up on the street just above it, the hearse had arrived and only a handful of people were still standing by the west door. He slowed his pace, waiting until everyone else had gone inside ahead of him, and listened to the heavy bell above his head toll the brief years of Clayton's life. Thirty-five. It was a hell of a thing to die at thirty-five with so much to live for, leg or no leg.

He glanced up at the bell and then back at the church doorway. And there, to his utter astonishment, he saw a face he had never wanted to see again. Much less find one day here in this isolated corner of Cambridgeshire.

He brushed a hand across his eyes, certain that in the bright sunlight he'd been mistaken. That in his distress over the Major's death, other memories had forced themselves to the forefront of his mind. It would be too cruel—

But no. There he was, bold as brass, smiling and chatting with one of the men in uniform next to him. There could be no mistake.

Captain Hutchinson. *What the hell was he doing here?* He hadn't known Clayton, had he? Why was he among the mourners?

Quickly stepping back into the shadows cast by a large tree overhanging the street, he tried to think.

Hutchinson must have traveled up from London with the Colonel. That would explain his being here. Hutchinson was always quick to see an advantage. Or had he somehow discovered that Clayton's sister was inheriting everything and fixed his eye on her? There was a well-set-up estate in Gloucestershire, and the older property here in Burwell, presently occupied by a tenant. Both would bring in a tidy income.

It would be like Hutchinson, to curry favor before the will had been read, to prove he was no fortune hunter. But he was.

He felt ill, perspiring in the late summer heat like someone with a fever, his legs trembling.

The last of the mourners had stepped inside the church, the coffin had been lifted out of the hearse and shouldered to follow the Rector down the aisle of the nave. And still he stood where he was.

He couldn't—*in God's name he could not now walk inside*. He couldn't share a roof with Hutchinson. Not even for Major Clayton's sake. Not with the man who'd killed Mary.

He closed his eyes, trying to steady himself.

A woman's voice came from just behind him.

"Are you all right, sir?"

"Yes. Yes, I'm fine. Thank you," he said hoarsely, and in spite of himself, in spite of everything, he started moving toward the church door.

But that was as far as he could go.

Turning on his heel, he walked quickly back toward the shelter of the shadows under the tree. It was as good a vantage point as any from which to keep watch.

Standing there during the service only hardened his resolve. He would be absolutely certain before he left Burwell. It was imperative that he be sure his own emotional state hadn't made him mistake someone else for Hutchinson. But when the service was over and the mourners began to file out, preceded by the coffin, he saw Hutchinson quite clearly. He was *there*, a few feet from the Colonel, his hand on Miss Clayton's elbow as she walked with head bowed, her shoulders shaking with her sobs.

If he had had a weapon of any sort, he'd have used it then and killed the bastard. He could feel the rifle in his hands, the familiar smoothness of the wood, the heat of the barrel from long hours of use, the weight of it, so real to him that for an instant he could almost believe it was there. And with all his heart he wished it was true.

The procession was moving on toward the churchyard.

But just before the procession turned into it, something happened that held him pinned where he was.

Hutchinson lifted his head, like prey scenting the air, and for an instant he was sure that the Captain had stared directly at him.

It was impossible, of course. It was his imagination.

The moment passed, Hutchinson's back was to him now, and he almost went down on his knees, to vomit.

He stumbled away like a drunkard, away from the church and the churchyard, and somehow, he was never sure afterward just how, he made it to the sanctuary of his house. The first thing he did was to pour himself the stiffest whisky he'd had in five years. The second was to open the wardrobe door and reach far into the back where he knew the Lee-Enfield was hidden.

Drawing it out, he felt on top of the wardrobe for the cartridges. They were still there behind the carved pediment. He wasn't supposed to have brought either the weapon or the ammunition back. But he had, because the rifle had become a part of him. And no one searched his kit.

Thank God he had.

He was already loading the rifle, hurrying to reach Burwell and the churchyard in time.

And then he stopped, reason finally overcoming the strain and emotion that were driving him.

Foolish to do such a thing. First of all, it would mar Major Clayton's last rites. And that would never do. Secondly, he'd be taken up at once and tried and hanged. He would be *damned* if he'd hang for the likes of Hutchinson.

The man deserved to die. But not this way. Not sacrificing himself.

He removed the cartridges and put the rifle back into the wardrobe, shutting the door firmly.

There had to be a better way.

Look at it from a different perspective. God had brought this man to him once. He would do it again. All he had to do was wait. However long it took.

He began to read the newspapers, as many as he could find. Cambridge, Ely, Burwell, the *Times* from London. Even the racing news in nearby Newmarket. And he burned them in the grate as soon as he'd finished them, to be certain that once the deed was done, there was nothing lying about that would cause talk or arouse anyone's suspicion. He traveled as well, to Boston and King's Lynn, to Bury and Colchester, as far south as St. Albans, looking for anything that might be useful in carrying out his task. He studied people, the way they moved and talked and behaved. It became something of an obsession, the need to survive what he was about to do. There was no satisfaction in it otherwise.

His patience paid off.

Captain Hutchinson was to be a guest at a fashionable wedding to be held in Ely Cathedral in three weeks' time. His name was there, leaping off the page of the Ely newspaper, even though his was only one of a great many other names. Hutchinson was, it appeared, a cousin to the bridegroom.

The first of September.

He was ready. He'd already laid the groundwork. Now it was just a matter of fitting the plan to the place. Thinking through each step, finding flaws, looking for opportunities on the ground, and looking as well at possible escape routes. He covered the Fen country on his bicycle until he knew every lane and track, until he felt he could reach any point in the dark of night. And then he walked the length and breadth of it.

The Fens were dangerous for the unwary. Narrow flat fields stretched for miles, where a boot in the rich black soil would leave its mark for the hunter to find. Irrigation ditches, sometimes crossed by a road or a bridge over a pump, where a false step could mean falling in and drowning. And the roads themselves, running arrow straight, so that any movement could be seen, even at a great distance. No trees, no buildings to hide behind until the chase had passed. Indeed, nothing to offer cover at all, unless one had learned beforehand where to find it.

He'd thought he'd known the countryside well all his life. Now he knew it intimately.

He was ready.

And Hutchinson would come to *him* for the killing.

Chapter 2

The day of the wedding in Ely, a small crowd had gathered to watch the arrival of the wedding party.

A barricade had been set up so that only the bride, her father, and her attendants could drive directly to the Cathedral door. The bridegroom and the wedding guests would walk across the grassy Palace Green to the church, a parade of handsomely dressed gentlemen and their ladies, a sprinkling of men in uniform, and a dash of clergymen, for the bride's family included several deacons and a Bishop.

By the Cathedral clock, it was two hours before the ceremony. Last-minute preparations were under way, flowers and candles being carried in, a carpet being laid down the long aisle, the organist practicing for the following Sunday's service. But for the most part, the afternoon was quiet, an island of serenity before the excitement of the ceremony.

No one noticed the elderly man on an equally elderly bicycle who came up the street from the direction of the school and the Cathedral offices, his thin white hair blowing in the light wind as he pedaled. It wasn't unusual for pedestrians coming up the road to pass in front of the west door on their way to the busy streets on the far side of the church.

He paused by the wall enclosing the Cathedral precincts and wiped his brow, looking tired and thirsty. But he mounted the bicycle once more and got as far as the abutments that reached up to the tower. There was a narrow recess there where he could leave his bicycle out of sight.

The old man appeared to be a knife and scissors sharpener, his clothes threadbare and his canvas carryall dusty from the roads. He started to leave the carryall on his handlebars, walking away before thinking better of it. He went back, picked it up, and put it firmly under his arm, then stepped into the shadow of the Galilee Porch that led to the west doorway, leaning there, as if the shade was welcome, this warm afternoon.

No one challenged him. No one paid him any attention. Behind his back, the enormous Cathedral seemed to crouch, waiting.

After a while he turned and went inside, into the wide space beneath the towers. Beyond, in the nave, the choir was just finishing a last rehearsal, and someone was putting a final touch to the flowers, pinching off any wilted blossoms. No one turned to look up the long handsome aisle to see who had entered. The sound hardly reached the nave.

He stood there for a moment, then turned and made his way to the right, where there was a door to the tower. It was a long walk, fifteen feet or more, and he was at his most exposed.

No one came out of the nave to call to him, to ask his business or demand that he clear off.

The tower door was unlocked, as it had been the last three times he'd tested it. He looked back over his shoulder. No one was in sight.

The old man slipped inside the tower door, closing it quietly behind him, then began to make his way up the long flights of stairs, taking his time. It was dim and musty in the shaft, the bell ropes swaying a little, making him feel light-headed, and he dared not look down. The canvas carryall seemed to grow heavier with every step. He was winded when at last he reached the stone parapet just above the chamber where the bells were hung.

They wouldn't ring until the wedding party was leaving the sanctuary. He would be gone by then. One way or another.

Sitting down on the warm, sloping cone of the roof, he waited for a quarter of an hour, letting his heart rate settle again. Then he opened his carryall and began to assemble the rifle. It had served men like him well in France. It would serve him now. Better than the older versions.

A pigeon landed on the parapet, staring unwinking at him, and he stayed where he was. Finally satisfied that the carryall held nothing edible, the pigeon took off again.

He waited with infinite patience, as he'd been taught to do. There was no hurry. His quarry would come to him. Finally he heard the great organ begin to play once more, this time the first of the set pieces selected by the bride's family. There was a stir below as onlookers who had gathered behind the barricades to watch the guests arrive saw the first motorcar pull up. A ripple of applause quickly followed.

It was time.

Getting carefully to his feet, keeping low, he made his way to the outer wall, peering between the battlements. A motorcar moved away as several more behind it took its place. As the guests alighted, others moved up in line. Unseen from below, he took out the German scope and attached it to the rifle. They hadn't used scopes during his training. And the Germans in France had taken great care to prevent theirs from being captured and turned against them. The first time he'd looked through this one, he'd been surprised by the clarity it had added to his own keen eyesight.

He scanned the guests as they crossed the Palace Green toward the west door, but he didn't recognize any of them. Earlier in the week he'd paced the distance from where the motorcars stopped and where he himself would be waiting. He knew he was well within range of his target. He could take his time and wait for the perfect angle.

Not too soon. Not too late. He knew, almost to the blade of grass, where he wanted his victim to be. He could see the Russian gun clearly, at the opposite end of the Green from the West Tower, the long muzzle of the cannon pointing outward, as if its intent was to protect the Cathedral from the townspeople.

Kneeling there, his weapon beside him, he was fairly sure he was invisible from the ground, but to be safe, he pulled an old dark gray hood out of the scissor sharpener's blouse and draped it over his head and shoulders. It was, he knew, almost exactly the same color as the stone around him.

Once more, he settled down to wait.

It was ten minutes to the hour when he saw his quarry alight from a motorcar that had just pulled up. Another man and a woman arrived with Hutchinson, chatting quietly as they turned toward the Cathedral. He could see the man's face clearly now, smug and satisfied with himself, a slight smile lifting his lips as he spoke to the woman beside him.

The angle was excellent. The target unsuspecting. He let the Captain come a little closer across the greensward, just clear of where the motorcars were stopping, steadied his breathing and emptied his mind of any emotion. Then he took careful aim, almost without thinking adjusting to the man's measured pace and the light wind. Old habits die hard.

And calmly, slowly, he squeezed the trigger.

The echoes against the stone were deafening, but he took no notice, his scope still trained on the quarry as Hutchinson's body reacted to the hit before he could even flinch from the sound of the shot.

Without a word, he crumpled to the ground and did not move. Only the red stain spreading across his stiff white shirtfront showed that he had been struck.

The woman, her hands to her face, was screaming, and everyone at the barricade turned to stare in her direction, then looked wildly around for the source of the shot. The other man was kneeling, frantically trying to loosen Hutchinson's cravat and open his shirt. But it was useless. That had been a heart shot, there was nothing to be done. Still the man kept working, unable to believe that it was hopeless.

Satisfied, the scissor sharpener ejected the single cartridge casing and began to disassemble his rifle, taking his time, ignoring the screams and cries below. He knew what was happening, he didn't need to look. Some were running to the assistance of the fallen man, others fleeing toward the street behind them, toward The Lamb Inn, out of range for fear there would be a second shot. A few would be scanning the rooftops and windows of buildings on either side of the grass, looking in vain for the shooter. The greeters at the door had rushed into the sanctuary, crying havoc. He could hear the unnerved guests as they hurried out to see, and all the while, the organ music went on, as if in the loft the organist was unaware of what was happening below in the nave. Then the last notes trailed off as he must have realized something was wrong.

The scissors grinder made his way to the stairs and started down them, taking his time, careful not to lose his footing. When he reached the bottom step, he peered out a crack in the door, then opened it wider. No one. Either they were cowering in the nave or already outside. The bride's motorcar was just arriving, adding to the chaos.

He began that long walk again, taking his time, reaching the Galilee Porch and the open doorway. Appearing bewildered and afraid, he stared vacantly around. No one paid him any heed. He inched sideways, making his way to his left. His bicycle was where he'd put it, but he didn't mount it. Instead he walked it down the quiet street, back the way he'd come, toward the school. Several people from there were running toward the Cathedral, and one or two called out to him, asking what had happened.

He shook his head. "Terrible," he said, "terrible." His voice was shaking, he looked as if he might fall down from the shock, and they ran on. He continued his slow, painful way to the arch by the school. There just as the police were passing, he mounted his bicycle and pedaled sedately off, a graying scarecrow with a lined face and bony knees.

T he police spent five hours searching the streets around the Cathedral, searching inside it despite the anxious wedding guests waiting to have their statements taken.

A constable reached the church tower, walking out into the narrow space around the battlements. He was an older man, staying on because the men who should have replaced him had long since rotted in the graveyards of Flanders or had come home without a limb or with other injuries. He looked down from this height at the target area and felt his stomach lurch as a wave of dizziness overcame him. Swiftly concluding that it was impossible to make such a shot from this position without being seen, he hurried back to the stairs, staring anxiously into the dim abyss, and nearly lost his dinner. By the time he'd reached the last step his heart was jumping in his chest.

"Nothing up there but the bats," he told another constable on his way to climb to the Lantern tower over the crossing where the transepts met.

When it came time to take statements from those by the barricade, everyone's attention had been focused on the arriving guests. They had seen nothing. As one constable put it, "A herd of green pigs could have come by, and if they were dressed to the nines, no one would have taken a bit of notice."

In the end, the wedding went off at six o'clock, the bride red-eyed from hysterics, the bridegroom grim-faced. Captain Hutchinson had been in his family's party. It was generally accepted that only a madman could have done such a thing, with so many people to witness it.

Wherever the madman was, he had cast a pall over the day, and more than one guest leaving after the ceremony had felt his hackles rise as he skirted the place where Hutchinson had fallen, expecting to hear the report of a rifle once more.

Two weeks after the murder, the police had made no progress at all. It was then that they called in Scotland Yard.

But not before the killer had struck again.

Chapter 3

The by-election was scheduled for the next week. The popular Tory candidate, Herbert Swift, arranged a torch-lit parade down the High Street, to end with a speech at the market cross. It was Medieval, the cross, the last seven feet missing. But the base was still intact, and Swift was to stand on it so that he could be seen as well as heard.

All went according to plan. The parade began at the pub named for Hereward the Wake, the eleventh-century hero of the Fens, and some thirty supporters followed their candidate down to the cross, chanting his name, their torches smoking and leaving a reeking trail behind them. The constable, a man named McBride, walked along with them, with an eye to keeping the peace, but the marchers were orderly and in good spirits.

It was all very dramatic, Swift thought, enjoying the spectacle. His rival, the Liberal candidate, was a dour man with no sense of style in his dress, his voice rough and his language rougher, and his meetings in a hired hall were enlivened only by the occasional snore from one of his audience.

Swift reached the plinth of the cross and prepared to step up on the base. He looked at the gathering crowd, many of them villagers come for the show, and felt a sense of satisfaction. It was a better turnout than he'd expected.

The torchlight flickered in the darkness, casting lurid shadows up and down the street and across the eager faces waiting for the speech to begin. The shops on either side of the two village Commons had closed for the day, their windows unlit and blank. Above the shops most of the shopkeepers or their tenants had already drawn their curtains. And the trees by the pond were dark sentinels at the far end of the second Common. This had been an ideal setting to hold his rally, and broadsheets had announced it for three days.

Swift savored the moment as he took his place on the broad footing of the cross and turned toward his supporters, his back to the pond. He was a student of history, and he thought that the scene before him could have taken place a hundred—two hundred—years earlier. It added a sense of continuity to what he was doing: standing for a seat in the House of Commons. A long line of men stretching back in time who were prepared to serve King and Country to the best of their ability were in the shadows of those trees, he thought, watching this twentieth-century descendant, judging him, and with any luck at all, approving of him.

He raised a hand for silence.

"The war is over," he began, his voice carrying well, as it always did, giving his words added power. "And we are embarking on a peace that will last through our lifetime and that of the generations following us. *Their* children will not know what war is. Men have gathered at Versailles to hammer out the terms of that peace, and we here in England have paid a very high price for it. We are still paying. Even now our families don't have enough to eat, work is hard to come by, and what work there is doesn't bring a man enough in wages to keep his—"

His face vanished in a spray of blood and bone, and before anyone could move, he crumpled without a sound into the startled crowd just as the single shot rang out and seemed to fill the night with endless, mindless reverberations.

Chapter 4

London, September 1920

Rutledge stepped into the office of the Acting Chief Superintendent with some trepidation.

He had had a loud and vituperative argument with Markham at the end of his last case, accused of following his own instincts rather than official direction. The fact that in the end Rutledge had been proved right had added to Markham's displeasure. He was a hardheaded, straightforward man who viewed intuition with suspicion and put his faith in the obvious. The dressing down had been personal as well as professional.

Keeping his own temper with an effort, Rutledge had drawn a deep breath, asking himself if every inquiry in Yorkshire, where Markham had come from when Chief Superintendent Bowles had had his heart attack, ended in a tidy packet tied with righteous ribbons. He had grimly withstood the storm, and then Markham had calmed down sufficiently to ask him if he was absolutely convinced of his facts.

He was. And said as much. Markham had thanked him and then dismissed him.

This morning Markham was finishing a report as Rutledge crossed the threshold, and looking up, he nodded in greeting.

"Cambridgeshire—the Fen country. Know it?"

"Around Ely? Yes, a little."

"Someone's walking around up there with a rifle, and so far he's killed two people. A Captain Hutchinson who was about to attend a wedding, and a man named Swift who was standing for Parliament—just as he was beginning a speech."

"A rifle?" Rutledge frowned. "They were turned in before we left France."

"Then someone failed to do as he was ordered."

"Are the two victims related in any way?"

"If Hutchinson was his intended target, no. If he got Hutchinson by mistake, we don't know. The wedding that afternoon was to be attended by prominent churchmen, members of the government, a number of the aristocracy, and military men. If his target was one of them, it will take weeks to interview them and find a connection."

"Was Swift a wedding guest as well?"

"He was not."

"Are we certain the killer was a soldier?"

"We're certain of nothing but the fact that we have two men dead, and too little to go on. Which is why the Yard has been asked to take over the inquiry." He paused, considering Rutledge. "It would not do to hear of a third murder by this madman."

In short, a swift conclusion to the inquiry was expected.

"I'll remember that," Rutledge said, not smiling.

Two hours later, he'd cleared his desk, packed his valise, and set out for Cambridge in his motorcar.

He spent the night there and the next morning headed north.

The sunny weather of yesterday had changed to damp, lowering clouds that obscured the unmade road, and the motorcar's powerful headlamps bounced back at him from the soft, impenetrable wall of mist. At the crossroads, the narrow boards giving the names of villages in each direction appeared and disappeared like wraiths, and sound was muffled, confusing. At one point he could hear a train's whistle in the distance but had no idea how far the tracks might be from where he was.

He drove with care, for the country could be treacherous. Lose one's sense of direction in this flat, featureless landscape and the motorcar could plunge into one of the many drainage ditches that ran arrow straight across the Fens. A missed turn could land him into a field of soft black earth, miles from the nearest house. For that matter, he hadn't seen a dwelling, much less another vehicle, for nearly half an hour.

The sounds of the train faded, then vanished altogether. It was, he thought, as if everything he knew, all that was familiar to him, even his senses, had been taken from him, leaving him to cope in a silent emptiness that had no yesterday or tomorrow, only the obscure present. Rather like death . . .

It was beginning to aggravate his claustrophobia.

Some time later, when he thought surely he must be nearing Ely, out of the mist came a strange sound, a clacking that he couldn't place. A hay wain? No, because he couldn't hear the jingle of harness or the familiar thud of hooves on the hard-packed roadbed.

Slowing, he peered through the windscreen, then stopped altogether. The last thing he wanted was to hit someone or something. Getting out, he walked forward a step at a time. He could see fewer than three paces ahead.

In the back of his mind, a voice was warning him to beware, but he had to know whether he was still on the road—or not.

Out of the gray mist, something stirred, then disappeared. He waited. In time it stirred again, creaking. He frowned, listening before going forward. But now there was silence.

What the hell was out there?

He moved on. Suddenly there was grass beneath his boots, where there had been road before. He turned and realized he couldn't see his motorcar.

In the same instant, the creaking seemed to come from directly above him. His immediate reaction was to duck.

A breath of air touched his face, and it pushed aside the veil of the mist for a few seconds. Something loomed just above his head, and he tensed.

He stood stock-still, waiting for whatever it was to reveal itself. And again there was the faintest rift in the white curtain, and he realized that he was standing only a matter of feet from a windmill. Its sails, laden with damp, were creaking as if complaining of the weight.

A few more steps and he'd have collided with the nearest sail.

But where the devil was he? Surely he'd already passed Soham. Many of the windmills had been replaced with steam pumps, ugly black fingers of chimneys reaching skyward. But Soham's still stood.

The sail above his head creaked again. Listening, he thought he could hear a pump somewhere in the distance.

A voice came through the mist.

"Who's there?"

"A visitor," Rutledge answered. He couldn't make out the accent. "I think I've lost my way."

"Do you need help?"

"Only to be told where I am. What is this mill?"

"Wriston Mill."

And how the hell had he got to Wriston? It lay south of Ely, and a little west. Where had he missed his turn?

The voice said, "Are you walking? On a bicycle?"

"I have a motorcar. I left it back there. I didn't know what the creaking sound was, and I got down to investigate."

"Yes, well, you'd be better with a horse out here. They know what they're about."

"I didn't have a choice in the matter. I'm—from Cambridge."

"Schoolmaster or don?" the voice said, and from the tone of it, either occupation was equally to be despised.

"Neither. I'm trying to reach Ely. On a matter of business."

"Well, you won't make it alive in this. Foolish to have tried."

"That may well be," Rutledge answered. "But here I am."

There was silence for a moment, and then Rutledge heard footsteps walking away.

Swearing to himself, he stood where he was, peering through the fog, trying to find something besides the windmill to serve as a landmark. This kind of mill stood by water, a pump, and he dared not choose the wrong way.

And then he heard the footsteps returning.

"Your motorcar is safe enough where it is. Follow me."

But Rutledge couldn't see him. All he could do was walk in the direction the footsteps were taking now, and that was a risk. His hearing had always been acute, not as sharp as Hamish MacLeod's had been in the trenches, but more than sufficient to serve him now.

He couldn't go wrong if he watched each stride, looking no more than one or two ahead. And so he followed the sound and soon was off the grassy sod, back to a road that seemed to be no better than a lane. They were walking along it now, he could hear the difference in the footsteps leading him. When he had gone some thirty paces, he knew he couldn't possibly have returned to his motorcar again. He stopped and said, "Where are you leading me?"

"Just along here. Another twenty or so feet. There's a house. You can shelter there until this passes."

The voice was odd in the mist. Distorted. He wasn't sure he could recognize it again in more ordinary circumstances. All he could do now was to trust it.

Eighteen. Nineteen. Twenty. He'd gone the twenty feet. He stopped.

The footsteps ahead of him stopped as well.

"To your left. There should be a gate."

Rutledge turned, reached out. His hands touched nothing. He put out a foot. Ah. There was indeed a fence here—iron, he thought. Leaning forward, his groping fingers found an iron picket, the top shaped like a flower. As he moved closer, he could just make out more of them. And there, just beyond, was the gate. His ghostly guide had been right on the mark.

Rutledge called, "Thank you."

But no one was there. That sixth sense so many people possessed told him so, and yet he hadn't heard the man leave.

He walked up what appeared to be a short path and found himself at a blue door. There was a knocker with a brass footplate. He lifted it and let it fall.

After a moment the door opened. A woman stood there, and even against the lamplight that made her appear to be no more than a silhouette, he could see her surprise.

He wondered fleetingly if his unseen rescuer had just come from her and she had expected—hoped—he'd returned. Or was she expecting another caller? The man in the mist had questioned him. Looking back, Rutledge wondered if he was waylaying someone.

"Sorry," he said, smiling. "I'm rather lost. Somehow in the fog, I made a wrong turn. I was on my way to Ely."

She blinked, as if his answer was unexpected. "Were you walking in this? I'm astonished you didn't fall into one of the ditches. Come in, then."

As she stood aside to allow him to pass, he said, "My motorcar is somewhere near Wriston Mill."

As if that explained everything, she said, "Just as well to leave it where it is. I was about to make a pot of tea. Would you care for some?"

In the lighted room he could see that she was quite pretty, dark haired and dark eyed. She was studying him as well. Behind her the front room contrived to look both smart and comfortable. A small fire burned on the hearth, and on a rug beside it a white cat lay curled up and asleep.

"That would be very kind. Yes."

He followed her through to the kitchen. It was a pleasant room, warm and friendly, but the windows showed only blankness beyond the panes. He felt suddenly anxious, claustrophobic because he couldn't see a world outside.

She was busying herself with the kettle and the tea. "You're a stranger, aren't you?"

"I drove up from Cambridge this morning."

"At the university, are you?"

He wouldn't have pegged himself as an academic and yet twice now he had been asked if he was. He was briefly amused. No Oxford man cared to be mistaken for a Cambridge man. "No, sorry. I have an engagement in Ely. This afternoon. I expect I shall miss it."

She glanced at the windows.

"It might clear," she said doubtfully. "But I shouldn't like to raise your hopes."

"Is there anywhere I could stay the night? If this doesn't lift, it would be foolish to press my luck."

"Indeed it would. We're hardly more than a village. But there's a small inn where hunters came in season. For the waterfowl. The hunters haven't been here since the war. I hope the shooting won't start up again. I don't like the sound of the guns. And it's cruel to hunt the birds. There's been some talk about protecting them. It's been done in other places."

The kettle was beginning to boil. From a shelf she took down two cups and saucers, two spoons, and the sugar bowl, setting them on the table. Then she went through a door next to the large dresser, returning with a small jug of milk. "There."

While the tea was steeping, she said, "I'll take you to the inn. Priscilla will be glad of the money."

"If you tell me how to go, I'll find it myself. You shouldn't be out in this mist alone."

"You'd find it very easy to be turned around. I'm used to it."

"You grew up here?" he asked as she lifted the teapot's lid, stirred the leaves, and let them settle again before pouring.

"I lived here as a child. My father was the village doctor. We moved away when I was seven or eight. My mother was insistent that we live in a place with better schooling. And so we went to Bury St. Edmunds."

"But you came back."

She frowned. "Yes, I suppose I did." It was an odd answer, but he didn't press.

They sat across the table from each other, and an awkward pause followed.

"I don't know your name, Mr. . . . ?"

"I'm sorry. Ian Rutledge." He smiled. "You really shouldn't invite strangers into your home. It isn't wise. But I'm grateful you did."

She nodded. "Marcella Trowbridge."

He inclined his head in acknowledgment. "Tell me about Wriston," he said. "I know where it is on a map of Cambridgeshire. Besides the inn, what else is there?"

"Shops and houses, of course. An old market cross. Cromwell took a dislike to it and destroyed the top. I'm told there's a very nice drawing in Christ Church in Cambridge showing how it once looked. One of the early abbots at Ely kept a journal, it seems, recording his travels. We owe him a great debt, because he described the village. It was hardly even that then. Our church was only a pilgrimage chapel in Saxon times, but as Wriston grew, so did it. There's a Green Man on one of the ceiling bosses. A very old one. As a child I used to stare up at it, certain that it was staring back at me, watching to see if I was behaving." She smiled whimsically, remembering. "The abbot must have been taken with it as well, because he mentioned it in his journal along with one of the gargoyles. The windmill, on the other hand, has been here since the reign of James the First, although it's been rebuilt many times. It's one of the few that haven't been replaced by steam, because it's really all but redundant. Drainage elsewhere stole Wriston's thunder, as it were. But in heavy storms, we're still grateful for it."

She realized all at once that she had given him more information than perhaps his question had intended. Shrugging a little, she added, "Otherwise it's rather a small, unprepossessing village."

He noticed that she had said nothing about Wriston's latest and less reputable claim to fame. The murder. He hadn't intended to come here until he'd spoken to the Ely police. But here he was and he should make the most of his opportunity.

"And that's the entire history of Wriston?"

She was still all at once. "I'm afraid I don't quite—I don't understand your question."

He let it go. She had taken him in and been kind. "I was wondering if Cromwell had done other damage to the town, perhaps in the church itself."

She visibly relaxed. "There's the usual story, that he stabled his horses in the nave. He was willing to run roughshod over the beliefs of others. In school I always found him a less than sympathetic character. That didn't sit well with my history mistress, who rather admired him." Making a face, she added, "It was whispered that the body in Westminster Abbey in London wasn't his. That it was hidden here in Cambridgeshire from the wrath of the Royalists."

Rutledge remembered the tale—that on his Restoration, Charles II had had Cromwell's body taken from its resting place in the Abbey and hanged, then beheaded, the head left to rot on a pike.

"Tell me. Was this the mill keeper's cottage?"

"That's on the far side of the mill. I'm not surprised you didn't see it. It burned down before the war and was never rebuilt. If you'd tripped over the foundations, you could have been seriously hurt. My father bought this cottage for my grandmother after she was widowed. She went away for a time, then decided not to return to Bury. Instead she lived here for many years, and then left it to me."

Finishing his tea, he looked up at the windows. There was a difference in the light now, although the fog hadn't thickened as far as he could tell. "It will be dark soon. Perhaps you should tell me how to find that inn."

"Yes. Of course."

She rose and led the way to the front of the house and the door. Rutledge had left his hat in the motorcar along with his valise. But it would be impossible to retrieve either of them until this weather broke.

Miss Trowbridge reached for a shawl on the back of a chair and spread it around her shoulders. "Stay close. Stray and I shan't be able to find you."

"Yes, all right."

As she came to the gate, she said over her shoulder, "This could go on for days. It has, sometimes."

"I'll say my prayers tonight."

She laughed. It was an odd sound in the mist, as if there were an echo.

They turned to their left and walked along the road. He could see her, but not very clearly. There was nothing but the soft cotton wool that touched his face with clammy fingers. If anything, he thought, it appeared to be getting chillier.

Miss Trowbridge stopped. "You'd better take my hand. The road bends just here."

He clasped her soft fingers in his, and they set off again. For all he knew, he thought wryly, she could have been leading him down the road to hell. And then she dropped his hand.

"Here. Do you see the steps?"

And he did. Just. He wondered if she'd been counting off strides, as the man earlier must have done, to bring him safely here.

"I'll wait until you've gone inside," she said. "But I should think Priscilla—Miss Bartram—will be at home."

He climbed the steps, but before he lifted the door knocker, he said, "Will you be all right?"

"Yes, of course."

He let the knocker fall.

A woman a few years older than Miss Trowbridge came to the door. "We're closed," she said.

Miss Trowbridge's disembodied voice said, "Priscilla? This is Mr. Rutledge. He's lost his way in the mist. Can you give him a room for the night?"

"Marcella?"

"Yes, I discovered him wandering about lost. I brought him to you." Nothing was said about offering Rutledge tea. He took note of that.

"A good thing. What brought *you* out in this?"

"I was looking for my cat," she said. "Clarissa. And found Mr. Rutledge instead."

"Well, then. Come inside, Mr. Rutledge. Marcella, are you coming too?"

"Thank you, no, Priscilla. Clarissa is probably waiting for me by the gate."

Rutledge was ushered inside, the door closed behind him.

"Will she be all right?" he asked, still concerned for Miss Trowbridge.

"Oh, yes. She'll find her way." She led him down a dimly lit passage to a sitting room. "Do you know Marcella well?"

"In fact, not at all." He took his lead from Miss Trowbridge's comments about the cat. "She rescued me. I nearly walked into Wriston Mill."

Miss Bartram crossed the room to turn up the lamp. He saw that she was wearing a man's trousers and shirt, but her short hair was becomingly cut, framing her face. He thought she must be in her early thirties.

She looked him up and down. "Where are you from, Mr. Rutledge?"

"I was on my way from Cambridge to Ely," he explained once more.

"Indeed. You're well off the right track." She gestured to the hearth and several comfortable chairs set in front of it. "You see the sitting room. Now, if you'll come with me?" Leading the way upstairs and down a short passage, she said, "This room has been aired. I'll put you here." Holding the door for him, she waited for him to enter.

The room was smaller than he'd hoped, seeming even smaller with the white world outside the windows. The bed boasted a blue coverlet that matched the curtains.

There were two chairs and a table that could serve as a desk, a washstand and basin, and an armoire, crowding together around the walls.

From the shelf above the bed, a pair of stuffed waterfowl in a glass case stared back at him as she stepped in and lit the lamp. Their glass eyes reflected the flare of her match and then the increasing light as the wick caught, giving them a haunted look. Rutledge found himself thinking that if he'd had his hat with him, he could have flung it over the mallards.

"No luggage, then?"

"It's in the motorcar."

"It will be there tomorrow. No one will touch it," she said complacently. "Now, will you be wanting a light supper?"

"Yes. That would be very kind."

"Then come along downstairs when you've settled in."

She left him then, and he went to wash his hands. He gave her five more minutes and then, not turning out the lamp, he took her at her word.

Looking into the sitting room once more, he realized she'd lit a second lamp and that other waterfowl were set here and there, some on shelves enclosed by glass, smaller ones in bell jars, and others in what appeared to be specially designed glass cases.

Each display had a small brass plate giving the name of the bird. COOT. BITTERN. SEDGEBIRD. A kite and a hawk. RUFF. SPOONBILL. AVOCET. REEVE. Even a snipe. There was also a rather unusual copper-colored butterfly perched on a bare twig. He gave up reading the labels. To his eye the specimens seemed tired, their feathers lackluster.

For her usual guests, they might be an advertisement of what to expect when they took their guns out. Or what had been there in the distant past, perhaps in her father's or grandfather's day. He remembered what Marcella Trowbridge had said about hunting. Seeing this display, he had to agree with her.

Down the passage he found the kitchen. Priscilla was just taking a meat pie from her oven. He wondered if she'd intended it for her own dinner, then realized that there was another just behind it. The table had already been set, and he could see that he would be dining here.

"I hope you don't mind," she said, looking up in time to see his glance at the table. "It's a lot of extra work, opening up the dining room. With only myself here, I have no need of it."

"This is fine," he assured her. "Thank you, Miss Bartram."

"Everyone calls me Priscilla. I haven't used Miss Bartram in ten years. Now. Sit down and I'll just dish up."

Rutledge took one of the chairs, saw that the tea was steeping, and was about to get up and move it to the table.

"No, just sit there, if you will. Better than getting underfoot."

Besides the pie there was cabbage and parsnips, with an excellent chutney.

"I made it myself," she said as he tasted it, and he told her it was very good.

She began to ask questions about his encounter with Miss Trowbridge, and he could see that she was a gossip by nature, reinforced by what must be a rather lonely life.

"If it hadn't been for her cat, I'd have still been lost in this mist. Or worse," he replied. "I don't know how she found her way here."

"We're used to it, I expect." Finding that topic a dead end, Priscilla asked if the news of their late disturbance here in Wriston had reached as far as Cambridge.

"The papers carried the account. A Mr. Swift killed as he was starting to address his constituents."

"Well, hardly an address," she said. "He's standing for office, and he was making his opening remarks when the shot rang out. But he was already falling, disappearing out of sight, and the cry went up that he'd been hit. Then Mrs. Percy exclaimed that she'd seen a monster. There was general pandemonium after that. The constable—we've only got the one—had run toward Mr. Swift, and by the time he looked around to where she was pointing, there was nothing to be seen. You'd have thought the shot fired itself. And try as he would, he couldn't discover anything more. This, mind you, following on the heels of that poor man killed in Ely not even a fortnight ago. They've made no headway in finding *his* killer, either."

"Were you in the square when Mr. Swift was shot?"

"I was. Most of us went for the entertainment, you see. There's not much else to do of an evening, and the torches were coming down the road from The Wake Inn. Like a parade, you might say. Then Mr. Swift was stepping up on the stump of the old market cross, and the crowd quieted down to hear him speak. He's—he was—a much better orator than the Liberal candidate. We expected to be well entertained. And just like that he was falling, cut off in the middle of a word. The noise seemed to come from everywhere at once, giving me the shock of my life. The butcher, Mr. Banner, was standing beside me, and he ducked, and so did the owner of the pub, as if expecting more shots. I don't think I could have moved if my life had depended on it. Mrs. Percy began screeching at the top of her lungs. I thought she'd gone into strong hysterics. After a bit she calmed down a little and I heard her claiming that it was a monster, up there at the ironmonger's window. What's more, the constable and afterward that Inspector from Ely, Warren is his name, tried but they couldn't shake her account. We don't run to hobgoblins here in the Fen country. I ask you!"

Rutledge smiled. Her vehemence told him otherwise. "Whatever she saw, it must have frightened her. Where was she standing, in relation to where Mr. Swift was speaking? Did you see her?"

"Not before she cried out. She was a little behind him, on the far side of the cross. She had her hands over her face. I thought she was shocked by his death—she was close enough to see what happened to him firsthand. Someone told me later his blood was on her apron."

Enough to shock anyone, he thought. It also meant that while looking up at the speaker, she must also have been looking almost directly at the killer. Had movement caught her eye just as the shot was fired? Most certainly not in time to warn Swift, but in time to absorb the fact that a monster had been there, looking down at his handiwork. While everyone else faced the speaker, watching him break off and begin to collapse, what had she actually seen?

The question was, who else had been in that same position and why hadn't he or she come forward? Were they afraid to be made a laughingstock? Apparently Mrs. Percy was not . . .

"How well does Mrs. Percy see?" he asked

"Well enough to be a gossip. She must wear spectacles for close work."

"Then what manner of monster?" Rutledge asked. "How did she describe what she believes she saw?"

"Now that goes to the heart of the matter. What she *believes*. All she would say was, there was a monster's face looking out at her from the ironmonger's dormer window. Bold as brass. Then it vanished. But by the time everything was sorted out, and Constable McBride went up the stairs to the dormer room, there was no sign anyone had ever been there."

"Did Mr. Swift have any enemies? Anyone who might want to see him dead?"

"There's the other candidate, of course, but I'm not convinced that any of that lot would have thought of shooting Mr. Swift. They're more likely to set upon him as he walked home afterward. Cowards, all of them."

When he'd finished the pie, Miss Bartram brought out a cake baked with sultanas and offered him a slice. She was an excellent cook, and he rather thought that her culinary skills, not the long-dead waterfowl, had brought her regulars back year after year.

"Was Swift married?" he asked, returning to the earlier subject.

"A widower. His wife and the babe died in childbirth. Late 1914, early 1915? That sounds about right." She sighed as she began to collect their dishes. "I don't remember the last murder here. I wish I hadn't seen this one."

Miss Bartram failed to hide her disappointment when Rutledge said good night after the meal ended, and went up to his room. A lonely woman, she would have enjoyed passing the rest of the evening in the sitting room with her guest. But it had been a long day, and the next would be even longer.

He worked at the table desk for a time, making notes on what he'd been told and adding questions that had come to him as he listened to Miss Bartram. Satisfied that he'd overlooked nothing, he went to bed. Later he would compare her remarks to the statement she'd made to the police.

But he couldn't fall asleep. The bed was comfortable enough, but the small room seemed close, and the mist wrapping the house beyond his windows was oppressive—a solid, impenetrable wall where even sound was trapped, for he could hear nothing out there. Not a dog's bravado bark or the hooves of a passing horse. He had the feeling that nothing existed beyond the wall of his room, and tried to laugh at such a fanciful notion.

Hamish didn't laugh. "That's what death is like. Nothing. Not sight nor sound nor friendship nor love."

And Hamish ought to know, Rutledge thought grimly. For he was lying buried in a grave in France, dead since the summer of 1916 and the Battle of the Somme. Rutledge shivered at the memory of that dawn. For as he had looked down at the still body of his corporal, he himself had nearly been killed by a shell landing too close to the trench and covering the living and the dead with unspeakable black earth that reeked of everything that had rotted in it. When he had finally been pulled out, more dead than alive, he had brought Hamish with him. Not just the man's body, taken up by the burial detail, but the young Scot's presence. Not the man's ghost—he could have understood a haunting—but an unwavering sense of guilt over the circumstances of Hamish's death. It had seemed easier at the time to accept the voice than to exorcise it by facing why Hamish had refused a direct order, and why he, Rutledge, had had to make an example of Corporal MacLeod, one of the best men who had ever served under him.

He had brought the voice back to England, an unbearable burden. He had toyed with the idea of killing himself to be rid of it. But to do so was to kill Hamish as well—a second time. And he couldn't bear to do that.

One night—one agonizing dawn—he might still find the courage or the strength to do what the Germans had failed to accomplish. If they'd killed him that week—the next month—even the next year, it would have been all right. He could have accepted that death. It would have been fitting, lifting from his soul the weight of guilt for taking his own life. Instead he'd come through four years in the trenches with little more than flesh wounds, seemingly invulnerable, and the bitter irony was, his men had thought him extraordinarily brave when, in fact, he was courting death.

Rutledge abruptly shut down the stream of memory. It wouldn't do to frighten Miss Bartram out of her wits by screaming the house down. She didn't deserve that.

And so he lay there, holding on to his wits by sheer will and refusing the dreams that would start whenever he shut his eyes.

When as last he did drift into sleep, his nightmares overtook him. He awoke with a start, his body cold with sweat, on the brink of shouting to his men to put on their masks as he clawed his way through the heavy ground-hugging fog of gas.

He was never sure afterward what had disturbed him. The dream or something more than a dream. The house was quiet, he'd heard nothing from downstairs, yet he felt a distinct sense of unease. He turned toward the window, and as he did, he saw that the moon had broken through and was shining across the floor of his room in bars of bright light. He got up and went to look out.

Between the two cottages across the way, he could see for what seemed like miles across the flat landscape. Except for the village itself there was no sign of habitation, no light in a farmhouse window, no headlamps as a motorcar made its way along the thin ribbon of road. And the street below was just as empty. He found himself thinking that even the companionship of the white cat—Clarissa?—would have been welcome. A living presence sharing the night with him.

Instead of what had walked in the fog.

Shaking off his mood, he went back to bed and slept quietly for a few hours.

After breakfast, he settled his account with Priscilla Bartram and thanked her for taking him in without any warning.

"I was glad of the company," she said. "There's no knowing what's abroad on such a night as we had. I haven't seen a mist that heavy in some time."

But someone else *had* been abroad last night. He was sure of it. Trained by four long terrible years in the trenches of France, he'd survived by knowing such things. By intuition and quick thinking, by experience and by the driving need to protect his men where he could.

Whoever it was, he must have stood outside the inn for a time, but Rutledge was nearly sure he hadn't come inside.

As Miss Bartram closed her door behind him, Rutledge turned to look up at the house where he'd spent the night. There was a sign above his head, made of iron. It bore a silhouette of geese in flight and beneath them, on what appeared to be water, was the name, THE DUTCHMAN INN. And he realized that unlike its neighbors, the inn looked more Dutch than English with its stepped gables. He'd seen paintings of Holland with just such fronts to the houses. He wished he'd thought to ask who had built the inn. But above the door there was a stone set into the facing of the lintel, and he could just make out the date, 1647, although he was fairly certain the inn as it stood now wasn't that old.

He'd intended to go directly to search for his motorcar. Instead he turned to walk down the street into the village proper.

Fen villages tended to be either new and without much character, thanks in part to the railway, or quite old. Wriston was one of the latter. Like Ely, it had been built on higher ground, an island of dry land rising above the once-waterlogged Fens. Some of them, like Ely or Ramsey, had begun with a church or abbey. Others were home to the fiercely independent men who eked out a fair living here and who had fought long and hard to stop the draining by the Dutch engineers hired for the purpose centuries ago. They had wanted no part of newcomers bringing in new ways. An independent and contrary lot they were, according to one historian he'd read, and content to be left alone.

In fact, long before the Dutchmen were brought in by an English king, Hereward the Outlaw had defied William the Conqueror's Normans in this watery landscape of the Fens. It wouldn't be the first or the last time that the inhabitants had gone their own way.

The question was, what had stirred them to murder in 1920? As far as he, Rutledge, knew, there were no new drainage plans, but it would be worth looking into. Was Swift contemplating changes that his future constituents would object to violently enough to turn to killing the man? And where did Hutchinson come into the picture?

Wriston spread out along the ridge of its high ground, a ridge too narrow to have been chosen for an abbey or even a small priory. What must once have been a small meandering stream had been forced into a channel on one side of the village, while fields encroached on the other, defining it for all time.

To Rutledge's surprise as he walked toward the stump of the market cross, he saw there were two elongated greens stretching to either side of it. The second one possessed a pond occupied at the moment by a dozen or so gleaming white ducks. Cottages and shops huddled together, facing the open space, many of them roofed with a distinctive thatch, very different in style from the beetling brows of the West Country. Here it was more like Cromwell's Puritan crop.

The small church appeared to have been added as an afterthought—he could see its tower beyond the second green at the far edge of the village—although Miss Bartram had indicated that it had Saxon roots. Ely and Peterborough cathedrals had been thriving houses long before the Normans took them over. At the far end of the village, where the road turned toward distant Ely, he could see the pub where the rally had begun.

He wondered which of the religious houses claiming Wriston had set up the market cross. What had been brought in for sale in those days? Eels for a certainty, fish and waterfowl, and whatever subsistence farming they'd been able to wrest from the wet land. It was, he thought, an ideal space in which to set up a market. Or a political gathering.

He stopped within a few feet of the cross, and turning in a circle, he began to study the nearest rooftops.

As Swift had begun speaking, all eyes would have been on him. And the shot therefore must have come from behind most of his audience. But which direction had he been facing? Surely toward the first green, his back toward the one with the pond. He had come from the pub, after all.

Very well, he asked himself, weighing each possibility in turn, if I were stalking that man with a rifle, where would I choose to wait? And from how far away could Mrs. Percy have seen me and called me a monster?

Hamish was on the point of answering him when a voice from just behind Rutledge said, "There's nothing to stare at. Move along, if you please."

He wheeled to find a constable standing there. He'd been so absorbed in his own thoughts he hadn't seen the man come up behind him.

This was not the time to introduce himself.

Rutledge said, "Thank you, Constable," and walked on. But he'd seen the dormer above the ironmonger's shop, and it offered both the clearest view and the best protection. Mrs. Percy had been right. But he'd wanted to see the setting for himself.

And it had brought home another truth.

Whoever he was, the killer was not suicidal. On the contrary, he'd planned his murders with an eye to disappearing as soon as possible after he'd dropped his man.

Rutledge walked on as far as the duck pond before turning around. The morning was fair and there were any number of people on the street now, going in and out of shops, stopping to chat with one another. Some of them cut their eyes to look at the stranger in their midst, and he caught the ripple of uncertainty, of wariness, as he passed.

Just beyond Miss Bartram's inn, on the other side of the road, he could see Miss Trowbridge's cottage ahead of him, the black iron pickets around the front garden distinctive. It was most certainly not as far away as it had seemed last night, and yet he'd have been lost a dozen times over if he'd attempted to find the inn himself.

The tiny space marked off by the fence was lavish with flowers, unlike its neighbors, whose seedy grass sometimes reached from the road to the door. Compared to Kent or the West Country, there was a noticeable lack of flowers, as if the rich black soil were too precious to be wasted on anything that didn't bring in pounds and pence.

A small sign on the gate—invisible in the mist last night—identified the cottage as THE BOWER HOUSE. Rutledge smiled. Miss Trowbridge had said that her father bought the cottage for his widowed mother. Who had named it, tongue in cheek, for a hideaway? Situated as it was at the bend of the main road?

Miss Trowbridge had been right about the mill. It was not very far away, and she must have grown up listening to the sails turn whenever she visited her grandmother. It was a squat mill, tall enough to allow the arms to sweep almost to the ground, clearing the high grass at its base by inches rather than feet.

The remains of the mill house were beyond as well, and Rutledge realized how perilously close to them he'd come in the mist. The blackened timbers were gone, of course, but the ragged foundations were a trap for unwary feet. Closer to he could see what appeared to be the traces of rooms, raised footings where the walls had once met the foundations. He winced at the thought of breaking a bone tripping over them in the fog. Even in the dark it would be far too easy to stray in their direction and take a nasty fall.

In the sunlight the mill was ordinary, its sails turned to catch the light wind. Painted black with white trim, it stood at a bend in the road. And behind it, as far as the eye could see, were those long flat fields, far lower than the ground on which he stood.

He remembered reading somewhere that as the Fens drained and the peat that made them so dark and fertile dried, the surface had sunk lower and lower with each passing year, until it reached a point where it stabilized. And the early practice of burning the peat to clear the land had enriched the soil but also left it vulnerable to east winds off the stormy North Sea. Indeed, some of the fields must be four and five feet lower than the road he'd been traveling. Only the embankments designed early on to hold back the water protected the unsuspecting traveler from stumbling into a field or, even worse, into a ditch.

He walked on and found to his chagrin that his motorcar had been as near to disaster as he himself had been. For the road he'd been traveling rose over an arched stone bridge across a pitch or waterway. And on the near side of the bridge, instead of continuing in the direction he'd expected, the road curved sharply to the right, skirting the strategically placed mill and the cottage where Miss Trowbridge lived, before running straight for the village, cutting it in half. He could easily have crashed into the ruins of the mill keeper's house, injuring himself and doing considerable damage to the motorcar.

To reach Wriston instead of Ely, somewhere he'd missed an important turning.

Looking out across the fields, he could see a stand of trees in the far distance, and rising above them was a church tower. Closer to but still some distance away, a line of pollarded willows marked another track. A third wandered off to his right.

Hamish said, in the back of his mind, "It was foolish to go on."

It was true, in hindsight. But he'd expected to run out of the mist eventually, or to find his way into Ely.

The motorcar seemed to be just as he'd left it, but then he noticed that his valise, which had been in the rear seat, was not precisely where he'd remembered setting it. If he hadn't been looking for it, he'd have never noticed the difference, but he'd suspected that the man who had rescued him had gone to have a look at the motorcar—and perhaps its contents.

He snapped the latches and scanned his possessions. Nothing appeared to have been disturbed, and everything seemed to be there—his gold cuff links were the only thing of real value that he'd packed, and they were under his shirts, where he'd put them. Still, someone had searched his belongings. He was fairly sure of it.

"Ye canna' be certain it was the man in the mist," Hamish pointed out. "It could ha' been anyone. The moon came oot in the night."

Hamish was right, of course, but someone had been curious about a strange motorcar abandoned in the middle of the road.

Still, there was nothing in the vehicle or the valise to indicate that he was from Scotland Yard. He carried his identification in his pocket.

Cranking the motor, he got in and reversed. Shortly thereafter, he found the turning he wanted, which must have been all but invisible last night, and was well on his way to Ely once more. The road ran true for some time, until it reached Soham, and there it headed north.

Now he could see the profile of the massive Cathedral across the flat landscape, rising above it like a great mirage floating on a flat green sea. It must have been, he thought, quite amazing in Medieval times to see it there, a wonder to behold in such a wet landscape. The Isle of Ely it truly was. And in the haze of sunlight, it was still quite magnificent. The town surrounding it seemed not to exist at all.

Inspector Warren looked up as Rutledge was ushered into his office.

"You're a day late," he said, rising to greet his visitor, noting the dark stubble of beard and the unpressed suit. "Did you sleep rough?"

"Near enough. I was caught in the weather yesterday. But that put me close enough to Wriston to have a look at the market cross this morning."

Warren raised his eyebrows. "Wriston? You *were* well and truly caught out, weren't you? All right. Sit down."

Rutledge took the empty chair by the desk. The other was piled high with paper. Statements, he realized, with a sinking feeling. Days' worth of work before any progress could be made. That was, unless Inspector Warren was prepared to sort them for him.

Warren wore a harried air. A tall man, stooped and fair, his hairline only just beginning to recede, he had a strong face, with laugh lines that crinkled at the corners of his eyes.

But the Inspector was not in the mood to laugh at the moment.

"Since you've been to Wriston, I'll start there. Did they tell you half the village had followed the victim to the market cross, where apparently they were met by the other half? We interviewed every one of them. Not all of them were constituents, mind you, but Swift usually gave good value at his rallies, and the curious had come to hear him as well. I expect there were a number of hecklers in the crowd, but he was dead before they could interrupt him. We searched the buildings nearest the cross, but of course by the time we reached the scene, there was nothing to find. We settled on two vantage points. The roof of the ironmonger's shop has a dormer. He and his wife live above the shop, but both of them were in the street." He gestured to another stack of papers. "A dozen people saw the ironmonger and his wife. They're in the clear. Nobody locks anything, worst luck, and the killer could have helped himself to half a dozen vantage points. Cheek by jowl to the ironmonger's, there's a fine pair of chimneys. The greengrocer's shop. But if he'd chosen *them*, he couldn't have got away unseen. My money is on the dormer window."

"Then the shooter could have easily come and gone through a rear door without being seen or disturbing anyone."

"Oh, yes. It was dark, all the light was in the square, torches smoking enough to blind a regiment. But Mrs. Percy, our only witness, claims she saw a face in the dormer window. That has to be where the man with a rifle was standing, not the chimney pots. I believe her. Not, mind you, a monster's face, which is what she initially described to Constable McBride and then to me. But something." Warren grimaced. "As if we didn't have our hands full enough with what happened here in Ely."

"I must agree with Mrs. Percy, from my own observations this morning. Especially if the wind was blowing the smoke away from that window. But what she saw wasn't a man with a rifle."

"Yes, well, there's that. But you won't convince me that there were two people in the dormer."

"How did she describe the face?" Rutledge asked.

"She wouldn't. She told me it was monstrous, the stuff of nightmares. My words, there, but close enough. She was badly frightened then and later when I came to speak to her. What's more, she is a little hard of hearing. She couldn't get any closer through the crowd of people, and being rather short, she moved around behind Herbert Swift. Lucky for us."

"There are several possibilities. Someone wearing a gas mask from the war—although that would make firing his rifle more difficult. Someone badly burned. Or even someone who wrapped his head, to be certain he wasn't recognized."

"That last would mean someone local."

"Very likely." Rutledge paused. "There's been no trouble in Wriston before this? You said no one locked his door at night?"

"They do now," Warren replied grimly. "But no, nothing major. Petty crimes, quarrels, that sort of thing. The last murder in Wriston was back in the 1890s."

Rutledge remembered what Miss Bartram had said about being glad of someone else, even a stranger, in the house last night when it was impossible to see who—or what—was outside the windows.

"Did Swift have enemies? Had he stepped on any toes in announcing he was standing for office?"

"Not that we can discover. The general view was, he was well liked, and likely to win. The other camp had only put up a token candidate to oppose him. Mind you, he wasn't here during the war. Any friends—or enemies—he made while he was away are another matter."

"That's when he could have met Hutchinson."

"Possibly. Yes. But proving it will be difficult."

They moved on to the first shooting, in Ely.

Warren stood up and said, "Come with me, you'll want to see this for yourself."

They walked from the police station to the Cathedral. Warren was saying as they went, "We've enough statements to fill the nave. And they come down to a single fact. We have damned little to go on. I'd hoped, when word reached us about what had happened in Wriston, that he'd made a mistake we could use, but he hasn't."

Ely's Cathedral Church of the Holy and Undivided Trinity came into view then. It was unique among English Cathedrals with that elegant octagonal tower, called the Lantern, set above the crossing of the transepts and the nave. Now, as the two men approached, the massive, battlemented West Front loomed before them. There was a small double-arched west door, and few of the embellishments or niches for saints to decorate the opening. Compared to Salisbury, for one, or Lincoln, it was more or less plain. And yet it was both elegant and powerful.

Warren said, pointing, "Here is where the motorcars pulled up. At the top of the Green. Arriving guests descended and walked toward that west door. Captain Hutchinson was among the last to arrive, in the motorcar belonging to the Honorable Reginald Sedley and his wife."

"Why was he with them? Any particular reason?"

"He was staying with them. I gather they hadn't met before. The bridegroom's family had arranged accommodations for many of the out-of-town guests, and Hutchinson was up from London."

"Go on."

"According to the statements from the Sedleys, they were talking about the wedding as they moved toward the west door. And behind them, another motorcar had followed their own, stopping to set down its passengers. That was the bridegroom and his best man, as we were to discover. The chauffeur of that motorcar was already moving on, making room for the one behind it. This meant that the bridegroom was only a little way behind Captain Hutchinson, and perhaps about five feet to his right. And then everything seemed to happen at once."

Warren moved forward, then stopped again.

"Hutchinson went down just here. The reverberations of the shot shocked everyone for an instant, and then Mrs. Sedley began screaming for a doctor as her husband knelt to try and help the victim. When we were finally able to speak to her, it was clear she hadn't seen anything but the Captain collapsing at her feet. Nor did Sedley, for that matter. He was intent on doing what he could to save Hutchinson. But of course that was hopeless."

Now Warren pointed toward the Cathedral. "There was general pandemonium. Guests who hadn't yet entered the west door and local people who were standing behind a barrier set up just there, to keep them out of the way of the wedding party"—Warren pointed to the spot—"while watching the show, ran in every direction, expecting more shots to be fired."

"It must have been difficult to account for everyone who was a potential witness."

"Believe me, it has been a nightmare."

"Better you than me."

"Yes, well, I hope they give you more than they have given us. There was an artillery Major, man by the name of Lowell, who more or less took charge. He sent someone for the police, another man to find a doctor who was amongst the wedding guests, and ordered everyone within hearing to stay where they were. Unfortunately, he himself had been standing just inside the church doorway and couldn't tell us where the shot had come from. But he informed us at once that it had been a rifle. And of course that was borne out by the distance. Still, it saved an inordinate amount of time trying to sort out the various accounts."

"Very convenient. Could he have fired that shot, then hidden the weapon?"

"I don't see how. He arrived just before Hutchinson and was speaking to one of the canons by the door. In plain sight. There were other former officers attending the wedding, but they had taken their places in the nave with their wives. Lowell is unmarried and was in no hurry to go inside."

They were walking now toward the West Front and the door to the Galilee Porch. Warren was saying, "Those buildings to your right belong to the Cathedral. We searched them as well as the Cathedral itself. Top to bottom. The Gallery—that's the wall there, still to your right—encloses the church grounds, offices, and the homes of various churchmen. We discovered a ladder placed up against the wall on the inside, out of sight from where we are, of course. See there, where that woman with the small child is passing? We left it where it is. I refused to allow them to move it because no one would admit to putting it there, not a churchman, not a gardener, no one. It's possible our man used it as a fallback position. Climbing it and resting his rifle on the top as he fired, then ducking out of sight. The problem is, he'd have been visible to anyone in the grounds who looked that way. Still, it offered the best means of escape. The artillery Major told us the angle was wrong, unless the killer was going for a head shot."

Rutledge looked toward the wall and then turned to the spot where Hutchinson had fallen. "Yes, Major Lowell is right."

"Our next possibility was to the left of the Cathedral door. There, see that makeshift wall? It runs out from the Lady Chapel and then turns down by the lane." Warren began to walk in that direction. "And there's a door in it. It's closed now, but it was standing ajar that day. We found a single cartridge casing on the ground, just about where you'd step through and then step back. It had rolled into a clump of grass by the wall, half hidden by the door. He didn't have time to look for it." He stopped, waving in that direction. "The doctor and the Major disagreed over that one."

Rutledge looked at where Hutchinson had fallen and then turned back toward the gate. "It would be a fairly easy shot," he replied. "It wouldn't take a marksman to do it. As long as the people at the barrier were out of his line of fire. Why did they disagree? The doctor and the Major."

"Lowell felt that the gate was a possible shot, just as you said. But when the doctor examined the body, he claimed the shot had come from above. Up there."

Warren pointed up at the west tower. "A constable climbed all the way up there and told me the slope of the roof would have prevented a decent shot. People were walking toward the door, and anyone stand-ing up there with a rifle was bound to be noticed."

Rutledge shielded his eyes from the sun as he stared upward. "Surely there was room to kneel."

"He says not. And no one has brought it up save for the doctor. Of course, Dr. Bradley has had no military experience, but later during the postmortem, he showed me the course of the bullet. It would seem he was right, although the only evidence, the casing, was here."

"What did Lowell have to say about that?"

"At the time, he never turned Hutchinson over. There was no reason to." Walking on toward the Cathedral, Warren added, "By the time we arrived, there were at least two hundred people milling about. Wedding guests, bystanders, those drawn from the school down there to your right. Ordinary people who heard the shouting and screams and came to see what had happened. My men began to sort them and take down names to collect statements. And I began to realize that no one had seen anything useful. By this time, the bride's father was pressing us to allow the wedding to go on, late as it was, and as soon as the body was removed, we really saw no reason to prevent it."

"Are there any statements in particular I should pursue?"

"There are several it wouldn't hurt to look at. Oddly enough, the bridegroom was convinced he was the target, while the bride, arriving in the middle of the chaos, thought he was the victim and was hysterical. It would probably have been wiser to postpone the affair."

By this time, they had reached the west door and Warren pulled it open.

"Is it usually closed? This door?"

"As a rule it's open during services and for occasions such as the wedding."

They walked inside. It had been some time since Rutledge had been in this Cathedral. Beyond the porch, to his right the lobby spread out toward the shorter twin towers overlooking the wall where the ladder had been left. Ahead, through another set of doors, he could see the unusual painted vault of the nave. It was quite long, leading down to the crossing, which supported the Octagon, which in turn supported the Lantern overhead. Thence to the choir. Ely was, in a way, a glimpse of what churches and Cathedrals must have looked like before the Reformation, when there were frescoes and painted statues and ceilings. The Victorians had reveled in adding color too, but not always successfully.

As he made his way down the aisle, he looked to his left and saw a rose petal, dried now, the color faded, that had escaped the cleaning women. It was caught under the edge of one of the kneelers, a sad reminder of the wedding's chaos.

Silence surrounded them in the nave, their footsteps echoing to the stone walls. It was cool and dimly lit after the warm sunny afternoon outside. Warren's voice was subdued as he said, "We had people out in the Lady Chapel, up on the roof, up in the Lantern, searching all the buildings in the Cathedral precincts, the Bishop's quarters, everywhere we could think of. This place is a rabbit warren, did you know that?"

"Most Medieval buildings are. Do you suppose the killer was

dressed as a priest or the like, someone who wouldn't be noticed because he appeared to belong in a church?"

"Carrying a rifle?" Warren went on toward the choir. "But then he could have hidden it in a valise, a musical instrument case. Still, he'd have to open it, wouldn't he, and assemble the rifle. A grave risk."

"Was there a published schedule for the guests to arrive?"

"No, none. He couldn't have known when to be prepared."

"And so he must remain invisible until he was sure."

"The organist brought a large portfolio with him. His music. But he was playing when the shot was fired. There are dozens of witnesses to that. The florists brought in long boxes full of flowers for the arrangements. Some of the flowers were quite tall at the back of the baskets. We searched the lot. Even the van they came in. Under the seats. The organ loft. Behind the organ pipes—have you ever looked behind those pipes? I had the altar cloth and the misericords in the choir searched. Everywhere we could think of, in the event he'd hidden his rifle and planned to retrieve it later. But he hadn't. Or else he'd extracted it before we got to him."

There was nothing to see, Rutledge thought, but the beauty around him.

He started back toward the West Front. "Without the rifle, there's no way to learn where he got it. The Army, most likely. But when? At the Armistice? Was he still in France then? A few must have been smuggled into the country without the Army's knowledge. Still, they were damned thorough." Then over his shoulder, he added, "Why did Captain Hutchinson have to die? And on that day? Was there a particular order in the two deaths? Was it opportunity or was there a pattern behind the order?"

"I can tell you why that day. Hutchinson had come up from London for the wedding. It was very likely that he'd return to London on Sunday evening at the latest. There were a number of parties and dinners before the nuptials, of course. But they were private and by invitation only. That means that his arrival here at the Cathedral would be his only public appearance, so to speak. The local newspaper carried several accounts of the wedding festivities, mostly after the fact. My wife had read them, and so I looked them up. Hutchinson was mentioned several times. And the wedding in general created quite a stir."

"Which means our man—the shooter—could be local."

"Yes, very likely," Warren said harshly. "More's the pity."

"Why was Swift running in the by-election?"

"That I can answer. Swift had been a solicitor before the war. There was no one to take over for him during the war, and his chambers were closed. When he came home again, the view is his heart wasn't in it. He must have seen standing for the seat of his late MP as offering a way out."

"What happened to him?"

"Mr. Davidson died of cancer in the early summer."

"If Hutchinson was related in some way to the bridegroom, was Swift connected to the man as well? However distantly? Grandmothers, wives, great-aunts? Any questionable inheritances?"

"I asked the bridegroom that question. He's not related to Swift in any way. But whether Swift and Hutchinson are related is another matter." Warren took a deep breath as they left the Cathedral and stepped out into the late afternoon sunlight. "I can't walk in there without thinking of that Saturday. Where was I? Oh. For what it's worth, I think they're random, these killings. Targets chosen for no other reason than that they are *there*, wherever the shooter wants to try his luck again. I don't envy you having to get to the bottom of this one. I'll help you in any way I can." He began to walk briskly back toward the police station. Over his shoulder he said, as Rutledge followed him, "But the truth of the matter is, with all due respect, I don't believe you'll have any better luck than I've had. You can see for yourself, it's hunting shadows."

Chapter 5

Rutledge took the man's comments as they were intended, a measure of his frustration. Warren had had nearly ten days to solve the first murder and four to tackle the second. That in itself was trying; add to it the necessity of calling in the Yard, and the man had every reason to feel he had failed in the eyes of his own Chief Constable.

"Do you think the killer is satisfied? Or will he find a new target?" Rutledge asked after a moment. "Now that he's twice successfully evaded the police?"

"Who knows what's in his mind?" Warren sounded tired. "The question is, is he moving west, looking for victims? Or is he choosing a village or town and then picking someone? Mind you, these aren't ordinary folk—the butcher's boy, an elderly seamstress, the dairyman. Hutchinson had something of a reputation, I'm told—he moved in the best London circles, and all that. Swift was a solicitor, standing for public office for the first time. God knows who might be in this killer's sights next."

Rutledge had already considered that possibility. If there was no personal connection between these men, then it had to be something else. And fame, however minor, might draw someone's attention if he was searching for another target.

They carried on in silence, and when they reached the station, Rutledge stopped by his motorcar. "Anything else I should know?"

"We've covered every possibility. Everything but a hot air balloon. But I'm at your disposal if you think of anything. There's an inn close by the Cathedral. The Deacon. I've booked a room for you there."

"Thank you."

Warren put a hand on the bonnet of the motorcar, brushing at an invisible speck. "I like tidy murders, if I must have one. Something I can follow through to a reasonable conclusion. Most of them are like that. If I don't know what's going on, my constables will, and in the end we'll find our killer. The wife, the brother, the lover, the husband. Or the jealous neighbor, the childhood friend, the man who owes money he can't repay." He stopped.

"This inquiry could turn out to be as simple."

"Yes, well, pigs fly." Warren hesitated. "I was never in the front lines. They put me in charge of transport. We ran the gauntlet of submarines, but no one was shooting at us. You said you could have made that shot. Were you serious?"

Rutledge bent to turn the crank. "A good marksman could have done it easily. At any one time I had ten men in my command who could have made either the shot here or the one in Wriston. Hutchinson must have been moving at a walking pace, conversing with friends, and in no hurry." He nodded. "A woman could have made it as well, if she'd been trained. It's not necessarily a man we're looking for."

Warren smiled, dusting his hands. "You've just doubled the number of your possible suspects."

"Was Hutchinson married?"

"His wife is dead. Has been for a number of years. Early in the war. So I'm told." Warren hesitated. "You can't believe we're looking for a woman."

"If we can teach shopkeepers and the sons of farmers to shoot straight when they're being shot at, why can't a woman learn to do it as well?"

"If I brought a rifle into my house, my wife would run screaming out the door. She doesn't care for weapons of any kind."

"Then we should hope our killer has a wife who feels the same way."

"When you're ready, I've got the names of witnesses you might wish to speak to. A list I've drawn up."

"Now is as good a time as any."

Leaving the motorcar quietly ticking over, Rutledge went inside the police station. The list was on the blotter of the desk, and Warren handed it to him.

"Tell me what you think after you've spoken to them."

"What about the artillery Major who was so helpful? Lowell, wasn't it?"

"Nothing there. He didn't know Hutchinson at all."

"But he was with the police at every turn. I'd like to speak to him."

Warren quickly added that name to the list. "Anything else?"

"Just tell me how to find The Deacon. That will do for now."

He was unpacking his valise, putting his clothes into the armoire, when Hamish spoke into the silence. "Ye ken, he's washed his hands o' these murders."

"At least he's been helpful."

He crossed to the window and realized that it looked out toward the Cathedral.

"Ye ken, if a woman knows her husband has a rifle, she's too afraid to report it, for fear of losing him to the hangman."

"There's that," Rutledge agreed. Over the rooftops, the Cathedral's Lantern gleamed in the late afternoon sun, its windows holding the light. It dominated the town, although Ely was building out from its center, as many prosperous towns were beginning to do before the war and would surely continue to do. Did the killer live here? Or was he a Wriston man? Or had he come from the half-dozen other villages scattered over the Fens where the ground was high enough for habitation.

Where then to begin? He took a deep breath.

The bride and bridegroom. Their marriage had set the wheels of murder turning. Or at least it appeared to have done so.

He shaved and changed his clothes, leaving the wrinkled suit to be pressed while he was out. After asking directions from the clerk behind the desk he decided it was too far to walk and went to his motorcar.

The Fallowfields had returned from a brief wedding trip and were staying with the bride's family before traveling on to London. The house was in a fashionable part of the town, and when he'd been admitted and asked to wait in the drawing room, he could see that there was old money here.

The furnishings were elegant and the carpet was new, replaced, he thought, for the wedding. The walls were a lovely shade of blue, set off by white trim, and the hearth was white Italian marble. A dark blue vase filled with white roses graced the small table beneath the windows.

Fallowfield had done well for himself, Rutledge found himself thinking as he waited. Was that why the man had expected to be the victim rather than Captain Hutchinson? That his good fortune was too good to last?

After several minutes, the door opened and a young, fair-haired man came into the room.

"Inspector? Jason Fallowfield. I'm sorry to keep you waiting. My wife asks to be excused. She's tried to put the events that day out of her mind, and it hasn't been very easy for her." He gestured to one of the chairs and took another just across from it. "She arrived after the event, there's nothing she can add."

"I can understand her distress. A wedding should be memorable for its joy."

"Yes, thank you. I don't know how I can help you. But I'm at your service."

"How long have you known Captain Hutchinson?"

"I saw him from time to time when we were children, and to tell the truth never really took to him. Then we served together in France. At Passchendaele. Sort of thing you don't forget, surviving that. We kept in touch afterward. Both of us live—lived—in London, and there was the occasional dinner or a weekend where we were houseguests at the same party. Tennis. Golf. The usual sort of thing when you move in the same circles."

"Tell me a little about his background. We're looking for anything that could point toward his killer."

"When I stop to think about it, I realize I didn't know him very well. And yet I thought I had. He was a private person, you see. He told me his father left him enough to be comfortable, and then before the war he married a rather wealthy woman. I never met her. She died while we were in France. There was some gossip at the time—I'm not precisely sure what it was about, but I gathered it had to do with her possible suicide. At any rate, Gordon should have gone home on compassionate leave, but there was a push on and I heard he was moved to another sector instead. By the time we met again, we were in Paris, of all places, on leave. And when I offered my condolences, he said something that I interpreted as a reference to a stillborn child. That would certainly explain why people believed she'd taken her own life, if she'd died soon after. I had the feeling he'd been hurt by the rumors of suicide. Although I must say, he appeared to be handling it well by that time. God knows, childbearing is a common enough cause of death. As a married man, I've begun to worry about it myself. But what can you do?"

"Who were his friends? His enemies?"

"I have no idea. I mean to say, he appeared to be well enough liked. He never lacked for invitations, at any rate. If there was any trouble, it never reached my ears." He hesitated, then added, "He *collected* people. That was my impression of him. He seemed to know everyone who was important. It was sometimes a matter for amusement, the way he could make friends. Like a chameleon, changing himself to match his surroundings, as it were. It sounds like an unpleasant quality, but in reality he could be great fun and a very good friend."

"Does he leave any family?"

"Only a sister. I've been on the telephone, speaking to her. She's in London. She couldn't face coming north alone to accompany the body home. I can't say that I blame her."

"How were you and Hutchinson related?"

"Our mothers were distantly connected. To tell the truth, most of my friends never came home from France. I daresay it was true of Gordon as well. Kinship matters then. Sometimes that's enough to stave off loneliness."

Rutledge understood what he was saying. Many of his own friends were dead or had gone on with their own lives while he was struggling to rebuild what was left of his.

"Why did you invite him to attend your wedding?"

Fallowfield was surprised. "It never occurred to me not to. I mean to say, we were talking about it one day, and I simply told him I wanted him to come. We were cousins, after all. We'd served together."

There it was again, that bond between men who had served together. Rutledge understood it well.

"Had your wife met him before the wedding?"

"Yes, on several occasions when she was in London and I escorted her to parties."

"Did she like him?"

His face flushed. "What are you suggesting?"

"Only that women are often more intuitive about people. They will dislike someone for no reason at all, and only later understand why they felt that way."

"I don't think she ever expressed an opinion one way or the other. Certainly when I added his name to the list of wedding guests I gave to her mother, she made no objection."

"I'm trying to discover any reason why someone should dislike this man enough that when he came to Ely for your wedding, he was killed. Even at the cost of nearly stopping the ceremony altogether. I understand it was several hours before the police would agree to the marriage going forward."

Fallowfield got up and walked to the window, his back to Rutledge. After a moment he said, "To tell you the truth, I thought at first I myself must be the intended target."

"Why?"

Fallowfield cast a glance over his shoulder. "Egoism, I expect. I was the center of attention, so to speak, the bridegroom. It never occurred to me that one of my guests might be shot. It's unheard of."

"There must have been a better reason than that."

Fallowfield turned and crossed the room to stop in front of Rutledge. "I was *there*. Not five paces from Hutchinson. With my best man." His face was intense, his voice tight. "I was expecting to hear a second shot—intended for me. I even turned toward Harry to warn him to move away. And then I realized there *wasn't* a second shot. It was—harrowing. I came through the war somehow. It flashed through my mind that it would be unthinkable to die on my wedding day."

"I still don't understand why you were so certain Hutchinson was not the target."

He paced away again, too agitated to sit down. "I suppose I never quite believed my luck. I survived France. Barbara was waiting. She waited for *me*." He turned back, his expression deprecating. "You see, Barbara could have had her pick of suitors. I've never quite understood why she accepted me."

"Is she—I'm sorry, but I must ask—is she wealthier than you?"

"Oh, not at all. I'd say we were about even. But her family goes back to the Domesday Book, and mine made its money in the previous century. In South Africa, with Cecil Rhodes. Hardly an aristocratic background, is it?"

"And you saw nothing, there by the Cathedral?"

"I saw Hutchinson start to fall, just as I heard the shot. I was nervous, for God's sake—I daresay anyone is, under the circumstances. Will everything go off well, will I muddle what I'm to say, will Barbara's little goddaughter be sick halfway down the aisle? It's a very long nave, you know. Especially for an anxious child. What if I drop the ring? What if it rolls under someone's feet and I'm down on all fours, scrambling after it? I wasn't thinking about murder. If anything I was feeling grateful that it hadn't *rained* all day."

"Your best man?"

"Harry saw Gordon fall. He thought he must have tripped, and then the report followed almost at once." Fallowfield smiled wryly. "Harry went down flat on his face. He's done that before, when a motorcar backfired. He's more than a little ashamed of that. I can't fault him. I'd have done the same, if I'd had my wits about me."

Rutledge smiled. His first Guy Fawkes Day after the war had been a nightmare, with fireworks going off right and left. "What can you tell me about the artillery Major—Lowell, his name is—who was so helpful when the police arrived?"

"I hardly know him. He's older, you see. His father and Barbara's father went to Eton together. Nice enough chap, career officer. He spent most of his time talking to Barbara's parents. His father isn't well, he must be into his late seventies now. I expect he was asked in place of the elder Lowell for the sake of an old friendship."

"What did he say to you after the shooting?"

Fallowfield frowned. "He hustled me into the building next to where I was standing, and I didn't see him again until the reception. The usual congratulations then, rather subdued, of course. Harry told me I mustn't go to Barbara. She'd just arrived, I could hear her crying. He told me I must stay where I was. Bad luck, you know, to see the bride before the wedding. It seemed so silly, in light of what had just happened, but I was terrified the police or the Bishop might not let the wedding go on. Even so, it was a near run thing. If the police had had their way, everyone would have been sent home. Barbara's father persuaded them that it was unfair to the guests who would be leaving on Sunday." His voice was wry as he went on. "They remembered to fetch me when Inspector Warren allowed the ceremony to continue. I did hear Barbara's father say that he was grateful Lowell was there, he'd been a sane voice in the chaos. To tell the truth, I think that my father-in-law would have been glad to see Barbara marry the man, if Lowell had been closer to her age. For the sake of the friendship."

It was an interesting comment.

And interesting too that the groom hadn't taken charge in Lowell's place. If only to impress his future father-in-law.

Fallowfield said into the silence that followed, "Is there nothing you can tell me about who did this murder?"

Rutledge gave him the usual answer: "I've only just arrived. It's too early to know where the inquiry will take us."

"But Inspector Warren has had nearly a fortnight."

"He hasn't been idle, I assure you." Rutledge rose. "You've been very helpful, Mr. Fallowfield. And I appreciate your assistance. It can't have been easy to relive that afternoon."

"God, I can hardly put it out of my mind. I try for Barbara's sake."

Fallowfield saw him to the door and closed it after him, Rutledge thought, with sheer relief.

But there was nothing here to be going on with. In some respects it had been a wasted hour. Fallowfield had been absorbed in the wedding, and rightly so. Rutledge doubted, in all fairness, that the man would have noticed much of anything until his vows had been said and he could walk up the aisle with his bride.

He went next to call on the Sedleys, hoping for more useful information.

They lived one street over from the bride's family, and both came into the drawing room to speak to him. They were a handsome couple. Sedley had an air of the successful man about him, and he looked the part: of good height, distinguished, with the first threads of gray showing in his dark hair. His wife was still an attractive woman, and the dark green scarf she wore in the neckline of her paler green dress was just the color of her eyes.

Rutledge asked more or less the same questions as he had before, and got much the same answers. Neither of them had seen anything except Hutchinson crumpling at their feet. And neither of them could suggest any reason why the Captain should have been a target.

In fact, Sedley's view was that his death was related to something in London. "I can't quite believe that someone followed him all the way to Ely to kill him. I mean to say, whoever it was took a dreadful risk. Still, there you are. The other possibility is that someone in the town had it in for the Captain, but he mentioned at some point that he'd never been to Ely before."

Mrs. Sedley added, "We ran him by the Cathedral after we met him at the railway station. He was interested to see it."

Both Mr. and Mrs. Sedley answered freely, with as far as he could tell nothing to hide. The shock of death arriving so close to them still had not quite worn off, and they appeared to be glad to help in any way they could.

"What can you tell me about Major Lowell?"

"Surely, you can't believe—" Sedley began in some consternation.

Rutledge smiled. "Not at all. He offered his assistance to the police, and Inspector Warren was grateful. I wondered what his background might be."

"Artillery, of course. Career officer. I didn't have much opportunity to speak to him, but he was quiet, competent, a good man in an emergency. You must remember that Eugenia and I were there with the Captain. Within touching distance when he was shot. Fallowfield and the best man were just behind us and as stunned as we were. Lowell had been standing by the entrance to the Galilee Porch, and so he was not immediately involved in what happened to Hutchinson. He ran to help me, saw that it was hopeless, and then he got the groom out of there as quickly as possible. There hadn't been other shots, but of course who knew? We were all targets in that moment, and I was worried for my wife. I couldn't leave the Captain, not lying there dead, and Eugenia refused to leave me. Lowell simply dealt with everything quietly and efficiently."

"No one challenged his right to take charge?"

"One of the other guests, Colonel Rollins, spoke briefly to him, and then left him to it. I did see that exchange. When it was perfectly clear that there was no further danger, people were converging on the Cathedral. The Colonel got all the wedding guests back inside and shut the doors to the nave. I didn't know where the bride and her father were taken, but I learned later that the chauffeur had had the presence of mind to drive on as fast as he could until they were certain it was clear. Very sensible of him."

Eugenia Sedley added, "It didn't take the police very long to arrive, but not in sufficient numbers in the beginning to make a dent in the confusion. It was fortunate that Major Lowell was there."

Rutledge had been watching her. From the start she had answered without apparent reservations. And yet there was a niggling feeling that she was holding something back. He wasn't sure what was behind that feeling, except for the fact that Hamish had noticed it too. Eugenia Sedley was too well-bred to speak ill of the dead. Was that it?

Rutledge acknowledged her comment and then, keeping his voice pleasant, more inquisitive than pressing, he said to her, "Often a hostess notices more about a houseguest than anyone else. I wonder if you saw anything that would be useful?"

Mrs. Sedley glanced at her husband, then answered Rutledge. "As a houseguest, he was charming and agreeable and no trouble at all. The servants were shocked that he'd been killed." Hesitating for only a moment, she added, "But Barbara's family has a long history, and over the centuries there have been quite a few distinguished members. Among the wedding guests was the Bishop, of course, and Colonel Rollins, and then someone from the Foreign Office, a man named Tuttle. I began to think that Captain Hutchinson was—seeking to make powerful new friends."

Her husband said impatiently, "We should not speak ill of a man who died while he was a guest in this house. I can't think your remarks have any bearing on what happened."

She sighed impatiently. "No, of course not, I can't imagine that they would have done. But, my dear, it's precisely *because* he's dead I must tell Inspector Rutledge what I think. He must be the judge of whether it's helpful or not. We want the Captain's murderer found, don't we? It will do no good to pretend he was perfect."

"Did anyone seem to take offense at his attempt to impress the more important guests?"

"I don't know that anyone realized precisely what was happening. It was a very busy few days. And he was quite good at it, you see. But as I was his hostess, I was sometimes anxious that he might be becoming a little obvious, ingratiating himself. Just happening to find himself next to the Bishop or the Colonel or Barbara's rather influential father a trifle more frequently than was usual in a guest who was not of the immediate wedding party. I must say, he was interesting. They seemed to enjoy his company, but I witnessed the maneuvers that made it possible for him to stand or sit next to one of them. And I wondered if someone else might have noticed. Barbara's mother, for one. She doesn't suffer fools lightly. And she wouldn't care to be used in that way."

Sedley said, "That's a little harsh."

"Yes, I suppose it is," his wife responded. "But if the Captain was behaving like this in Ely, perhaps he had behaved in the same way in London."

"I appreciate your honesty," Rutledge cut in, before Sedley could say more. "It's something to bear in mind. Jealousy is a powerful emotion." He hesitated, then added, "I know it will be very painful, but could you tell me what happened as you walked across the grass toward the Cathedral?"

She turned slightly to look toward the drawing room window, and at first he didn't think she intended to answer him. Then she said, bringing the moment back in her mind, "I had just turned to Captain Hutchinson—I can't even tell you what I was about to say. Something trivial, it's completely gone from my mind now—when his face changed. I've never seen anything like it. Shock? I don't think it was pain. Just—surprise that something was happening to him. And suddenly noise was everywhere, and the front of the Captain's white shirt was turning red. All this before he began to fall. As if time had stopped, somehow. To my surprise, I was screaming for help, and my husband was on his knees, trying to stem the flow of blood. But there wasn't much of it after all." She shuddered, and her husband put his hand over hers.

"That's enough," he said. "You've upset her enough, Rutledge. We've told you we saw nothing. How could we, we didn't even know where to look."

But Rutledge had got what he came for—a first insight into the dead man. And from that he would have to build a case.

There was time for two other interviews in what was left of the afternoon. First was a young man who had been behind the barricades. One of the several dozen people who had collected to watch the spectacle of a fashionable wedding.

The reason this witness had been of interest to Inspector Warren was because he was deaf. He hadn't heard the shot, he hadn't been distracted by the screams.

His name was Teddy Mathews. He had come to the barricade wondering why people were gathered there, to see what had drawn them—what was happening.

Rutledge found him at the house where he lived with his sister. It wasn't far from the Cathedral, and it was Mathews's custom to walk there on the grounds every day for exercise.

When Rutledge arrived, it was the sister, Sadie, who admitted him. He asked to speak to her brother and added, "I'm not sure how to manage the interview."

"I'll translate for you, of course. And he can read lips as well." She led him through to a sitting room where Mathews was reading by the window, and made the introductions as her brother rose to greet their visitor.

He was slim, with dark hair and very bright blue eyes, and his handshake was firm.

As they were seated again, Rutledge explained why he was there, and the young man nodded.

"I'll help in any way I can," he replied as his sister translated his signs. "But first I must ask. Do you know who it was who did this thing? I've found it hard to sleep, thinking about it."

"We're hoping to make an arrest soon," Rutledge answered. "Anything you tell us will be useful."

"Yes, I can see that being deaf might have its uses here." He smiled, but his sister couldn't quite bring herself to answer it with one of her own.

"I saw people at a barrier, and wondered what was happening. There was obviously going to be a wedding, judging from the guests who were arriving on the other side of the Green, and I stood there for a moment or two, enjoying watching like everyone else. I had no idea who the bride or groom was, mind you. It was just a way to pass the time. There was a lull in arrivals, and I was about to turn away when another motorcar pulled up and three people got out. A very beautifully dressed woman and two men. I was staring at her when two other men arrived just behind them and started toward the Cathedral as well. I couldn't ask anyone, but I rather thought one of the two men with the woman must be the bridegroom. The tall one, perhaps thirty or so, fairly handsome. It was something in the way he carried himself. As if he knew his worth. I was looking directly at him when he was hit." He broke off, then went on more slowly. "I didn't know what was wrong. He just stopped short for the briefest moment, and then fell backward. I wondered for an instant if his heart had given out."

"You couldn't hear the shot at all."

"No, not at all. I'm totally deaf. But I could very quickly see from the faces around me that something was badly wrong."

"What happened then?"

"I turned to the man beside me, asking for an explanation. But he was very upset, and I couldn't read his lips."

"You were turned to face the Lady Chapel at that moment?"

"I was."

"Did you see anyone near the wall or the gate into the Cathedral grounds?"

"I don't think so. I was struggling to understand what the man was saying, why people were jostling us now, pushing to get away as fast as they could. I couldn't tell why they were so frightened. Still, if something had been going on in that direction, something unusual, I think

I'd have noticed. Inspector Warren has already asked me the same question, and I keep trying to remember anything that might help."

"Have you remembered anything?"

He shook his head, unhappy. "Sorry. No."

"Go on."

"When I turned back, I realized that the man was hurt, was even possibly dead, and people were rushing out of the Cathedral just as the bride's motorcar was turning into the street and starting in our direction. An Army officer and another man were bending over the fallen man, and then the officer stood up and began to look at the buildings on either side and then up at the Cathedral, as if searching for something. I realized then that nothing more could be done for the man on the ground. It was shocking. I couldn't begin to imagine what the bride must think, seeing all this turmoil. I left shortly afterward, because it was distressing not to know what was going on. It wasn't until later, when the police came to our door, that I realized the man had been shot and that I'd been mistaken in thinking he was the groom."

"How did the police know to find you?"

"I believe someone there at the barrier recognized me. I hadn't stayed long enough to see the police arrive. They wanted to know why I'd left, but my sister explained about my deafness. I think they understood."

Mathews was, Rutledge saw, a very good witness, clear about what he'd seen, even though he'd only partially understood it at the time. It explained why Warren had suggested that Rutledge speak to him.

"When you left, how did you make your way home?"

"I turned away from the barricade, walked straight to the next street, and made my way home from there. On foot."

"Did you see anyone or anything unexpected as you turned away from the Cathedral? Workmen with their tools, a priest carrying anything unusual, a person with a large bundle or package?"

Mathews watched his sister's busy hands, then nodded. "By that time, other people were hurrying toward the Cathedral. There was a sweep, I remember, his tools over his shoulder, and a priest, and then there was the man with a barrow. He'd been going in my direction, but he turned and hurried back toward the Cathedral, leaving his barrow standing in the road. A number of people stopped me to ask questions. I couldn't tell them what I'd seen. By the time I reached my house, I was shaken, I admit it. I wouldn't go out at all the next day. I don't like to feel—different. But this brought it home to me very clearly that I was."

There was anguish in his face as he finished. He had, Rutledge thought, managed to come to terms with his deafness. And then, caught in the midst of chaos, he'd kept his head until he'd reached the safety of his house. Only then had he given in to the shock.

"The man with the barrow. Could you see what he was carrying in it?"

"I seem to remember it was covered with a ragged cloth. I didn't think about it again until the constable came to interview me."

It had been the last thing on Mathews's mind, that was clear.

"Are you sure he'd been leaving the Cathedral area?"

"I don't know. He was ahead of me on the street, but he could have come from the pub just there or one of the shops. I expect I assumed he was going about his business when the excitement began." His brows twitched together as he tried to remember. "People do cut across in front of the Cathedral. Every day. But I was at the barrier, and I hadn't seen him there. He could have come from that lane running down beside the Lady Chapel."

A man with a barrow. Anything could have been under that cloth.

It was a place to start.

Rutledge thanked him, and Mathews's sister showed him to the door.

She said, as he stepped out into the late afternoon sunlight, "My brother is a good man. He manages quite well, actually. But he was very upset when he reached the house. I hope this is the last time you will need to interview him. It's difficult to relive what happened."

"We'll try to spare him, Miss Mathews. But we're searching for a killer."

"Ask someone else, then. There were dozens of people there. Perhaps if they *heard* the shot they can tell you where it came from." She closed the door, leaving him there.

His last interview was with a Mrs. Boggs, who was going to market, noticed the cluster of people by the Cathedral barrier, and stopped to see what had brought them there. Someone told her it was a wedding, and she'd stayed in the hope of seeing the bride arrive.

She lived in one of the poorer sections of Ely. She walked home daily from her work as a washerwoman for one of the large homes not far from the Sedleys'.

She was surprised and more than a little flattered to find Scotland Yard at her door.

As he asked his questions, he realized that she was more astute than he'd realized. Her red face, strawlike fair hair, and rough hands were a badge of her occupation, not her mind.

"What I know about guns," she said, "you could put in a thimble. But I was watching that Captain Hutchinson coming across the grass. He was a well-set-up gentleman, and I saw him step out of his motorcar and offer the lady with him his hand."

It had been Sedley's motorcar and Sedley's wife.

"Tell me about him," Rutledge asked.

She cocked her head. "Nearly as tall as you are, a man to take notice of. Now the gentleman with him was quite handsome, but a little old to be the bridegroom. Still, you never know, do you? The Captain—they told me his name when they took my statement—was smartly dressed, as if his valet had taken special care. I do know something about valets. They like their gentleman to be well turned out."

"What did you see just before he was struck by the bullet?"

"The lady was speaking to him, but he looked up, as if he knew something was about to happen, and then he was shocked, as if he couldn't believe what it was. At first I thought the lady had said something unpleasant, but we heard the shot in the same breath, only I didn't know what it was, I couldn't think for the sudden noise. And he was falling over, and everyone was screaming." She shook her head. "I never saw anything like it."

"What do you mean, he looked up?"

"The way you do sometimes when you hear something you don't believe."

And Mrs. Sedley couldn't remember what it was she was saying to Hutchinson just as he was shot.

"Did you see anyone by the gate that led into the precincts of the Cathedral, the one close by the Lady Chapel? Or anyone at all who seemed to be out of place? Either the way he looked or because of what he was carrying."

"There was no one by that gate. Not that I saw. Why should there be? You couldn't very well watch all the finery from there. As to anything out of place, I do remember something that struck me as a little odd. But for the life of me I can't bring it back. Just something ordinary, you know, but I was in a state by that time, and it clear went out of my head."

Try as he would, Rutledge couldn't coax whatever it was from her memory. In the end he had to thank her and ask her to notify the police if she brought it to mind.

Back in the center of Ely once more, he found a telephone and put in a call to Sergeant Gibson in London.

Gibson's voice as he came to the telephone had a cautious note in it.

Rutledge said, "Two of the people involved in these murders in the Cambridgeshire Fens came from London. I shall need whatever you can find about one Captain Gordon Hutchinson. He's the victim in Ely. The other man is the bridegroom here, Jason Fallowfield. He was walking very close to the victim and might well have been the intended target. They're distantly related, although they called themselves cousins. Most particularly I need to know if the second victim, the one in Wriston, had any connection with either of the other two men. Herbert Swift is the name. There's no link we can find here—it must lie in London. Finally, there's an artillery Major, one Lowell, first name Alexander. Does he have a connection with Hutchinson or Swift? He couldn't have been the shooter. But he may have been involved in some way."

Gibson said only, "That's a tall order. Sir."

Rutledge smiled grimly. Whatever was happening in London must be requiring a good deal of manpower, and Gibson was alerting him to the possibility of delays before he received any information.

So much for Markham's dictum. Unless there was a break here in Cambridgeshire, there was no possibility of an early arrest.

He thanked Gibson, adding, "Give it your best try. That's all that matters."

Gibson was silent for a moment—Rutledge could hear voices, as though several men were walking past where the sergeant was standing. Finally in a rush the sergeant said something that was nearly unintelligible coming down the line, then added "Sir" before ringing off.

Rutledge would have sworn that what he'd heard was *new broom*.

An ominous sign.

Chapter 6

Shutting the door behind him as he walked into his room under the eaves, Rutledge sat down in the only chair and gave the problem facing him some thought.

He'd seen the mountain of interviews that Inspector Warren had painstakingly collected. It would take days to sort through the rest of them, in the hope of finding something, anything to be going on with. His time was better spent elsewhere.

But there was still the question of the man with the barrow.

Rutledge made a note to deal with it tomorrow, and went out to find himself some dinner before going to bed.

But the room felt still, airless, when he came in again, and a little after two in the morning he could stand it no longer. He got up, dressed. The streets were empty and quiet when he let himself out of the inn door and walked as far as the Cathedral.

In the nearly full moon, it was at once imposing and mysterious. The silvery light shone through the Lantern, giving it a ghostly glow that seemed to emanate from inside. Where it could be seen from his vantage point, the roof gleamed like dull pewter, while below it the stone walls seemed to squat in darkness with very little definition, the occasional spire rising into the night sky, like fingers pointing to God.

The Palace Green stretched before him, full of shadows, the Russian cannon that Queen Victoria had dedicated on a visit to Ely black and ugly. Looking at it, he thought it had been an odd welcome for the wedding guests, but then it had stood there so long it was likely that no one noticed it.

He began where the motorcars had drawn up, at the top of the Green, then took the route that Warren had pointed out to him. There was no one else about, although he thought he heard an owl in the distance. He walked across the grass, now damp with dew, and stopped where Hutchinson had fallen. Standing there, he did what Major Lowell had done, turning slowly in a half circle, his gaze taking in every possible vantage point and then discarding them one by one.

There was no clear line of sight from the Diocesan buildings. It would have had to have been a head shot. But the killer had gone instead for the heart. Why?

The high stone wall, which began next to the Cathedral's own walls, stretched down the road toward an arch that led into the school grounds. The same wall where a ladder had been placed. Neither Inspector Warren nor his constables had discovered who had put the ladder there. But again the angle was wrong. A bullet from there would have had to traverse the chest, exiting below the left arm after striking the heart. The head would have been a more certain target.

Hamish spoke into the silence. His voice seemed to echo ominously through the darkness. "Yon battlement."

Looking up at the dark mass of the great west tower, Rutledge was inclined to agree with him. But a constable had climbed up there and found nothing. And it was very exposed, more so than the gate on the far side by the Lady Chapel. Any of the arriving guests might have looked up at the wrong time, attracted by movement—even a pigeon flying up—and spotted the killer. He would have been well and truly trapped, no way out but through that single tower door inside the Cathedral itself. He couldn't have hidden, unless he was dressed as a guest and could mingle easily. But that meant abandoning the rifle until it was safe to go back for it. Where in hell's name could he have hidden it? The killer must surely have known that someone would climb up there to have a look. But he couldn't have come through the tower door with it, hoping to secret it somewhere else. Even broken down, it would have been difficult to conceal. Inspector Warren had even searched the organ pipes.

And yet, if he'd been the killer, Rutledge knew he would have taken his chances there because it was the most certain platform from which to make his shot.

While the gate on the north side was exposed as well, at least there were choices of direction for the man's escape. And that's where the cartridge casing had been found.

But a cartridge casing could be dropped anywhere, far from where it had been ejected. The killer could have come down from the tower, left the Cathedral by a different door, and then as he came around the apse and the Lady Chapel to that gate, lost the casing without knowing it.

Misdirection? Both the ladder against the wall and the dropped casing?

"Ye ken," Hamish said after a moment, "it isna' sae important to know how it was done. He's sae verra' clever, he's killed twice withoot being seen, save for the auld woman who swore she saw a monster."

"Not much to go on, that monster," Rutledge answered aloud with a wry smile.

"Aye, it's verra' similar to the problem here."

"Yes," Rutledge answered slowly. "Misdirection again. But tomorrow I'll climb to that tower."

And shortly after breakfast, when the sun was bright and a mist clung to the lower-lying villages, hiding them from sight, Rutledge came back to Ely Cathedral, and without much notice being taken of him, he wandered about for a time. Much to the horror of Hamish's Covenanter soul, who had a distaste for ornamentation and splendor that smacked of Popery.

He'd walked down to the choir and thence to the Lady Chapel, exploring as a policeman rather than a worshipper, made his way back to the Galilee Porch, and from there went unchallenged to the tower door. It was a climb. Two hundred eighty-eight steps, unless he'd missed his count. But in the end he came out onto the battlemented top of the tower.

It was a dizzying height. Two hundred feet or more, with splendid views over Ely and across the surrounding Fens.

The constable had been right, the slope of the roof made it difficult to walk around, offering little or no space for footing.

Instead of walking, he got down on all fours and crept around to the position he was looking for. When he came to a spot where he could look down, he saw that he had a perfect view of his field of fire.

He could see where Hutchinson had fallen so clearly that he himself could have taken that shot.

He knelt there, thinking it through, ignoring Hamish in the back of his mind.

There was still the problem of getting the rifle safely away. But the man couldn't have made the shot with any other weapon. It was too far for a revolver, and by the time Captain Hutchinson had come that close, the man would have had to stand to aim.

There was no proof he was right, of course. But it had been a daring plan, if this had been the place the killer had chosen.

And that was a measure of what the man had felt toward Hutchinson. A savage hate, to take such a risk. Or a cold one?

Which meant, Rutledge realized, that of the two victims, it was Hutchinson who had been the more important one. Herbert Swift could have waited. Days. Weeks. Hutchinson would only be within reach for a stated length of time. And as Inspector Warren had pointed out, the wedding ceremony was the only public appearance the Captain had made. The private parties and dinners hadn't been announced, there was no way to plan for any one of them. But here—here at the Cathedral, Hutchinson would be certain to appear, and *that* fact had been known for some time.

Rutledge couldn't blame Inspector Warren for not working it out the way he himself had. Warren had been the man on the scene, he'd had to deal with the bride's irate father, the Bishop and the Colonel and all the other important men connected to the family. He'd had to depend on his constables to do much of the legwork. Those endless statements had taken time, and the pressure to find the killer had built with each passing day. But Warren had only had a handful of days. Swift was killed then, and a second inquiry had been set in motion, stretching his resources to the limit.

Damned on every side, he'd at least had the courage to ask the Yard to send someone. And he had cooperated fully when Rutledge arrived, knowing he was acknowledging his own failure.

Rutledge could respect that.

He made to rise and move away from the space between two blocks of stone where he'd been crouching, when he realized what it was Hamish was saying to him.

Caught on a bit of rough stone was a single gray strand of cloth, so nearly the same color that it was all but invisible.

He gently tugged at it and brought it free. Worn cloth, he thought, and easily snagged. But how had it got here? More important, *when*? That was the question. And unfortunately there were any number of answers. All the same, if he'd been a betting man, Rutledge would have wagered that it had been the cloth with which the killer had wrapped himself and his rifle, shielding both from view. It made sense. The color alone was not likely to have come from a casual visitor's clothing. It matched too perfectly.

Taking out a clean handkerchief, Rutledge laid the tiny strand of cotton there and folded it again.

Satisfied, he left the tower and climbed down the multitude of steps once more, carefully opening the door and finding it a simple matter to slip out of it unnoticed. But then there was no wedding today. He had just reached the west door when a man in clerical dress came out of the sanctuary. Rutledge turned.

"Beautiful building, isn't it?" the man said, his accent strong Scots.

"It is indeed," Rutledge answered.

The man nodded and went on his way.

Rutledge watched him as he strode out of sight, his mind elsewhere.

After a moment he said, "I'm going back to Wriston. There are too many people involved in what happened in Ely. If I find anything there, I can backtrack to this place."

Hamish said, "Aye, but will you tell yon Inspector what you found?"

Rutledge shook his head. "Not yet. Not until I can be sure."

Inspector Warren was not best pleased to hear that Rutledge was already leaving Ely.

"Giving up, are you?"

Rutledge said, "Early days for that. No, I've spoken to those witnesses, and I've looked at the ground. I don't know that we can learn any more here at this stage. What I hope to discover in Wriston is whether or not someone else saw Mrs. Percy's monster. Surely someone did, and hasn't had the courage yet to come forward. Would you willingly admit you'd seen something that you couldn't explain?"

"I probably would, if asked by a policeman," Warren answered stiffly.

"Yes, perhaps you'd speak to him. But not to your local constable, who would be sniffing your breath or wondering if you'd fallen down and hit your head. You would know full well the constable would file away your vision along with Mrs. Percy's and remind you of it later, when next he saw you staggering down the High at closing."

Warren grudgingly agreed, striving to keep amusement out of his gaze.

"Our quarry was faultless here. He'd planned meticulously for this kill. He couldn't have got away with it if he hadn't. And then he tried again. He might have been careless." Rutledge paused. "And if he wasn't, he could well be searching for a new target, because he knows we can't touch him. Yet."

"I hope to God you're wrong." Warren took a deep breath. "The Chief Constable is already demanding answers, and he'll be in *your* face if there's another murder. The wedding was bad enough, given who was attending, and then Swift on top of that."

But there was very likely to be a third, Rutledge thought. He could almost feel it.

He was halfway to the street when he remembered the barrow. Turning, he went back to Warren's office, poked his head around the door, and said, "The deaf fellow. Mathews. He saw a man with a barrow walking away from the scene. After any number of people had rushed past him toward the Cathedral, he left the barrow and went to see for himself what the excitement was about. He's not likely to be our man, but if we don't follow up on him, we'll never know for certain."

"Any idea what was in that barrow?"

"According to Mathews it was covered by a cloth." He thought about the strand of gray cotton in his handkerchief. Had it come from that barrow? It would be luck indeed if it had. But where was the barrow's owner now? Much less that cloth—long since tossed into a tip?

Inspector Warren was nodding. "Very well, I'll see to it. Do you think Mathews can identify him? There must be twenty or more men with barrows in Ely."

"We'll have to trust that he can." Rutledge thanked him, went back to The Deacon, thought about it, and walked on to Teddy Mathews's house.

He was in and alone. Rutledge apologized for coming in unannounced, when the man's sister was away.

Mathews shrugged. Rutledge said, speaking clearly, "The barrow the man abandoned to run back toward the Cathedral. You said there was a cloth thrown over the contents."

He handed his notebook to Mathews, who took up the pen and wrote on the first empty page he came to, *I expect I ought to have said sacking. It was so filthy you could hardly tell that once it had been yellow.*

Yellow, then. Not gray.

He'd probably sent Warren's men on a wild-goose chase. Still, he was reluctant to rescind the request. And who knew what lay under the sacking? Whatever color it had been.

He thanked Mathews, who scribbled something more on the page, then passed the notebook back to Rutledge.

I'm sorry I couldn't be more help.

"You're a good witness," Rutledge assured him, then took his leave.

At The Deacon Inn, Rutledge asked Reception to hold his room but took his valise with him and set out for Wriston, stopping briefly for petrol.

It was a village, not a town. Fewer people were involved. Ely was the proverbial haystack, and for all anyone knew, the needle was already back home in Soham or Burwell, even London. Wherever he'd come from.

Hamish said as Rutledge threaded his way through Ely to the Cambridge Road, "For a' anyone knew, he was walking the mist in Wriston."

Chapter 7

Now that he was in the village in his official capacity, Rutledge's first duty was to call on the constable.

He'd arrived at Wriston by a roundabout way, crisscrossing the Fens to explore several nearby villages, and there was not much to choose between them save for size. Isleham was smaller, Soham a little larger, and Burwell, the largest, a bustling town with a fine church. And the fields that ran for acre after acre in their long narrow beds for the most part held the same variety of market crops—oats, peas, and barley.

It was late in the afternoon when he walked into the police station, across from the duck pond. Constable McBride was at his desk, reading an Ely newspaper.

He was a burly man with thinning brown hair, and he looked up at Rutledge with some surprise, recognizing him at once as the stranger he'd chivvied along only yesterday for excessive curiosity about the site of Swift's murder.

"Back again, are you, sir? Anything I can help you with, then?"

But there was a guardedness in the offer.

Rutledge handed him his identification, and McBride studied it for longer than necessary, and then, getting to his feet, he said in a slightly aggrieved voice, "I'm sorry, sir, but you didn't tell me who you were."

"I hadn't yet reported to Inspector Warren in Ely. I'd been caught out in that mist the previous night, got thoroughly lost, and when I realized that I was in Wriston, I wanted to take a preliminary look at that cross."

"Yes, I see." But it was clear he didn't. "Is there anything new, sir? From Ely?" He held up the newspaper still in his hand, then set it aside. "There's nothing in here. And the last report I'd had from Inspector Warren was three days ago. Even that was not what you might call informative."

"What does the Ely paper have to say about the murders?"

"Precious little. A nine days' wonder, as it were. It's no longer on the first page." Gesturing to the chair on the other side of the desk, he sat down. "How can I help you, sir?"

"Tell me what happened here in Wriston."

"Surely Inspector Warren has already done that."

"I'd like your point of view. You live here."

McBride gave him a concise report. It differed very little from what Rutledge already knew. "We searched and we found nothing. Not even a cartridge casing. The shot must have been a difficult one. Night, flickering torchlight. I'd not have tried it, I can tell you that. I mean to say, what if he'd missed?"

But whoever it was had had no problem making his shot count.

"The question is, what ties these two deaths together? There has to be a very good reason. For one thing, they were killed within days of each other, and only a matter of miles apart. For another, they were fairly prominent men. This wasn't a grudge killing between neighbors, because they weren't in any sense neighbors."

McBride shook his head. "I've spent hours thinking about that, sir. I can't see how they could have known each other. Perhaps someone only believed they did."

Which, Rutledge thought, was a very perceptive comment.

"The war. Is there a connection there?"

"I can't think how that could be. The Swifts have been farmers here for generations. Our Mr. Swift spent most of his war in Glasgow, serving with the Navy as a civilian. Still, he liked Scotland, it seems. He wrote the Rector to say that when he could, he'd take long walks. He thought it cleared his head. He was still mourning his wife."

"Did Swift have enemies?"

"We haven't found any. If you want my opinion, whoever did this isn't a Wriston man, and that means the quarrel, if there was one, didn't have its roots here. Mr. Swift wasn't one to visit Ely or Soham or Burwell often, but he went there if it was a matter of business. I'd say look at his clients or *their* enemies. A quiet man, and well liked. He'd have won, you know. Hands down. I daresay his killing could even have been political, although that's a stretch, in my view."

"What about his opponent?"

"I doubt he could be bothered. What he liked best, if truth be told, were the free beers his supporters bought for him down at The Wake."

"What was Mr. Swift talking about the night he was killed?"

"He was hardly into what he'd planned to say. It had to do with the war ending, but the legacy of the war was still with us. I doubt anyone would argue with that."

"His private life, then."

McBride smiled. "As to that, his wife ruled the roost until she died in childbirth. It nearly killed him as well. I don't believe he'd have gone on, if the war hadn't changed things. Scotland was good for him, taking him away from here."

"Someone wanted him dead."

"It's true, but try as I will, I can find nothing in his life to explain that. Unless . . ." McBride's gaze stared into the past, somewhere behind Rutledge's left shoulder.

Rutledge felt an instant burst of panic, then caught himself. No one could see Hamish where he kept watch at Rutledge's back, as he had done so often in the trenches.

"There was something before the war. Mr. Swift was serving as a witness in a trial in Ely. There was a man sent to prison for putting another man in hospital with a skull fracture and broken ribs. It was claimed the victim was thrown down a flight of stairs. The man swore it wasn't true, that the victim, after an argument, turned to have the last word, lost his balance, and fell. But the jury thought otherwise." McBride lifted a shoulder in a shrug. "That man might've held a grudge against Swift, because he gave evidence against him, but I can't see how Captain Hutchinson fits into it."

"Do you remember the man's name?"

"That I don't. The only reason I remember the trial at all is that my wife's brother was bailiff at the time."

"Then I'll ask him if he recalls the trial."

"Dead on Passchendaele Ridge," McBride answered somberly. "More's the pity. A good man."

"Turn it another way. Who has such a rifle?"

"There's the catch," McBride agreed. "They aren't lying beneath every bush, are they? The question is, did he keep it back when he left France, or was it one used to train troops?"

It was time to mention Mrs. Percy.

"I've been told that at least one of the onlookers described our man."

McBride pushed aside his newspaper. "Mrs. Percy. I don't know who spoke to you about her. But I'd discount what she said, if I were you, sir."

"Why? She saw *something*. It wasn't what you expected from a witness, perhaps. But it was information we have to investigate."

"Sir, I can't see how we can explore what she described. She's an elderly woman whose eyesight is not the best. I mean to say—a monster."

"The question is, was she the only one who looked up just as the shot was fired? There may be other witnesses who don't want to come forward. We need to find them."

"There's nothing in the statements we collected that show information has been withheld."

"I'd like to question her, all the same."

"She's still that upset, sir, I doubt she'll make any sense."

"Then I'll go alone. She might speak more freely. Tell me where to find her."

Mrs. Percy lived in the last cottage on the lane called Windmill Row.

There was no windmill now. Instead the fields began not twenty feet beyond her door, and a bulwark of earth separated them from the end of her lane. He could just see the darker green of late season crops growing several feet below the level of the higher ground on which her house sat.

She was snapping beans in the kitchen when Rutledge tapped at her open door. "Come," she called, and he stepped inside, following the sound of her voice. She was a small woman, gray hair pinned up on her head, blue-veined hands working with the beans in a large earthenware bowl. He didn't think she even looked down at them, her fingers busy on their own.

"Who are you?" she demanded, peering at the tall stranger who'd just appeared in her kitchen. "I was expecting the butcher's boy."

"My name is Rutledge, Mrs. Percy. London has sent me to Wriston to find out what I can about the death of Mr. Swift. I understand you were by the market cross that evening, when he was shot."

"I was. It was a warm evening, no clouds, and I felt like walking up to the cross to see what the shouting and those torches were all about. When I got there, the smoke made my eyes water. I pushed my way around behind Mr. Swift, where it was a little better, and just then he started to speak. I'd hardly got settled when he dropped like a stone." She shuddered, her hands pausing in their work. "I wish I'd never gone up. I wish I'd decided to do my mending instead." Her fingers found their rhythm again.

"Had anyone else moved around behind Mr. Swift, to get away from the smoke?"

"Paul Ruskin was there—he's the cooper from Soham. I knew his father. But most everyone wanted to be out in front, of course."

Another name. So much for McBride's pessimism.

"Anyone else?" Across from where he was sitting, a pair of worn wooden stilts were standing in the corner, and on a shelf just above them, a pair of wooden skates for use on ice. A hundred years or more ago, men had walked the fields on stilts, and they'd been quite good at it, striding out boldly and swinging across ditches, fording streams.

Mrs. Percy considered his question, then shook her head. "No, I think it was just Paul and me. Mr. Ruskin and me."

It was time to ask the question that had brought him here. There was no way to soften it, to draw her out. But he tried.

"Scotland Yard was very pleased to learn there was a witness to the shooting, someone who could describe Mr. Swift's killer."

Mrs. Percy lips thinned to a tight line. "Well, they're wrong," she said after a moment, when he didn't press.

He listened to her fingers snapping the crisp flesh of the beans.

"Have they made light of what you told them? The constable and then Inspector Warren?" he asked gently.

"I didn't see anything. I told you. The smoke was making my eyes water. All I saw was smoke."

The damage was done. Rutledge couldn't shift her. And that he laid at the door of those who had questioned her in the beginning. A monster was not evidence. And in their own desperation, they had hounded her to make sense of the senseless. Now she was refusing to acknowledge her own statement, denying she had seen anything after all.

She rose, the beans half filling the bowl, the sack that had held them empty now.

"I have to cook my dinner," she said, dismissing him. "There's the door."

Rutledge swore to himself. He needed her testimony, he needed to watch her face as she described the monster she'd seen. But he would have to come back—as often as necessary until she relented.

Meanwhile, there was still the man in Soham.

Thanking her, he turned and found his way back to the door where he'd come in.

The question, he thought as he made his way back to the market cross to stare up at the dormer window once more, was how much he could discount the monster as part of her shock or as part of her eyes watering. He squinted, distorting the window as much as he could, but the circumstances were very different here on this sunny day.

And it was possible that someone else besides Ruskin had had a similar vantage point, but what had been done to Mrs. Percy would have been a warning that the truth would be rejected out of hand. And so any hope of locating those witnesses—if they actually existed—was small.

He drove on to Soham, finding the High Street and the square, then asked a man crossing it toward the shops how to find the cooper.

The man nodded. "Out that way to Fox Lane. You can't miss it."

And he didn't. The front of the shop was open, and the scent of fresh-cut wood filled the air. He found Ruskin in the yard, gathering staves together one by one in a raising hoop, frowning as he worked. Perhaps in his late thirties, he had graying hair and a strong face. He looked up, nodded to Rutledge, and without stopping what he was doing, he asked, "Help you, sir?"

"I'm looking for Paul Ruskin."

He straightened. Behind him in the shed was a shelf with the tools of his trade, and beyond them against the far wall was a row of his finished goods. Butter churns, coal scuttles, a firkin and a bucket, dwarfed by a pair of hogsheads.

"You've found him, then."

"I've come from Ely. My name is Rutledge. Scotland Yard sent me to help Inspector Warren find the man who killed Captain Hutchinson and Mr. Swift. I understand you were in Wriston the evening Swift was shot."

Ruskin set the staves aside and considered Rutledge. "Who told you I was there?"

And Rutledge realized that this man hadn't been questioned by the police. That somehow in the chaos, he'd left Wriston before McBride could collect all his witnesses. If Mrs. Percy hadn't recognized him, he'd have been in the clear.

Rutledge sat down on a finished barrelhead. "Someone saw you and reported it to me. Why? Did you have anything to hide?"

"No." But there was a wariness in the man's voice. When Rutledge said nothing, he added, "I saw no purpose in hanging about. The man was dead, and I'd had aught to do with it."

"Sensible of you," Rutledge said affably. "What brought you to Wriston?"

"I'd delivered a half-dozen barrels for one of the farmers. Burrows, his name is. I stopped off at The Wake after delivering them. There was talk that Swift was planning to speak. He came in just after that, walking around, having a word with everyone. And I decided to hear what he had to say. It'ud been a long day for me, but I wasn't ready to go home. My wife and I'd had words that morning, and I didn't want to open up the quarrel again."

"So you followed the torchbearers and the others to the market cross?"

"I did. But I'm not a Wriston man. I didn't care to draw attention to myself, like. Not that I didn't have every right to be there, you understand, more a question of not wishing to push in."

It was something Rutledge had heard many times before. A village only five miles away could be as foreign to its neighbors as if it were fifty or five hundred miles distant. This was a Wriston rally.

And so Ruskin had moved away from the main body of Swift's followers and found himself next to Mrs. Percy, behind the market cross.

"Did you see Swift fall?"

"I couldn't help but see it. One minute speaking, the next pitching over, and half his head missing." Something changed in Ruskin's face. "It brought back the war. I can tell you that. I thought I was done with the dead falling at my feet and the sound of gunfire. I'd put it behind me, and it all came rushing back. So I left. I saw no need to stay. There must have been forty some people who could talk to the police. They didn't need me."

That explained his leaving. It was something Rutledge could understand. And Hamish as well, stirring in the back of his mind.

"What did you see?" Rutledge asked quietly. "Up there in the dormer window?"

"God knows. It happened so fast, I thought it was a flashback to the war."

"Describe it for me."

Ruskin shook his head. "No. I don't want to remember. It made my blood run cold. I told myself I was wrong, and that I'd imagined it. And so I set it aside."

"Did you see the rifle?"

"No. No, not that."

"Then what?"

He shook his head.

"You must tell me. I can't find this killer if I don't know what I'm searching for." He waited. "Ruskin, I can have you arrested for refusing to cooperate with the police. Don't make me take that step."

The man looked directly at Rutledge then, his eyes haunted. After a moment he said, "Will you go away and leave me alone? I don't want the police here, hounding me. I don't want to dredge it up again and again."

"I won't tell Inspector Warren. Or your own constable. No one knows I'm here anyway. I came on my own."

Barely satisfied, Ruskin searched Rutledge's face. And then, against his will, Ruskin stood up.

"A helmet," he said. "I saw a German helmet. I know, it's impossible. But that's what I saw. "

And with that he walked away, disappearing into the back of his shop.

Rutledge sat where he was for a moment.

Hamish was saying, "He saw what he feared to see. Only that."

Taking a deep breath, Rutledge got up and walked back to his motorcar. Across the rooftops facing him, he could see the elegant tower of the village church. He bent to turn the crank and got into the motorcar.

Had Ruskin imagined the helmet? He must have done, Hamish was right. Shocked by the rifle's report and the dead man almost at his feet, he'd reverted to what he knew, the war and the trenches. Who else would be shooting at him but his German foes?

Still, the fact remained. He *had* seen something.

"Will ye tell the ithers?" Hamish demanded. "Ye gave your word."

"Warren and McBride? The constable here? No. We'll see what comes of it."

Reversing the motorcar, he added, only realizing too late that he'd spoken aloud. "Who's behind this business? Who is using the war to exact his revenge?"

I f he was to remain in Wriston for several days, he needed somewhere to stay. Rutledge wasn't certain that Priscilla Bartram would accommodate him. It was one thing to take in a stranger lost in the mist. Quite another to go to all the trouble of opening her inn to someone who might spend only a night or two there. Still, he hadn't seen any other lodgings in the village. The Wake Inn was small, more pub than hostelry.

Then he remembered something Miss Trowbridge had said. *She needs the money.*

Leaving the motorcar by the police station, he walked down the High Street to The Dutchman Inn.

Hamish said, "She willna' be pleased ye didna' tell her who you were."

There was that. But he rather thought Miss Bartram would choose company in the evening over turning him down out of pique.

Whether she would talk as freely once she knew he was Scotland Yard was another matter.

When she came to the door, it was clear she was happy to see him again, telling him almost in the same breath that his room was still available.

"Have you finished your business in Ely?" she asked, urging him toward the sitting room. "Well, then, you've earned a bit of time to yourself. Not that spending it here in the Fen country is anything special, when the waterfowl aren't coming in."

Her face, however, changed when he told her who he was. She wasn't best pleased.

"Scotland Yard, then. You could have told me when you were here.

I'd have said nothing, you know, not even to Constable McBride, if you'd asked me not to. As it was, I may have said too much. About the people here. Mr. Swift."

"I had yet to report to Inspector Warren in Ely. It was proper to do that first. In fact, it was happenstance that I came here first at all. It wasn't where I intended to be."

"You told me you'd come from Cambridge. Not London." There was an accusing note in her voice now.

"And so I had come from there. I thought at the time you might prefer someone from Cambridge to a stranger from London."

"Did Miss Trowbridge know? What brought you here?"

"She never asked," he said carefully. "After all, if it hadn't been for her cat, I'd have likely stumbled over the ruins of the mill keeper's house and broken my neck."

That mollified her, but she said stiffly, "What brings you back here now?"

He told her the truth. "I came to confer with Constable McBride. And to speak to Mrs. Percy. Although she appears to have withdrawn her remarks about a monster. She now claims she saw nothing at all."

"Yes, well, who can blame her?" Finally satisfied, Priscilla Bartram relented and invited him to join her in the kitchen. "I was just about to put the kettle on."

Rutledge followed her and sat down where he'd had his dinner the night of the fog. It had been a very different evening. Now the sun came through the windowpanes in golden shafts of light that fell across the well-polished floor, and the door to the yard was standing open. The light breeze carried in a sweet scent from the cut-flower garden just outside.

"Well now. Scotland Yard. My heavens. I never thought I'd be speaking to Scotland Yard," Miss Bartram went on, the kettle filled and beginning to boil, the tea things set out.

"I remember looking at the waterfowl in the glass cabinets. Which reminded me of the reason this inn is here. Was there any hunting with a rifle?"

"My grandfather and his father owned a flat-bottomed boat, with a screen made of reeds raised above the bow. The hurdle maker made a new one each season. There was a duck gun hidden in it, only the barrel visible. A great noisy thing. One shot from that could bring down a dozen or more birds, and their dogs were hard-pressed to bring them in. But that was for market, you understand. In my father's day, he'd take out guests in his boat and they'd wait for the birds to come in of an evening. A shotgun was all they required. There was nothing in the Fens of a size to warrant a rifle."

"Perhaps someone used to do a little deer stalking in Scotland? Or shooting in Africa? Bringing his gun along to show the other guests."

She smiled as she turned to the teakettle. "None of our guests had such lofty ambitions. They were shooting for pleasure and for the table. Mostly they'd come up from the south. London, some of them, and the Home Counties. One man was writing a book on migrating waterfowl. He drew the birds he brought back, then used watercolors to fill in the outlines. Quite lovely, the drawings were. Very clever. He'd pin the birds up into position against a painted backdrop, then start to work. Every feather in its proper place. When he'd finished with them, his wife plucked and cooked them."

Not a very fitting end for the man's models, Rutledge found himself thinking.

"How well did you know Mr. Swift?"

She went to the pantry and brought back slices of meat and bread, and the chutney he'd liked before. "Of course I never had any need of his advice. My father's solicitor was in Burwell. Still, I'd met him here and there, but more a nodding acquaintance than *knowing* him. When he returned from Scotland and reopened his law business after the war, he kept to himself."

"What was his background? Was his father a solicitor as well?"

"His father was a farmer, and he married more acres. There was money enough to send the two sons to university, but Swift chose the law, while his brother wanted the farm. They had words when the father died over what to do with the land. Swift wanted his share of the inheritance."

"Trouble?" He took the sandwich she'd made up, and realized how hungry he was.

"In fact they came to an amicable agreement. I'll tell you where there might be jealousy, though. There was a third boy. Wild oats, before the elder Mr. Swift was married. Still, he acknowledged the lad, paid for his education and the like, but he wasn't legitimate and there was nothing for him in the will. He was apprenticed to Ned Miles. The barber. And the day the father died, Anson left Wriston and has never came back."

"Was he in the war? This Anson Swift?"

"If he was, nobody knew of it. He didn't join with the local men, if that's what you mean."

She brought the pot to the table and poured Rutledge's cup.

He thanked her and then said, "No one seems to think that the Swifts were acquainted with the first victim, Captain Hutchinson."

"Well, you never know," she said, considering it. "Stranger things have happened. But on the whole, I'd say it's not likely. Did you know that the Captain was here in the Fen country some months ago?"

Rutledge nearly choked on his tea. "What? Are you sure?"

"Well, not in Wriston, of course. But he came to a funeral in Burwell. The only reason I know of it is that later I recognized his photograph in the Ely newspaper."

"Tell me."

"I went to the service myself. The dead man, Major Clayton, was from Burwell, although he lived in London. His father was a military man before him, but their roots were here in Cambridgeshire. My father had known the family, you see, and I felt I ought to go. At any rate, there was a Colonel to give the eulogy and this Captain Hutchinson came north with him."

"Have you told Constable McBride about this? Or Inspector Warren?"

"I thought surely they must already know."

But Inspector Warren had been concentrating on Ely, and by extension, on Wriston. He'd said nothing about Burwell.

Rutledge sat there, trying to think. Was this the only time that Hutchinson had come north, before the wedding? Or had he had connections here that no one knew about?

Hamish, stirring in the back of Rutledge's mind, said, "Ye ken, it changes everything."

It bloody well did.

"Was anyone else from Wriston at Major Clayton's funeral?"

Priscilla Bartram frowned. "I don't believe so. No, I don't remember seeing anyone I knew from Wriston. But that's not surprising. I told you, Major Clayton lived in London. I never met him myself."

The question now was, why hadn't the murderer taken that opportunity, if he'd been intent on killing Hutchinson? Why wait for the far more public venue of Ely Cathedral and the wedding?

And the answer, Rutledge thought, was that Ely offered the killer a better chance of escape.

"Did Captain Hutchinson travel to Burwell with anyone in particular?"

"I have no idea. When I saw him, he was generally with the Colonel or the Major's sister. There was no reason to pay particular attention to him, it was just that he was a rather handsome man, and you tend to notice such people."

What had Mrs. Sedley told him? That the Captain had managed to find himself in the company of the prominent guests more often than was usual? A man who courted the wealthy or the powerful . . .

It was the first break he'd had. And he was going to make the most of it.

"What sort of man was Hutchinson?" he asked Miss Bartram.

"Well, of course I didn't speak to him. I was just one of the mourners. But he was very pleasant to everyone. It seemed to me that the Major's sister was grateful for his support when we went to the graveside. But then he left with the Colonel after the luncheon, while Miss Clayton was staying over with friends, unable to face the journey south that same day. At least that's what I heard someone say. I really didn't know anyone there, you see. I expect that's why I noticed what was happening."

Which must have been unpleasant for Miss Bartram, but very useful for the police.

Rutledge asked, "Was Herbert Swift at that same funeral?"

"I don't believe he was. I never saw him if he was there."

"How did you learn about the funeral in the first place?"

"There was an obituary notice in the Ely newspaper."

Rutledge finished his tea and thanked her. She reminded him to leave his valise in the sitting room, and he saw to that before going out.

Ten minutes later, he was back at his motorcar and reversing to drive to Burwell.

It was necessary to pass Wriston Mill on his way, and at that moment Miss Trowbridge was opening her gate and stepping out into the road.

She was surprised to see him again and stopped by the gate.

Rutledge slowed. "Thank you for rescuing me. I spent a comfortable night at Miss Bartram's inn," he said, smiling.

"I thought your business was in Ely. Are you returning to Cambridge, or have you misplaced the road again?"

He was amused, but there was another side of the coin that had to be addressed, and laughter was not the best way to handle it. "Neither, as it happens. I'm afraid my business in Ely is only a part of what I'm here to see to. Miss Trowbridge, I'm an Inspector, Scotland Yard, here to investigate the murders of Captain Hutchinson and Mr. Swift."

Her expression had been friendly, surprised, and a little pleased to see him again. But at his words it changed. "Indeed," she said coldly.

"I have fences to mend," he replied wryly. "But the fact is, I hadn't reported to Inspector Warren in Ely. I was still—en route."

"Are you not still an Inspector, 'en route'?"

"Yes. In truth. But it's not always pleasant to be reminded of duty." She had nothing to say to that.

"You and I didn't discuss the murders. It was not official, that encounter."

"Indeed," she said again. "I shall remember that when we meet again."

There was nothing for it but to touch the brim of his hat in acknowledgment and drive on.

It was a straight run across the built-up embankment that comprised the narrow road to Burwell. He could see trees in the distance, and the church tower reaching above their green tops long before he could pick out the village itself.

Larger than Wriston, and more of a town than a line of cottages strung along a ridge, Burwell was still a village. Trees shaded the streets and filled the churchyard, unlike Wriston, which had perhaps only a dozen trees to its name, and those mostly by the church on the far side of the second green.

He found the church of St. Mary's easily enough, and began to look for the Rectory. But when he knocked at the door, he was told by the middle-aged housekeeper that Rector was in the church. There had been a death to register.

Rutledge went back to St. Mary's. There he found Mr. Hurley just coming out the west door.

Greeting the Rector, Rutledge introduced himself.

"Scotland Yard?" Hurley peered over his glasses. "Is anything amiss? What brings you here?"

"Is there somewhere we could speak privately?"

"Yes, of course, my study." They turned to walk toward the Rectory, and Hurley went on mildly, "You make this sound very mysterious."

"Not intentionally. No. I'm looking into a death. I'm told that you conducted a funeral some time in the summer for a Major Clayton."

"Ah. Yes, I remember that one well. A number of the men who'd served under him came. They spoke highly of him."

"Why did he choose to come back to Cambridgeshire to be buried?"

"He'd wanted to rest next to his parents, even though he hadn't lived in Burwell for some time. When he made the request several weeks before the end, he wrote that his only ties in London were military. His sister lives there, at least for the moment. But she's engaged, and when she marries she'll be living in Norfolk. I expect he thought she might find it easier to visit his grave from time to time if he was laid to rest here." They had reached the Rectory steps. Hurley turned to look up at Rutledge. "Does this have to do with the Major? Is that why you're here?"

"No. Not at all. But there were several guests from London, I believe. Not including the men who'd served under him or who knew his sister. Do you remember a Captain Hutchinson?"

"Yes, indeed, he arrived with Colonel Nelson, who was to speak at the service. And quite a nice eulogy it was, I must say. I gathered he'd known the Major personally."

They went inside, stepping into the dimly lit hall after the bright sunlight outside. Hurley led the way to his study, down a passage from the door, and gestured to the chairs arranged around his desk.

"Please. Hutchinson is the man whose death you're investigating? Yes, I should have realized. A terrible tragedy, that and Herbert Swift's murder. I hope you find whoever is responsible," Hurley continued as he took his own chair behind the desk.

"Do you know if the Captain had visited Burwell before the funeral?"

"I don't believe so. He asked me about the terrible fire we'd had here some years ago. It too was a tragedy, one most of us would rather forget, as it killed a great many people, all of them family members or friends. No one was spared grief. And of course he was curious about the Fens. Most people are. The Colonel was asking when steam had replaced the windmills."

"What was your impression of the Captain?"

"I can't say I formed one. There were half a hundred people here. I managed to speak to most of them, but there wasn't time for more than the niceties and words of sympathy. I was concerned for Miss Clayton. She was in some distress. But I did suggest that the Colonel speak to Mr. Harvey, who loves nothing better than to discuss our windmills." He hesitated. "I will add this. The Captain was a pleasant man, and he had a knack for putting people at their ease. Once or twice I had the oddest impression that it was an—an act. Wrong of me to speak ill of the dead, but I must be frank with the police. I'm sure I was quite wrong in my judgment."

Rutledge understood what Hurley was getting at. That while the pleasantness, the openness were accepted at face value by most people on casual acquaintance, it did not come naturally to Hutchinson.

"He wasna' born with a silver spoon," Hamish said quietly in the back of Rutledge's mind. "He had to make his ain way."

And yet Jason Fallowfield had suggested that Hutchinson's father had left him in comfortable circumstances. Was it that Hutchinson had had to learn early in life that to succeed, he must cultivate his betters? And leave the impression he'd come from money? That would have allowed him to move more freely in some circles.

Hutchinson wouldn't be the first man to learn such a lesson. Not quite ingratiating, not a hanger-on, but making every effort to be likable, accepted. Even when it went against his own nature.

It would be interesting now to hear what Sergeant Gibson had to tell him about Hutchinson's past. Rutledge made a note to find a telephone as soon as possible.

Hurley could add very little more to what he'd already said about Hutchinson. Shrugging, he smiled wryly. "I never dreamed—none of us did—that it would matter months down the road. Or that the man would be dead before the summer was out."

"Still, no one thought to tell Inspector Warren about this visit?"

Surprised, Hurley said, "But nothing happened here. It didn't seem to be important. After all, it was an Ely matter."

The old way of life, of isolation from one village to the next, here in the Fen country, where water had separated everyone and made foreigners of people ten miles distant. Even draining the land had pitted the old villages making their living from the marshy waterways against the new ones springing up to tend the vast fields and keep the land dry.

As if he'd heard what Rutledge was thinking, Hurley said, "My great-grandfather hated the changes to this part of Cambridgeshire. He told his children that nothing good would come of it, that the land would feed a few generations and then be worn out. He was wrong, of course, but there was nothing to show at the time that he wouldn't be proven right."

Rutledge said, "Did you notice any other strangers at the service?"

"One or two. A Miss Bartram spoke to me. Her father and Clayton's father had known each other years ago. It was kind of her, and Miss Clayton remembered Miss Bartram's grandfather as well. He had brought a doctor from Ely when the elder Clayton had appendicitis. Then there were the people up from London, strangers to me, but they all seemed to know each other from the Army or they were friends of Miss Clayton's, here to support her through her ordeal. I don't recall anything that was said or done that would give even a hint of what was to come. More to the point, Captain Hutchinson was here for only a matter of hours. What harm could be done in such a short period of time?"

Rutledge asked the name of the family with whom Miss Clayton had stayed while in Burwell, and he found Mrs. FitzPatrick at home. She agreed to see him—more, he thought, out of curiosity than to impart any information—and the young maid showed him to a sunny room where Mrs. FitzPatrick had been writing letters.

She was a small woman, perhaps thirty-five, with fair hair and brown eyes. Greeting him, she said, "I can't think why Scotland Yard should wish to see my husband or me, but of course we'll be happy to help in any way we can."

"The Rector gave me your name. I'm looking into the funeral service for Major Clayton, and he tells me that Miss Clayton, the dead man's sister, stayed with you while she was here in Burwell?"

Frowning, she said, "Yes, of course, but is anything amiss with the service? I can't think what it could be."

"There was an Army officer who came up from London with Colonel Nelson. A Captain Hutchinson. Do you remember him?"

"Yes, of course," she said again, "he'd served with Major Clayton, he said, and he was very kind to Vera—Miss Clayton—on the journey up from London." Then the frown deepened. "Are you telling me—is this the man who was shot in Ely a fortnight or so ago? I couldn't imagine it was. My husband agreed that Hutchinson wasn't an unusual name. I went to school with a Gracie Hutchinson in Kent."

"I'm afraid it was the same man."

"Oh, dear. I'm quite shocked. But are you investigating that—that murder?"

"I've been sent here by the Yard to look into the Captain's death as well as Mr. Swift's," he said.

"Mr. Swift. We knew *him*, you see. Socially. I was never so shocked as when I heard of *his* death. Who on earth would wish to do him any harm? He was encouraged to stand for the vacant seat, but I don't think he was very enthusiastic about it. Still, he had a sense of history, and he thought perhaps he might do some good. My husband felt that Herbert—Mr. Swift—found himself surrounded by too many memories when he came back to Wriston after the war, and that that had played a part in deciding to stand. He'd never really recovered from the death of his wife."

"Did he have enemies? Either personal or through his work?" When she looked confused, Rutledge added, "Not everyone is happy when a will is read."

"Yes, but you don't blame the solicitor, do you? And he wasn't the sort of man to attract trouble, if you know what I mean. Even his opponent had little to say against him. He was a good man."

"And Captain Hutchinson?"

"He was considerate, charming—very solicitous for Miss Clayton's welfare. It was very hard for her, you know. Her brother had been in hospital since before the end of the war. In December 1918 gangrene set in, and although they took the foot, it moved slowly upward. The stump never healed properly, according to Vera. In the end, they went up to the knee, and then almost to the hip. After that, it was only a matter of time. He couldn't leave hospital, but she visited him nearly every day. I'm very pleased that she's marrying soon. It will be good for her to put the past away."

"Was her fiancé here for the service?"

"No, he's been in Canada. His grandfather died just before Major Clayton. But he's expected back any day now."

"What was your impression of Captain Hutchinson?"

"My husband didn't care for him. He thought the Captain was

paying too much attention to Vera. He was a widower, after all. But of course, without her fiancé, she was alone through this ordeal. Friends were with her, yes, but I think because the Captain had known her brother, it was a comfort to her. The Colonel was an older man, while the Captain was more her brother's age. And of course he didn't stay—he went back to London that evening, which was quite proper."

"Where did he serve with Clayton?"

The frown returned. "To tell you the truth, I was never really clear about that. It was just—accepted. I did hear the Captain say that one felt the need to support the family of a fellow officer. 'I would hope someone would do as much for my sister.' Those were his words. I thought them very respectful."

"Did Miss Clayton indicate how long she'd known the Captain? Did he come often to visit her brother in hospital?"

"That was months ago. I've hardly given the man any thought since then. I did ask Vera if she had met him during her visits to her brother, but apparently he came most often at night, because he was busy during the day with his duties."

Mrs. FitzPatrick approved of the Captain. Her husband hadn't. But he, according to his wife, was presently out in the fields having a look at one of the ditches, and he wasn't expected home before dinner at the earliest.

"Sometimes voles burrow into the earthworks that protect the fields. It's very trying, because they can do so much damage. He took Bob with him—the terrier—in the event that was the problem. But I don't think my husband can add much more. We spent only a matter of hours in the Captain's company, after all."

Rutledge thanked Mrs. FitzPatrick and took his leave. Walking through the town for a time, he listened to Hamish in the back of his mind, but it was the Rector's words that seemed to follow him.

What harm could be done in such a short period of time?

There had been no quarrels, there had been no unsettling remarks that would lead to murder months later, Hutchinson had stepped on no toes, and perhaps more important he hadn't encountered an old friend or an old enemy here in Burwell. He had simply escorted a grieving sister of a fellow officer to her brother's funeral, and then left, his duty done.

Perhaps it was the Colonel whose company Hutchinson had really sought, and escorting Vera Clayton had been a way of putting himself in the presence of the Colonel and made it possible for him to travel back to London on the same train.

Mrs. Sedley had indicated that Hutchinson had been busy cultivating the bride's relatives during the events before the wedding. And yet neither in Ely or here in Burwell had the man put anyone's back up. He seemed to know just how far to go in his push for attention, surely indicating he'd had a great deal of experience over the years.

That brought him back to Hamish's comment.

It was time to speak to Sergeant Gibson, at the Yard.

Rutledge inquired of a passerby if there was a telephone in Burwell that he could use to put in a call to London, but there was no public telephone, and he hesitated to carry on a conversation about Hutchinson or Swift within hearing of interested ears in a private household like the FitzPatricks.

In the end, he walked again to the church and then went inside. He tried to picture the funeral in his imagination, searching for anything that might help him explain Ely and then Wriston. But that led nowhere. As far as Rutledge could judge, it was nothing more than happenstance that Hutchinson had come to Burwell some months before he traveled to Ely.

He drove back to Wriston in the late afternoon, watching the shadows shift across the long lines of green fields. He stopped halfway there, got out of the motorcar, and walked along the road for some distance. It was a strange land, if you were used to the rolling countryside of Somerset or the Downs of Kent. And yet very different from the marshy coast of Norfolk or the long stretches of reeds and tidal rivers along the Essex coast. No one in sight for miles. Just the heat of the sun, the smell of the damp, rich earth, and a sense of isolation that was in its way claustrophobic.

No trees, no grazing horses or cattle, no sheep, no birds hopping along the rows in the fields, not even the distant sound of a dog barking.

Just—emptiness.

Rutledge was nearly to Wriston when he met someone coming the other way. An elderly man on a bicycle, a knife and scissor sharpener, pedaling slowly home after a day of making his rounds.

Chapter 8

Rutledge had nearly reached Wriston when he saw a signpost on a rutted lane that led in an irregular fashion to a farmhouse in the distance. He'd passed it on his way to Burwell but had missed the significance of the small bird painted on the sign.

A swift . . . Swift?

On impulse he turned down the lane, disregarding the warning from Hamish that he would rue his decision. But before very long he had to abandon the motorcar where it was and continue on foot when the lane dwindled to little more than a track. How anything but a horse, he thought, could manage this, he didn't know.

Ahead he could see the farmhouse. Like so many others here, it was built on one of the tiny bits of dry earth rising like islands in the peaty marshes of the Fens. It had been rebuilt at some point, possibly around 1900, Rutledge thought, for now it was two stories, brick and substantial.

This track led not to the door of the house but to the farmyard, where farm equipment and a pony cart, a small carriage and a stable, were fitted into the space like a puzzle, using every inch of high ground. To one side was a small kitchen garden, cut out of the surrounding fields and protected by banks. One of the rows held flowers for cutting—zinnias, marigolds, stalks of what must have been foxglove.

Walking around the house he could hear voices in the kitchen, but he proceeded to the front door, smiling when he saw the newer lane that led up to it. He had come in the back way, probably the original approach.

He knocked, and after a moment a woman in an apron came to ask his business.

"I'm looking for Mr. Swift. Brother to the man who was killed in Wriston."

She stared at him, uncertain what to do.

"I'm from Scotland Yard, I've taken over the inquiry into what happened to Mr. Swift and Captain Hutchinson."

Her frown disappeared in an uncertain smile.

"Do you have anything to prove who you are?"

Rutledge took out his identification, and she looked at it carefully.

"I'm sorry," she said when he had put it back in his pocket. "But we've been worried, you see. We saw you coming down the track, and we didn't know . . ."

He understood her alarm. Nodding, he said, "I didn't know there were two ways into the property. I'm sorry if I disturbed you."

She led him to the sunny kitchen where her husband was standing, clearly listening to what had transpired at the door. Rutledge saw that there was a shotgun leaning against the wall behind him.

"Mr. Swift? I'm from Scotland Yard. My name is Rutledge. As you may have heard, I'm here to look into the death of your brother."

"I'm Swift," the man said, his accent definitely Fen country, his face browned by the sun, and his hands rough from working the land. His hair was rather long and bleached almost to whiteness, it was so fair, and thinning. Rutledge thought he must be older than his wife by several years. But that might also have been put down to the life he led. "I'll trouble you for that identification, if you don't mind."

He studied it as his wife had done, then passed it back to Rutledge.

"Sit down, then," he said, nodding to the chair nearest Rutledge. "The two men who work for me are in the fields today. I didn't see a weapon, but then I don't think my brother did either."

"Were you in Wriston that night?"

"No, I wasn't, thank God. Summer work on the land goes on to dark, and then you're up at four to start again. I don't see Wriston from week to week."

"I understand your brother chose the law and you chose the farm."

"There was some trouble over that in the beginning. He wanted his share of the land to pay for setting up his chambers. But we settled it to suit us, in the end. If you're asking if I still carried a grudge, the answer is no. I expect I've done better than he did. In many ways." He glanced at his wife.

"You work harder for your living than he did."

"If I'd shot him twelve times over, what good was his law to me?"

"Surely you inherit?"

"After burying him, there's the wait for the will to be settled. And then I'll have to find someone to buy the house where he had his chambers. I'll see nothing for a while. Besides, if there was a bad year on the land, I could borrow from him. I always paid it back, and he knew I would. So he helped when I asked. That's finished. And I don't think his death will bring me any new way of finding the money."

"I should think the farm pays well."

"It does. But it's not selling the crops that matters. It's the buying of the seed and sowing and waiting to learn what sort of spring we're to have, then seeing that the crop is watered enough and not too much, looking out for it in the storms and watching for breaks in the banks that guard the ditches. We have ten milk cows on another part of the farm, it came with my wife, and we have a man to take care of them. I make a living, a good one in good years. I also pay the wages of the men who work for me."

Rutledge couldn't decide whether the man was listing his troubles to impress Scotland Yard with his very different life from his brother's or to prove he had no reason to kill him. And Hamish was silent on the subject.

"Did your brother have enemies?"

"I doubt it. He wasn't the sort of man who would make trouble or look for it."

"He was a widower, I understand."

"Yes. He worked in Glasgow for the Admiralty during the war, couldn't stand to be alone in that empty house. He studied charts, checked them for accuracy, that sort of thing. He was a civilian, all the same, and perhaps that's why he came back calmer than he'd been when he left. I think he stayed too busy to think. It was what he needed."

"His wife died in childbirth? With the child?"

"Yes. A fever took her, and the child didn't thrive. I thought he'd run mad with grief. He shut himself up in the house and wouldn't see anyone or talk to anyone. He gave Susan good references and told her he didn't need her anymore. It took Ruth, here, three days to put my brother's house to rights after he'd left for Scotland. You'd have thought it had been lived in by Travelers. We were glad he came to his senses and found a new housekeeper to keep him in good order up there."

"Who is Susan?"

"She works at the Rectory now. A good woman, steady and dependable. Rector says she's a blessing. But she nursed my brother's wife during those last months before the child was born. Eileen should never have got pregnant in the first place, and it was trouble from the start. The doctor told my wife he didn't think it would end well. And it didn't. But they were over the moon with joy about the child, it was what they both wanted. Or thought they did. I wondered sometimes if he regretted it when she died. If he blamed himself."

Rutledge remembered what Jason Fallowfield had told him about Hutchinson's wife, that there had been whispers of suicide when she lost her child. The hazards of childbearing were many, from complications to fevers to stillbirths. That grief Swift and Hutchinson had shared.

"Did your brother often go to London? On behalf of a client, perhaps? Or for a holiday with his wife?"

Swift laughed. "I doubt he'd been farther south than Cambridge, where he read law. He dreamed of Greece and Rome but never strayed far from the Fens until he went to Glasgow."

"So everyone says. But he might have gone farther, without telling you."

"There's that. But I'd not like to take a wager on it."

"There's no reason you can think of for your brother to be killed?"

"None. And it's what keeps me anxious."

"But if he had no connection to the Captain who was killed at Ely, why did his murder follow hard upon the first death? And why should yours follow hard upon your brother's?"

"The only man who can answer that shot them both. If I had to answer to God tomorrow, I can tell you I had nothing to do with it."

"Were you in the war?"

"Six months in 1915. I lost three toes to frostbite and was invalided out."

"Did you bring a rifle back with you as a souvenir?"

He laughed without humor. "I spent two of those months in hospital. How was I to bring home my rifle? They took it from me when I was carried by stretcher to the aid station."

Rutledge believed him. He'd seen the alarm in Mrs. Swift's eyes and the wariness in her husband's when he'd arrived unannounced. Born of fear, not guilt.

"I understand there was a third brother. Anson."

"He left Wriston as soon as my father died and the will was read. There's been no word of him or from him since then. And if it was Anson, why would he shoot that Captain? It would make more sense to come for the two of us."

Rutledge thanked them and left. It was one hell of a struggle to turn the motorcar and retrace his steps to the main road.

So much, he thought, for exploring out here on his own.

W riston was not on the telephone, Rutledge was told when he arrived at the inn and went up to his room to wash his hands. It would be necessary to travel to Ely to find one.

He thanked Miss Bartram and avoided a question about how he'd spent his day.

He wasn't ready to talk about Hutchinson and Burwell, although he knew very well that Priscilla Bartram was eager to hear more. She would have no trouble guessing where he'd gone. He could pass it off lightly, and make no mention of his visit to the Swifts.

And so when he came down later to join her for dinner, he was prepared.

She had roasted a hen, and with it there were potatoes and a dish of stewed apples. Serving him, she asked, "Did you find your way to Burwell, then?"

"Larger than Wriston, isn't it? Interesting church, as well. But a wasted journey, all the same."

Miss Bartram had clearly hoped her information would prove to be more useful.

"Did you speak to the Rector there?"

"I did, and he recalled meeting you. Apparently Vera Clayton, the sister of the dead man, remembered your grandfather."

She smiled, pleased. "Yes, I did tell her of the connection. I wasn't sure she was old enough to have any memories of her own grandfather. He was interested in collecting stories about the old days in the Fens. There's a family that claims descent from Hereward the Wake, who fought the Normans when they tried to bully their way north. Did you know? They called him an outlaw. He interviewed the family to see if they could tell him more about Hereward, if there were family documents or legends or the like. Hereward's something of a hero to Fen people. And there's no proof he was executed or exiled. Perhaps he made his peace with the Normans in the end."

Rutledge encouraged her to tell him more about the elder Clayton, and she was soon confiding in him that the inn had once been the home of one of the Dutch engineers who had drained the land and set up the first windmills.

"The village is named for him. Wriston. Although of course that wasn't his name, it was as close as anyone could come to it."

The conversation moved on to the fishing that was once a popular sport in the Fens, and he wondered if somewhere in this house there might be displays of pike and roach and bream, with whatever else her father or grandfather had caught.

It was still early, and he decided after his dinner to drive back to Ely to find a telephone. He reached the Yard without difficulty but was told that Sergeant Gibson wasn't there. The gruff Inspector who had answered the call added that Gibson was away on official business and there was no certainty when he'd be back.

Rutledge hadn't given his name, he'd simply asked for Gibson. He was glad afterward that he'd been circumspect.

It was late when he reached Wriston. It would have made better sense to stop at The Deacon Inn. But his valise was at The Dutchman, and he knew Miss Bartram would be watching for him, for he had given her the impression he intended to return.

He left the motorcar in front of the inn and decided to stretch his legs. There was no mist tonight—the wind had picked up a little and small clouds were scudding across the sky, promising a change in the fair weather.

Turning in the direction of the mill, away from the village greens, he saw the ghostly shape of a white cat walking toward him down the road.

Kneeling, he called to her by name, and she came trotting to him, wrapping herself around him. But when he tried to lift her, to carry her back to the house, she turned and scampered away.

He followed her, and after a moment or two, he saw Miss Trowbridge, not at her gate or even in her doorway as he'd have expected, but standing in front of the mill, looking up at the arms moving above her head, the creak of their wooden parts almost soothing in its regularity. Like a rocking cradle, he thought, for no reason at all.

Afraid of startling her, he called, "I was out for a walk and encountered Clarissa."

Miss Trowbridge turned quickly, as if he'd interrupted something he shouldn't have seen.

"Mr.—Rutledge." She was pretending to have difficulty recalling his name, but he knew very well she remembered it.

"Looking up at the stars? When I was in France, on clear nights I watched for Orion as we moved toward autumn. He was familiar. Comfortable."

"Yes. The hunter."

He realized that she was referring to him obliquely.

And then she surprised him. "I was just going to put on the kettle. Would you care for a cup of tea before you go back?"

He thought she assumed he was staying in Ely. He answered only, "Yes, I'd like that. If it isn't too late."

She said nothing, just walked to the gate, opened it, and preceded him up the path. The cat was there, a white streak in the darkness, leaping through the door almost before there was room for her to pass.

When he entered the cottage, Clarissa had already claimed her chair, as if to warn him off.

He followed Miss Trowbridge to the kitchen, as he had before, and watched as she put the kettle on.

Hamish, in the back of his mind, was asking why this young woman had invited him into her home at such an hour—it must be going on ten o'clock. But the answer could be that she had no near neighbors to gossip.

Did she also want to know how the inquiry was going?

That suspicion brought with it the question: was it curiosity or was there some other motive?

Not that he suspected her of firing the shots. But was she fearful that she might know who had? Or thought she might know?

She turned, reaching for the cups and saucers in the dresser, carrying them to the table.

"Do sit down," she said, as if his standing there made her nervous. "Or we could carry our cups into the front room."

"I would feel awkward sitting there, carrying on a one-sided conversation with Clarissa," he said lightly, and that brought a smile.

"For heaven's sake, you sat in the kitchen before."

"I did." He pulled out a chair. "I'm staying at Miss Bartram's again. There's not much I can learn in Ely—" He broke off as she almost dropped the bowl of sugar.

Flushing a little, she set it down on the table and disappeared into the pantry for the jug of milk.

"Why is Ely a—a dead end?"

"Too many people, Miss Trowbridge. They witnessed the—er—murder, but they saw nothing useful. Looking in the wrong direction at the moment the shot was fired. Inspector Warren has interviewed most of them, I've interviewed a handful myself, and we've got almost nothing to be going on with. But here in Wriston, someone saw the killer."

"Mrs. Percy," she said flatly, setting the small jug next to the bowl of sugar. "But what did she see?"

He was intrigued. When he'd first met her, the night of the fog, she had avoided any mention of the murder here in Wriston. Now she appeared to want to talk about it.

"That's the question."

"No, I mean, she saw something, a monster. I've heard the gossip. But of course there's no monster running about with a rifle in his hands. What did she really see?"

"I wish I knew."

The kettle came to a boil. She went to it, her back to him again, and began to make the tea. He wondered if Miss Trowbridge had been waiting for him, the kettle filled and ready to set on the heavy black range in her kitchen. But she couldn't have known he would walk that way.

Was it someone else she'd expected? He remembered the man in the mist. Where had he been going? Or coming from?

"It makes no sense anyway," Miss Trowbridge was saying as she brought the teapot to the table. "Killing Mr. Swift, much less that man in Ely."

"Did you know Swift?"

"Everyone *knew* him. He was the solicitor. But I don't suppose anyone really knew him well. He'd been away, for one thing, and he wasn't a gregarious sort. I think he had grown used to his own company and his books."

"Did he handle your grandmother's will? Leaving you this cottage?"

"No, that was a man in Bury. She lived here in the cottage, of course, but she was a very private woman and she felt that her business was her business."

"What do you think was in that dormer window?" he asked.

It caught her off guard. They had left that question behind.

"I don't know. Someone who wished for a better view of the speech? Everyone leaves his door unlocked—or did. Someone could have gone up to that dormer window and looked out."

"Were you there, that evening?"

She took a sip of her tea after stirring in the sugar. "No. I really had no interest in the by-election or hearing Mr. Swift speak."

"But you'd have voted?"

"Yes, of course, one does."

"Then you'd already decided which candidate you supported?"

"I'd already decided which man would represent us best in London."

A very different way of putting it.

"If the shot didn't come from that dormer window, where was the killer?"

"I know nothing about firearms. I expect Constable McBride and the other men present that evening would have a better idea about the direction." She was toying with her teaspoon. "But does direction really matter? Wherever he fired from, Mr. Swift's murderer got away."

"The problem is, we have so little to go on. Anything Mrs. Percy tells us could be useful in tracking him down."

Miss Trowbridge rose, collecting their cups. "I'm afraid I'm no use at all."

"It depends. On whether anyone passed your door directly after the shot was fired. It isn't that far from this house to the market cross. You'd have heard the report, surely, and wondered what it was. You know a few people still come here in autumn and winter to hunt. But this isn't the season for shooting. Did you go to your door and listen to see what was happening? Or stay here, the door shut tight, because you were afraid to know?"

Color flared in her face. "What are you accusing me of? I will tell you straight out that I had no reason to want anyone dead."

"But you did hear the shot?" Rutledge persisted. "I can't believe you didn't."

She was standing there with their cups and saucers in her hands. "Yes, all right, I heard the shot. Clarissa was in and safe. I didn't want to go rushing out to see what it was."

"Still, you heard someone pass your door. Who was it?" His voice was cold now.

"I was here in the kitchen, putting away the dishes from my dinner. You can't hear someone passing, unless he's on horseback or in a motorcar. And not always then." She crossed to the sink to set down the cups. "I think you should go now. I shouldn't have suggested tea in the first place. But you were a stranger here, and I know what loneliness is."

Turning her back to him, she stared out the windows that overlooked her small back garden.

And so he left, walking briskly to the door and closing it behind him.

Chapter 9

When Rutledge reached Miss Bartram's house, she was waiting for him, calling his name as he came through the door.

"Mr. Rutledge? I thought perhaps you'd like a cup of tea after your long drive from Ely. Or perhaps a small whisky. We always kept a little here for the hunters, coming in cold and wet of an evening."

"Thank you, Miss Bartram, but I have a long day tomorrow and I think I'll go directly up."

"Yes, of course," she said, disappointment in her voice. And then, as if she couldn't stop the words, she said, "I noticed half an hour ago that your motorcar had returned." Unspoken was the follow-up: *Where have you been?*

"I was tired, and I thought if I walked for a bit, I'd be ready to sleep."

"Oh. Then I'll bid you good night. Breakfast at seven-thirty?"

"Yes, thank you very much." With a smile, he turned and went up the stairs.

The next morning he paid an early visit to the police station and found Constable McBride just opening the door.

"You're still here, Mr. Rutledge," he said as Rutledge walked up.

"I've a question about the night that Swift was killed. You've told me that most of the village was present. What about those who weren't, someone living on the outskirts of Wriston. Did anyone there notice someone leaving the village while most people were rushing to see what could be done for Mr. Swift? Did they hear a motorcar passing, or a horse?"

"No one saw or heard anything unusual. Or if they did, they aren't speaking up."

"But surely the sound of the shot reached every house in Wriston. Did no one hurry to a window or a door to see what the matter was?"

"The only way the killer could have gone was toward the mill. He'd have been seen if he'd chosen to go past the church instead. It's too open. We did question everyone in Wriston. Those present for the speech, and those who stayed at home."

"Even the person who lives out by the mill? The cottage with the gate?"

"Miss Trowbridge? She couldn't help us. No one came that way as far as she could tell."

"The killer couldn't have vanished. Or had he disappeared across those fields?" Rutledge asked impatiently.

"If he knew what he was doing, he could follow the narrow path along the top of the hummock that separates the edge of Wriston from the fields."

Rutledge had seen such a mound at the end of the lane beyond Mrs. Percy's house.

"You're saying that a stranger couldn't depend on the path taking him to safety."

"I should think if he came here to shoot Mr. Swift, he would have reconnoitered an escape route. He must have done, to decide he could use that dormer."

"And yet no one saw a stranger walking about, looking out for such places."

"He could have done six months ago. No one would remember him now."

Or he could have come at night, Hamish suggested. When he could be sure he wasn't seen . . .

"What about Anson Swift? He wouldn't need to explore. He knew Wriston well enough."

"How did you hear about Anson?"

"The question is, what became of him?"

"He left here and never came back, to my knowledge. I did hear a rumor that he went to Australia. I expect it was just that. A rumor. And if it was Anson, why would he kill the Captain in Ely? Just to frighten his brothers?"

Rutledge could sense how defensive McBride was. The man had done everything he could—everything he could think of doing, and here the stranger from London was questioning him as if he had somehow failed in his duty.

"I was hoping we'd missed something, that's all." Rutledge smiled. "This killer manages to appear and disappear like a magician. I thought perhaps he'd disguised himself as a priest in Ely, where he wouldn't be noticed coming in and out of the Cathedral grounds. The question is, what disguise would work here?"

"That seems to point to someone local," McBride said, not at all mollified.

"It could. But more likely it's someone whose presence wouldn't draw comment. Take myself, for instance. Scotland Yard, every right to be here asking questions. No one would take issue if I went into the church or called on the constable or sat by the duck pond to eat my lunch."

"We've had no weddings this past six months. Only one funeral. Three christenings. Are you saying that someone came here to look around Wriston and find out what he needed, all the while pretending to be a mourner at the funeral or one of the family at the christening?"

"I know, it's far-fetched. On the other hand, if I were a quarter of an hour early for something like a christening, I could wander freely around Wriston, passing the time, and no one would look at me twice—or remember me after I'd gone."

"Six months ago no one knew Mr. Swift would be standing for Parliament or for that matter, that Captain Hutchinson would be attending a wedding in Ely."

McBride was taking his suggestion literally. Rutledge let it go for the moment.

"Well, it was worth pursuing. Anything might trigger a memory that could help us."

McBride nodded. "I haven't had to deal with murder these past five years. And then it was straightforward. A drunken brawl that ended in a killing. I don't like the feeling that we're vulnerable. I don't like to think of someone planning murder on my patch and then getting away with it."

"No, I'm sure you don't. Inspector Warren feels the same."

"I'd say the connection starts in London, not here. Only Mr. Swift hadn't been to London. He hadn't been elected."

"If it wasn't London, it was somewhere else. The problem now is to find out just where the paths of these two men crossed that of their murderer."

Rutledge left the police station and walked toward the church, Hamish busy in his mind. It was the frustration of dead ends, he knew that, but Rutledge felt the past creeping into the present, and he knew that the safest thing to do was find a place where he could let it happen, out of the public eye.

The inn wouldn't do. Not with Miss Bartram hovering . . .

Reaching the churchyard, he scanned the tombs, the trees, anything that would offer shelter, privacy. There was nothing, only the tombstones and one mausoleum with an iron gate in front of the iron door. He could just make out the name carved over the gate, but it would not help him now.

Pressed for time, he opened the church door and stepped into the dimness, cool and quiet. Above his head was a wooden ceiling similar to many in this part of England, beautifully carved, dark wood, barrel-vaulted.

He quickly searched the small church, but it was empty. Sitting down on the stone steps of the pulpit, worn smooth by centuries of feet climbing up them to deliver homilies and eulogies and sermons, he pressed against the stone so that it was a bar across his back. It was the nearest he could come to hiding himself.

He waited.

Just as the darkness came down, he looked up and saw the face.

The Green Man. The carving that Miss Trowbridge had watched on Sundays, a child sitting through the long service. It was the decorative knob where the ribs of the ceiling crossed each other.

It was still there some twenty minutes later as the darkness and the sounds of battle slowly receded. He was trembling, his mouth dry, his heart beating rapidly.

He concentrated on the carving until his heart rate and his breathing steadied. The guns faded, the shouts and screams, the firing that had seemed to reach a crescendo in his head.

And then it was over. He took a deep breath and, badly shaken, buried his face in his hands.

This had been one of the worst daylight relapses into darkness that he could remember in some time.

Getting to his feet at last, he was about to turn and walk back up the center aisle when a voice said, "My son, are you all right?"

Rutledge froze. He'd been alone, he was sure of it. Where had this man come from? And what—*in God's name, what had he heard?*

Realizing in that same instant that he must be facing the Rector of the little church, he said, fighting to keep his voice steady, "I'm all right. A—a touch of sun."

The elderly man came toward him. "Does it happen often, this return to the war? For surely that must be what it was."

The man couldn't have heard the guns or the screams or the shouted orders . . .

But he was saying, "I've seen it before, you see. And you needn't worry, I have no intention of giving you away. You're the man from London, aren't you? The Inspector from Scotland Yard. My name is March. Andrew March."

Rutledge didn't give his own name. Instead he replied, "I'm all right."

"You are now. Yes. Come with me, we'll find a place to sit."

He led the way to the nearest pews, not looking over his shoulder to see if Rutledge was following. Sitting down, he patted the wooden bench, as if inviting a child to sit with him. Rutledge leaned against the nearest pillar, watching him.

"Have you lost your faith? Is that it? Or is it just the unbearable past that haunts you?"

"A little of both, I think," Rutledge answered against his better judgment. Part of him was urging flight, getting out of this church as quickly as he could, his secret intact. Another part of him wanted the peace of confessing. And that was denied him. He moved inadvertently, still rattled by what he'd just been through.

The Rector nodded, misinterpreting it as a need to go. "Yes, it happens. Well, they say that time is the healer. But it isn't, always. If you want to come to the Rectory and talk, you can generally find me there."

And he turned and walked toward the altar, leaving the way clear for Rutledge to reach the west door unhindered.

* * *

He walked out into the sunlight, blinking a little, and then went to where he'd left the motorcar.

For the rest of the morning he drove through the Fen country, stopping in each village and walking, as he had done in Burwell, learning the landscape.

Soham, with its larger mill and handsomer church and quiet streets. Tiny Isleham with its beautiful church set apart in its churchyard like a grande dame presiding over her charges. And then back to Wriston, and dead ends.

The journey hadn't done much to sweep away any lingering cobwebs, but he was hungry now. He found a small shop that served sandwiches and ordered the first item on the pretty hand-printed menu.

The middle-aged woman who served him said as she brought his meal, "You're the man from London. Scotland Yard."

"That's right. Were you standing by the market cross when Mr. Swift was shot?"

"I was. I shut my eyes almost at once. It was the most horrible thing I'd ever seen. One minute he was speaking and the next his head had just—fallen open." She shivered at the memory. "I couldn't sleep that night, or the next either."

"And so you didn't see anything—who was shooting or from where."

"No, I didn't even know what had happened at first. I didn't recognize the sound of the shot because it was so sudden, just everywhere all at once. Deafening. Echoing."

Shaking her head, she added, "He was dead. Just like that. People were screaming."

"Do you think anyone else besides Mrs. Percy saw the man with the rifle?"

"No," she said quickly. "No, I'm sure they hadn't."

But it was too fast, almost as if she wished to shut off speculation or questions. Confirming his suspicions, she turned to move away to greet an older woman who had just come into the tea shop.

Rutledge touched her arm, stopping her.

"There wasn't a monster," he told her. "The flickering torchlight, the movement of the smoke, and the sudden shock produced him. Even the most ordinary person looks different in such circumstances. Remember that."

She stared at him for a moment, then almost tripped over a chair at the next table in her haste to go.

Hamish said, "It will be all o'er the village by sunset."

Yes, Rutledge silently answered him. That was the point.

When he'd finished and paid his bill, a younger woman came to the counter to help him. The middle-aged woman was studiously wiping down a table by the window.

It was time to call on the ironmonger. He should have done it earlier, but when the darkness came down, he had had to accommodate it.

Walking through the shop door, Rutledge was met with that familiar, slightly metallic scent that seemed to be a part of such places.

The shop was empty, except for a portly man with black hair liberally streaked with gray and the shadow of a heavy beard. When he looked up and saw that it was Rutledge, he came hurrying toward him.

"Mr. Rutledge, is it?" he asked, a slight echo of Wales in his voice. "My name is Ross. Martin Ross."

"I'd like to have a look at your dormer window, if you have the time to take me upstairs."

"I'd thought you might come to speak to me first thing—Constable McBride told me you were in Wriston."

"I came as soon as I could. I understand that you weren't at home that night, that you'd gone out to hear Mr. Swift speak."

"Yes, yes, my wife and I and our grown son. The shop was closed, but the house was open. I mean to say, we hadn't thought to lock the doors, back or front. I feel responsible, somehow."

"You couldn't have foreseen that someone would use your house in such a way. He could easily have broken in."

"That's true enough. But people seem to be avoiding the shop. It's worrying. Both Constable McBride and the Inspector from Ely, Warren his name is, both of them went through the house inch by inch. There was nothing. No spent cartridge casing, not even a mark on the sill of the window. He hadn't tracked in mud or stopped to help himself to the biscuits in a box on the kitchen table. And yet he was *here*. At *my* window. Where else could that shot have come from, I ask you?" His words spilled over each other with barely suppressed anxiety, a man caught in a situation he didn't know how to cope with.

"He left no traces of himself in Ely," Rutledge reminded him. "I wouldn't have expected him to betray himself here." He said nothing about the gray thread still folded into his handkerchief.

"Yes, but don't you see? He was *outside* in Ely. Everyone says so. He was in *my* house. My wife hasn't been able to sleep, knowing he was here. And when people come into the shop, they look around uneasily, as if he's hiding amongst the hammers or under the table where the nails are set out. Someone dropped a spanner the other morning, and I saw two people start, as if they thought it was a gunshot."

"The man who came into your house cared nothing for you, Mr. Ross. He chose your window because it was convenient. He won't be returning."

"Still, I have the strongest feeling my neighbors blame me." He led the way down a passage that opened into a small room. The rear door stood open, and beyond it was an empty space where there must have been outbuildings at one time.

Noticing his glance, Ross said, "We had a shed and a small barn— for the horse, of course. They blew down in a windstorm the third year of the war, and I never replaced them. Well, the Army took our horse, of course, and never brought him back."

There were only two houses on the lane that ran behind the shop, and beyond them was the embankment that bordered the fields. Just as he'd seen it at Mrs. Percy's cottage. He leaned out for a better look. It went as far, he thought, as the raised bridge where he'd stopped his motorcar the night of the fog.

That was how the killer had come, then. Unseen, because everyone was drawn to the torch-lit parade down the street.

He turned and followed Ross up two flights of stairs to the second-floor room where the dormer let in light and warmth. What had once been a small bedroom for servants or a nursery was now given over to a collection of boxes and barrels, a few outworn chairs, a woman's dress model, and other oddments accumulated over the years.

He threaded his way through to the window. The sash was raised, a warm breeze drifting in.

"Do you leave this window open?"

"Yes, in the heat of the day. Someone generally comes to close it each evening. It allows a little circulation of the air, you see. It was warm that night, there was no expectation of rain, and I was in a hurry to shut up the shop before the crowd moved down the street. I didn't think it mattered. I could easily have come up the stairs and shut it. But it seemed unimportant. Still, he could have opened it, couldn't he? It wouldn't have mattered if the window had been shut."

So that, Rutledge thought, was the source of the man's anxiety, that he'd made it easy for a killer to do his work. One small oversight . . .

And yet—if the killer had had to open the window, he might have been seen by someone as he rose to raise the sash. Mrs. Percy might have seen more than a monstrous face.

"You didn't look this way when you heard the shot?"

"I don't know that I've ever heard a rifle being fired before this. The report seemed to come from everywhere at once. I don't think I even registered the fact that it was a shot, I was too shocked by what I was seeing. And then people were pushing back, away from where the body had fallen, and there was general panic. Only afterward, when Constable McBride was looking for a source of the shot, did we consider my window. It was the butcher who was first to Mr. Swift's body. I closed my eyes, feeling a little sick, trying not to think about what had happened."

Rutledge looked down, saw the market cross clearly. "Swift was standing on the base of the cross?" He made a point of leaning out the window.

"Yes, it raised him above the crowd just enough that we could see and hear him. I'd have said the ideal place for a speech. That's why we all saw him die."

And panic had taken over, giving the killer a chance to escape.

Rutledge noted the sill, but Warren's reports had already confirmed that there was no mark where the rifle had rested, and not enough dust for a footprint to be found.

"Thank you, Mr. Ross, you've been very helpful. I wish I could say that there was something here to help us catch our man, but he's been very clever."

Ross was nodding, drinking in every word. "Yes, yes, that's true. I'll tell everyone who comes in. Thank you."

They went down the stairs again, and as they turned at the first-floor landing, Ross said, "I wonder if you know. There was an ex-soldier passing through here not three weeks ago, looking for work. He'd been a cobbler, he wanted to set up by the market cross, but Constable McBride wasn't having it. He said that we'd soon have every mendicant in Cambridgeshire wanting to do the same. But Rector took pity on him and let him set up by the church. I don't know how many shoes he mended, but he was gone the next morning. I was told the butcher's lorry gave him a lift to Ely."

It was clear to Rutledge that Ross had been racking his brain for any memory that might divert attention from his shortcomings and the now-notorious dormer window. Still, it would have to be pursued.

Thanking him, Rutledge went directly to the police station to speak to Constable McBride.

"For one thing," McBride told him, "this ex-soldier came through nearly six weeks ago. Not three, as Mr. Ross led you to believe." He sorted through a handful of papers from the side drawer of his desk and passed a sheet to Rutledge. "For another I spoke to him myself. His name is Peter Jenkins, he comes from Warwick, and he was a corporal in the Buffs. He'd been a cobbler in Warwick before the war and until the shop closed last spring—the owner had died and the widow couldn't carry on. Nor did Jenkins have the money to buy the shop from her. He had no choice but to take to the roads. But we can't have every Tom, Dick, and Harry setting up at the market cross on days when there's no market. And so I told him. When he'd moved on, I sent a query to Warwick, and his story was confirmed by a Constable Godwin."

"Well done," Rutledge told him, glancing through the information on the sheet.

"I can't think he'd give me his right name if he was here bent on mischief. But we've had no trouble in this village, and the next peddler might be a Traveler, out for what he can find. Still, when the Rector took pity on him, I let it go."

"There's no one else who came through?"

"No, it's been a quiet summer. And we're a little out of the way, you see, not on a direct road anywhere. Did you have a look out that window while you were calling on the ironmonger?"

"I did. You couldn't ask for a better position for a shot."

"No," the constable said morosely. "It's too bad Swift didn't find another site for his speech. He might still be with us."

"I wonder," Rutledge said, "if the killer came late at night, when the village was asleep. He could have stayed in the shadows, learned whatever it was he wanted to know, and then gone away again without arousing suspicion."

"How did he know what Swift was planning?"

"That shouldn't have been too difficult. Surely it was no secret, that rally."

"True enough," McBride said.

"I'd like a list of every man in the village who served in France during the war. And if you will, send a request to your opposite numbers in the surrounding villages asking them to draw up one as well and send it to me here in Wriston."

"Here, you're saying that one of *ours* is this killer."

"No. But once we know the names of men who can handle a rifle, then we can find out if any of them knew Hutchinson."

Rutledge was just about to take his leave when someone came galloping down the High Street on a lathered horse. He was a tall man, lean and weathered.

"There's been another shooting," he called as soon as Constable McBride and Rutledge appeared in the police station doorway.

"Where?" the two men replied almost in unison.

"Over by the Burrows farm. It's all right, Mr. Burrows wasn't badly hurt. But he like to had a heart attack afterward. It was that close run a thing."

Rutledge was already sprinting for his motorcar, McBride at his heels.

"Where is the farm?" he asked the constable.

"It's over toward Burwell. You'll see a line of trees going into the farm. Not a large place, there's not enough land for more than a house and a few outbuildings. He keeps some of his larger pieces of equipment in Burwell."

Rutledge reversed the motorcar and headed for the Wriston windmill, letting McBride show him the way from there.

They came to a long straight road—not the one Rutledge had taken on his way to Burwell, but half a mile distant. As they turned into it, he could see the line of trees that McBride had described. When they reached the track, he realized that the farm must have been there for a very long time. The track was rutted and uneven, and the house was low, rambling, as if it had been designed to fit into the flat profile of the land around it, then added to as necessity or money dictated.

But the steps to the door were swept, there was a fresh coat of paint on the outbuildings, and a small bed of marigolds where the path widened added a dash of color.

Someone had heard the motorcar arrive, and a tall, thin woman held the door open for them.

"Do come in," she said in a voice thick with unshed tears. "My father is in the front room."

They followed her through to where an older man was sitting in a chair, hands on the arms, his face flushed. There was a red streak across one cheek, and someone had tried to wash away the worst of the blood. It still stained his shirt and coat.

Looking up, he nodded to McBride and said to Rutledge, "And who might you be?"

"My name is Rutledge. I've been sent by Scotland Yard to look into these shootings."

"Well, it wasn't soon enough," Burrows said, glaring up at him. "It's a wonder I'm alive. I can't think how he came to miss." He added, "Do sit down, it hurts to twist around like this."

"I think you should start at the beginning, Papa," the woman said as Rutledge took the chair offered and McBride went to stand by the window.

"I was on my way home, on horseback. I'd gone into Burwell after a part for the pump in my kitchen. The road was empty. I'd swear to that. Nothing to be seen anywhere, midday and quiet. And then a face appeared over the edge of the bridge across the ditch. He'd been hiding there like—like some sort of water creature. I'd hardly taken it in when something stung my face and the report of the rifle frightened the hell out of my horse. It took off at a great pace, and by the time I'd got it under control again, I wasn't about to go back the way I'd come. And so I took a roundabout way home, my face bleeding all over my coat. I couldn't stop it."

He put up a hand, touched the crease gingerly. "It's still wet," he finished.

"Leave it alone, Papa, you'll only make it worse," Miss Burrows told him.

"Don't fuss, Meg," he warned her sharply.

"Describe what you saw," Rutledge asked after a moment.

"I told you, it was like something out of a tale, this wormlike thing with a face you didn't want to look into twice. Cold and hard. Eyes that had nothing human about them. He must have kept the weapon under him until he was ready to fire. I tell you, I should be out there on the road, dead, a bullet through my skull. All I can think of is that he couldn't bring the rifle up properly, lying on it like that. There's no sense to it, else."

"But why should he wish to kill you?" Constable McBride demanded. "Did you know Mr. Swift, or that Captain in Ely?"

"Of course I knew Swift. Everybody did," Burrows answered testily. "As for that Captain, I doubt I've ever clapped eyes on him. I was too old for the war. And I've never been any farther south than Cambridge. Rumor has it he was a London man."

"He was," Rutledge replied. "But he was in Burwell recently. For the funeral of a Major Clayton."

Burrows started to shake his head and stopped abruptly. "I knew a Clayton years ago. He bred horses. He died in '05 or '06, I think it was."

"Inspector Warren never told me that Hutchinson was in Burwell," McBride cut in to ask. "When exactly was this?"

"Earlier in the summer," Rutledge answered. He'd been watching

Burrows's face, and he thought it likely that the man was telling the truth. He didn't know Major Clayton or Hutchinson. "Tell me, Mr. Burrows, do you own any weapons?"

"I've a shotgun. I expect everyone in the Fens must have one. But this wasn't a shotgun, I tell you, else he'd have taken my head off, not cut my face."

"Yes, I understand. But Constable McBride here has been making a list of men who'd served in France. It's possible that someone who worked for you was a soldier and brought back a souvenir."

"Two of my men died in France. The other came home without his arm. The only souvenir he brought back was one of those helmets the Hun wore. With the spike on top. Bloody silly thing to wear in the trenches, if you ask me."

But these were parade helmets. In the trenches they were covered, the spike removed.

Rutledge was suddenly reminded of what Ruskin had told him, that he'd seen a German helmet.

"Where is this helmet now?"

"His wife made him get rid of it."

"Could that be what the man was wearing?"

Burrows glared at him. "I know the difference between a helmet like that and the face I saw."

"It would be best if you went to a doctor. I'll drive you there, if you like," Rutledge suggested, watching a thin beading of blood reappear along the line of the cut every time Burrows impatiently dabbed at it.

"Meg is better than a doctor when it comes to taking care of me. What I want to know is when are you going to bring in this fool? Before someone else is killed. And the next question is, will he come looking for me and mine, now he's missed his chance? I don't relish walking around with eyes in the back of my head or looking over my shoulder. And there's Meg here. What if in the dark she's mistaken for me?"

"To tell you the truth, I don't know if you're still in danger—or if he's satisfied that he marked you. But I'd stay close to the house for a day or two."

"I can't stay close to the house. I've a farm to run, and I'm short two men as it is. Three if I had my way. Who is going to see to things if I don't?"

"A few days, Papa," Miss Burrows interjected. "It's not time for the harvest. Surely you could spare a few days?"

"I won't be kept prisoner in my own home. By God, I won't."

But it was half bluster, Rutledge thought. Burrows had been thoroughly frightened, and there was no mistaking the stiffness in his body as he sat in the chair. Or his uncertainty about the future. Having looked Death in the eye, so to speak, he was not likely to do something foolish.

And then Burrows said, "I'll keep the shotgun to hand, and if he comes nosing around this house, I'll shoot first and ask later."

"Just be sure," Rutledge warned, "that you're firing at the right man. You don't want to make any mistakes. Or you'll be up for murder yourself." He rose. "I need to report what happened to Inspector Warren in Ely. Will you describe that man again?"

"I never really saw him. Just that wormlike body and a face as cold as death. As if he could look down at my corpse without feeling anything except—satisfaction."

Miss Burrows turned away, biting her lip to hold back tears.

"Which of your enemies will feel satisfaction at your death?" Rutledge asked.

"Good God, I don't know any who would shoot me down in the road. There's competition in this business. A better yield, finding a stronger seed. That sort of thing, but not murder. I'd done nothing a man might want to kill me for."

When they had left and Rutledge was driving with care through the ruts and holes of the road leading up to the farmhouse, McBride said, "What do you make of Burrows, then?"

"He couldn't have shot himself. And I don't think the daughter could have shot him. Besides, she was frightened for him."

"He knew Swift."

"Yes," Rutledge said slowly, trying to ignore Hamish in the back of his mind. "But so did everyone in Wriston. Still, it's worth keeping in mind. Show me where this ambush happened."

McBride gave him directions, so that they came up on the bridge just as Burrows had done. Rutledge stopped the motorcar well short of the spot and got out. He could see droppings on the road some fifty yards back. Testing the light wind, he realized that it was blowing toward the bridge, which meant that the horse probably hadn't caught the scent of the man who was waiting. Farther along, the turf on the right side of the road was torn, where the horse was startled, and started dancing, fighting the bit, before taking off in fright.

Rutledge stood there, looking down toward the bridge.

It was a clear shot, the man's head well above his mount's, and the distance was good, the wind hardly a factor, the pace steady as the horse trotted home.

He asked McBride to stand in his place while he walked down and over the hump of the bridge.

The late season grass was matted where someone had been lying there waiting. In some places it was already beginning to spring back. He couldn't judge the height or the shape of whoever had lain there. But there was enough evidence to verify what Burrows had claimed.

Rutledge scanned the area, looking for anything the killer had left behind—a cigarette stub, a cartridge casing, anything that would be useful. But the man had left no trace other than the bent blades in a patch of grass.

He stretched out full length, to see what the killer had seen.

From this position, it would have been easy to watch Burrows coming from at least a mile away, even if the sound of hooves hadn't alerted the killer to his approach. And yet the height of the old bridge concealed the waiting man until he had lifted himself long enough to aim and fire.

Rutledge rose slightly, raising an imaginary rifle, then bringing it to bear on McBride.

It was an easy shot. Easier than peering over the edge of the parapet at Ely Cathedral, easier than shooting at Swift through the wavering torchlight and wafting smoke. Why then had the killer missed?

Hamish said, "The horse. As soon as he moved, yon horse would see him."

It was very likely. Even a slight shift by the horse could have made the difference between life and death. The other two victims had either been standing or walking slowly.

And that was a miscalculation on the part of the killer, if he'd known nothing about horses.

The question now was, had Burrows been the target? If so, how had the killer tracked him to this particular place? Had he seen him in Burwell earlier?

Or had the man with the rifle missed at the last minute when he realized that Burrows was not the rider he was expecting?

Finally, would any target have done? Was this a third attempt to murder? Or just a tactic to muddle the issue?

Rutledge got to his feet and walked back to McBride, who jogged forward in his turn to have a look at the far side of the bridge.

Driving on to Wriston, Rutledge said, "I'm intrigued with Burrows's description of what he'd seen. I want to go back and speak to Mrs. Percy. And then I'll continue on to Ely. Get me that list of men who were in France. I'll need that when I get back."

But Mrs. Percy wasn't moved by Burrows's close call or his description of the killer.

"I never saw anything," she told Rutledge a second time. "When

I gave my statement to Constable McBride, I'd been blinded by the torches and all that smoke. And there's an end to it."

"It isn't the end. You signed your statement. By doing so, you were swearing to the truth of it. Is the memory of what was in that window too frightening to think about now?"

"How can I be afraid of something I didn't see?" she countered.

"If you won't describe it, will you try to draw it?" Rutledge took out his notebook and held it out to her. "I'd like to show it to Mr. Burrows."

But she refused to take it, and finally he withdrew the notebook.

"I didn't see anything to draw. There was only a man with a rifle in his hands."

He didn't think she'd seen a rifle. He wasn't sure she would even have recognized the difference between it and a shotgun. Not in the few seconds she'd had to take in what she was looking at. According to McBride, there had been no mention of a weapon in her original statement.

But she'd been questioned. Not only by the police but just as surely by her neighbors, curious about her monster.

And in the end, she had recanted. *A man with a rifle in his hands.*

What was acceptable to the world. What would never again make her a laughingstock.

"A pity. We might have confirmed what you'd seen, on the basis of what Mr. Burrows has reported. It would have vindicated you."

Something flickered in her eyes. "That's as may be. It was daylight when *he* saw what he saw. There's a difference."

He thanked her and left. He was just bending down to the crank when he noticed that in the house next to hers a curtain twitched.

Mrs. Percy's neighbor would be over as soon as he had turned out of the lane, out of sight, to find out what the police had wanted. And the news of Burrows's wounding would spread like wildfire.

It couldn't be helped. He'd had no choice but to tell Mrs. Percy she wasn't alone in seeing something incomprehensible, hoping that the fact that the killer had struck again would encourage her to talk to him. Putting together her evidence with Ruskin's and Burrows's, he might just have something more definitive than *monster*.

Rutledge stopped to tell McBride that he'd got nowhere and would be driving on to Ely.

McBride shook his head. "Stubborn woman. But the main question now has to be where does this man go when he's not using that rifle? Cambridge? Peterborough? King's Lynn? Even Inspector Warren doesn't have enough men to look everywhere."

"Nor can we take a chance that there's another target out there who might not be as lucky as Burrows."

"Do you think he'll try to come back for Mr. Burrows? Just wounding him might not be enough."

"God knows. But I think Burrows will stay close to his house for a while. Which is probably his best protection just now."

"But not in the long haul."

Rutledge took a deep breath. "True. He could bide his time, whoever he is, and try when we've given up. Or brought him in."

"A soldier. A solicitor. A farmer. It makes no sense."

When Rutledge reached Ely and reported to Inspector Warren, he heard the same comment. *It makes no sense.*

"If he's satisfied," Rutledge pointed out, "he can disappear as easily as he appeared. If he isn't, Burrows won't be his last target. We don't have time to worry about motive or connections. We've got to find him."

"Will he come back for Burrows, do you think?" It was the same question that McBride had asked, but this time it was from a different perspective. "Do you think we could use that possibility to trap him?"

"God knows. It depends on why he shot at him. How deep his feelings went. What worries me is that he missed. It was a clear shot, an easy shot. Was it the shifting of the horse? Or was he having qualms of conscience?"

"My money is on the horse. He's shown no signs of a conscience so far, interrupting that wedding and then killing Swift in front of women and children."

"I've asked McBride to send out word that I'd like a list of all the ex-soldiers in each village. Can you draw up one for Ely?"

"It will take time, we'll have to go door to door. It's the only way to be sure we have all the names. Do you think it's one of them?"

"If they didn't do the shooting, they could have brought back a rifle as a souvenir for themselves or someone else. Or know who did. Meanwhile, I've spoken to Swift's brother. He seems to think he's a likely target as well. I must say, isolated as the farm is, he could easily be picked off from a distance. The question is, how to protect a population as scattered as it is here in the Fen country. You can't watch them all. On another matter: What do you know about Hutchinson's sister? Did you inform her of her brother's death, or did Fallowfield?"

"Fallowfield asked if he could tell her. I thought it best. He also identified the body and saw to it that the remains were taken to London as soon as they were released, accompanied by a man of the cloth, someone related to the new Mrs. Fallowfield. He felt responsible. After all the man had come to Ely for his wedding."

"Burrows swears he had no connection with the other two men. That could mean that whatever links them is in the mind of the killer. Not something we can easily track down." Hamish was saying something. Hearing him, Rutledge asked, "Do you have ghosts, phantoms, or other specters in the Fens here?"

Surprised by the question, Warren laughed. "Do you think our killer is a phantom?"

"No. But if he can appear and disappear at will, perhaps he keeps himself out of sight in some place people are afraid—or unlikely—to go."

"We have a great hound—Black Shuck—who is a sign that something is about to happen. A harbinger, so to speak. I don't know anyone who has seen him in the last few years, but I was told that he was spotted near Isleham the day before we declared war on Germany. It was never confirmed. Excitement was running high then, and people were ready to believe in any omen."

"Is this Black Shuck like Conan Doyle's Hound of the Baskervilles?"

"Oh, yes, the story. Our black dog hasn't been known to harm anyone. On the contrary, he's a warning. Then there's the black mill at Wriston. People have always thought it was haunted. A man was killed there a century or more ago, hung up on one of the arms. An accident most likely—no one was ever taken up for the crime. Several of the old mills have stories attached to them. And one of the old lagoons had a legend about something that lived in the water. That's gone, along with the lagoon. Not much help, I'm afraid."

It wasn't.

Rutledge went back to the telephone he'd used before—in the passage to Reception at a hotel—and this time he found Sergeant Gibson at the Yard.

"There's not much to tell," Gibson said. "I spoke to the Captain's sister. She was upset, said no one could possibly hate her brother, and told me that it must have been a madman that shot him."

"What's their background?"

"Hutchinson and his sister were orphaned young and shifted from relative to relative until he went to Sandhurst. He was a young Lieutenant when he met and married a woman who had money of her own and a house in London, where they went to live. There was some story she'd been engaged to another man, but I couldn't confirm that. Hutchinson had his first taste of war with the Expeditionary Force that went over in those early days, trying to stop the German advance. He was wounded at Mons but not sent home. His wife lost the child she was carrying, and her death was put down to despair. The short of it was, she didn't want to live. The sister—she lived with him and his wife—says it was a very happy marriage, but another source claims the wife was unhappy."

"No foul play suspected in the wife's death? If he married her for her money, he could have killed her for it as well."

"It appears he was in France at the time."

"What about the jilted lover?"

"Never heard of again. I'd guess he decided he was well out of a bad bargain. The sister couldn't even remember his name. She said it was never official, their engagement, just something understood from childhood."

"Did Hutchinson's wife have any relatives who might have felt she was married for her money and then neglected?"

"None the sister knew of. There was an uncle who was her guardian, but he's long since dead. I did speak to the Rector at Mrs. Hutchinson's church. St. Timothy's, in Warwick, where she's buried. He was inclined to agree with the official cause of death. I did learn that a maid disappeared from the London house not long ago, but she wasn't there when Mrs. Hutchinson was alive."

"What became of her? Did you ask Miss Hutchinson about her?"

"I was told there was probably a man involved. The girl had come highly recommended, and she did her work well, they had no complaints of her. But she was young, unused to the city. Then one day she seemed very unhappy and just walked out. Miss Hutchinson called in the police after she failed to return by the end of the week, but they had no luck finding her. She wouldn't be the first to wind up in the river. Miss Hutchinson says she was young enough to believe promises made to her by a man, only to find herself deceived."

It was not uncommon.

"She wasn't pregnant, was she?"

"There's no way of knowing the answer to that. But she hadn't confided in anyone at the house."

"What about Hutchinson?"

"The sister says he was away more often than not, and she was indignant that we should think her brother had interfered with the maids. Besides, there's no evidence of that anywhere. The staff said he left the management of the house to his sister and treated the staff with indifference."

Digesting what Gibson had said, Rutledge could see that Hutchinson had probably married for money, using that charm several people had spoken of to find himself a rich wife, then ignored her. He'd been kind to Major Clayton's sister, but more or less as his opportunity to spend time with Colonel Nelson. It was a pattern of sorts. A housemaid would hold little interest for him.

"Turning to Fallowfield. What did you learn?"

"Well liked, no skeletons that I could discover. The same with the Sedleys. Above reproach, I was told at Mr. Sedley's London club. A good man, according to his solicitor."

"That leaves Swift."

"He's never been to London. At least if he came, he kept himself to himself and left no trace. He was to come down the week after the election to look for a flat that would serve when he was in Commons. He'd written to ask if there were any likely places close by Westminster. He was told there was no such list, he'd have to find something for himself before the House sat. I had that from an acquaintance at Westminster. He said Mr. Swift would wait until he was elected before making living arrangements. But it appeared that with his lackluster opposition, he was the most likely to win the by-election, and the general view was, he'd be a happy backbencher."

That corroborated all he'd learned in Ely and Wriston about Mr. Swift, the solicitor.

"There are two new names for you to look at. Anson Swift, the illegitimate brother of the dead man. And a farmer named Burrows. Any luck with Lowell, the artillery Major?"

"Good officer, careful of his men. A bachelor. Steady. No vices."

"Good." Lowell, it seemed, was not a suspect.

"There've been changes here, the new broom and all that. Constables reassigned. And speaking of that, the Acting Chief Superintendent was wanting to know if there was any news from Ely. Sir."

"Yes, well, it's more complicated that we had anticipated."

"That may be, but Himself is looking for an arrest sooner rather than later."

"I'll keep it in mind," Rutledge said dryly and broke the connection.

He sat there in the little enclosure for the telephone, thinking over what he'd learned.

Nothing useful. Nothing that would lead to Hutchinson's death in Ely in the summer of 1920.

Somewhere there had to be a strand of information that would help in the inquiry. A list of ex-soldiers was not likely to produce a killer in time to make Markham happy. But there would have to be a report in a day or two, and Rutledge accepted that with a sigh. Even if it offered no motive, no suspects, and no evidence to be going on with.

Leaving the telephone closet, he went back to the police station, but Inspector Warren, he was told, had already gone home for the evening. He scribbled a note to leave on the man's desk. It said simply, *Nothing useful from London.*

On his way back to Wriston, Hamish was busy in the back of his mind.

Trying to ignore the probing, the querulous demands for answers, the unsettling reminders of France, he looked up at the western sky. Clouds were streaked across the horizon, a blaze of color, and visible wherever the road took him, because of the flatness of the land and the lack of woods or towns or hills to break the view.

A fiery gold in the last bank of clouds, a blazing red above that, and then, as the red faded to rose and the rose to lavender, the earth seemed to reflect the light.

Not a night to be looking for a murderer, he thought. But he had the feeling that he should not linger on the road, he should be in Wriston by nightfall. It was an odd feeling, very like the one he'd had when he woke to find the fog lifted, as if someone had been there, looking up at his window.

And yet the sky held him in thrall, for the light seemed to fill the motorcar, to warm his face, and as he drove he watched it slowly fade until there was nothing but the afterglow.

When at last he could shut out Hamish no longer, he heard what the voice in his head was telling him.

"He can see ye as clearly as he saw yon farmer. Ye're a target. Ye're Scotland Yard, and he knows ye're after him. This land is no' as empty as it seems. Ye'll be dead before ye hear the shot."

Was it a reflection of his own mood, or was Hamish warning him?

By that time he was less than two miles from Wriston. Beside him in the ditches and the fields, insects and frogs set up an invisible chorus. Over the quiet running of the motor, it was unexpectedly loud. And as he drove into the village, his headlamps picking out the road ahead now, that sense of vulnerability seemed to increase.

Death could be lurking anywhere. Behind the buildings, among the trees, in the shadows by the church . . .

In this inquiry, McBride and Inspector Warren, with the best will in the world, had come up empty-handed. Scotland Yard was expected to find those elusive answers.

And right now the killer had no way of knowing that Rutledge too was getting nowhere, had so far learned nothing useful.

Chapter 10

The list of ex-soldiers arrived the next morning by a special messenger who came roaring into Wriston on his motorcycle, his goggles and cuffed gloves a souvenir of France.

Leafing through it, Rutledge could guess how many men had set out from this handful of villages to fight the Kaiser. Perhaps less than half had returned. He remembered the small corner of Isleham churchyard where a memorial had been set up, and the long rows of names on the plinth of the cross. He had not paused there. It had seemed too much of a burden to carry with him just then.

The constables in the various villages had been thorough, giving him ranks and sometimes other brief notations by some of the names.

Lost his leg.
Lost his arm.

Blind.
Gassed.
Troubled.

Rutledge needed no explanation of that last. Men who had brought the war home with them, physically or mentally.

He could mark off the severely wounded, those who couldn't manage a rifle, much less the stairs in the ironmonger's house or those up into Ely's tower. They might hate as much as the next man, but they weren't the killer he was after.

Still, he'd have to interview the troubled men. He could feel his stomach clenching at the thought.

McBride, who'd heard the roar of the Indian coming down the road, had hailed Rutledge and was trotting toward him.

"Inspector Warren has been thorough," he said, looking up from the sheaf of papers in his hand.

"I can't see that it will help all that much," McBride commented. "They're not likely to confess when you walk in the door."

"If someone has a rifle hidden in the thatch of his roof, he'll find it hard to deny it to my face. And that just might give him away."

"I doubt you'll find him in Wriston."

"Possibly not. On the other hand, if he does live here, he knew the risk he was running, and he's found a way to keep you in the dark."

It was clear McBride disagreed, and Rutledge let it go.

They crossed to the police station. Rutledge sat down at McBride's desk to make notes on the sheets while the constable paced restlessly, then left on his rounds.

Finally satisfied that he'd narrowed down the numbers, Rutledge sat back, waiting for McBride to return.

Hamish was saying, "It's likely he lives alone, this man. Else, how has he kept the truth from his wife or his bairns?"

"He could have a cowshed or some other—"

He could hear McBride returning, and broke off, aware he'd answered Hamish aloud.

"There's a problem," the constable said almost before he was through the door.

"Another shooting?" Rutledge asked, quickly getting to his feet.

"No. Monster fever," was the sour reply.

"What brought it on?"

"Sam Turner was walking back from the pub last night. He swears he saw something moving out in the fields. Lights, he said. And it wasn't a man with a lantern. It didn't stand on two legs, it was up in the air. Leaping and turning, without rhyme or reason."

"How drunk was he?"

"Fairly. He admits to it. His wife is a termagant, and he spends most of his evenings at the pub. Still, he swears it was real. He's telling half the village to lock their doors."

"Someone searching for something?" Rutledge asked with interest. "Or merely stirring up trouble?"

"Turner says spirits. A lost soul, looking for peace. He's fairly clear about that. He claims it's Burrows. That he's dead."

Rutledge came around the desk, folding the papers in his hand in half. "No one has come in from the farm, bringing the news. We'll have to drive out there and see for ourselves."

"It could be, no one's found him yet," McBride agreed.

They hurried to the inn, where Rutledge had left the motorcar, and on the way McBride asked, "What do you think the chances are that something—or someone—was out there? That it wasn't just the drink that made Turner see the lights?"

"Fairly poor. But if they were real, I'll wager whoever it was used stilts. Like those I saw in Mrs. Percy's kitchen. There must be other old pairs lying about. If not, it would be easy enough to make new ones. It's the most likely explanation. We could search for prints, but even if we found them, they wouldn't tell us much more than we know already."

McBride whistled as he bent to turn the crank. "I never thought of stilts. My father had a pair when he was a lad. I could never get the hang of them."

Remembering the man in the mist, Rutledge asked as he drove over the bridge by the windmill, "There's another possibility. What was he wandering about in the dark looking for? Or perhaps that ought to be *who*? Surely not Sam Turner."

"It won't matter to Turner or to half of those he's told. There are old tales about lights out in the Fens. Fox fire. Someone will remember them."

They fell silent then, and it wasn't until they were turning in on the long track that led to the Burrows house that McBride brought up something that clearly had been worrying him for some time.

"There will have to be another by-election. With Mr. Swift dead, the seat in Parliament won't go by default to Mr. Johns, the other candidate. There's been some talk. Most people think Johns won't stand now, for fear of being shot in his turn. But if you ask me, he wasn't all that eager to begin with. The party needed a name, and he was persuaded. Nor did he exert himself overly."

"Knowing that Swift was likely to win."

"I'd say that was his thinking. But who will stand in Swift's place? I'm hearing whispers that no one appears to be that eager to fill *his* boots."

Inspector Warren had raised that question as well.

"Who would be likely to come forward? Surely not Swift's brother? Or Burrows?"

"I doubt you could pry either man off his land. Certainly not for London."

"Then we'd better unravel this puzzle quickly."

They had reached the house now, and Miss Burrows must have seen them coming, for she was at the door, calling to them, "Has there been any more trouble?"

"We've come to look in on your father. How is he?" McBride asked.

"Well enough. Last night he was planning what had to be done in the fields. Today his face is hurting, and he's using the wound as his excuse not to go outside. How long will that excuse hold up?"

"There was a—rumor in Wriston today that he was dead. Your father," Constable McBride said.

"Started by whom?" she asked anxiously. As they joined her in the doorway she led the way to a sitting room. It was comfortable and well kept, but the furnishings were late Victorian, the wallpaper dark.

"A man walking home from the pub said he saw lights out in the fields. He claimed they were the souls of the dead." McBride was wishing he'd said nothing about Burrows having died. Shrugging uneasily, he added, "A silly business, but we can't ignore the story."

"No. But who was out there in the field? Was it someone coming in this direction?"

"He said the lights were just—there. Not that they were moving in a particular direction."

Rutledge added, "On the other hand, we felt it was a good idea to look in on you."

"I don't like it," she told them flatly. "It's strange, all of this business. The monsters, the faces, the lights. I don't believe in such things. But there's got to be some truth to it. Some explanation that makes sense."

"Or—he was drunk. This man was walking from the pub to his house. McBride tells me he'd stayed until closing, as he sometimes does, and had to be turned out. Everyone else had already left. He was in the street alone. His imagination could have played tricks on him."

"And there's a pair of owls that live in the church tower," McBride put in. "Some people don't care for them."

McBride was trying to ease Miss Burrows's anxiety. But the best view of the fields was looking down Windmill Lane, past where Mrs. Percy lived, well before the churchyard. The power of suggestion? Rutledge wondered again. Or had the man actually seen something?

They could hear someone moving about on the floor above, and after a moment footsteps on the stairs.

"My father," Miss Burrows said, adding quickly. "Please, say nothing about the lights. At least not until you *know*—" She broke off as her father came through the door.

It appeared he'd been sleeping, his hair mussed and his face slightly flushed. The mark on his cheek was still inflamed, and Rutledge suggested again that a doctor should have a look at it.

"I don't want a fuss made," Burrows said testily. "What brings you here? Is there fresh news?"

"Nothing to report," Rutledge said easily. "We thought it best to see how you were faring. You had a narrow escape."

"I don't think I slept a wink last night," Burrows said morosely. "The face burned like fire, and I woke with a start at every noise. But he didn't come. I sent my daughter to a neighbor's for the night. I didn't want her here. And I didn't want her coming in every half hour to ask me if I was all right and getting the shotgun in her face for her trouble."

And so he must have sat up, guarding the house, possibly from an upstairs window where he had a full sweep of the approaches. Rutledge knew that he should have sent McBride out to keep the man company, but he wasn't convinced that the killer would return. And McBride was needed in Wriston. The danger—if danger there still was—would come later, when Burrows's guard was down.

Burrows had been the third choice on the killer's list. Was that significant? Where was the pattern? Or was there a pattern?

"Where are the two men who work for you?" Rutledge asked.

"I sent them away home. I trust them, of course I do. But last night I didn't want them lurking about."

But Rutledge wondered if it was a matter of trust after all. Burrows hadn't seen the face of the man firing at him.

"You could come into town for a few days," Rutledge suggested.

"Miss Bartram has extra rooms, she can put you up. It might be more comfortable for you and your daughter."

To his surprise, Miss Burrows added her own arguments to Rutledge's.

"It might be as well, Papa. What do you think?"

"I won't be run out of my home," he said tightly. "Go if you like. I can fend for myself. I managed well enough for both of us after your mother died."

"I don't want to leave you."

"I'll take Miss Burrows back with me if you like," Rutledge offered.

"It will be all right after tonight," her father answered. "Bill Waters is bringing me one of his dogs. A big brute, bark like a railway locomotive. No one can slip up on me if the dog is here. He'll see him or smell him before I do."

But a man with a rifle could stay downwind and kill from a distance. It was a fragile line of defense.

"I'll come back tonight, shall I?" Rutledge asked. "To spell you. We can watch turn about."

Burrows hesitated, then shook his head. "If I'm alone, I know who's out there. And I'll shoot first, ask his business later."

"Not a good idea," McBride began.

But Burrows said stubbornly, "You've lived here all your life. Do people walk about out there in the dark? Not God-fearing souls. Only someone bent on trouble, and you know that to be true as well as I do."

Rutledge was reminded again of the man who had helped him in the mist. He'd appeared and disappeared like a wraith.

McBride was saying unwillingly, "I'd have to agree with that. After midnight, the frogs have the ditches and the fields to themselves. But I don't wish to come out here in the morning to find you with a body on your hands and a story that you thought it was someone else you were firing at."

"Never fear," Burrows told him grimly. "If I fire that shotgun, I won't miss. And I'll have the right man."

Miss Burrows wouldn't accept their offer to take her into Wriston. She was closer by at a neighbor's house, could come in the morning to prepare breakfast for her father and the men who helped him in the fields.

"I'll be all right, it will be daylight and he'll hear me walking up the track."

But the truth was, Rutledge thought, she wanted to be near enough to hear the shotgun go off in the night. Or the rifle . . .

Rutledge and McBride left them to it and turned back toward Wriston.

"Stubborn old fool," McBride said under his breath.

Rutledge was of the same mind.

"What about the men who work for him? Were they in the war, are they on our list?"

"The older one, Bill, was in the Navy. He's not likely to be our man. Steady and quiet and never a troublemaker. I don't see him shooting anyone. Besides, how was he to get to Ely to kill Captain Hutchinson? It's quite a way."

"By bicycle?"

"Possible, if he had all day to do the journey. No, my money would be on the younger one. I say young, he's thirty-five if he's a day. He's a good worker, and to be trusted. But he's a moody bastard, and about once every six months, he takes a day off and drinks himself blind. The next morning he's back at work as if nothing happened."

"I doubt the killer did his work in a drunken stupor."

"No, there's the rub. Besides, the two men share a cottage over by the cattle byre, and there would be no hiding a rifle in there. You'd stumble over it sooner or later."

"On the farm there must be a dozen safe hiding places."

"Still, it would come to light. And someone would ask whose it was. Bound to. No, I don't think Burrows has anything to fear from his help."

Back in Wriston, Rutledge went to the little café for his lunch, the menu running to sandwiches, and then he set about interviewing the names on his abbreviated list of Wriston's ex-soldiers.

Seven of them had been in the square the night Swift was killed, and witnesses had verified their presence. That was made clear in the statements Constable McBride and Inspector Warren had collected. Two men had stayed home with their wives because they didn't intend to vote for Swift. Three others had remained in the pub, not interested in what the candidate had to say. Another had a sick calf to watch over, and one had a teething child, walking the floor with it by turns with his wife.

The last two on his list had no alibi and no apparent reason to do murder. Still, he put a question mark by their names.

Conferring with McBride later, he learned that one of them was "too shiftless" to be troubled by revenge, and the other was courting a girl at one of the farms.

The next day Rutledge set out for Soham and spent the morning looking up the ex-soldiers that Constable Peckham had included in his list.

The cooper was on there, but Rutledge had already spoken to him. One by one he tracked down the others, and one by one he cleared them.

Until he came to the rat catcher.

The man lived down by one of the small streams that still criss-crossed the area. His house, if it could be called that, was hardly more than a hut, a single room that served for sleeping and eating. A narrow cot in one corner was his bed, a table in the middle of the room must be where he ate his meals, and he cooked over a small open fire just outside the door where boards had been nailed together to form a rough lean-to that kept out the rain. A tan and white terrier lay sleeping by the door, his muzzle on his paws.

The man was tall and rangy, with long fair hair and a scruffy beard. His eyes were a light gray and never wavered from Rutledge's face as he gave his name and why he had come.

"A policeman," Jeremiah Brenner said, looking him up and down. Then he added, "I haven't been to Ely since the war."

"Then you've nothing to hide," Rutledge said. "What did you do during the war?"

"I don't remember." His gaze turned to the wall, and Rutledge realized that there was a large rat in the cage sitting on a shelf. "He's tame. I call him Isaac. I found him when he was no larger than my thumb, pink and blind. So I kept him. He doesn't judge me, I don't judge him."

There was something about the man that put Rutledge off. He wasn't sure whether it was the light eyes that seemed as cold as icy water, or if it was the rat.

"Do you make a good living as rat catcher?"

"Does it look like it? But my father was rat catcher before me. And it's all I'm fit for now. I drink too much."

And yet Rutledge was sure the man was cold sober just now.

"I drink to forget," Brenner went on, as if he'd heard the next question in Rutledge's mind. The cool eyes came back to Rutledge's face.

"What do you want to forget?"

"Ah, that would be telling. Is there anything else?"

"Did you know Herbert Swift?"

"I know who he is—was."

"And Mr. Burrows?"

"I've caught rats in one of his barns. Twice the size of the barn cat, they were."

"Did you know the man who was shot in Ely?"

Brenner smiled. "I knew of him. Only I wasn't the one who shot him."

"Then who do you think did?"

"Even if I knew I wouldn't tell you. Whoever it was, he must have had his reasons. Some of us didn't like our officers."

And that was all he could learn from Jeremiah Brenner. He put a question mark by the name. But if there was a rifle in the bare hut, Rutledge wasn't sure where it could have been concealed. Still, the rat catcher answered to no one, and he could have found half a hundred places to keep the rifle safe.

Rutledge drove next to Isleham. The day was hot now, the air heavy. He left his motorcar in the shade cast by the trees in St. Andrew's churchyard, and walked to each of the addresses on his list.

The first three names were easily eliminated. One had actually come to Wriston to hear Swift, "to make up my mind, once and for all," he'd added. What's more he had been seen to give Swift a hand when the man stepped up on the base of the market cross, just before he'd begun his speech.

The other two had perfectly good alibis, one working behind the bar at the local pub, and the other playing cards with the brother of the Isleham constable. They had been together most of the evening.

Numbers four and five had no alibi, but one had served in Egypt, well away from France where Captain Hutchinson had spent his war, and the other had been a conscientious objector and had served as an orderly in a hospital in Devon.

Their names received a question mark, but after the interview he was inclined to think they were in the clear. And Hamish agreed.

The sixth name lived just below the church in a house set back from the road. Rutledge's first impression was that Lieutenant Thornton must be one of the more prosperous denizens of Isleham. There was a garden on either side of the steps, and the path leading up to them branched there to go toward a small folly, like a round Greek temple that must serve as a garden house. It reminded him vaguely of the Temple of the Winds he'd seen in a book on Athens. And one of the two small wings on either side of the house was mainly glass, a conservatory, he thought.

The middle-aged woman who answered his knock wore the uniform of a housekeeper. He gave her only his name, asking to see Lieutenant Thornton.

"I'll see if he's receiving visitors, sir. A moment, please."

He waited several minutes for her to return.

"Mr. Thornton will see you now," she said. "This way, if you please."

He followed her into a central hall and down a passage that led to a very masculine sitting room, framed maps on the wall and a large globe on a stand in one corner.

Thornton was standing by the cold hearth. A tall slender man with fair hair and blue eyes, he greeted Rutledge pleasantly and offered him a chair.

"Is this about the Memorial Fund?" he asked. "I've been intending to send in my contribution. I'm sorry someone had to come all this way on my account."

"I'm from Scotland Yard, sir. I'm here in connection with the murders of two men, Captain Hutchinson in Ely and Mr. Swift in Wriston."

Thornton frowned. "Yes, a tragic business. I'll help in any way I can, but I don't precisely know how I can be of service."

"Had you ever met the Captain? While you were serving with the Army during the war? Or perhaps afterward, in London."

"I may have met him somewhere in France. If I did, I don't recall it. But I never served under him, if that's what you're asking. I don't often go to regimental functions and the like." He smiled grimly. "My rank is a battlefield commission. I joined as a private soldier and was promoted more or less against my will."

Rutledge gestured to the room they were in, indicating the house in general. "You could have trained as an officer."

"I didn't want the responsibility for the lives of others. Rather selfish of me, perhaps. I killed Germans when I had to, but sending other men out to die on my orders was something I couldn't face. Were you in the war? Yes. Then you'll know what I mean."

Rutledge did. All too well.

With Hamish rumbling in the back of his mind, he answered, "No one did that by choice. Only by necessity."

"Very true. Still, I was happy to serve under someone else."

"I understand Captain Hutchinson was in Burwell for a funeral several months before traveling to Ely for a wedding. A Major Clayton's services."

"I knew the Major, of course. I served under him. But I make it a point not to attend funerals. There have been too many. Men are still dying, although the war is nearly two years over. I didn't know the Major's sister very well—I'm sure my absence wasn't noticed."

"And Mr. Swift?"

"I've heard him speak, of course. But I'm not interested in politics. I do my duty, I vote. I don't mean that. Still, I haven't seen this better world we were told we were fighting for. If you want the truth, it's something I try to avoid thinking about. The future." It was his turn to gesture to the room at large. "I stay in the past, where it's safely, unemotionally over." A wry smile accompanied the remark. "I can do nothing to change the past and I have no responsibility for it."

"If you were in the ranks, you were given a rifle. What became of it?"

"*My* rifle? I daresay I had more than one whilst in France. The last one I turned in with the greatest relief when I was given my commission. That was in the last days of the war. I don't think I shot anyone after that. I tried not to. There were rumors of Armistice. It was all about to end, and I couldn't see any reason to kill another man whose only hope was to live a little longer and then possibly go home." He shrugged. "Not that they didn't do their best to kill us."

"Do you have any idea who might have wanted to see these two men dead? Or who shot at Mr. Burrows the day before yesterday, narrowly missing him?"

"Burrows? The farmer? My God," Thornton said blankly. "As for the other two, I don't know enough about the matter to do more than hazard a guess. And that would be someone who hasn't finished his war. For whatever reason. Rather frightening to think about. I have my own nightmares, God knows." His eyes were suddenly different, his features twisting with pain. "Mostly about the machine guns. I can't hide from them, and I know I'm going to die. The doctors told me this might pass. So far . . ." He shook his head, unable to finish. Getting up, he walked to the window and stared out at nothing until he could turn to face Rutledge again.

"Is there anything else?" he asked. "I'd rather not talk about the war any longer."

"Are you married? Do you have a family?"

"Sadly no. I thought I was engaged once. And then the war came along. I don't think there's anyone now who would wish to share this life. How do you explain to a woman who hasn't been to war what it was like, and why you have changed so much?"

Rutledge had no answer to give him. He'd carried his love for Jean throughout the war as a promise of happiness when it was finished. And instead he'd had to find the courage to set her free, rather than tie her to the shambles he had become. To add to his pain, he could see how relieved she had been, how happy to walk away and not have to deal with what she didn't understand and didn't want to face. Very soon thereafter, she'd married someone else.

And there was Meredith Channing, who had also left him to find the man she was married to, and whom by her own admission, she hadn't loved.

The room around him seemed to close in, and he made his escape before he could say or do anything that Thornton could recognize. *Shell shock.* Disgrace and cowardice and lack of moral fiber . . .

Outside he walked on to the churchyard, tree-shaded and quiet, avoiding the memorial to the war dead. It struck him that this island of tranquility was only a matter of miles from the hustle and bustle of Newmarket, the center of horse racing.

Someone was coming in through the lych-gate, carrying a pot of flowering plants and a small trowel, walking toward a fresh grave he could just see near the apse. Avoiding the woman, he turned and went into the church.

It was lit by the small but elegant clerestory illuminating the dark framework of the magnificent hammer-beam roof. He stood there and stared up at it, letting the conversation with Thornton fade. The emotions the man had roused were always too near the surface, like exposed nerves, sensitive to the touch, even to the air. No matter how many times he might tell himself he had begun to heal, he could see that Thornton had not, and it was a reflection of his own guilt.

And then, concerned that the woman planting the flowers might well come into the church to say a prayer for the dead—remembering how the Rector in Wriston had come upon him unexpectedly—he hastily turned to leave.

Taking with him, unwittingly, the thought that there had been no Green Man here, only angels decorating the ceiling above his head.

I t was tempting to go to the rambling old Red Lion pub for a drink, but Rutledge had other calls to make.

Finishing those, he walked around the village a little, looked at the old priory that had become a barn, and then made his way back to the motorcar. And still Hamish was there in his mind, refusing to go, reminding him again and again of his encounter with Thornton.

Giving up, he drove back to Wriston. Had it been a mistake to interview the ex-soldiers? But where else was he to turn for answers, if not to men who had handled rifles, knew them intimately, and could probably still shoot as well with them as they had in the trenches.

Priscilla Bartram was on the lookout for him, and met him at the door, for all the world like a wife awaiting her husband's return from the fields or the shops. Her life was a lonely one, and he could understand that his presence was at once comforting and comfortable. But there was nowhere else in the village to stay.

She offered him a drink, but he was no longer interested in a whisky. Instead he told her he would work in his room, writing up the day's report for Inspector Warren in Ely.

"You'll be down later for dinner? I found a nice bit of beef at the butcher's."

"In an hour, then." He smiled and went up the stairs.

But not to work. He stood by the window for a time, then sat down at the desk to take out the stationery there, imprinted with the same scene that was on the iron sign outside.

He wrote a note to his sister, Frances, telling her where he was— she had not been in London when he left—and adding that it would probably be a longer inquiry than he'd expected. He asked her to collect his mail and then could think of nothing else to say.

In the end, he balled the note up and tossed it aside.

Thinking better of leaving it for Miss Bartram to find, he collected it from the floor and put it in his luggage instead.

It was while he was putting his valise back in the armoire that he had the thought.

And Miss Trowbridge had unwittingly given it to him.

The Green Man.

A face, often smiling without real humor, in a circlet of leaves, as if the man were poking his head out of them to see what was happening around him. Sometimes the leaves grew from his head or his face, half concealing it, like a man's hair and beard. A pagan symbol, yet popular in churches or in the names of pubs in a few places he'd been. Something so commonplace and conventional that he'd missed the significance.

And now, suddenly, it had triggered what must have been in the back of his mind from the start, but locked away in his other memories of the war.

Chapter 11

How many times had he and Hamish worked with a sharp-shooter, turning him from a British soldier into a tree or a mound of straw or a ragged edge on the trench wall, creating their own Green Man, so to speak, but with deadly intent? Changing his face, disguising his body, wrapping his rifle so that it was invisible to the enemy?

It had taken patience and ingenuity, and the Germans were quick to see through whatever scheme they'd come up with. It was an ever-changing battle of wits.

But then the Germans had had snipers—sharpshooters—from the very start of the war. Trained men who were very good with a rifle and equally good at concealing themselves. Some would lie in wait for days, or from the middle of the night to midday, invisible in bits of straw or sacking, using whatever came to hand. Shell-blasted trees or stumps, the ruins of a building, or even the rim of a shell hole. Their targets were any head that popped up above the top of the trench—in the beginning the British soldiers had worn soft caps, not helmets—to see what was happening on the opposite side. Making the British and the French keep their heads down also left them blind.

In fact, the German telescopes were so good that sharpshooters were ordered not to let them fall into enemy hands.

It was an old concept, sharpshooters, not new to the Great War, but the British had been reluctant to employ such tactics. Sharpshooters had been used in the Second Boer War, but the British had had to begin all over again when they finally saw the necessity of fighting fire with fire in 1914. Even so, it was thought to be not quite the thing. Not sporting to take out a chap who didn't even know anyone was there, who didn't have an equal chance to kill as well as be killed.

And the men who did this work were often shunned, generally considered beyond the pale. They seldom boasted about their skill, passing themselves off outside their own companies as regular foot soldiers. But sometimes when the truth did leak out, they were pariahs. Even back in England they told no stories, never bragged about their best kills, and often kept to themselves . . .

"Like Thornton?" Hamish asked.

That jarred Rutledge. He hadn't considered the possibility. Yes, Thornton was reclusive, but he was also a very different sort of man from the sharpshooters Rutledge had dealt with. Scots, most of them, and often retainers on an estate where deer stalking was popular in the autumn, and for the rest of the year, they were more than a little feared by poachers. They possessed the eye of an eagle, one Highlander had told him, and steel nerves. It was all that was needed to take such a skill to war.

But now someone had brought that skill home with him, and for some reason had begun to shoot again.

It wouldn't be the first time Rutledge had dealt with a sniper. Then he himself had been the target.

The question now was, had the war returned to *this* man, or had he found his former skill useful when he decided to commit murder?

Hamish said, "It doesna' matter which came first."

And Hamish was right. It didn't. But to know might make it easier to find a killer.

Those lists of ex-soldiers he'd asked Inspector Warren to draw up were useless now, Rutledge could see that. Finding out who among them had served as a sniper would mean searching the War Office records. What's more, he himself had often enlisted the help of the best marksman in his company, unofficially putting him to work when faced with a German sharpshooter who was pinning his men down. That had seldom gone into any records, a tacit agreement when the request was made. But they had got their man, and he'd been grateful.

Still, it hadn't hurt to let these village men know that they were under scrutiny by the Yard, whether one was the killer he was after or not. Somewhere on the lists was the name he was looking for, and if he was getting close—whether he knew it or not—it might force his quarry to keep a low profile for a while.

"Ye ken," Hamish went on, "that he's verra' guid. He didna' copy what he'd seen in the trenches."

That was true. This killer could think for himself. He could plan, he was patient, and he was willing to risk everything when he saw his opportunity.

And that made him all the more dangerous.

Rutledge considered whether or not to speak to Inspector Warren or possibly even Constable McBride. It was information that could be valuable.

And yet, if what Rutledge suspected ever became common knowledge, his advantage would be lost.

But he had his explanation now for the monster Mrs. Percy had seen. And it had been real enough. Only she hadn't known how to interpret it . . .

He wondered if the cooper in Soham had suspected the truth. It could explain why Ruskin had quietly left Wriston without giving McBride a statement.

Better to hunt the shadows alone, as long as he could.

Downstairs, he waited until his dinner was nearly finished. And then he said, "Tell me about the housemaid Herbert Swift dismissed after his wife died. Susan, her name was."

"Well, he was leaving for Scotland, of course, and Susan's roots are here in the Fens. She didn't want to go north. Nor did he want to take her. She'd been his wife's maid, she reminded him every day of his loss. I can't think she felt ill done by. And she's been such a help to the Rector."

"Perhaps she'll remember something that might be useful."

"It was so long ago, of course. Water under the bridge since then. But then Mrs. Swift came from Ely, didn't she? As I remember, she was a Phillips before she married."

That name hadn't come up in connection with the wedding guest list, not as far as he knew. He made a mental note of it.

"I was just a girl when she came to Wriston, and I thought her the most fashionable person imaginable." Miss Bartram smiled at the memory. "I looked forward to seeing her Sunday morning, and I tried sometimes to copy her hats." The smile turned wry. "But of course it wasn't very successful. She was one of those women who could wear pretty hats, and I'm not. Still, it was a pleasure for me. And I expect for my mother as well. But it had an unhappy ending, didn't it? I don't think Mr. Swift ever looked at another woman after his wife died. Mrs. Prescott asked him how he expected to entertain in London, if he didn't take a wife. She's Teddy Prescott's widow, you see, and hopeful. But he told her he was intending to serve his constituents, not set himself up as a Londoner."

"Then after dinner I think I'll walk to the Rectory and have a word with Susan."

It was a quiet evening, and Rutledge stood for a moment, watching the ducks floating on the pond, gliding above their reflections and finally climbing out to waddle toward wherever it was they roosted at night. One of the dogs outside a house on the far side of the Green gazed after them with bored interest, then rested his head on his paws again with a drowsy sigh.

He had put it off long enough. It was time to face the Rector.

But March gave no indication that he mistook this call as a cry for help. He listened with courtesy to Rutledge's request, called to Susan to come down and speak to the Inspector, and then left them alone in the small Rectory parlor.

She was older than he'd expected, her reddish hair threaded with gray, but her face was still smooth and her eyes were a bright blue.

"I'm trying to find something in Mr. Swift's life that may have led to his death," Rutledge began easily. "You worked for him for some time, and I wouldn't be surprised if you'd kept up a kindly interest in his well-being in the years that followed."

Susan Tompkins smiled. "He was a good man, you know. He had a love of history, and he was concerned about his clients, always looking out for those who needed his help but couldn't pay his fees. Once he took a pig in place of what he was owed, then he never had the heart to butcher it after it'ud grown to a good size. He said he couldn't bear to touch the meat."

"By history, do you mean the history of the Fens, the background of the people who lived here?" It was always possible that Swift had stumbled onto something that could mean trouble for a family or its holdings. Even if he kept it to himself.

"I can't count the times I dusted his bookshelves. There were books on Rome, six or seven, and weighty ones, you'd not dare drop one on a foot. And then there was Egypt. He bought all he could find.

He told me once he'd have liked to go there. But of course there was no money for such a journey. Not for a country solicitor. I don't recall any books about the Fens."

But then as a solicitor he might have learned more than he should about his clients. He might not have needed a book.

"He had financial problems?"

"No, sir, he was comfortable enough, but it came from what he earned. And of course his wife's money. Not that that was excessive, but it was what he called a nice cushion. That's why he decided he might stand for Parliament now."

An interesting point.

"Why did he go to Scotland?"

"His wife had just died, sir, and he was at his wit's end. He wanted to close up the house, walk away from it. And then he was asked to go to Glasgow, for the Admiralty. Something to do with the ships on the River Clyde. Mr. Swift showed me where it was on the map. He'd always liked the sea, he even wrote to the Admiralty offering his services. And they took him on. It was, he told me, as far away as he could get from his memories. 'There'll be nothing there to remind me,' he said. 'I can step out my door of a morning and even the air will be different, and the weather, and the look of the land. I can shut out the pain and bury myself in my work.' And that's what he must have done because when he came back to Wriston, he was a different man."

"How different?"

Susan considered the question. "Settled in himself? I don't think the law was ever his calling. It was just a better way of making his living than farming. And in Scotland he'd done different things. It seemed to me that this made it possible for him to say yes when he was asked to stand for the vacant seat. He hadn't gone to Rome or Egypt, but he was no longer really here in Wriston, if you know what I mean. He'd tried to take up the law again, but his heart wasn't in it. I think perhaps it must have palled."

She was a perceptive woman, Rutledge thought. "Tell me about Mrs. Swift."

"Ah, she was the loveliest thing. Slim and fair and pretty as a picture. Her father spoiled her, but she had a sweet nature that made everyone love her. I was promoted to lady's maid when she was sixteen, and I came here to Wriston with her. My own father was from here, and I still had two aunties here. They're dead now, of course, but on my days off I'd go and visit them. So I wanted to stay here, after Mrs. Swift went. There was nothing left for me in Ely, you see, my parents being dead by then. Rector was happy to take me on."

"Swift must have taken a flat in Glasgow. Who looked after him there?"

"He wrote soon after he got there, to say he'd found a flat not far from the Cathedral, and there was a girl he'd found to come in twice a week. 'Nothing like you, Susan, which I must say is cheering for me. I don't care to look back. Not even to the happy times. But I hope you are content where you are. I want you to know I'll be all right, in a bit.'"

It was clear Susan had treasured her conversations with Swift, and that first letter. Rutledge could hear a slight change in the tone of her voice as she quoted her former employer. A softness too, that told him she'd been fond of the man.

But nothing in her memories helped him, as far as he could tell.

"After his return from Scotland, were there many visitors to Swift's house? Someone he'd known in Scotland or served with there?"

"I have no idea, but I think I'd have heard sooner or later, if there had been. Someone was bound to tell me if he'd had anyone in particular come to call. I could still serve at table if he had guests. Rector wouldn't have minded." There was the smallest touch of wistfulness in her voice. She wouldn't have left the Rector, perhaps, but the past still held her heart. She'd have gone to help Swift if he'd asked it of her.

"I believe Mrs. Swift was a Phillips before her marriage, and from Ely." He listed the names of Barbara Fallowfield's family and the Sedleys and several other people closely connected to the wedding, and asked if the Phillips family had known any of them.

But Mrs. Swift hadn't moved in such exalted circles, although her father had been a prominent barrister. Which meant that her marriage to a solicitor in Wriston hadn't been quite the step down he'd thought it might have been.

"Although pretty as she was," Susan said, defending her mistress's choice of husband, "she could have aimed higher. But she'd fallen in love, you see, and Society as such didn't matter to her. Still, I think her mother might have been pleased if she'd married better. She was more ambitious than Mr. Phillips."

A dead end, Rutledge told himself. Nothing here to lead him to a murderer. For all he could see, Swift had led a quiet and exemplary life.

Thanking Susan, he rose to leave, and then she said something that stopped him in his tracks.

"I remember one thing. It's probably not important. But perhaps I ought to mention it all the same. I'd like to see whoever shot Mr. Swift brought in and tried for it. Mr. Burrows's wife—she's dead now, she died of the influenza—told me once that Ben Montgomery and Mr. Swift had courted the same girl before Mr. Swift went to Ely for a trial and met Miss Phillips. She didn't marry either man, as it happens. But before she looked elsewhere, they'd come to blows over her. Out there on the Green, mind you, in front of half the world. I don't think they spoke again for years and years, Ben Montgomery and Mr. Swift."

"Who was this girl?"

"You'd have no way of knowing, of course, being a stranger here, but she was Miss Trowbridge's mother. Up from Bury to spend a summer here with the Montgomery girls."

The Montgomery family, it seemed, had owned one of the larger holdings, and it lay hard by the Swift farm in the direction of

Soham. It was run now by the husband of one of the daughters of the house, Randolph Abbot.

The next morning, following Constable McBride's directions, Rutledge found the drive leading up to the farm and was met there by a large Irish wolfhound who sniffed his boots and followed him up the broad pair of steps.

The house was a little grander than that of the Swifts or the Burrowses, and there was a large bed of flowers where the drive looped in front of the door. Although as Hamish was pointing out, *drive* was more or less a courtesy term for the hard-packed clay that made up the roads, tracks, and lanes in the Fen country.

A young woman answered his knock and told him that her mother was in. He was led to a sunny room in the back of the house where a new sewing machine had just been set up and was being tested.

Mrs. Abbot was plump, there was no other word for it, and as her daughter brought a stranger through the door, she looked up, her face flushed from attempting to thread the machine's needle.

"Mama, this is Mr. Rutledge, here to see you. He's from Scotland Yard," the younger woman informed her mother.

"Indeed," she said, straightening up. "Do have a try, Charlotte, your eyes are better than mine. Now then, Mr. Rutledge, how can I help you?"

"I understand Miss Trowbridge's mother used to come to Wriston in the summer and was a houseguest of yours?"

The pinkness was fading from her face as she gestured to a chair, and she said, "My goodness, that was years ago. However did you discover she'd been here? Did Marcella tell you?"

"It was someone in the village."

"I wonder who. Well, then, what can Miss Trowbridge's mother have to do with Scotland Yard?"

"I understand that Mr. Swift and your brother vied for her attention one summer, and it resulted in a quarrel between the two men."

Mrs. Abbot laughed. "Hardly men. I think they must have been all of seventeen. I was ten, and my sister was nineteen. She had gone to school with Helena in Bury, and in the summer holidays she invited Helena to stay with us for a few weeks. Of course with a new and pretty face about, all the lads were falling over themselves to attract her attention. When Herbert and Ben fell to, it was more a scramble than a fight, and Helena was dying of embarrassment. As I remember, it began with a promise Helena had made to Herbert Swift to come and see the new foal at his father's farm. The lads didn't speak for a fortnight or so, and then Helena was gone, back to Bury."

"But would your brother have told you if that resentment had lasted?"

"They were far too young to be thinking of marriage. It was a summer's infatuation, nothing more. Two years later, Helena was engaged to James Trowbridge."

"Who was the village doctor in Wriston, as I understand it. Until his wife persuaded him to live in Bury."

"Well—yes, that's true. But you must understand that Helena had been brought up in Bury, her father had friends in Cambridge, and she was often taken to concerts and plays and the like. She enjoyed her summer fling on a farm, it was not her life."

He was listening to something Hamish was saying—that Herbert Swift had not been happy as a farmer's son.

Rutledge said, "Was it the visit of this girl from Bury that made Swift decide to become a solicitor rather than farm with his brother?"

Mrs. Abbot's eyebrows flew up in surprise. "I'd never thought about that, to tell you the truth. Perhaps it was. But of course he married a girl from Ely. Not Helena."

Still, Helena's visit must have sown the seeds of discontent. Even a gentleman farmer's lot was not going to satisfy a young man who had glimpsed another world, one where he had seen himself lacking the polish and sophistication to enter.

The question now was, how had that visit changed Ben Montgomery?

"And your brother? What has become of him?"

A cloud passed over her face. "Ben chose the Army. He went to Sandhurst, over his father's objections. We'd had a military band come to Ely that summer, and we all went to hear them play on Palace Green. Ben talked of nothing else after that. It broke my mother's heart. She was never the same afterward."

"Where is he now?"

"Ben? He lives in London. We don't see him very often. The Army changed him. He was such a sweet boy, kind to Shirley and me, always helping Papa and the men on the farm, and of course was the heir to it. But when I married he asked my husband to take it on." She looked around the room. "I was born in this house, you know. I still live here."

"And your older sister?"

"She married a trainer down in Newmarket. She loved horses, I wasn't surprised when she brought Ted home."

"How did the Army change your brother?"

"He was always such a skinny lad. You wouldn't know him now, his shoulders as wide as a door, and three more inches in height. But that was all right, you know. It was the grimness about him that made him a stranger to us. When I said something about that, he told me that he killed men for a living, and it was expected of him to live with it. I asked him why he didn't walk away, and he said he liked the Army, most of his friends were soldiers, and he didn't know what else he might like to do." She glanced toward her daughters, then turned back toward Rutledge. "I shouldn't have told you that. I can't think why I did. I doubt I've mentioned Ben to anyone in a long time."

"He survived the war, then?"

"Oh, yes. He was wounded several times and has the scars to prove it, so he says. But he's still a serving officer."

He asked for Montgomery's regiment and she told him.

It had seen heavy fighting in the first days of the war.

"Is he married?"

"He was courting someone, but nothing came of it. The Burrows girl. But her father wasn't keen on their marriage. And she's never found anyone else."

A tangle of lives, he thought, and it would be up to him to sort out whether or not Marcella Trowbridge's mother had set in motion something that had seen two men killed and one wounded.

"Did your brother know a Major Clayton? Or Captain Hutchinson?"

"I have no idea," she said, shaking her head. "It's not something he'd mention in his letters. They're usually no more than a few words to tell us he's well and to ask after us. As if he doesn't know what else to say."

"Mama," the younger daughter interrupted diffidently. "Charlotte has the needle threaded at last."

"Wonderful, my dear. Thank you. Is there anything else, Mr. Rutledge? I don't think I've been very much help."

But she had. He thanked her and left.

What he'd learned from Mrs. Abbot warranted traveling to London, but he was reluctant to leave the Fen country just now. He drove back to Wriston, intending to go on to Ely, but as an afterthought he stopped at Miss Trowbridge's door and asked if he could speak to her.

She greeted him coolly but allowed him to come inside.

For once Clarissa was awake, and she examined him with interest, picking up the scent, he thought, of the Irish wolfhound.

"I've just called on Mrs. Abbot," Rutledge began, taking the seat he was offered. "I understand your mother came one summer to visit the Montgomery sisters."

"She did. It was her first visit to the Fens. I don't think she'd have come again if she hadn't met my father. She liked Society, and there's very little of that in Wriston." Echoing what Mrs. Abbot had said, Marcella Trowbridge added, "Farmers and their wives work from first light to last. There isn't time for visiting art galleries or attending the theater or musical evenings. It was the way my mother had been brought up."

"And yet you—and your grandmother, who had this cottage before you—have been happy enough in Wriston."

"You don't know if I'm happy or not," she retorted sharply.

"Yes, that's true. Sorry. I was also told that Herbert Swift and Ben Montgomery quarreled over your mother."

She smiled suddenly, lighting her face with brightness. "I've heard that story. They were only boys. The fight was broken up by the man who kept the windmill. Angus."

"Angus?"

"He was a Scot. At a guess he left the Highlands to seek his fortune, and very likely he got no farther than Cambridgeshire before his money ran out. I do know he was more or less adopted by the old man who kept the mill at that time. Mr. Sherborne had no son, and Angus had no father. They hit it off, and Angus took over the mill when Mr. Sherborne was too ill to work it any longer."

"Where is this man Angus now?"

"I should think he's dead. He left Wriston years ago, but I remember him from my childhood. A quiet, lonely man. He liked my grandmother. But at the end of each December he got terribly drunk—some sort of Scottish holiday—and then was completely sober for the rest of the year."

"Hogmanay," Hamish said, in the back of Rutledge's mind, and before he could stop himself, he repeated the word aloud.

"I'm sorry?" Miss Trowbridge said, uncertain.

"It's the Scots' new year," Rutledge replied. "Celebrated with food and whisky."

"I don't think Angus was very much interested in the food. But he did enjoy his drink."

"You call him Angus. What was his full name?"

"I don't think I ever heard it. He was always just—Angus."

Another false lead.

"Why did the mill house burn?" he asked, curious.

"I don't really know. There are any number of stories. It was a windy, stormy night, and I expect a lamp blew over. Our roof was damaged as well, and two of the blades of the mill were broken. There was more trouble in the village. Slates from the church roof, a few trees down, a chimney, and even a few flowerpots dislodged from steps and doorways." She gestured toward the world outside. "It's so flat, you see. There's nothing to stop the wind for miles, and then suddenly there's a village in its path. Without the mill we feared there would be extensive flooding. But the rain passed with the wind. That was all that saved us."

He had a feeling she hadn't told him the truth. But why would she lie?

He thanked her and rose.

"The mill house is said to be haunted. Or was," she went on as she followed him to the door. "I don't know if fire destroys ghosts as well as buildings."

"How was it haunted?"

"Angus claimed it was haunted by his wife. I hadn't known he'd been married, and I asked if she had died. He told me that not all ghosts are dead. I thought it an odd thing to say. But Mr. Sherborne claimed it was haunted too. I never knew him, but apparently he often told the story that two of the Dutchmen brought over to drain the Fens had played cards there one night. There were two versions of the story. One version held that it was on a Sunday that they were play-ing, and the Devil came and took their souls, leaving only their bodies with nowhere to go. The other version claims that they fought and one killed the other, but not before he'd been gravely wounded himself.

And he died later of his wounds. He goes back to the house, looking for his friend, to make certain he's dead."

She lived here alone, out by the mill, Rutledge thought, but the stories seemed not to trouble her. If ghosts walked, she didn't see or fear them.

But he thought she must be haunted in some way. He remembered finding her staring up at the mill, as if searching for something. Or waiting for someone?

"Who looks after the mill now?" Rutledge asked. "It's still a working mill, is it not?"

"Yes, it is. Currently it's the ironmonger who sees to it. It's a hobby, I think, that he's grown tired of, but no one else has come forward. The Rector offered, but then when it comes to machinery, he's rather at sixes and sevens."

I n the afternoon Rutledge drove to Ely, to try again to reach Sergeant Gibson.

Clouds were building on the horizon now, and the air had that oddly heavy feeling that presaged a storm.

Rutledge paid a courtesy call on Inspector Warren before going on to the telephone, to report what he'd learned—but not what he suspected about the killer.

Warren smiled wryly. "You've not made much progress."

"I've brought that list of ex-soldiers." He took it out and spread the sheets across Warren's desk so they could study it at the same time. "This is what I've discovered thus far. What do you know about the sort of war these men had? The ones with the question mark by their names. I've spoken to them, but I wasn't satisfied when I left that they were in the clear." He stepped back and waited.

"A little. But I'm not sure what you're after," Warren said, parrying the question.

"Have they been troublesome in the past?"

"The only trouble has been occasional public drunkenness and assault. It's not unusual for a man who served in the war to find himself in an altercation with someone who wasn't. I've told you, we don't run to murders, here. Although you'd think, given the isolation of the Fens, that we'd regularly find a body or two in the ditches or under one of the bridges. There are people in Newmarket who might wish to be rid of a troublesome debtor or the like. But the thing is, people down there don't know the Fens; they couldn't hide a body as well as I could, for one. And since you can see for great distances, someone stopping a motorcar to toss a corpse into a ditch is more likely to be spotted than someone around, say, Norfolk, with its low hills."

Whoever his man was, Rutledge thought, he hadn't hurried into murder. He'd waited, and rid himself of his target in such a way that he wasn't a suspect.

"Thornton. Ruskin. Brenner. What do you know about them?"

"Nothing professionally. Thornton's family goes back a long way in the Fens—to the fifteen hundreds, I expect. There are memorials in the churchyard at Isleham to many of them. I'd be surprised if he turned out to be our man. Quiet, respectable, and no history of violence. Ruskin and Brenner haven't been quite the same since the war. But they've done nothing out of character that I got wind of. Brenner was drunk once or twice, but as a rule he's sober, and even if he's drunk he stays in his house. Ruskin keeps to himself, is surly sometimes with his custom, but no better nor worse than the others."

"It doesn't mean they don't have another life."

"If they do, then they've managed to keep it quiet. There's been no gossip."

"What about Ben Montgomery?"

"I don't think he's been home again more than three or four times in ten years. You're out of luck, Rutledge." He smiled to take any sting out of the words.

"Brenner knew Hutchinson. I'd swear to it."

"Did he, by God?" Inspector Warren said, rapidly rethinking his rather cavalier dismissal of Brenner and the others.

It was Rutledge's turn to smile. "And Montgomery is in the Army in London. What are the odds that he hasn't at least encountered Hutchinson? He most certainly knew the Swift brothers and Burrows."

"What else haven't we uncovered?"

"That's the question." Rutledge began to collect the lists.

"Are you going to London, then?"

"Not yet. But I shall have to if I'm to question Miss Clayton and Montgomery. And find out how Brenner knew Hutchinson."

"Miss Clayton? Captain Clayton's sister? I knew him before the war."

"Hutchinson came to his funeral. In Burwell."

"I'll be damned." Warren stared. "Are you sure of that?"

"It helps," Rutledge said, "to remember that even people we think we know well can kill."

The call to London yielded no fresh information. Sergeant Gibson had found little to pass on. "There's not been much time," he explained.

Still, Rutledge gave him the three names he'd mentioned to Inspector Warren. "I don't think you'll find skeletons in these closets, not unless we're very lucky. But I have to be sure."

He had intended to stop at The Lamb for his dinner. It was close by the Cathedral and even older than The Deacon, where he'd stayed earlier. But wind was already tossing the trees as he went back to his motorcar, and the sky in the east was black. He had no wish to be crossing the Fens in a driving rainstorm, and it appeared that that was what was coming.

He could hear the thunder behind him as he drove out of Ely, and it rode his coattails out across the Fens. There was the faintest line of sunset on the western horizon, and it seemed to intensify the darkness behind him. The storm loomed like a great black beast, shot with lightning and roiled by the wind.

Halfway to Wriston, he heard a motorcycle coming up behind him, throttle open, racing the storm. It passed him with a roar, but he could see it long after the sound had faded into the distance. Then it was over one of the humpback bridges and lost to sight.

Not five minutes later, great drops of rain, driven by heavy gusts, hit with the force of hail, and Rutledge picked up speed, putting the large motorcar through its paces on the straightaway. The duck pond was empty as he reached the second green, and the trees near the church were thrashing like tormented souls. He came to a skidding halt in front of The Dutchman Inn, and made it through the door just as a crash of thunder followed a blue flash of lightning.

"Mr. Rutledge?" Miss Bartram's voice came from the sitting room, sharp and anxious.

"Yes, I just missed the storm," he called, his words almost lost as the rain came down in wild sheets, pounding the roof and making the windows rattle.

She came to meet him, her face anxious.

"Something's happened," she said. "Constable McBride was just here, asking for you."

Chapter 12

Rutledge looked out at the High Street, almost invisible in the blowing sheets of rain. Lightning flashed, thunder crackling almost on its heels, and Miss Bartram cried out.

He slammed the door against the still-rising wind.

"Has anything happened to Mr. Burrows?"

"I-I don't know. I don't—Constable McBride didn't say—just that it was urgent."

He could hear the wind rising as the thunder moved toward them, and he debated trying to reach the police station. Almost at once he thought better of it.

Whatever had happened, it would have to wait. There was nothing either he or McBride could do just now.

Miss Bartram said, "I was intending to put the kettle on. I—" She broke off as thunder seemed to shake the house. The glass drops on the tall lamp behind her tinkled discordantly, and in the kitchen something fell with a crash. "I do hate these late storms so!" Turning, she hurried into the sitting room and sat down. "It will be over soon, that's the one saving grace. Meanwhile—" The lightning was blue, reflected in the glass of the displays, seeming to surround them. The next clap was deafening.

Standing in the doorway between the sitting room and the short hall, Rutledge said, "I think that struck something. But not here. It should be moving on now."

And he was right. They could follow the storm as it swept westward. In a few minutes the worst had passed, leaving behind a hard rain. Lifting the curtain to look out at the street, he could see that it was awash with puddles, and that surely meant that the ditches were full, nearing capacity. It was a sobering thought.

With a word to Miss Bartram, Rutledge opened the inn door. Turning to step outside, he encountered Miss Trowbridge, umbrella in hand, hurrying toward them. Her skirts were wet and heavy with mud.

"The lightning struck one of the arms of the mill. We need to repair it as soon as possible."

"Who do you need?"

"Mr. Ross. He'll know what to do."

"Come inside. I'll find him."

"My shoes are muddy—"

"Never mind, come inside."

He waited until she was safely indoors, took her umbrella with him, and got the motorcar started. Reversing in a spray of muddy water, he drove down to the ironmonger's shop. Ross was inside, tidying up the table with the boxes of nails.

As soon as he saw Rutledge striding through the doorway, he said, "Was it the mill?"

"Yes. I'm afraid so. One arm, according to Miss Trowbridge."

"Right. I'll get what I need and collect the others."

He turned toward the back of his shop as Rutledge said, "Can I help?"

"We've repaired it before. We'll manage."

Following him, Rutledge could see the fields beyond the shop, glistening with water as the sun tried to break through the heavy clouds in the east, a single ray lighting up the sky for a moment and then vanishing just as quickly.

Ross was right, he seemed to have everything in hand. Rutledge turned, went out through the High Street door, and made his way through the rain to the police station.

McBride was at his desk, and he rose as Rutledge came in.

"You're soaked, man," he said. "Were you on the road when this hit?"

"I made it as far as the inn in time. But there's an arm of the mill that's down. Lightning. Ross is collecting his people to see to it."

"I'm needed, then. This came for you. An hour ago." He passed an envelope to Rutledge. "Special messenger."

The motorcycle.

Rutledge tore open the envelope and pulled out a sheet of paper.

The message was from Jason Fallowfield, forwarded by Inspector Warren.

I've spoken to Mr. Lowell, the father of the artillery officer, Major Lowell, who offered his help to Inspector Warren. His son will be in Ely this evening, passing through from Lincoln. I thought you'd want to know. If you could call around seven, I'll be happy to arrange for a meeting.

Rutledge took out his watch. There was barely enough time to reach Ely.

"I must go. Miss Trowbridge is at the inn. Give her the umbrella. And tell Miss Bartram that I'll probably be staying over in Ely."

And he was out the door, back in his motorcar, and setting out for Ely. He could watch the clouds lift, and the Cathedral appear like a mirage again, floating above the steaming fields. The road under his tires, slick clay, with puddles concealing the pits and ruts, was treacherous and took all his concentration. He was aware of Hamish in the rear seat, just behind his right shoulder, but had no time for him. The bottoms of his trousers, one sleeve, and across his back where the rain had soaked his clothing felt the cool wind of his passage, but there was nothing to be done about them.

The Cathedral clock was showing five minutes after seven o'clock as he caught sight of it passing Palace Green. And it was nearly ten after the hour when he pulled up in front of the house belonging to the bride's family.

It was still raining as he walked up the path, and he could feel the wet soaking through his coat, damp against his flesh now.

The same maid opened the door to him. "Mr. Rutledge?"

"Yes, that's right."

"Mr. Fallowfield and Mr. Hale are waiting for you in the library. If you'll come this way?"

He followed her down the passage, where he was shown into a large library, shelves ranging around the room, and long windows looking out on a garden dripping and windblown.

Jason Fallowfield and his father-in-law rose to greet him, and Fallowfield made the introductions.

"Major Lowell is just changing for dinner. He was held up by the storm. Are you all right?"

"I'm afraid I was caught in it as well," Rutledge said. "It's kind of you to arrange this meeting."

"Not at all. I'm glad to have been of some use."

Hale, who was tall, slender, and graying, said, "I really don't see what can be gained by this meeting, but Jason here tells me you were very anxious to meet Alex."

"He was there," Rutledge said. "He may have noticed something that the rest of us have missed."

"I am astonished that no progress has been made—" He broke off as the library door opened again and the Major walked in.

Fallowfield introduced Rutledge and then said, "I'm sure you'd like to speak to Alex alone. Mr. Hale and I will join the ladies in the drawing room."

It was clear that Hale would have preferred to stay. And Rutledge could understand why—after all, it was the wedding of his daughter that had nearly been ruined by the shooting. But Fallowfield showed unusual resolve in ushering him out of his own library.

Rutledge had used the moment to judge Lowell.

He was of medium height, his carriage that of a career military man, his fair hair already graying at the temples. He came forward, took one of the chairs, and said, "I have only a few minutes. I've given my statement to Inspector Warren, but I understand that you have several questions about that day."

"You seemed to take charge very efficiently."

"There were no policemen. Hale hadn't hired any to handle the traffic, as the motorcars were to stop at the top of the Green. I myself sent someone to bring the police to the Cathedral. Young Fallowfield seemed to be thunderstruck, and I got him out of the way as quickly as possible. My first thought, God knows why, was that the man with the rifle had meant to kill *him*. Hutchinson wasn't even in the wedding party, a guest only, and certainly Fallowfield thought it likely as well that he must have been the intended target."

"I'm afraid I don't understand the logic of that. Why should someone wish to kill the groom on his wedding day? Surely the man with the rifle knew what he was doing?"

"Who else would anyone be shooting at?" Lowell countered. "We most certainly had no idea why Hutchinson should be killed. Hale was arriving with his daughter; the other important guests had already been seated. The groom was there, a matter of feet away. I heard the shot, of course, and I looked at every possible vantage point. I saw no one. No one at all. Whoever it was hadn't stood there gloating, he'd vanished. But that didn't mean he wasn't going to take a second shot from another position. With the groom safely away, I waited for the police, who came promptly, I must say. And with all due respect, Inspector Warren hadn't been in France. He was doing his best, but he was as shocked as the rest."

"Where was the killer?"

Lowell frowned. "I would have said that the shot came from above my head, but the doorway confused the sound, it echoed and changed it. I don't know Ely very well and wasn't aware until later that one can go up into the tower. Still, the most likely source was by that gate into the Cathedral grounds. It was most certainly his best chance of getting away unobserved."

"You don't think he took a greater risk, using the tower?"

"I was there in the doorway. He'd have had to pass me."

"But you weren't. You ran forward to make sure Fallowfield was moved to safety, and the doorway was unguarded. I've climbed up there. It takes time to make your way down."

Staring at him, Lowell considered the matter. "Yes, of course. You're right. I should have remained where I was. But I didn't. And I don't know that anyone else stayed there."

"Did you see a man with a barrow?"

"A barrow. No. I don't believe so. Or I should say I never saw the barrow. But come to think of it, as I was motioning Hale and his daughter to leave the scene as quickly as possible, I did see a frightened old man with a bicycle. I don't know where he came from, but after I'd shut Fallowfield in the Bishop's quarters, I noticed him being buffeted by people running up the street from the school."

"Was he carrying anything?"

"No, both hands were on the handlebars, as I remember."

"Did you mention him to Inspector Warren when you gave your statement?"

"I don't believe I did. Until you asked about the barrow, I'd quite forgot him. Besides, he was hardly a threat."

There was a tap at the door. It opened on the heels of that and Jason Fallowfield said apologetically, "Sorry. But they're going in to dinner."

"I've kept you too long, Major. Thank you for your help."

Fallowfield politely accompanied Rutledge to the outer door, saying, "I must apologize for my father-in-law. He's still rather bitter about what happened that day. And I can't fault him for that. But we were there, and if we can help the police in any way, so much the better."

"I'm grateful," Rutledge said. "We'll have our man in the end. It's just a matter of time."

But as he walked back to his motorcar in the light rain that was falling now, Hamish was reminding him that he had been rash to promise.

He drove not to The Deacon Inn but to the house Teddy Mathews shared with his sister.

They too had just sat down to their evening meal, and Miss Mathews was reluctant to interrupt it.

"We have guests. It would be more convenient if you could return tomorrow."

"I won't be in Ely tomorrow," Rutledge told her. "And it's rather urgent."

She went to fetch her brother, and apparently he'd seen her displeasure, for he asked almost at once, "Has something happened?"

"I need to clarify one point in your statement," Rutledge said carefully. "Did you see an elderly man with a bicycle standing with you behind the barricade?"

"I don't believe I did," he answered slowly. "Should I have?"

"I can't be sure until we find this man. But thank you—and you as well, Miss Mathews—for taking the time to assist the police."

From there he went to the house of Mrs. Boggs, the washerwoman.

She had just finished her tea, and affably asked him if he'd had his.

"Yes, thank you, Mrs. Boggs," he told her. "There's just one question I'd like to ask. Did you notice anyone with a bicycle walking past the Cathedral doors just after the shot was fired?"

"A bicycle? I can't say that I did." She cocked her head to one side, as if listening to an inner voice. "But now you mention it, I did see an elderly man coming out of the church. I don't know where he went. I expect he'd been in one of the chapels, praying. Certainly not one of the wedding party."

"Did he have anything in his hands?"

"I don't believe he did. Just an old man looking as if he were ill."

He thanked her and left.

Inspector Warren had gone home for his own dinner when Rutledge called in at the police station. He was directed instead to a young constable who worked with Warren.

Constable Nash said, "Do we have a statement from the elderly man seen coming out of the church? I'll look, sir, but I don't recall that statement in particular. Was he one of the wedding guests?"

"I understand that he was not."

Constable Nash led him to Inspector Warren's office and went around the desk to open the center drawer. Taking out a list, he scanned it. "I don't think he's here. Unless he's that one." He pointed to a name on the second page. "He was with his daughter, as I remember."

"It's likely he was riding a bicycle."

"A bicycle, sir?" Nash scanned the list again. "Are you sure he was coming out of the church?"

"One source says he was on a bicycle. The other that he was coming out of the church."

Nash shook his head. "I must say, he's not on our list. But people had come from the direction of The Lamb, you know—that is, from the street behind the barricade—and simply kept going. They hadn't been present when Captain Hutchinson was killed, they'd just been attracted by the sound of the rifle and then hurried on after they saw a man lying on the Green." He smiled deprecatingly. "It was a Saturday, sir, and a fair day. Everyone was out and about, doing a little marketing, taking their children or their dog for a walk. We have well over a hundred statements here."

"Yes, I understand. It's probably of no importance, then. Thank you, Constable. I shan't disturb Inspector Warren tonight. Will you leave a message for him? That I spoke to Major Lowell, and I think he can be removed from the list of suspects."

"I'll do that, sir. Thank you, sir."

It was close on nine now, and the rain had finally stopped. Rutledge had lost his appetite and decided to drive back to Wriston after all.

Clouds were still scudding across the sky, and the frogs had begun a chorus in the flooded fields and the ditches. In one place the embankment had been breached, and water covered the road. He tested the depth and changed his mind about driving through it in the dark. Reversing, he went back to the last crossroads, and found the turning for Isleham.

He was nearly there when close by the priory barn he saw a man out walking, keeping to the shadows.

Rutledge slowed, and watched for a moment. There was something furtive about the man's movements, and he was carrying something in his left hand.

Hamish said, "He doesna' move like a man full of the drink."

Rutledge had been thinking the same thing. After a moment, he left the motorcar where it was and, walking across the wet grass toward the priory barn, followed the shadowy figure. It had disappeared around the corner of the building, and Rutledge went after him.

He'd just reached the corner and was about to turn it, when someone came around from the far side and nearly blundered into him.

"Who the hell are you and what are you doing here?"

Rutledge said, "I could ask you the same thing. I'm Scotland
Yard."

The man moved back. "Indeed. Rutledge, is it? I'm Thornton. You
interviewed me."

"What are you doing out here?"

"I saw someone lurking about in the churchyard. I was just
coming home—I'd got caught in the rain over in Soham. I watched
for a minute or two, couldn't decide what he was doing, and started
after him to ask his business. But he went out through the lych-gate,
doubled back, and disappeared in this direction. I'd like very much to
know who he was."

"Where did he go?"

"That's just it. I lost him on the far side of the barn. He simply disappeared."

"Did you go inside?"

"The door is locked. To keep the young people out, and to prevent
the Travelers from using it to sleep rough."

"What did he look like?"

"I've no idea. I never got a good look at him." Thornton raised his
left hand. "I brought a stick with me. Just in case. There's seldom trouble here in Isleham, but after the shootings, it puts the wind up when
you see someone hanging about like that. At this hour of the evening."

"Was he carrying anything?"

"I don't know. It looked like it. A satchel or something. Or it could
have been his dinner and his bedroll. It was too dark to be sure."

Then which man had attracted Rutledge's attention? Thornton
with his stick? Or the interloper with his bedroll? It was impossible to
tell. And yet there was no reason for Thornton to be sneaking around
in his own village unless he *was* following someone else.

"Let's have another look."

Together they walked around the barn, but there was no one to be seen.

"He could have gone through the fields, but I doubt it," Thornton was saying. "The thing is, they're wet, and the pitches are running high. What brings you to Isleham? Still interviewing ex-soldiers?"

"The road from Ely to Wriston is flooded."

"Not surprising. There are low places along there. And sometimes the banks are weakened and the water comes through. I'll report it."

"Can I give you a lift?"

"Yes, that's kind of you." They walked together toward Rutledge's motorcar. "What brings you out at this hour?"

"I was in Ely. Police business."

Thornton smiled, a flash of white teeth in the darkness as he turned toward Rutledge. "Successful, I hope."

"Early days," Rutledge answered.

It was not far to Thornton's house. Rutledge stopped and his passenger got down.

"Thanks. If I discover who it was, I'll let you know." He turned and walked up to his door, setting the stick to one side before going inside.

Rutledge watched him go.

And then he went back to the priory barn and searched a second time. But no one was there. Where had the man gone?

He stopped at the barn door and tested it, even though Thornton had told him it was kept locked. It swung open, a greater darkness inside.

"Anyone there?" he called, his voice echoing around the walls.

There was no answer. He stood there, testing the darkness. He'd left his torch in his motorcar. After a moment, he moved forward, working his way around the walls. But when he'd made a circuit of the interior, he found no one there. And no one had slipped out the door, he was nearly sure of that.

He went back to the motorcar and took out his torch. When he shone the light on the door, he saw that the lock had been broken. Someone then had forced his way inside while Thornton was moving around the walls outside.

He turned on the torch and cast the light about. Except for a few wet footprints on the dry, dusty floor, there was no other sign of whoever had come inside.

He must have escaped while Rutledge and Thornton were driving away. And where he was now was anyone's guess.

Rutledge went back to his motorcar and slowly drove up and down the streets of Isleham, but the only thing he saw was a dog trotting homeward. Rain had kept most people close.

So who had been out in the wet, lurking, as Thornton had put it, in the churchyard? Or had the man been a figment of Thornton's imagination?

Dissatisfied, he headed for Wriston, coming in from the direction of Burwell rather than the flooded Ely road and over the bridge past the mill.

In the flare of his headlamps, he could see the bald new repairs where the arm had broken. There was very little standing water, but Ross and his men had been quick, thanks to Miss Trowbridge's warning. Even so, he could hear the rush of water beneath the bridge, and there was the glitter of pooling in the ruins of the mill house.

A light glowed in the windows of Miss Trowbridge's cottage, and the door opened a little to let the white cat in. If she saw Rutledge she gave no sign of it, shutting the door as soon as Clarissa darted inside.

He continued to The Dutchman Inn and pulled up near the steps.

There was water on the street, puddles everywhere he looked as he splashed around the motorcar to the door. Miss Bartram had been watching for him. He walked in to find her just coming into the hall.

"I've put some dinner aside for you," she said cheerfully. "I thought perhaps there wouldn't be time to find anything in Ely."

It was kind of her, and he ate the food she warmed for him. But he couldn't satisfy her curiosity about what had taken him so long in Ely.

He wasn't sure he knew the answer to that himself.

Fog followed the rain. When Rutledge woke in the middle of the night, he could see the thick white mist outside his windows, wrapping the house in the eerie silence of three o'clock in the morning.

He went to the window to look out, but he could barely make out his motorcar.

Listening, using his ears rather than his eyes, he could have sworn he heard a bicycle being pedaled along the High. Was it his imagination, that half-asleep, half-awake moment when one is roused in the middle of the night? He couldn't be sure, and then the sound vanished, lost in the darkness.

What he heard next, he recognized instantly: the sound of a horse being ridden fast, coming from the direction of the mill.

He found his clothes without turning on the lamp, and slipping downstairs, he let himself out as quickly as he could.

The horse had gone past, he couldn't tell where, but he could no longer hear hoofbeats.

He began walking, using the High Street to guide him, staying in the middle of it. It wasn't long before he could hear voices in the distance, and using those as his goal, he walked on. The mist, mercifully, wasn't as thick as it had been that first night.

At length he could make out what sounded like McBride's voice, and then someone responding, urgent and frightened. A woman's voice? Miss Trowbridge, as far as he knew, didn't keep a horse. Who then? Miss Burrows?

"McBride?" he called, suddenly galvanized into action.

"Rutledge?" McBride answered. "I didn't know you were back. You'd better come."

He followed the voice, and there in front of a house door, not the police station, was McBride, his uniform donned over his nightshirt while Miss Burrows was holding the reins of her horse, peering anxiously into the mist.

Seeing him finally, she said, "I heard the shotgun. I was afraid to go to the house—in this. And so I came for help."

"You can't drive in this," McBride said to Rutledge. "You don't know the roads."

"I can try," Rutledge said. "But I think Miss Burrows ought to stay here."

"*No.* No, it's my father, I want to go." She hastily secured the horse while McBride was trying to persuade her to wait.

"We're wasting time," Rutledge said. "Are you coming, McBride?" He turned, hoping he could find his way back to the inn. The mist seemed to thin, thicken, and thin again. He recognized the dormer window of the ironmonger's shop and knew he'd passed the market cross without seeing it. And then the motorcar came into view. He bent to turn the crank as McBride hurried to open the rear door for Miss Burrows. Rutledge spared a fleeting thought for Hamish as she slid into the seat, then he was behind the wheel, reversing to drive back toward the mill.

It was difficult. He saw the gate to Miss Trowbridge's house and then nearly missed the turning over the bridge. Soon Miss Burrows, reaching over from the rear seat, pointed.

"There—the road you're after."

It was a straight run then, until the last of the trees lining the lane into the Burrows farm loomed to his left, and he made the turn with ease.

The problem was how to approach the house. He drove with care, missing the ruts he could see, slipping and sliding in the wet clay. Then the lights of the house glowed through the mist.

Out of the darkness came the most ferocious noise that Rutledge had ever heard. He stopped, and even as he pulled up the brake he realized it must be the dog that Burrows had been planning to borrow.

McBride was saying, "Good God, it's Black Shuck."

Miss Burrows countered with, "It's the dog. Something's wrong."

"We don't know that," Rutledge argued and blew the horn several times.

"Burrows?" he shouted. "It's Rutledge. And Constable McBride. We're here with your daughter. I'm coming in."

The shotgun fired, and even over the dog's barking, Rutledge could hear the pellets raining down in the trees on either side, ten feet ahead of his bonnet.

"Damn it, man, have you run mad?" Rutledge bellowed, angry now.

"Papa?" Miss Burrows cried, her voice breaking. "Please. Are you all right? What has happened? Please—I want to come in."

She was opening the door, getting out. Rutledge reached over the back of his seat and caught her arm.

"No. Stay where you are. He's going to shoot as soon as you come into range."

Miss Burrows fought him, crying and calling to her father.

Rutledge, keeping his eyes away from where Hamish should be sitting, pulled her back inside the motorcar.

And then through the mist Burrows shouted, "Is it you, Betty?"

Suddenly still, Miss Burrows said in a husky voice, "That's my mother's name. Betty."

"We'll have to wait for sunrise," McBride said. "But what if he's hit someone, and he's out there, wounded?"

"There's nothing we can do," Rutledge said quietly. "Walking up there is suicide."

"Betty?" Burrows called again. "Where are you?"

"Something's wrong," Miss Burrows was saying, "His heart—"

But Rutledge didn't think it was the man's heart. "Answer him. Let him think you're his wife."

"I can't."

"You must, if you expect us to help your father."

"Dear, is that you?" she responded, her voice trembling. "Why have you got out your shotgun? I want to come in. Will you let me?"

They sat there, waiting.

And then Burrows called, "McBride? Is that you, Constable?" The barking stopped. "What are you doing out here in the middle of the night?"

"I got word you'd seen something. I've come with the Inspector to see if you were all right."

"You aren't walking, are you?"

"No, we're in Mr. Rutledge's motorcar."

Rutledge turned the headlamps off and then back on again.

"Come in. Hurry. There's someone out there, and I don't think I missed him."

"All right. We're coming in," McBride called. "Don't shoot. We'll stop in front of the house."

And Rutledge eased in the clutch, moving slowly forward, prepared to reach for the brake if Burrows fired again.

This time he let them come as far as the steps of the house. Miss Burrows was out of the motorcar almost before Rutledge had stopped.

"Papa?" She ran into the house, calling her father. They could hear the dog's deep, throaty growl. McBride was out and racing after her, calling to her to wait. Rutledge was at their heels.

They found Burrows sitting by the window of the front room. At his feet, its hackles rising, lay the largest brown dog Rutledge had seen in some time.

"Be quiet, Hector," Burrows said, then noticed his daughter. "I thought you were over with Ed and his wife."

"I was. I heard you fire. I didn't know what to do." She reached out to touch his shoulder and drew her hand back almost in the same movement.

"He's burning up with fever," she told the two men in a low voice.

Rutledge moved the lamp in order to see him better. One side of

Burrows's face was swollen twice its size, red and inflamed where the bullet had grazed him.

"Hello," Burrows said now, as if they had come to call. He set the shotgun down by the chair, and added to his daughter, "I don't feel particularly well. Perhaps I ought to go lie down, now that you're here."

She turned quickly to Rutledge. "What are we to do?"

"He needs a doctor. As soon as possible," Rutledge said, moving around Burrows to put the shotgun out of reach, then leaning down to look at his face. The dog growled again, getting to its feet. "It's infected. The wound. I thought you'd taken care of it."

"He wouldn't let me. Not after that first day. He said it was healing."

But it hadn't.

Straightening up, Rutledge said, "Where is the nearest doctor?"

"Burwell."

"Then let's get him into the motorcar. The sooner he's there, the better."

But Burrows was rising to his feet, and the dog stood by him as if daring anyone to touch him. "I'm thirsty. I think I'll have a little water before I go up."

"Papa, we need to go to Burwell. To the doctor. Come with me, won't you?"

"I don't need a doctor," he said testily. "I'm all right. Just tired. What time is it?"

Rutledge stepped forward. "Mr. Burrows. Your daughter isn't feeling well either. I think we ought to take her to see a doctor. Will you come with us? I think she would be more comfortable if you did."

Burrows frowned as he looked at Rutledge. "Who are you?"

"I've come from London, Mr. Burrows. We need to hurry. Will you go with us?"

"All right," he said docilely. "If McBride thinks it best. Stay, Hector." The dog subsided, although it seemed uncertain.

"I do, I most certainly do," the constable said quickly.

Between them, Miss Burrows and McBride got her father outside and down to the motorcar. The dog followed as far as the door, then stopped.

Burrows, turning to look at it, exclaimed, "Here. Where's my shotgun?"

Rutledge answered him quickly. "It's in the boot."

"Well, then." He got into the motorcar, and Rutledge could hear Hamish in the back of his mind.

It was difficult reversing, but soon they were on their way down the dark drive, the headlamps trying to pierce the fog and getting nowhere. Behind them they could hear Hector howl once, and then he was quiet.

Burrows turned to his daughter, and said, "There's a mist coming in."

They managed to reach Burwell without mishap, but twice McBride had to get down and find the road ahead. All the while Burrows was complaining querulously that he was tired and wanted to go home. Passing the churchyard and then the Church of St. Mary's, where Major Clayton's services had been held, Rutledge said quietly, "McBride?"

"Down that street—to your left. Yes, that's right. Turn left again at the next corner." After a moment, he added, "There. The house just there. Dr. Harris."

"Go to the door. He'll know you, I think. Miss Burrows and I will bring her father as soon as the doctor answers."

It was nearly two minutes before a light came on, and then a figure appeared in the doorway.

"What is it? What's the emergency?" a man's voice asked.

"We've a sick man here, Doctor." McBride turned as Rutledge coaxed Burrows up the walk and to the door. Harris opened it wider to allow them to pass, and they stepped inside. In the lamplight, he stared at Burrows's swollen face.

"What happened?"

"He was shot," Rutledge said. "And neglected the wound. He's delirious." He quickly explained the situation.

"This way." Harris led them down a passage to the door that opened into his surgery. "Let me light the other lamp."

As the light flared, Harris said, "All right, Mr. Burrows. Let me have a look at your face."

But in the end, Rutledge and McBride had to hold the man in his chair while Harris examined the wound. Miss Burrows, stifling sobs, stood in a corner out of the way.

"The wound's badly infected," Harris said. "I need to clean it, and then we'll see what's to be done."

He worked steadily while Burrows assured him that all was well, he didn't need a doctor. Fifteen minutes later, he said, "I think he ought to stay here for what's left of the night. I can't take his temperature, as agitated he is, but it's high enough. I'll give him something for that, and also to help him sleep." He took out two powders, put them into a glass of water, and said, "Are you thirsty, Burrows? Drink this, if you will." When the glass was empty he added quietly, "Wait here."

He came back shortly and said, "The room's ready. I've prepared a bed for Miss Burrows as well. It will help her father if she stays."

By this time the sedative was beginning to take effect. They got a drowsy Burrows to the narrow room made up for him and put him to bed. Leaving Miss Burrows to sit with him until he was fully asleep, the doctor led the way back to his examining room.

"When was he shot? Tell me the details."

Rutledge gave him an abbreviated version of events, and Harris nodded. "It's going to be touch and go. I dressed the wound with a septic powder, but we'll know by tomorrow if it will work. Are you staying in Burwell?"

Rutledge said, "No, there's something we must attend to. We'll be back tomorrow."

"Very well. I'm glad you brought him in when you did."

He saw them to the door, and when McBride had turned the crank and joined Rutledge in the motorcar, he said, "Where now?"

"Back to the house. First of all to take care of the dog. As soon as it's light, we'll see if there's a body there. Or if Burrows was just firing at shadows."

McBride took a deep breath. "Think he'll be all right?"

"It's anyone's guess. Harris was worried."

By the time they had reached the Burrows house the mist was beginning to lift, helped by a light predawn breeze.

Hector was reluctant to let them in, but Rutledge finally managed to calm him.

They sat in the front room, McBride dozing in his chair, until the dawn had brightened, no more than a dull glow in the shredding mist, and then they went out to search.

It didn't take long. Hector, allowed outside, ran nose to the ground around the perimeter of the house and outbuildings, then trotted back to Rutledge and McBride.

"No body, then," McBride said. "It was all his fever, wasn't it?"

"I'm not sure," Rutledge said. "Look there." He pointed to where Hector was sniffing with particular interest in the thicker grass that grew around the tree nearest the house. He knelt for a better look. "Is that blood?" Reaching out, he touched one of the drops Hector had found. His fingers when he turned them over were a rusty red. "He hit something. Or someone. I wonder who . . ."

Burrows was no better in the morning. Rutledge had waited until full daylight to leave the farm because he wanted to look for more signs that Burrows had actually shot someone. But if there was anything to find, it had been so diluted by the damp ground that it was all but invisible. The first spots had survived only because they were by the trunk of one of the trees and well enough protected.

He and McBride took Hector back to his owner, watching the huge dog nearly twist himself in knots with joy at the reunion. Then

Rutledge drove Constable McBride to Wriston, before turning back to Burwell.

Dr. Harris couldn't tell him with any certainty what the outcome of the infection would be.

"It could spread. Once in the soft tissue, it's harder to kill. I had one man come in with a small scratch, the infection got into his bloodstream, and there was nothing we could do. But Burrows is healthy, he has a chance. My wife is looking after Miss Burrows. She's been too upset to eat, but I'll give her something a little later to help her sleep. She won't do Burrows any good collapsing over his bed."

"I think when Burrows fired his shotgun last night, he hit someone. You haven't seen any wounds of that sort, have you?"

"Not so far. No. I'll report it if I do." He paused for a moment. "You know, I'm sure, that Captain Hutchinson was here for the funeral of Major Clayton. Earlier in the summer, that was."

"Yes, I've been told he was in Burwell. Only for the day."

"I don't like to spread gossip. But the man was murdered. You're here to conduct the inquiry. All the same, I wouldn't have sought you out. But now you're here . . ."

"Is there something you know about Hutchinson?"

"Not really. No, not about Hutchinson. My wife's cousin lives in London. Apparently she knew Mary Hutchinson rather well. They grew up in the same village."

"Mary Hutchinson? His sister?"

"His wife."

"I believe she's dead," Rutledge said, not sure where the conversation was heading.

"Yes. I wonder—I wonder if you've looked into that."

There had been no reason to look into Mary Hutchinson's life. Or her death. She had been a part of the background of the victim.

"What can you tell me about her?"

"That's just it. I can't. It's my wife who told me. When her cousin

Alice learned about Hutchinson's death, she wrote to my wife. She'd said nothing for all these years, but with Hutchinson dead, she felt free to speak. It seems she'd been very worried about Mary for some time. There was a letter that Mary wrote to Alice shortly before she died. Alice sent it to my wife to read." He coughed in embarrassment. "This is awkward. Perhaps you should speak to my wife."

"Perhaps I should," Rutledge said, "if she can shed any light at all on these murders."

"I doubt she can do that. Just go through the passage there, turn left, and knock at the first door you come to."

Rutledge thanked him and followed his directions.

When he tapped lightly on the closed door, a woman's voice called, "Come."

He entered a small sitting room where a woman was working at a desk. She turned. Mrs. Harris was small, trim, and pretty, with the calm demeanor of a woman who knew her own worth. She said, "Mr. Rutledge," and rose to cross the room.

"Your husband tells me you know something about the late Captain Hutchinson."

Her mouth tightened as she gestured to the chairs by the hearth. "My cousin Alice is nobody's fool," she said after a moment. "I'll tell you that in the beginning. I'll also tell you that I met Captain Hutchinson when he was here for Major Clayton's funeral. I wanted to meet him, you see. To discover for myself what sort of man he was."

"What did you learn?" Rutledge asked.

"That my cousin was probably right about him. Charming and manipulative. He neglected his wife—Alice's friend—terribly. Mary was quite wealthy, you see. And her death was under questionable circumstances."

"What sort of circumstances?"

"To put it bluntly, suicide. It was decided that she had been grieving for her child, who was stillborn. But Alice believed that she regretted her marriage and couldn't go on with it. The charming man she thought she was marrying didn't exist. Mary was—how shall I put it?—Mary wasn't a very pretty woman. And the Captain was a very attractive man. She wouldn't be the first to be captivated by such attentions."

"Go on."

"I wrote to Alice to tell her I'd met the Captain, but it wasn't until he was killed that she sent me a letter she'd received from Mary only a few weeks before her death. I think you ought to read it."

She went to the desk, found the letter, and held it out to Rutledge.

"Are you sure your cousin wouldn't object to my seeing it?"

"Not at all."

Lifting the flap of the envelope, he took out the folded sheet inside. It was very brief.

Darling Alice, I'm so sorry I haven't written. I've been ill. It has not been an easy pregnancy. I think that was because I've been dreadfully unhappy. If this child lives, it will give me something to live for. If it dies, then I'll have nothing. And I don't know if I can go on. No, don't listen to me, it's that this business of having a baby is so trying. Did you feel so down when you were having your first? Tell me you did. It will cheer me to know that I'm not alone in this.

It was signed simply with an *M*.

"She appears to have been having a very difficult time. But I can't see that her death could be laid directly at the Captain's door. Nor does it explain these murders."

"No, perhaps not. But you're investigating the Captain's death. This shows you an entirely different view of the man from the effusive obituary that appeared in the Ely newspaper."

She went back to her desk and retrieved a card. "This is where my cousin lives in London. Perhaps you ought to speak to her. Alice Worth is her name."

He took the card and thanked her as he gave her back the letter and took his leave.

But as he was driving out of Burwell, Rutledge found himself thinking that Mrs. Sedley and Mrs. Harris had seen through the carefully cultivated facade that was the public Captain Hutchinson. Mrs. Sedley because she had watched him insinuate himself where he thought the greatest advantage lay. Mrs. Harris because she had wanted to find out whether her cousin had been right in her assessment of the man.

The question was, What did this have to do with Herbert Swift's death?

Or for that matter, the attempted murder of Mr. Burrows?

Chapter 13

Rutledge spent the rest of the day going through the list he'd made of ex-soldiers, this time in Wicken, but without any luck.

The constable there, a man called Lark, said, shaking his head, "I can't see that this is getting us anywhere, sir."

But somewhere, Rutledge thought, out here in the Fens or in a town close by, is the man who knows how to use a rifle and, more important, how to make himself invisible.

"Someone who came for the shooting?" Lark went on. "The autumn visitor. Or the winter. Miss Bartram over in Wriston knows who they were. Not many of them come now. But she must still have the names."

Rutledge said, "I can't see a connection to Swift and to Captain Hutchinson. Hutchinson hadn't come here until this summer."

"But he did come. And so the killing began."

It was an interesting way of looking at the murders.

"When did Swift come back from Scotland?" Rutledge asked. "Do you know?"

"Late 1918, as I remember. Constable McBride can tell you for certain."

"Close enough. Two years ago. And nothing happened to him. Then Hutchinson came to Cambridgeshire. The first time there was no time to plan. But when the Captain came again, he was killed. Then Swift, because he was already here, already available."

"But how does Burrows fit in?"

That was the problem.

Rutledge thanked Constable Lark, and turned back toward Wriston.

Where was the connection among these men?

Hamish said, "Swift would ha' left for London, if he'd won yon seat in Parliament."

"But his killer is here, not in London. And for some reason he can't go there."

"He couldna' carry the rifle with him."

That made sense. He could hide it here. He knew the land.

By the time Rutledge had arrived at The Dutchman Inn, he'd made up his mind.

The next morning, he left the Fen country for London, stopping in Cambridge for petrol.

I t was late when he reached the city, and later still when he walked into his own flat.

On the long drive south, he'd decided where to begin. Captain Hutchinson's sister.

She had lived with her brother in a house in one of the elegant squares that had seen their heyday in the 1890s. Number 7 was, like its neighbors, large, well kept, still handsome. There was black silk on the knocker, a reminder that it was a house of mourning.

The middle-aged maid who answered the door told him that she would inquire if Miss Hutchinson was receiving visitors. When she returned, she reported that Miss Hutchinson was resting.

"Please tell her that Scotland Yard would like to ask her some questions about her brother's death."

It was several minutes before he was led to a sitting room where Miss Hutchinson was waiting.

She was tall and slim, a striking woman rather than a pretty one. She kept him standing as she said, "Inspector Rutledge? Have you found out who killed my brother?"

"Not yet, Miss Hutchinson. I wish I could tell you otherwise. Did your brother know someone named Swift?"

"Swift? I don't believe so. I didn't know most of his friends. He was, after all, a serving officer in the Guards."

"I understand he lost his wife in the early years of the war."

Her eyebrows rose. "That's true. What does that have to do with what happened in Cambridgeshire?"

"I don't know. But somewhere in your brother's past something occurred that may have brought about his death. Tell me a little about Mrs. Hutchinson."

She turned away. "Mary was from Warwickshire. She met Gordon at a ball. It was love at first sight, I've been told. She was about to become engaged to someone else, and broke it off to marry my brother."

"Did she come to regret the marriage?"

"No, of course not. That's a terrible thing to suggest."

"But there was some question about her death."

"I assure you, this had nothing to do with Gordon being shot in Ely. I wrote to Jason. I told him that this business must be some terrible mistake. That my brother had had no enemies."

"Was Captain Hutchinson in England when his wife died?"

"He was in France. The war was just becoming a stalemate, he couldn't leave. He wasn't even here for her funeral."

But an officer serving in France would have been given compassionate leave if his wife and their child had died. If he'd asked for it.

"How well did he know Major Clayton? I understand he attended the services for Clayton in Burwell."

"He'd met him in hospital, on a visit to the wounded that Gordon made with Colonel Fisher."

"Was it Colonel Fisher who traveled to Burwell with your brother?"

"I don't believe it was. I didn't know the Claytons, and so I didn't go with Gordon. You're grasping at straws, Inspector." She was impatient now, a little sharp.

"Did your brother know someone in the Fen country by the name of Burrows?"

"Was he in the Army?"

"No. He's an older man. A farmer."

"Well, then, I doubt it. Really, Mr. Rutledge, I can't see where these questions are leading."

"Was this house yours, Miss Hutchinson? Or your sister-in-law's?"

She flushed slightly. "It belonged to Mary's family. It had been closed since her parents' deaths. My brother brought her to London and opened the house. She was pleased. She'd always liked it."

"And it's yours now?"

"Sadly, yes. As my brother's heir."

Hamish was reminding him of something. Mary Hutchinson's house . . . He said, "The staff here. Who hired them?"

"I suppose my brother did. It was fully staffed when he sent for me."

"There was no one who came to London with the new bride?"

"Yes, there was her maid."

"Where is she now?"

"Pensioned off, when Mary died. I already had a personal maid. There was no point in keeping her on."

"I'd like to speak to her. Can you tell me where to find her?"

She was exasperated with him. "Really, I don't know what Miss Newland could possibly tell you about something that happened in Ely."

"Nor do I. But I intend to find out. The address, if you please."

She went to the desk, found a small leather-covered book, looked up a name, and wrote the information on a sheet of stationery. Folding it, she turned and handed it to him. "I think you should leave now. There must be something you can do to find my brother's murderer. Searching out old servants doesn't seem to be very useful."

Rutledge smiled. "Scotland Yard prefers to be thorough," he answered and took his leave. She was frowning as he closed the door.

If Hutchinson had possessed great charm, most certainly his sister had none, he thought, driving toward Wiltshire. Perhaps with her brother providing for the two of them, she hadn't needed any.

When he arrived in Abbot's Green, he was surprised to find that the direction Miss Hutchinson had given him was a large, handsome brick house set back off the road on the far side of the small village.

He'd expected a pensioner's cottage, but it appeared that Miss Newland had found another position.

And this presented something of a problem. If Scotland Yard came calling, the mistress of the house would very likely insist that he interview Miss Newland in her presence. If he insisted on speaking to her privately, it would cast suspicion on the lady's maid. What had she to do with the police?

He drove up to the Georgian door, knocked, and asked for Miss Newland.

The maid who had come to the door said, "Who is calling?"

"My name is Rutledge. I'm here," he said blandly, "about a small legacy left to one of the staff at her former place of employment. I should like to trace that person, and Miss Newland might be able to tell me where to find her. A private matter, I'm afraid."

He was left to his own devices while the maid went to find Miss Newland. After perhaps five minutes, a woman in the severe black of her position came to the door.

"Mr. Rutledge?" she asked tentatively.

She was nearing forty, he thought, with fair hair that fought against the severity of the style that suited her dress, repressively impersonal. There was a small scar, round and rather unusual, on one cheek, near her mouth. It detracted from a pretty face.

"Yes." He looked up at the house. "Could we walk here in the drive for a few minutes? I'd rather not be overheard."

Mystified, she said, "You mentioned my former employer . . ."

"Mrs. Hutchinson. Yes. Will you walk with me?"

Reluctantly she came down the short flight of steps and followed him to the faun fountain that graced the circle created by the loop in the drive.

Certain now that he couldn't be overheard, he said quickly, "I'm from Scotland Yard, Miss Newland. I'm investigating the murder of Captain Hutchinson."

Shocked, she stared up at him. "Captain—but who—I didn't *know*."

She wouldn't have seen the London newspapers. He explained what had happened. "And we have very little evidence to help us with our inquiries."

Her face hardened. "Good luck to him, whoever he is. I hope you never find him." She was about to turn away and go back to the house when he stopped her.

"Miss Newland. I need your help."

"I told you. I wish whoever it is well."

"Perhaps you do. But he's murdered another man, and shot a third. We need to find a killer."

"I haven't seen the Captain since I was let go. After Miss Mary's death. What can I possibly know that would be useful to you?" With one hand she shielded her eyes from the sun, searching his face.

"I have no idea," he said truthfully. "But a woman whose cousin Alice Worth knew your former mistress suggested that I look into her death. I called on Miss Hutchinson, and she was less than helpful."

"That doesn't surprise me. She didn't care for the woman her brother married, and he only married Mary for her money. He wanted that lovely house and the position the address gave him. Once he had what he wanted, he changed toward her. Mrs. Worth—the Alice you spoke of—was her only friend. He'd discouraged everyone she'd known growing up from visiting her. It wasn't convenient—she didn't feel well—they'd made other plans. After a while, they stopped asking to see Mrs. Hutchinson."

"Was he that cruel?"

"I don't think it was cruelty. He didn't care for them, you see. They could give him nothing he wanted. He brought his own friends round, and they entertained lavishly. Miss Mary enjoyed that. They were invited to teas and concerts and the theater, to dinner parties and weekends in the country, but these were people the Captain—he was a Lieutenant then—wished to impress. He expected Miss Mary to use them as he himself did. To cultivate them and curry favor, to do small things to put them in her debt, whatever he thought would serve him best. She wasn't comfortable using people in that fashion. The only times I saw him angry with her were over small things she'd failed to notice or do. He accused her of not caring, of letting him down. But she hadn't. It wasn't her way to look for opportunities to put herself or her husband forward. She hadn't grown up in that kind of life, she had a position, she didn't need to push so hard for recognition. It was just that he wanted even more fashionable connections."

"And when the war came?"

"He was in his glory then. He expected to end the war as a Major at the very least. But he never seemed to find the right opportunity to shine. He could be very brave when he had to, but he wasn't a good leader. Do you know what I mean? Miss Mary said to me once, 'He climbs on the backs of other people. He's never understood that.'"

"Were there other women?"

Frowning, she considered the question. "Oh, he charmed them, when they were useful or related to someone important. It never went beyond that. Well, there *was* one, perhaps, if you believed the rumors. The housekeeper wrote to me that he'd taken a fancy to one of the maids. This was after he'd come home from France. The spring of 1919. I never knew him to look twice at one of them, so I was quite surprised. And I told her so in my next letter. But Mrs. Cookson claimed he was besotted with the girl. And then one morning she was gone. Her things with her. Just like that. I expect she wouldn't stand for what he wanted. God forgive me, I remember thinking that it served him right, to be disappointed."

Some men considered the staff in their houses as natural prey. A pert maid, always underfoot, smiling . . . it could be tempting. But pretty or not, a servant girl was seldom related to a Colonel or someone in the Cabinet.

And then Miss Newland's next words changed his mind.

"Mrs. Cookson told me she was a Scottish girl, pretty as a picture, with the most charming accent. Even the tradesmen who came round wanted to hear her speak. But an excellent worker for all that."

"And that's all you know about this girl?"

"It's all that she wrote."

"Where can I find Mrs. Cookson?"

"I should think she's still at the London house."

"Do you recall someone by the name of Swift coming to the house? Or Burrows?"

Miss Newland shook her head. "I never met the guests."

"Tell me a little about Mrs. Hutchinson's life before she met the Captain."

"She was not the prettiest girl in Warwick, but she was well liked. And she had a way of putting people at their ease. I never knew her to be a wallflower. She always had partners at any balls or parties. I was over the moon when I was told I would be her maid. It was the best position anyone could ask for. We went to Newmarket for the races— her uncle was mad for the horses, and he'd spend a week before the flat racing calendar, going from trainer to trainer, looking over the field and deciding where to bet. He was good at it too. There was a man she met at one of the dinner parties. She pointed him out to me once. I was certain she was in love with him, and he with her. It would have been a fine match. She said they were well suited to each other. But her uncle felt she was too young, she should wait a year, and before that year was out, she'd met the Captain."

"What was her uncle's name?"

"Thaddeus Whiting. Sadly, he died soon after Mary's death. I think it broke his heart."

"And the other man?"

"He came to Warwickshire once to plead with her, to beg her to change her mind. But the Captain was exciting, charming. She thought that was what she wanted. A pity she was wrong."

Newmarket was only a matter of a few miles from the Fen country.

"What was his name? This man. Do you remember?"

"I should. Of course I should. But I can't bring it back. He took Miss Mary to a party at Warwick Castle, and I went along as chaperone. That was the only time I met him—"

The door had opened and one of the maids was standing there, beckoning to Miss Newland.

"I'm wanted, Mr. Rutledge. I must go. I'm so sorry I couldn't help you more. I'd have done anything for Miss Mary, and she knew that."

"How did she die?" he asked quickly, before she could turn away and go back to her duties.

"Miss Mary? She cut her wrists. In the bathtub. There was a picture in one of the books in her father's study. A man during the French Revolution did that, and he was painted lying in that tub full of bloody water. She'd had nightmares about it as a child. I expect she remembered."

And then she was hurrying back to the house.

Rutledge knew the rather dramatic painting. Marat lying in his bathtub. But he hadn't slashed his wrists. He'd been stabbed by a woman. Rutledge searched for the name. Corday. Charlotte Corday.

But she hadn't been shown in the painting. Only the dying man. The child had remembered what she saw—but not what it meant.

When the door had shut behind Miss Newland, Rutledge went back to his motorcar and turned toward London.

He faced the same problem as before. Miss Hutchinson would either insist on sitting in on the interview—or would forbid it altogether.

Leaving the motorcar at the far end of the square, he walked back to Number 7, and this time went down the steps beside the iron railing to the tradesmen's entrance.

A scullery maid answered his knock and informed him that the housekeeper, Mrs. Cookson, was presently upstairs discussing the next day's menu with Miss Hutchinson.

"But you could wait in the housekeeper's parlor, if you like," she said with a cheeky smile.

He smiled in return and was led through the servants' dining room and down a short passage to the housekeeper's small parlor.

It was tastefully decorated with what must have been cast-off furniture from upstairs. There was a small table desk, a tea table with matching chairs, and a more comfortable chair next to a bookshelf holding cookery books, household hints, a volume on etiquette, and an older edition of *Debrett's Peerage,* well thumbed. He wondered if that had been a discard from upstairs.

He was still standing at the bookshelf when the door opened and Mrs. Cookson came in.

"May I help you?" she asked coolly. She was graying, her hair glossy and piled high on her head. There was a cleft in her chin, and her full lips were pursed in disapproval.

"My name is Rutledge. I'm from Scotland Yard. We're investigating the murder of Captain Hutchinson. I'd like to ask you several questions."

"The police were here the day after he—died."

"Yes, I'm sure you were very helpful." He smiled disarmingly. "But other matters have come to our attention since then."

"And they are?"

"How well did you know Mrs. Hutchinson?" he began.

Surprised, she said, "But she died during the early days of the war."

"I'm aware of that. Please answer the question."

"I was hired when the house was opened, while the Captain and Mrs. Hutchinson were on their wedding trip. I hadn't known her before that time. But she was quite lovely to work for, and I was as sad as anyone when she—she died."

"Why do you think she killed herself?"

"I—the inquest concluded she had cut herself in a fall. There was broken glass beside the tub."

"She brought her maid with her from Warwick. Did you know her well?"

"Miss Newland kept herself to herself. We were polite to each other, but not what you might call friendly."

And yet they had corresponded.

"Why did she leave?"

"After the funeral, she was given what was due her in Mrs. Hutchinson's will, and she chose to retire." Her voice was strained as she said the words.

He could hear Hamish telling him that she was hiding something.

"That's not what Miss Newland has told me." And Miss Hutchinson had said she had her own lady's maid . . .

"It was—there was some trouble about Mrs. Hutchinson's personal effects. I was told that Miss Newland claimed certain items as promised to her."

"What happened?"

"I wasn't there. Miss Hutchinson said afterward that Miss Newland was a thief and she'd told her to get out."

"And did she leave without a character?" Miss Newland had said nothing about the circumstances surrounding her departure. Was Mrs. Cookson given to exaggeration? Or had Miss Newland concealed the real reasons for being dismissed?

"She did. That very afternoon. I was sent to oversee her packing, as there had been the trouble over Mrs. Hutchinson's things. And she was blee—" She broke off, turning red.

"Bleeding?"

"I could only think that Miss Hutchinson had slapped her. One of her rings cut into Miss Newland's cheek." Without thinking, she touched her own face, where Rutledge had seen the deep scar on Miss Newland's.

The only way a ring could have cut that deep, he thought, was if Miss Hutchinson had struck her with the back of her hand.

"But she left, and that was the end of that."

"I did keep up with her. From time to time." Mrs. Cookson was walking the very narrow line between honesty and truth.

"In spite of the fact that she was accused of thieving."

Mrs. Cookson bit her lip. "She had known Mrs. Hutchinson since she was a small motherless child. Sometimes things are said. 'I'd like you to have this one day,' or 'It was my mother's. I'll leave it to you in my will, shall I?' Whether they are *meant* or not. I can see Miss Hutchinson's point as well. It was her brother's house, and he wasn't here to tell her his own wishes. There was no proof of promises on either side. Miss Newland must have been upset, close as she was to her mistress. She would have liked to take some small memento with her. In the heat of the moment, things are done and regretted later."

Mrs. Cookson was trying to be fair. Rutledge, reading her expression and listening to the tone of her voice, could see that she had had to side with her employer's sister, but she had been inclined to believe Miss Newland.

"I don't see why it should matter that Miss Newland left us when she did," she added, realizing that she might have said too much.

"It's not always possible to see the links. Tell me about the young woman who was taken on as maid at the end of the war. The one from Scotland."

"Catriona Beaton? You know about her as well? One of the maids left to be married, when the footman in Number 12 came back from the war. We advertised of course, and this young woman had excellent references. She was here some months. Nearly a year. She'd come down to London to make her fortune, and I wasn't convinced that service was the right choice for her, but I changed my mind in the end. A hard worker, never any trouble, knew her duties. And then one morning she was gone. Not a word, no request for a reference, not staying out her notice. Just—gone. I couldn't believe it."

"And you haven't heard from her since then?"

"I told you. Not a word."

"Why do you think she left?"

"She was young, eager to get on. I thought she'd found something better. That's why she didn't need a reference."

"There's more to it than that," he said quietly.

Mrs. Cookson took a deep breath. "I shouldn't be telling you this. It was the Captain. He'd been away, and he came home for a fortnight. She'd been here two weeks by that time. Even I could see where this was going. He'd never spared a glance for the staff before. I doubt he could recognize any of us on the street. Now he seemed to know which room she was working in, when she'd be coming to make up the fires or turn down the beds. I was worried, I can tell you that. He'd talk to her. About her afternoons off. About Scotland. About what she wanted to do with her life. I don't know what all. She asked me once what to do about him, and I told her, if he began to make her feel uncomfortable, I'd speak to Miss Hutchinson. One day she did come to me, saying that he'd asked if she'd have dinner with him one night. She didn't know how to refuse him. And so I went to Miss Hutchinson. She must have had a word with her brother, but it didn't do much good, I can tell you that. The night before she left, Catriona came to me, frightened and in tears. She wouldn't tell me what had happened. She just said she was afraid. The next morning, when she didn't come down, I sent one of the other maids up to wake her. And the room was empty. She'd gone."

"What did you think had happened?"

"That he'd offered to set her up in a house somewhere. As his mistress. I think she decided that the best way to cope with the situation was to leave."

"Had he set her up?"

"When he discovered she was gone, he went mad, accusing me of sending her packing, accusing his sister of the same thing, frantic to know if she'd left a forwarding address. And then one night he came in, and he was himself again. It was as if he'd never set eyes on her."

"He'd found her, then."

"No, I don't think he had. He'd just come to his senses. Or realized that he couldn't marry such a one. I don't know who it was spoke to him. Someone must have done."

Or he'd found her—and had it out with her.

What had become of the girl?

Hamish said, "He could ha' throttled her for leaving him."

The voice seemed to echo around the small room. Rutledge said quickly, "What do you feel became of her? She was here nearly a year. You got to know her well enough to judge her character."

"I was always afraid she'd done herself a harm. She was owed her wages, you see, and she never collected them. A girl like that? She wouldn't lose nearly a month's wages, if she could help it. And what about a reference?"

It was typical of the housekeeper to see the girl's death in such a light. She wouldn't want to consider that her late employer had driven a second woman to suicide.

Chapter 14

As Rutledge was opening the tradesmen's door, he glimpsed a motorcar just pulling up in front of the house.

He stopped where he was, waiting.

A man stepped out of the motorcar, walked to the door, and lifted the knocker. Rutledge could hear it clearly from where he was standing, the brass plate sounding sharply.

After a moment, the maid who had let him in greeted the caller and invited him inside, and the door closed behind him.

Rutledge stayed where he was, for the motor was still running.

Nearly five minutes passed, then the door above him opened again and Miss Hutchinson swept out, followed by the visitor. The chauffeur was standing by the rear door now, holding it open as the man helped Miss Hutchinson inside, then followed her.

The chauffeur shut the door smartly and went back to take his place behind the wheel.

And then they were gone.

Rutledge breathed a sigh of relief. It had been a near run thing. He didn't want Miss Hutchinson to see him again, not coming out of the downstairs servants' quarters. It was better for Mrs. Cookson if she didn't have to answer questions about his visit.

Leaving the area stairs, he walked back to where he'd left his own motorcar.

Hamish said, "It's a' verra' well to learn about the past, but it doesna' have a bearing on the murders."

It didn't. Rutledge had to admit it. But he'd discovered that there were at least two secrets in Captain Hutchinson's life. What were the others?

It was time to call on Mrs. Harris's cousin Alice Worth.

He found the card given him by Mrs. Harris, and discovered that Alice Worth lived in a tall, handsome house in one of the most fashionable squares in London. A dinner party was in progress when he knocked at the door—he could hear voices and laughter. What's more, the maid who answered his summons was uncertain what to do with the policeman on the doorstep.

She left him there, went to find her mistress, and in a few minutes he was whisked down a passage to a small morning room done up in pale peach and cream. Mrs. Worth swept in shortly afterward. A slender woman with fair hair and china blue eyes, she was wearing a very becoming evening gown of lilac and silver.

"I have guests, as you can see," she said abruptly. "I'm sure this could have waited until the morning."

"I'm afraid not," Rutledge replied pleasantly. "I'm inquiring into the death of Captain Hutchinson. Mrs. Harris, in Burwell, told me you could provide information about his late wife, Mary."

Her manner changed at once. Quietly shutting the door behind her, she said, "She was driven to her death. I'm convinced of it. If her husband wasn't guilty of killing her, he most certainly was morally responsible. I'm glad he's dead. I see no reason why I should help you find his killer. The man is to be congratulated on his good sense."

"Do you know who killed Hutchinson?" he asked, keeping his tone matter-of-fact.

"I am not required to answer your questions," she told him. "I'm not a suspect, and I have no proof. Therefore I will make no accusations."

"You do realize that whoever he is, he's killed another man, and a third is at this moment fighting for his life." It was only a slight exaggeration. But he could read her eyes, and she was unaware of what had happened to Swift and Burrows.

"Then I was mistaken," she said. "The person I suspected would not have done such a thing."

"Not even if he had been driven mad by Mary Hutchinson's death?"

"If he had been driven mad, as you put it, he would have found Captain Hutchinson and killed him a very long time ago. No, you're looking in the wrong direction."

"Revenge is best savored cold," Rutledge reminded her.

"Revenge or justice, I wouldn't know. I didn't kill him. Good evening, Mr. Rutledge."

With that she was gone, and the maid who had admitted him escorted him to the door and shut it firmly behind him.

Hamish said, "Ye canna' make her tell."

"She told me more than she realized. That whoever was in love with Mary Hutchinson is still alive and still has feelings for another man's wife. The question is, how well did she know this man? It's one thing to see Mary Hutchinson and whoever he is as star-crossed lovers, but Mrs. Hutchinson made her choice."

Still, it was frustrating to have come this far and be met with a stone wall. The letter sent to Mrs. Harris had given him the impression that Mrs. Worth was eager to see justice for her late friend. Instead she'd turned a policeman away.

Now the question was, should he make an appearance at Scotland Yard—or avoid it?

Looking at his watch, he realized that Acting Chief Superintendent Markham had long since left for the day. He found somewhere to have dinner, and then looked at his watch again.

The night staff would have taken over. Sergeant Gibson had most likely gone for the day as well.

But there were questions he needed to ask, and answers he needed to hear.

He drove on to the Yard, left his car some distance away, and walked in. His office was as he'd left it, several files still waiting for his attention. Nothing there from Gibson.

Dealing with the files quickly and efficiently, he carried them to Sergeant Gibson's desk and set them in the box for completed files. Then he swiftly searched the sergeant's desk.

He found what he was after and flipped through the pages, scanning the information they contained.

Gibson had found nothing new to report. And if Gibson couldn't, then very likely there was nothing more to be found.

Fallowfield, Lowell, Burrows, Swift, and his half brother Anson—they were all there along with Brenner and Montgomery, several with a mark by their names indicating the search for information had been conducted and the information conveyed to the Inspector who had requested it. In this case, himself.

Rutledge put the file back where he'd found it.

He was disappointed that nothing of interest had been discovered about Ben Montgomery, who had joined the Army and never returned to visit his family in Cambridgeshire, or about Jeremiah Brenner, he of the cold eyes and the need to drink to forget. They had been promising leads.

And then he left the Yard as quietly as he'd arrived.

Rutledge slept in his own bed that night and started for Cambridgeshire early the next morning. He stopped by the house that had belonged to his parents, where his sister Frances lived presently, and found her just having her first cup of tea in the small room overlooking the garden.

"Darling Ian, what a surprise. Sit down and I'll have Molly bring you some breakfast."

"I haven't time," he said. "Is there fresh tea in that pot?"

"Yes, help yourself. You know where to find the cups."

He did, and joined her at the table. "You've been away," he said.

"And so have you. I came round to call on Monday. Where have you been?"

"Cambridgeshire. The Fen country. And you?"

"I went to see Melinda in Kent. I wanted to tell her my news."

Rutledge smiled. She was engaged to be married now. Melinda Crawford was an old friend of the family, his parents' friend and now theirs. She would be one of the first people Frances would wish to tell.

That made it official. Real. He wanted nothing but happiness for his only sister. But when she had told him she was thinking of marriage, it had seemed that the bottom had unexpectedly fallen out of his world. It had taken all the will he possessed to smile and tell her he thought she'd made a good choice.

He had begun to come to terms with her engagement, but it had not been easy.

He drank his tea, listening to Frances's account of the visit to Melinda Crawford in Kent.

"She keeps asking me when you'll come to see her."

But he couldn't. Melinda had come from a military family, married into another, knew war and soldiers. He would betray himself, and she would know what haunted him. He cared too much for her good opinion to risk it.

Rutledge forced a smile. "The Yard takes most of my time."

"You could take leave, surely. You work too many hours as it is. A few days away from the Yard would be good for you."

"I'll try," he promised, and changed the subject.

Ten minutes later he was heading out of London, already considering where to look next.

Newmarket. Mary Hutchinson had fallen in love there. Who was the man? And how had he dealt with the breaking off of their engagement, after Mary had met Lieutenant Hutchinson?

Where was that man now? A loose end, and one that could matter. It was possible he'd not been free to pursue his revenge until now. If he'd returned to live in Newmarket, he could have killed Hutchinson in Ely and easily gone home without attracting attention.

Hamish was reminding him that a man who had loved Mary Hutchinson would have no reason to kill two other men, even if he'd shot her widower. Had Swift died only to distract the police from the real purpose of the crime?

That brought him back to why Captain Hutchinson had to be the first to die. The real target . . .

If that was true, then why shoot Mr. Burrows? An unnecessary risk, surely. And another dead end.

He spent the night in Cambridge again and arrived in Newmarket early in the morning. Horses were just coming in from their morning gallop, walking single file, their riders hunched in their saddles, thinking about breakfast.

The better part of the day, Rutledge and the local constable, an affable man called Henry, went searching for any evidence of Mary Hutchinson's presence here with her uncle before the war, any news of Herbert Swift, or proof that Captain Hutchinson had visited the town.

Swift, they learned, occasionally followed the horses, but he was generally the guest of an Ely solicitor, a man named Baron.

Captain Hutchinson had come once or twice in 1919, but always with a group of other young Army officers. No one could recall meeting him in 1914.

If the two men had crossed paths, there was no record of it.

As for Mary Hutchinson's uncle, Thaddeus Whiting, a few of the older trainers and jockeys remembered him and spoke warmly of him. Several recalled meeting his niece, but if she'd formed an attachment for anyone she'd met in Newmarket, they were unaware of it.

"Does anyone from Burwell or Wriston or Isleham frequent Newmarket?" Rutledge asked Michael Flannery, one of the trainers.

He smiled. "Of course they do. When they can. But they're not big punters, they come for the day, enjoy themselves walking around looking at the horses, and then go home. It's London and the shires that keep us afloat."

Rutledge thanked Constable Henry for his time and prepared to drive on to Burwell to look in on Burrows.

Constable Henry said, "I'll keep an ear to the ground, if you like, sir. You've given me the names. Where can I find you?"

"Wriston. Or Ely."

"That's fine, then, sir. Safe journey."

A safer one than his first visit to the Fen country, he thought as he drove into Burwell late on a windy afternoon.

Dr. Harris was pleased with the progress Burrows was making. "But it was a near-run thing. Infections like that can be very stubborn. Are you going his way? I'll release him if you are. He's to keep that face clean and dry. If he does, he'll be fine."

Rutledge waited while the bandages were changed and Burrows was given instructions about the care of the wound. And then the man came out. He looked better, his face less swollen and his eyes clear. He greeted Rutledge with a nod, turned to thank the doctor, and walked out to the motorcar. His daughter had already returned to Wriston to oversee the farm.

Waiting until Burrows was out of earshot, Rutledge said to Harris, "If you will, thank your wife for me, and tell her I did as she asked. But I'd like to know the name of the man Mary Hutchinson was engaged to before her marriage. If she can discover that, I'd be grateful. I'll be in Wriston until this inquiry is finished. Or in Ely."

"I'll pass the word. Thank you for listening to her worries. I don't know that it was helpful to you, but it will make my own life more comfortable."

Rutledge smiled. "I daresay."

Burrows was taciturn until they were well out of the village and on the road toward his farm. Even then his conversation turned to what he must do to make up for lost time and how well his daughter had managed in his place.

There were two questions Rutledge wanted to ask the man, and the first was the most innocuous.

"I see these fields," Rutledge said, gesturing to either side of the road. "You can't manage them with a handful of men."

"In the planting and the harvesting, I take on day labor. They know when to come. Some have been stringing the hops in Kent, or harvesting them. Others need work to put food on the table for winter. A few are Travelers—gypsies—who do whatever's to hand. I keep my eye on them. They're not to be trusted. But there's not much to steal. This year we've been lucky with the barley. The weather has held, save for the storm the other night. But it's time to bring it in." He touched his face. "Bloody man! He's cost me." It had been his own intransigence over keeping his wound clean that had sent him to Dr. Harris, but Burrows was having none of that.

"I assume you know many of the people who come to work. They're here year after year. Anyone among them who might have something against Herbert Swift?"

"I can't see why. They're in the fields all day, these workers. They don't go to the pubs, although sometimes they bring in beer without my knowledge. There's no time to waste in the villages. One or two of the young rascals, yes, but where would they come by a rifle, even if they'd wanted to shoot someone?"

"From their fathers in the war."

"Pshaw. That's as likely as my daughter shooting him. Except," he added hastily, "I don't have a rifle. But you have my shotgun."

"It's in the house now. You'll see it there. I'd put it away if I were you."

"All well and good." Burrows sat back. "I'll be getting myself one of these motorcars. One day. I've been saving for it. A good harvest this year will see me clear."

"Do you often go to Newmarket?"

He sighed. "Not as often as I'd like. There's the fields and the cows and never-ending work to repair the banks and keep up the buildings."

"Who else from the Fens goes there?"

"I've heard it said that Swift has been there a time or two since the war, with a friend from Ely. He's—he was no gambler. At a guess, he liked the excitement."

"Anyone else?"

Burrows named a dozen or so men, some of them ex-soldiers Rutledge had already interviewed. Among them was the man Thornton. "He's like so many of the others. The war changed him. He doesn't go to Newmarket or anywhere else there's a large gathering. I've noticed that."

"Know him well, do you?" Rutledge asked casually.

"Not very well, no. He's got more money than the rest of us put together. I hear he's thinking of buying steam tractors for his fields. I'd do it myself, but it's costly and so far I can find the workers when I need them."

"Ever see Captain Hutchinson in Newmarket?"

"If I did, I don't recall. He'd have been with a party of friends. We'd have nothing to say to each other except for hello and who do you favor in the next race, while waiting for a drink."

Burrows meant that as a generalization, unaware that he'd described Hutchinson well, a man who didn't waste his time with someone who couldn't advance his career or introduce him to someone even more important.

"What about Thaddeus Whiting from Warwick?" Rutledge asked as he pulled into the farm lane.

Burrows turned to him. "I haven't heard that name in—what is it?—five years or more. He's dead now. Why should Scotland Yard be interested in him?"

Because, Rutledge wanted to say, I spent five or six hours in Newmarket searching for information about the man and learned nothing.

"His name came up. Hutchinson's wife was his niece," he told Burrows.

"Well, I'll be damned. My daughter met her once. She wasn't married then, was she? It was the year before the war, 1913. Shy girl, but very pleasant."

"I'm told she was later engaged to someone she'd met at Newmarket before she was introduced to Hutchinson," Rutledge continued.

"Was she now? I can't think who that would be. My daughter might know."

But Miss Burrows, delighted and wary over her father's return, gave Mary Whiting Hutchinson scarcely a moment's thought.

"We didn't keep in touch," she said as her father carried on into the house, her gaze following him. "I liked her. But she wasn't engaged to anyone then. She'd have told me. There was someone she was seeing, I think, but I couldn't tell you whether he was at Newmarket or not that year." Miss Burrows smiled. "We spent an afternoon together. If he'd been there, she might not have had the afternoon free."

"If you remember anything else, send me word."

"I promise. But you're telling me that Mary was married to that man who was shot in front of Ely Cathedral?" He had her full attention now. Shivering, she said, "But I didn't know. How awful."

"Mary Hutchinson died in the first months of the war. In childbirth. She and the child didn't survive." It was a kind lie.

"How very sad. There's something that Mr. Swift and that Captain had in common, then. Both lost their wives in the same way."

But not quite the same. One was a beloved wife deeply mourned. And the other was a neglected wife who was wretched enough to take her own life.

Rutledge thanked Miss Burrows and was about to leave when he remembered the barrister in Ely who enjoyed Newmarket.

Burrows scratched his chin. "I expect that would be Thomas Bacon. No, Thomas Baron. Ask anyone in Ely, they can tell you where to find him."

Miss Bartram was delighted to see him again. When he told her he'd been in London, she was eager to hear about his journey.

Mindful of what had kept this inn in business for so many years, he asked her, "Does the name Thaddeus Whiting mean anything to you? Did he ever come to Wriston for the shooting?"

"And who is he, when he's at home?"

"He's from Warwickshire. He came sometimes to Newmarket. It's possible he also knew about The Dutchman Inn."

She shook her head. "I'm sure I'd have remembered if he had. I'll look in my father's book, of course, but I don't expect I'll find him."

In Ely, Rutledge was greeted by a morose Inspector Warren.

"I hope you're bringing me good news. I've spent the past two days reviewing statements, and I'm damned if they're any more useful now than they were when they were written."

"We took Burrows to a Dr. Harris in Burwell. He'd neglected that graze on his cheek. And I went on to London, since London hasn't been very forthcoming with information. I'm beginning to see why. There's very little to be had. At the moment I'm interested in finding a barrister by the name of Baron."

"Baron? Good God, you don't think he's involved, do you?"

"He isn't, as far as I know. But he sometimes went to Newmarket with Swift."

"Now that's interesting." Warren got up from behind his desk. "I'll go with you."

They found Thomas Baron in his chambers, and after the client who had been consulting him had left, he ushered the two men into his office.

Warren made the introductions, and Baron asked how the inquiry was progressing. "I knew Swift. We weren't close friends, but we had consulted on several matters. Before the war we'd travel occasionally to Newmarket, enjoy an expensive lunch, and talk about anything but the law."

"Did you meet any of these people while you and Swift were there? Captain Hutchinson, Thaddeus Whiting, Whiting's niece, Mary, her fiancé, or a farmer named Burrows."

"Hutchinson? The man who was murdered? Never met him, but there were usually a number of Army officers up from London in the season. He could have been one of those. They kept to themselves as a rule. Thaddeus Whiting. The name's familiar. Before the war? If he brought his niece with him, I never heard of it. Burrows I know by sight, but I've seen him there only once or twice. I'll tell you who is mad about the horses—or was. Surprised me. The cooper over in Soham. Ruskin? I think that's his name. Thornton, in Isleham, used to be interested in racing, but the war put paid to that."

"How well do you know Thornton?"

"Not well. He's an interesting man to dine with. Very well read. Before the war, he and Swift sometimes got into heated arguments over obscure points of history. Mind you, neither man had been to Athens or Rome, but to listen to them you'd think they were regular visitors."

And yet Thornton had said he barely knew Swift.

"How heated?"

"No, no, nothing that would lead to murder. It was more the pleasure of proving the other man wrong." He smiled. "It was generally a chance meeting, a casual remark, and they were off. An entertaining evening for everyone."

Rutledge thanked him, and they left.

Inspector Warren said, "Who is this man Whiting?"

"Mary Hutchinson's uncle and guardian. He's dead, but the question is, since he knew Hutchinson, is it possible he also knew Swift? Is that our connection between the two victims?"

"They are all three dead," Warren pointed out. "You're not likely to find out."

"What happened to the windmill keeper in Wriston?"

"After the cottage beside it burned, he left. Drank himself to death, if you ask me. That's very likely how the fire started. Although there are some who said the cottage was haunted and the old man burned it down to rid it of its ghosts. God knows what he thought he'd seen. The way those wooden arms creak, you'd believe in anything."

Rutledge remembered their creaking, the night of the mist, and how unnatural it had seemed. Unnoticed perhaps in the daylight, when one could see them move. But in the mist or late at night, it would be very different.

He left Inspector Warren at the police station and drove to the Cathedral.

It was beautiful in the afternoon sun, and he wondered as he always had when looking at these Medieval masterpieces how they had been designed and built by masons and workmen who might not have lived to see their work finished. A leap of faith, leaving something to the future. A name scratched out of sight on a gargoyle's ear, or on a beam high above the nave, or wherever a man could leave his mark unseen. To show he had been there, and created something.

"What will ye leave behind?" Hamish asked into the silence.

"Nothing," Rutledge said, and turned to go to the motorcar.

And then he wheeled, realizing that the man standing nearer the Cathedral, staring up at it as he himself had been doing, looked familiar.

Sure now that he hadn't been mistaken, he strode forward just as the man began to walk away.

Lengthening his stride, he called, "Thornton."

The man looked over his shoulder to see who was addressing him. Startled to find that it was Rutledge, he hesitated for a moment, and then stopped to wait for him to catch him up.

"Inspector."

"Mr. Thornton. Admiring the Cathedral?"

"I always come here when I'm in Ely. It's an amazing building. I'd like to have a painting of the view I can see across the Fens. I'd think about that view when I was in the trenches. That was my escape."

For Rutledge, it had been the poems of O. A. Manning.

"I understand you sometimes went to Newmarket before the war."

"Another lifetime," he said wryly. "I didn't have the heart for it when I came home from France."

"Did you meet friends there, or go alone?"

"Does it matter? Sometimes with friends, sometimes alone. I was young, fancy free. It was something to do. Farming doesn't let you escape for very long. At least not as far as London. Newmarket was close enough to waste a few hours there."

"Did you ever meet someone named called Thaddeus Whiting?"

"I may have done. Is he a trainer? A rider?"

"What about Herbert Swift?"

"Ah. You're remembering what I'd said earlier. That I didn't know him well. It's true. I never visited his home or anything of the sort." Thornton smiled. "We were single, we'd come down from Cambridge, although he was ahead of me and I'd never met him there, and we made fools of ourselves a time or two, showing off our knowledge of the classical world." He turned to look up at the tower, sadness in his face now. "It was a very different time. Carefree and happy. Nothing could happen to us in that bright, sunny world. He was married shortly afterward, as I remember, and that put paid to visits to Newmarket and drinking ourselves silly of an evening. I didn't know him, what he feared or what he loved or what made him angry. Just that he had a very sharp mind and I could test my own against it."

"Did you marry, as he did?"

"I'd grown up in Isleham, I wanted to see a little more of life before I settled down. Then Germany attacked Belgium and suddenly I was at war. Marriage seemed to be a luxury I couldn't afford, given what was happening in France."

Rutledge thought he was telling the absolute truth—but not the whole truth.

He said, "And Captain Hutchinson? Lieutenant Hutchinson, as he was then. Did you meet him?"

"At Newmarket? No. I don't believe I ever saw him there. Or if I did, I had no way of knowing who he was." He looked up at the Cathedral again. "I was thinking before you spoke to me that it was shameful to use this beautiful edifice for murder. Whoever he is, I hope you find him."

And with a nod he walked away.

Hamish said, "Ye ken, he's a canny one."

Rutledge nearly answered the voice aloud. Why do you think that?

"I wouldna' care to play cards with him."

What had taught Thornton to conceal his feelings so well?

After a moment Rutledge walked back to his motorcar. If Alice Worth had given him a name, would it have been Thornton's?

He stopped again at the police station to ask if Thornton had had any encounters with the police. There was often inconclusive evidence or a warning given that never made it into official reports. Yet they formed a pattern.

But when he was asked about the man, Inspector Warren shook his head. "Impeccable record. Although I was told that once before the war, he was warned in Newmarket for public drunkenness. But he went home and slept it off. It was put down to high spirits, and that was that. He's not the sort of man you'd expect to see brought up before the magistrate. A gentleman. This is twice you've brought his name up. Any particular reason why?"

"Curiosity. He served during the war in the ranks." But Rutledge was wondering to himself if that one night of drunkenness had been the same night he learned Mary Whiting was marrying Lieutenant Hutchinson.

Inspector Warren looked at him straightly. "That doesn't make him a murderer."

"True enough."

"Did you ask him about arguing with Swift?"

"He told me it was before the war, a mere acquaintance, not a friendship. He claims it was nothing more than a kind of boasting. Certainly Swift stopped coming to Newmarket after his marriage."

"That was probably true enough. Swift and his wife were insepa-rable. Her death nearly broke the man. Some men take to drink or become reclusive after a wife has died. Swift wanted to turn his back on everything that could possibly remind him of her. To shut out the misery. It took him four years to work up the courage to come home again."

"Still—"

"I can't think Thornton harbored a grudge for six years, thirsting for revenge because Swift got a date in history wrong."

But it wasn't arguing with Swift that interested Rutledge. Still, he could see that when it came to choosing a second target—if Hutchin-son had been the first and most important one—it might have appealed to Thornton to think of shooting Swift as having the last word. Rut-ledge remembered what he'd said to Alice Worth. That revenge was best savored cold.

"Is there any chance that Thornton was courting the woman Swift married?"

"I hardly think so. There have never been any rumors to that effect."

Rutledge shook his head. "Wherever I turn, there's no pattern to point the way."

"I don't like to say it, but so far you've done no better than I have in this search."

"Early days," Rutledge answered him grimly.

R utledge left the motorcar by the Wriston inn and walked on to have a look at the ruins of the mill keeper's cottage.

Had the man who was charged with the upkeep of the mill tripped over a lantern in a drunken state—or set a fire to burn out the ghosts that haunted him?

Rutledge could understand how that might happen.

It wasn't his inquiry, it had nothing to do with this one. It was the mill that actually drew him here again, and the memory of Miss Trowbridge standing near it, looking up at the sky. There had been more than stargazing on her mind that evening. He wondered what it was.

Something twisted around his legs, and he looked down to see Clarissa winding herself back and forth, leaving a thick coat of white hairs on his trousers. When she lifted her head to beg for stroking, he could see that one eye was pale green, the other a pale blue. A striking combination. Mewing, she waited, and he reached down to touch her head, setting off a loud purring that made him smile.

"She likes you."

He turned to see Marcella Trowbridge standing at her gate, a shopping basket over her arm.

"I'm fond of animals," he replied.

"Sometimes they're kinder than people." As if she suddenly regretted the remark, she smiled and added, "They don't disagree with you or dislike you because you're grumpy in the morning or prefer your tea without milk."

Rutledge said, "Tell me about the man who used to live here."

"I liked him. He was kind to a lonely child. He'd sit with me on the steps and tell me stories or make things for me out of wood or string. My father had never had time to do that, and I never knew his father. My grandfather had died when he was still fairly young. My grandmother liked Angus too, and she was a very good judge of character. Mother would have been shocked if I'd told her I was entertained by the man who looked after the windmill. I sometimes wondered why Angus chose to live here when he could have lived in Scotland with his own people. But perhaps there had been a falling-out. I was far more romantically inclined, preferring to believe he'd lost the only woman he loved and had exiled himself forever. Too much Sir Walter Scott, I expect. But perhaps it was she who haunted him. Something did."

Her face colored suddenly, and she broke off. After a moment she asked, "Why do I tell you such things?"

He thought he knew the answer to that. She was very much alone in the world. And loneliness brought with it longing. Or emptiness.

Was that why Mary Hutchinson had taken her own life?

Chapter 15

Walking back from the windmill, Rutledge continued on to the police station, in search of McBride.

"Burrows is at home. A chastened man. I think he'll let his daughter attend to that wound now."

"Blood poisoning. He could have died." McBride stood up and stretched.

"Tell me what you know about this man Thornton. In Isleham."

"Not much, sir. Just that he's kept to himself since the war. People hardly ever see him out and about."

And yet he'd been in Ely today.

"He told me he barely knew Swift. And I've learned since then that they knew each other rather well, before the war."

"I doubt that makes him a murderer. People change in six years. And Swift wasn't in the Army, he never went to France. They wouldn't have much in common now, would they?"

"Probably not. Was Thornton ever engaged to be married?"

"I haven't heard anything about it. Not to a local girl, at any rate."

Alice Worth had the key to that question. And she refused to give up the answer.

"I'm driving back to Burwell. I want to speak to several people there. And then I'll speak to Swift's brother again. It may be late when I return."

"I'll pass the word to Miss Bartram."

Rutledge changed his mind and went first to call on Swift's brother, finding him just walking in from the fields.

The man grinned and said, "You came the right way round this time."

"I did," Rutledge said, answering the smile. "I need to ask a few more questions about your brother."

"Come in, then. I think there's lemonade on offer."

Rutledge accepted the invitation and sat with Swift in the kitchen, sipping the cool drink.

"Nothing like it on a warm day. But the lemons are hard to come by. And dear at any price. What is it you want to know?"

"Did your brother go often to Newmarket?"

"Newmarket? A few times with a friend from Ely."

"Did he see a man called Thornton there? From Isleham."

"God help me, I'd forgot about Thornton. They shared a love of ancient history, and my brother relished their arguments. I use the word loosely. Showing off was closer to the mark."

"Did they visit each other in Wriston or Isleham?"

"My guess is, they never did. And it was about that same time that Herbert met his wife-to-be. After that, he lost interest in horses and Greek history and everything else, spending most of his free time running up to Ely to call on her."

"What about someone called Thaddeus Whiting?"

"I don't think I've ever heard him mention that name."

"Mary Whiting?"

"There was a girl—Mary? Margaret? I can't be sure what she was called—who caught Thornton's eye. He met her in Newmarket, and that evening talked about nothing else, even refusing to take umbrage at something my brother brought up about Rome. Herbert came home gleeful, claiming that he'd found Thornton's Achilles' heel. That was before he'd met *his* wife, and he thought it amusing. Funny you should remind me of that." He stared off into the distance. "I do fairly well, as a rule. The farm keeps me busy, there's no time to mourn. And then something like this comes along and I can see my brother's face as plainly as I see yours." He cleared his throat. "We were all young then. I'd been married a year myself. They called me the Old Man. I was all of twenty-eight. We didn't know what was to come, did we?"

Rutledge pressed, but that was all that Swift could remember. And then only because of his brother's reaction.

As he was leaving, he asked Swift if he was still worried about being a victim himself.

Shrugging, he said, "There's the farm. I don't have time to worry. But I keep a sharp eye out, all the same."

Driving on to Burwell, he sought out Mrs. Harris, telling her a little of what he'd learned in London.

"I can't think why Alice couldn't have helped the police. But she was Mary's only friend, and I expect she still feels strongly about what happened to her."

"And she said nothing to you about the man Mary had met, who he was, where he came from?"

"I don't think it mattered to her," Mrs. Harris said slowly. "He didn't come to Mary's rescue. No white horse, no shining armor. He left her to her fate."

"Perhaps he didn't know. Or perhaps she sent him away and asked him not to spoil her happiness."

"If he didn't know then, in the end I think he did. Alice wrote to him, I'm sure of it. She told me she was going to. I tried to talk her out of it, and she didn't mention it again. But I know her, you see. She wrote that letter and she sent it. She felt that strongly about what happened." She lifted her hand in a rueful gesture. "I always wondered what he made of her letter, if he was in France somewhere, fighting the Germans. Helpless to do anything. If he wanted to kill that man Hutchinson, why didn't he do it then? Men were dying every day."

"It's possible their paths never crossed."

"Well, there's that, I suppose."

"If you could persuade her to change her mind, I'd be grateful."

"That would be the same as sending him to the hangman. I'll have to think about that. I don't feel as fiercely about this matter as Alice does, but I'd hate to think my actions condemned anyone."

"It's possible he's killed two people."

"Yes, that's true. But why should he have shot Herbert Swift?"

And that was unanswerable. An opportunity to cast doubt on why Captain Hutchinson had to die? It always came back to that question.

Hamish said, "There could be two men. One who wanted Swift dead and the ither who wanted yon Captain dead."

That was possible. An unassailable alibi for one murder would tend to make the police think that that person was in the clear. But it was highly unlikely. How had the two men met and decided on murder? Why would they trust each other? And why should the owner of the Lee-Enfield need a partner when he could make his own kill so cleverly? It was the second victim that brought Scotland Yard into the picture—an unnecessary risk for Hutchinson's murderer, who had gone scot-free.

There had to be more than a love affair gone wrong to make someone kill twice and then wound a third victim. Unless the point was to confound the police. A cold-blooded decision.

He thanked Mrs. Harris and drove back to Wriston as quickly as possible, walking into the police station to ask Constable McBride for the key to Herbert Swift's house.

McBride said, "Everything was in order there. Inspector Warren was with me when I searched."

"I'm sure that's true. All the same, I'd like to look at some of his cases."

Reluctantly Constable McBride got to his feet, taking a key from the drawer of his desk. "It's beyond the second green. The Swift house."

They walked there in silence. McBride unlocked the door and stood aside.

The house smelled damp and musty, the faintest odor of cigarette smoke lingering in the air as well.

Swift had taken over a smaller house next to his, opened up a passage between them, and used that as his chambers. As they went down the passage, it creaked a little. And then they were in the cottage. The front room had become a waiting room, what would have been a bedroom had become an office, and the room in back was where his clerk must have worked.

"He had a clerk," Rutledge said. "What's become of him?"

"He went home to Norfolk," McBride said simply. "When we locked up here. These files will have to be turned over to someone to sort out."

Rutledge spent an hour going through past cases that Swift had handled. For the most part they were conveyances, wills, property settlements, and so on. Swift had been involved in three criminal cases. One was trespass, where two cousins had argued over an inheritance and the elder of the two had come looking for the younger, intending to teach him a lesson. Another was a drunken brawl ending in bodily harm, and the third was housebreaking, by what appeared to be a Traveler. They had been tried in Ely, and two of them had ended in guilty pleas. Only the two cousins had insisted on trial before they were satisfied. But there was nothing in any file to make Swift a target for revenge.

After a thorough search of the office, they went back to the main house.

If Swift had been guarding any secrets, they hadn't found them.

The sun was setting when they locked the door and walked down the green toward the police station. Once again the sky was radiant, ablaze with color from the softest lavender to a flaming red.

"I've never quite got used to the sunsets," McBride said into the silence. "I've only to step out of an evening, and there it is, surely different each time I look up. I was talking to a man who loved the mountains, and I asked him if he ever felt cut off, like. With no horizon, just more mountains shutting out the view. But it didn't appear to bother him."

Rutledge left him at the police station and walked on toward The Dutchman Inn.

A boy rolling a hoop came running down the street and nearly collided with Rutledge. Laughing, he ran on, the hoop bouncing and wobbling over the ruts in the road.

Hamish was asking, "Did ye no' think of leaving the farmer out of it?"

"Because he was wounded, when the man with the rifle could very easily have killed him?"

"Aye, it doesna' make sense."

"Unless his conscience troubled him."

"Aye, but would it? It's possible, ye ken, that he was intended to mislead."

"But the killer came back."

"Aye, someone did."

The presence of the dog had been a deterrent, because it meant that no one could steal up close enough to the house to see the man inside. And so there was nothing to show what the intentions of the intruder were. Still—he knew he'd missed . . .

Thornton had shown no signs of having been wounded by Burrows's shot. He didn't limp. There were no obvious bandages. Surely if he'd bled enough to leave traces on the ground, he'd have still been showing the effects of his injury.

"There's still Swift," Hamish was saying. "He claims he wasna' fashed with his brother o'er the inheriting of the farm. Ye have only his word."

"He was nervous when first I arrived at his door."

"Aye, he said he was afraid he might be next. But it's possible he was afraid of Scotland Yard."

"Why shoot Hutchinson first? If he'd been found out, Swift would still be alive."

"Aye."

He'd reached the inn, and for a moment considered walking on as far as the mill. There would be an even better view of the sunset from the little bridge.

On impulse, he did just that. He was watching the sun dip into the horizon when he was distracted by Hamish.

Frowning, he tried to see what was there in the middle distance. A man? Standing there for the same reason Rutledge had come to the bridge?

But the figure was in the middle of nowhere. What was he doing there? Where had he come from—where was he going?

Remembering the lights in the fields and the man he himself had encountered in the mist, Rutledge gauged the distance. Too far to run, but with his motorcar . . .

He turned quickly and ran in the opposite direction, toward the inn.

Turning the crank at speed, he nearly got caught by the backlash. Swearing under his breath, he got in and drove out of the village as far as the bridge.

The sun had gone down but the afterglow was dulling toward dark. He peered into the distance. The figure he'd seen was still there.

Turning in that direction, he headed straight for the figure.

And then it was gone. Rutledge blinked, peering out the windscreen. Whoever it was couldn't disappear into thin air.

Had the man seen the motorcar coming and chose to get off the road? But where to?

Down one of the embankments? Rutledge flicked on his head-lamps.

If he was wearing dark clothing, he'd be the devil to find against the black soil.

Arriving where he thought the figure might have been standing, he pulled over and stopped. Reaching for his torch, he began to search the fields on either side of him.

Where the devil was he?

Rutledge walked some twenty paces forward, casting the torch beam to either side. Then he walked back to the motorcar and kept going for another twenty paces or more.

Nothing.

How had he vanished? Where had he gone?

He moved the motorcar forward twenty yards, and tried again.

His torch skimmed the black, peaty soil, the browning stalks of what must be barley, and then he crossed to the far side of the road.

Frustrated, Rutledge spent half an hour hunting for whoever it was. He came up empty-handed.

Finally returning to the motorcar and carefully reversing on the narrow road, he went back the way he'd come. And as he drove toward Wriston, he had the oddest feeling that somewhere in the darkness out there to either side of his headlamps, the man he'd seen was watching him go, and laughing.

O ver dinner he asked Priscilla Bartram who might be out late, walking on the road.

"Hard to say. One of the farm tenants coming back from the fields? He'd know his way. Or a Traveler, up to no good. Even a tradesman, caught out after making a delivery."

But what tradesman walked? What goods could he carry, without so much as a barrow or bicycle?

He must have appeared to be skeptical, for Miss Bartram glanced at her kitchen windows, where the curtains had been drawn against the night.

"You don't think it could be the killer, do you?" She crossed to the door into the kitchen garden and tested the latch. "One can't be too careful. I've been thinking of getting a little dog. For company. I hear Mr. Taylor's bitch has had a litter."

And for protection?

How long had she lived alone in this house, without feeling the need for a dog?

A moth, drawn by the light, in spite of the curtains, threw itself at the glass, and she nearly dropped the spoon in her hand, turning toward the window. Then, feeling a little embarrassed, she said, "I shan't forgive whoever it is who did these murders. He's taken away my peace of mind."

"I don't think you have anything to fear."

"He walked into the ironmonger's house, didn't he? How did he know they weren't at home? What if Mrs. Ross had been lying down with a headache, and her husband had left her there while he went out to the rally? What then?"

It wasn't the first time Rutledge had wondered about such a possibility.

But he said, "He could have knocked at the door out to the kitchen garden. And when no one came, he walked in."

"I still say, what if Mrs. Ross was resting, a cool cloth over her forehead, and didn't hear the knock."

He had no answer for that.

The next morning brought news that Ruskin, the cooper in Soham, had gone on a rampage in the night, wielding a side ax. It was a blade that was razor sharp on one side and dull on the other, with the typical short handle that coopers used in the close-quarter work of their trade.

It could do serious damage, wielded as a weapon.

Because he'd been on the ex-soldier list, Rutledge went to Soham to interview him, and found him in the local police station with a heavy head.

Ruskin looked up as the cell door opened, and Rutledge stood there in front of him.

"What happened?" Rutledge asked. He'd asked the constable to stay in the tiny office and give him time alone with the man.

Ruskin buried his face in his hands. "I'd been to the pub, and I didn't want to go home. There's a cot in the loft of the shed, and I thought to sleep off most of what I'd drunk before my wife saw me. That's all I remember. Then I was back in Wriston, and the man in the window was shooting at *me*." He sighed, looking up at Rutledge. "Constable says I was running down the lane shouting and waving the side ax. I was looking for someone, and I was going to kill him. I'm told it was the hurdle maker I was chasing. I must have frightened him out of his wits. Then some men wrestled me down, took away the side ax, and held me until the constable came. One of them flung a pail of water over my head. By that time I was nearly sober. They clapped me up here for the night, all the same."

"Why were you searching for the hurdle maker?"

"God knows. I doubt I've exchanged a dozen words with him. Besides, it had more to do with the night Swift was killed. The nightmares came back after that. A time or two I've tried to drink myself into forgetting."

That didn't work. Rutledge had tried it, found it made the nightmares harder to escape, and gave it up. But Ruskin would have to learn it for himself.

"Nothing happened at your shop after you got there last night? No one came to see you?"

"How do I know? I don't remember, I tell you. It's a blank, until I started dreaming."

"Then it was what you saw in Wriston."

"It must have been." He shivered. "I didn't want to kill anyone. I didn't want to be killed."

But what had triggered this particular nightmare?

Looking at Ruskin, he thought it was likely that the man himself would never know. It was locked in his mind with the war he wanted to forget.

Still, Rutledge tried. He kept his voice level, quiet.

"Was it a sniper, Ruskin? One of our sharpshooters?"

"No. No." Ruskin shook his head. "Don't ask me, don't make me remember."

"Then it was German. Am I right?"

Finally, Ruskin looked up, his eyes dark with pain. "It was outside Ypres. I saw him. Staring straight at me. I knew he was going to fire. And I threw myself to one side. But the man behind me didn't see him. Not in time. And he took the bullet meant for me. It was my *fault*."

Rutledge put a hand on the other man's shoulder. "You needn't think about it again," he said firmly. "You've done your duty."

Ruskin didn't answer, enveloped in a misery that nothing could stop. After a moment, unable to watch, Rutledge left.

He went to speak to the constable.

"Now he's sober, sir, we'll let him go with a warning. If it happens again, I'll have to charge him. That side ax could cleave a man's skull."

"He can't help responding the way he has."

"That may be, sir, but we can't let him endanger himself or others."

The constable was too young to have been in the war. He'd been sent to fill the shoes of an older man on the point of retiring, and he took his duties seriously.

"Lost your father in the war, did you?"

"Sir, yes. Early on."

Rutledge thanked him and took his leave.

Driving out of Soham, he said aloud, "I find it hard to believe Ruskin saw a German."

"Aye, that's true."

"Perhaps he saw what he feared to see."

"Aye, it's why ye never look into a mirror."

Trying to ignore that remark, Rutledge knew the answer must be there, in the depths of memory. He couldn't quite reach it . . .

Something he'd been told? Something he'd seen? A passing comment, a remark overheard. *What was it?*

I nstead of driving on to Wriston, he decided to go to Isleham instead.

Rutledge found Thornton at home.

The man was surprised to see him. "I can't think why you've found it necessary to call on me again. But I'll help in any way I can," he said as Rutledge was ushered into the room with the globe and the maps and the books.

"I've been to see the cooper in Soham. The man called Ruskin. Do you know him?"

"I can't say that I've ever met him. Still, I'm sure we must own some of his wares. You can ask my housekeeper, if you like."

"He had a difficult war. Last night he ran amok, thinking he was being hunted by the man who'd killed Swift. He saw him, by the way. Just as Mrs. Percy had."

"Did he indeed," Thornton said, his eyes narrowing. "How did he describe this person?"

"He said he was a German sharpshooter."

Thornton stared at him. "Good God. He can't be serious."

"The hurdle maker didn't find it amusing."

"Are you saying Ruskin killed him?"

"Only that he was on a rampage and the hurdle maker got in the way. He wasn't hurt, as far as I am aware."

"But why did he think Swift's killer was German?"

"I'm not sure he did. But whatever he saw, it triggered that memory."

"They were devilishly clever at making themselves invisible. It was usually something in the landscape, something we'd never think twice about. That was early on, of course, before we knew what they were up to," Thornton said. "One of the worst we faced was in the stump of a dead tree. They'd reinforced it. We couldn't touch him. He was out of grenade range as well. Hardly the sort of thing you'd see in a dormer window."

Devilishly clever at making themselves invisible . . .

But *invisible* was the wrong word. *Invulnerable—*

There it was, the memory Rutledge had been looking for.

"They used a helmet sometimes," Rutledge said slowly. "Have you ever been to the Tower of London? I was taken there as a child, to see the ravens. The armor frightened my sister, I remember. Especially the casques, the helmets with the fanciful armorial figures. When the German snipers peered over the parapet of their trenches, they sometimes used a helmet, steel with slits for the eyes and mouth. Only much cruder, of course, than what's in the Tower. There was one man in particular. He was damned good. Something of a legend, I expect, on his own side, but someone we wanted badly. I never saw him, he wasn't in my sector. But when he was killed, in the next sortie someone found his helmet. That could explain what Mrs. Percy saw. Why Ruskin was so shaken." He paused. "Know anyone here in the Fen country who brought back such a souvenir?"

"No. I don't," Thornton said pensively. "Are you sure about this? I never saw it either."

Rutledge held out his hand. "Give me a pen and some paper. I'll draw it."

Thornton passed him what he asked for. And in that brief exchange, he could read the man's eyes, unguarded.

Speculation? Anger? Uncertainty? Or a succession of all three?

Sketching, Rutledge said, "A friend of mine described it." He finished and gave the drawing to Thornton.

It was more like half a cylinder than a helmet shaped to fit the head. Some of those for knights, he remembered, had even had ears. Here the eyes and nose had been crudely cut out, the mouth no more than a ragged slit. A face and yet more an ugly, terrifying rendering of it.

And Ruskin had seen it twice. In the trenches and in the upstairs window of the ironmonger's house.

Thornton leaned forward to examine it. "Nothing like that in our sector. Are you sure about this? Or is it apocryphal?"

"No, I think it actually existed. My friend knew what he was talking about."

He held out his hand for the drawing, and Thornton reluctantly passed it across the desk to him.

"I can see why this disturbed anyone who saw it. I'd hardly want that as a souvenir."

"But if you were—or had been—a sharpshooter yourself, you might find it interesting. Most particularly, if you were the one who'd killed him."

"Yes, I see. The question is, *who*?"

"I thought perhaps it might be you. You might have such a helmet."

"Me!"

"You lied to me about Swift. You knew him better than you were willing to admit."

"But why should I have shot the other man, Hutchinson?"

"If there's a reason, I shall find it," Rutledge said, rising. "I'll see myself out. Good day, Thornton."

Chapter 16

He walked out of the room, leaving the man sitting there, a frown on his face.

As Rutledge turned the crank, Hamish said, "Ye canna' search every house in the Fens. And ye ken, the helmet and the rifle could be anywhere."

But Rutledge was trying to remember the rest of what he'd been told about the German sniper. It had been a chance meeting with Captain Graves in France, and they had had very little time to talk. *What else had he said about that particular sniper?*

A Scots company had killed the man. Was that it? Rutledge couldn't be sure.

The cat was out of the bag now. Thornton knew he was a suspect. But then he must have guessed in Ely that Rutledge was suspicious of the lie he'd told—and been caught in.

In Wriston, he left the motorcar outside the ironmonger's house and walked down the lane where Mrs. Percy lived.

She called, "Come," as she had before, and he found her sweeping her kitchen floor.

"You again," she said tartly. "I've told you it's useless, I don't know anything."

He reached into his pocket, unfolded the sheet of paper with the drawing on it, and set it down on the table.

Curiosity got the better of her. She stood the broom against the doorframe, walked across the kitchen, and looked down.

He could hear her suck in a breath, the shock of what she was seeing hitting her like cold water in the face. She reached for the back of a chair to steady herself, then turned to him.

Her eyes were wide, frightened. She cleared her throat, then had to do it a second time before she could find her voice. Even then it was more a croak. "Where did you come by this?"

"It's a drawing of a face guard—a protective covering for the face— that the Germans sometimes used when they were shooting at us in the trenches. It's metal, smooth, dull metal. What you saw in that window above the ironmonger's shop was a soldier's disguise. Not a monster."

Her pale face flushed with rising anger. "You mean to say I was tricked?"

"Yes, in a way. If anyone was looking up when he took that shot, only that strange face could be seen. Its intent was to confuse and make people afraid." He waited. "Is this at all like what you remember?"

"It could be a twin," she said. "I haven't slept well since I saw it. I've been the butt of jokes. I've been questioned over and over again. I hope you find him and hang him, whoever it is."

"Will you give Constable McBride a new statement?"

"Of course I will." She wiped her hands on her apron. "I'll just fetch my hat."

Leaving him standing there, she walked away. Two minutes later, she was back, wearing a dark blue straw hat with pansies around the brim. It was the hat of a much younger woman, and he wondered if she had kept it all these years or had bought it at a jumble sale.

Rutledge accompanied her to the police station. McBride, staring at the sketch, said, "Well, I'll be—" He stopped in time. "But is this possible? How did he come by such a thing?"

"He was given it, he made his own from rumors he'd heard, or he stole it. We don't know. But there's your monster. Mrs. Percy has come to give you an amended statement. If you'll make a copy of it, I'll take it to Inspector Warren myself."

"Gladly. Thank you, sir. Now, Mrs. Percy, if you'll sit behind the desk here, I'll fetch paper and pen."

Rutledge left him to it.

He stopped at the market cross and looked again at the dormer window.

Given the torchlight and the smoke, the face peering down at the crowded square below, it would be easy to believe that a monster was up in that window. And because the killer had had to raise up to use the rifle, he'd needed a disguise.

And this reinforced Rutledge's belief that his man was an experienced sniper.

A master of disguises—no two the same. Keeping the police guessing, keeping witnesses too frightened to know precisely what it was they'd seen.

Who in Wriston—who in the Fens—had been a sniper and kept it hidden, a dark secret of the war?

Or had he learned the trade from someone else who knew it well? That too was a possibility.

Leaving his motorcar where it was for the time being, he walked back to The Dutchman Inn.

Priscilla Bartram, feather duster in hand, was putting the sitting room to rights. When she heard him come through the door, she hurried to meet him, duster still in hand.

"You were gone most of the morning," she said. "Is there any news?"

"I've been questioning a number of people," he said vaguely. "It's often the details that trip people up. Verifying this or that. Making sure that when someone says he was in such and such a place at such and such a time, he's telling the truth."

She would have preferred exciting information she could pass on to friends. Relenting, Rutledge smiled. "A dull morning on the whole, but I think we've discovered Mrs. Percy's monster. Just an ordinary man wearing a disguise."

He caught the apprehensive look she cast at the nearest window, as if expecting to see the face peering in. He didn't think she was the sort of woman whose nerves produced shadows where there were none. And yet the killing of Swift had given her cause to worry. After all, she had seen him die.

She led him back to the kitchen, where there was cool water waiting for him, and with it she offered a plate of biscuits.

He ate them to please her, and then was about to leave for Ely when she stopped him at the kitchen door.

"I was thinking," she said hesitantly, as if reluctant to be considered a meddler. "You asked me, didn't you, if I recognized anyone from Wriston at the funeral of Major Clayton."

"Yes. Have you remembered someone else?"

"Not precisely. There were several other people I recognized, from other villages. Is that important? If not, I won't bother you with it."

"Make a list for me. That would be very useful."

Happy to have been helpful, she nodded. "I'll have it ready when you come back."

Retrieving the motorcar, he set out for Ely.

But Inspector Warren wasn't as pleased as Rutledge had expected him to be.

"All well and good," he said. "But the Chief Constable was here late yesterday, a musical evening at the Cathedral. He stopped to see me and told me again how anxious he is to see this matter brought to a successful conclusion."

"We aren't dealing with an ordinary murderer. This man is clever, and winkling him out of wherever he's been hiding will be difficult."

"I understand. The point I'm making is that the Chief Constable doesn't. He was expecting the Yard to make swifter progress."

"And so we are," Rutledge said, smiling. But when he left the police station, his face was grim.

He shut himself in the hotel telephone closet, and gave what he was about to do some thought.

First the call to Gibson.

The sergeant answered in his usual taciturn manner.

"Anything for me?" Rutledge asked. He weighed the silence before Gibson spoke. Then he could hear the opening of a drawer, the rustle of papers.

"The servant girl. Catriona Beaton. Seems she left the house in the middle of the night, and wasn't seen again. But a body that might have been hers was found near the railway tracks in Hampshire some weeks later. There was enough clothing left to make a tentative identification. She'd been buried in a shallow grave in a stand of trees above the tracks, and her remains were washed out by that heavy rain. School-boys, playing the truant, found her. According to the inquest, she was murdered by person or persons unknown. Girls without references face a heavy go of it."

Rutledge asked, "Was she pregnant, do you know?"

"That couldn't be determined."

"Did Hutchinson own a motorcar? Did he have a chauffeur?"

"He did own a motorcar, but he chose to drive himself."

"What did Miss Hutchinson have to say about the girl's death?"

"That she'd been a good, hardworking young woman, and that it was a tragedy for the entire household. What's more, she paid for the girl to be buried decently. Apparently Miss Beaton had no family."

It was often those women without a family, without a protector, who suffered most from the attentions of their employers.

Neither Miss Newland nor Mrs. Cookson had told him anything about the girl's body being recovered.

"Did the police speak to the staff?"

"Miss Hutchinson told them it would be too upsetting—she'd break the news herself."

And she hadn't. The question was, why? Had she told her brother?

Or had she feared he'd killed the girl himself? Love scorned could lead to murder as quickly as love satisfied. It was very likely that Miss Hutchinson wouldn't wish the household to speculate and gossip—and reach unwelcome conclusions.

And Mary Hutchinson? He put the thought into words.

"And Mary Hutchinson?"

"Orphaned young, brought up by her uncle, married, and died of overwhelming grief after losing her child."

The attending doctor had been kind. They often were in cases of suicide.

"Any information on Anson Swift?"

"That's the lot. Except to add that the Whiting you inquired about died of natural causes."

Necessary information, although it left much unanswered.

Rutledge thanked him and put up the receiver.

His next call was to a friend at the War Office.

When he explained what he needed, the voice at the other end of the line said, "You do realize that this desk isn't an adjunct to Scotland Yard."

Rutledge laughed. "Where else will I find such an excellent source of information?" Then he added in a very different tone, "This man has killed twice. If he's reverting to what he did in the war, I need to hear about it. If he's using his training in France to rid himself of enemies in England, I want to know."

"How many names have you got?"

Rutledge told him, and heard the groan at the other end.

"It would be simpler to search Regimental records than hunt for a single man, regiment unknown, service unknown. If they used sharpshooters, it's usually found there. All right, give me the first ten."

When that was finished, Rutledge said, "And then there is Captain Gordon Hutchinson. Did he have anyone up on charges? Were any of his men taken up for cowardice and shot? What was his record?"

"I'll do my best."

Rutledge gave him the number at the hotel, and thanked him. "The hotel will forward any messages to Inspector Warren."

"You owe me a bottle of the finest whisky money can buy," the voice said, and rang off.

All I need is one good bit of evidence, Rutledge thought, not moving out of the telephone closet. But everywhere I turn, it's not there.

Hamish said, "Go to Warwick."

That was where Mary Hutchinson had grown up.

There was a tap at the door. He looked up to see a man standing there impatiently waiting his turn in the telephone closet.

Rutledge left him to it, and turned toward Wriston.

Whoever this killer was, he knew how to stay out of the public eye. Whether he was the old man, the owner of the barrow, someone from the Fen villages, or one of the wedding guests, he'd successfully evaded being seen by anyone. And while he had been visible in Wriston, he had given away nothing.

The one person Rutledge had spoken to in all the Fen country who'd impressed him as the most likely suspect was Thornton. The man was intelligent, clever, well read, and probably could outwit all of them put together. Brenner was more of a hothead, and while hotheads could be dangerous, these murders had taken meticulous planning.

Had Thornton been a sniper in the war? Or the spotter for one? Given his propensity for living as a recluse, it was possible. And there had also been men who were natural shots, who could hit targets with ease, once they were accustomed to their weapon.

And if the Chief Constable was pressing Warren, the Acting Chief Superintendent would soon be recalling him.

When he came down to dinner later that evening, Priscilla Bartram had gone to great lengths to make up for dining in the kitchen. The large round table with its eight chairs was covered with a pretty cloth embroidered with—not unexpectedly, given the glass cases in the sitting room—pheasants. He was glad to see there were none of the stuffed birds in this room, brought in to complement the cloth.

As he ate his dinner and carried on a conversation with Miss Bartram, he wondered what she would do if the wildfowlers didn't return to Wriston. Her chances of marrying were small, given the loss of a generation of men. Her chances of keeping the inn were even less. Marcella Trowbridge had said Priscilla Bartram could use the money, and he'd been generous when she'd set her terms for meals and lodging.

When they had finished, Miss Bartram carried their dishes out to the kitchen, then turned to Rutledge. "That list I promised you. It's in the sitting room. Shall I bring in a fresh pot of tea and a little of that cake you enjoyed last night?"

"Yes, thank you." He got up and walked to the sitting room. There, feeling the gaze of the glass eyes all around him, he picked up the list.

There were only a handful of names on the sheet, but her handwriting was an ornate copperplate and not easy to read.

Three men had come from Soham, and he didn't recognize the names, which meant he hadn't interviewed them. Ex-soldiers?

A third, from Wicken, he had already spoken to.

Miss Bartram came in with the tray, setting it on the tea table at his elbow.

"The first two names from Soham and the one from Wicken are fathers of men who'd served with the Major but hadn't come home," she said. "It was rather sad, really. Almost as if, since they couldn't bury their own, they could at least bury their sons' commanding officer. Adam Lindsay didn't stay for the luncheon. I wouldn't have known who he was, but one of the Soham men spoke with him. And that last name, the one in Isleham, was odd. He was there at St. Mary's but he never went inside for the service. He was still standing in the same spot when we came out. The only reason I know *his* name is that just before the war he came here with some others from Isleham for a Maundy Thursday service. That was when the roof of St. Andrew's in Isleham sprang a leak and the church had to be closed for the weekend." She smiled. "He certainly set the village girls in a twitter."

But Rutledge hadn't been listening. The final name, the one in Isleham, was Kimber Thornton.

He stared at it, then asked Priscilla Bartram to repeat what she'd just said.

She did, adding, "Is this useful at all?"

"Very much so. You say Thornton just stood outside St. Mary's? He didn't go in for the service? Did he speak to anyone?"

"He was never near enough to speak to anyone. And he didn't come to the committal service, either. By the time we walked back to the church again, he'd left."

"You are certain he didn't come to the luncheon."

"I'm positive."

"This is very helpful, and I'd appreciate it if you didn't say anything to anyone else."

"I understand." She was a little flushed with pleasure, but as his words sank in, she said quickly, "You're not thinking that *Mr. Thornton* is the murderer?"

"Every new bit of information fits into the puzzle," he said. "I shall have to ask him what he saw while he was standing there."

Mollified, she nodded. "I see." But he didn't think she did, and he was glad.

He excused himself soon after, and went out to the motorcar. It was a fair night, and there were no clouds on the horizon. It was later than he liked, but this couldn't wait.

Setting out for Isleham, he thought, A second lie on Thornton's part. He didn't attend Major Clayton's funeral—and he didn't know Swift very well. What else has he lied about?

Hamish said, "It wouldha' been better to wait until ye hear from London."

"It will take too long to sift through regimental records, and Gibson has already told me that he couldn't find very much about Thornton. I asked that he try again, but he's not likely to learn more than he already has."

"Still . . ." Hamish said.

Thornton, as it happened, hadn't gone to bed. But he had taken a walk, according to the housekeeper whose prim mouth indicated that Rutledge was out of order for calling so late.

"Where is he walking?"

"I don't know, sir. Sometimes he doesn't sleep well. And then he walks for a few minutes or for hours. I never know which it will be. I just leave the door off the latch, and he locks up when he comes in."

He could see that it was useless to ask to wait, at this hour.

Thanking her, he drove around to the far side of the church and left his motorcar there. And he walked the narrow streets of Isleham, looking for Thornton. He was nowhere to be found. Rutledge even stepped into the pub in the event he'd stopped in for a last drink.

If Thornton was in Isleham, he was invisible.

The only other possibility was that he'd called on someone. At this time of night?

Rutledge waited for a full hour, and still Thornton hadn't returned. *Where the hell had the man got to?*

Finally giving up, Rutledge drove back to Wriston. Priscilla Bartram had already gone upstairs and he was glad not to be asked where he'd been.

On the spur of the moment, he walked as far as the police station, but it was dark as well. London would still be lively at this hour, in many parts of the city, but in the Fens it seemed that people had little use for late-night revelry.

He went down Mrs. Percy's lane and stood for a time staring out at the fields.

Here was where someone going home from The Wake had seen lights bobbing in the fields. But there was nothing out there tonight. Everyone had assumed that the sighting had something to do with the murders. But perhaps they hadn't. Perhaps it had only been two boys making mischief or even oblivious to the stir they'd created, then were unwilling to step forward—

He heard something at the head of the lane and whirled.

Someone was pedaling down the High Street on a bicycle, hunched over the handlebars, as if tired and still a long way from home. The cyclist was heading toward the windmill. But where was he going from there? Burwell? Isleham?

His first thought was that this could be Thornton.

Racing up the lane toward the High Street, he skidded to a stop and looked both ways.

But the cyclist was nowhere in sight.

Had he heard Rutledge's footsteps on the hard clay of the lane and speeded up? Or was he approaching the windmill, said to be haunted, and hurrying to put it behind him?

One ghost avoiding another . . .

The thought passed through his mind, and Hamish said derisively, "Yon rider wasna' a ghost. Go after him."

Rutledge ran on to the motorcar, turned the crank, and leapt behind the wheel. But by the time he'd reached Miss Trowbridge's house and driven up and over the bridge beyond the windmill, he couldn't see the cyclist—or anyone else—along either of the straight lines of roads.

It wasn't until he had driven back to The Dutchman Inn that he realized that he hadn't looked behind the mill. A man could conceal himself and his bicycle there and outwait the motorcar at his heels.

Cursing himself for a fool, he went back to the windmill, on foot this time, carrying his torch with him. Flicking the torch on, he shone it into the high grass at the mill's broad base. Stems and blades had been bent and flattened. Very recently, because a few were already beginning to right themselves.

"Who's there?" A voice came out of the darkness.

He turned.

Miss Trowbridge was standing in the road, a shawl around her shoulders against the night's chill.

"Rutledge," he said, coming round the mill so that she could see him.

"What on earth are you doing behind the mill? What are you looking for?"

"Curiosity," he said, not wanting to frighten her. "I couldn't sleep."

"But I thought I heard your motorcar just now, passing by and returning."

"So you did. Did you hear anything else?"

"No. I told you. I'm used to the sound the bridge makes when something heavy, like a motorcar, crosses it. You probably haven't noticed the slight noise. But I know it well."

She must, living here on the outskirts of the village.

He walked through the high grass to where she was standing on the road. "Can you hear people on foot, say, or on a bicycle?"

"No, of course not." She hesitated. "Are you telling me that you believe this is the way whoever shot Mr. Swift left Wriston without being seen?"

"It's more likely," he responded, "that he left by running along the embankment that separates the village from the fields on that side."

"Yes," she said slowly, thinking about it, "but he would have to know what he was about. We played there as children. The Loon River, although it's presumptuous to call it that, once flowed on that side of the village. It's hardly more than a ditch with standing water now." And then she turned to him, her eyes large in the pale oval of her face, all he could see in the dark. "You're telling me that he—whoever he is—must be a local man. That someone from Ely, or Cambridge, or even Peterborough wouldn't have known he could escape that way."

"Unless of course he'd studied the land. He must have done in Ely to know where the best concealment was. He didn't intend to get caught."

"That's horrible to think about. That someone plotted to kill two men."

Rutledge said, "I don't want to frighten you. Still, since I've been here, I've seen Wriston so empty of an evening that you'd be hard-pressed to find anyone in the High or on the lanes. And yet someone has been abroad. On foot, on bicycles. Who do you think they are?"

She hesitated. "People do walk from place to place at night. I've wondered sometimes if they're Travelers, using the roads when no one else does. The windmill often seems to fascinate them for some reason. Clarissa pricks up her ears and stares in that direction, then after a bit relaxes and goes back to sleep. She must hear something, not just a mouse in the wainscoting."

"Does anyone come to your door?"

"No, never. Well, sometimes a London policeman lost in the fog." She said it with a wry smile.

But he himself wouldn't have found her door if there hadn't been someone else in the mist that night. Someone who knew there was a cottage here, and where to find the gate.

Someone who had searched his motorcar and his valise.

"I'm not afraid," she said, as much for her own benefit as for his, he thought. "I don't know why, but I've always felt very safe here in this cottage. As if my grandmother's love still surrounds me."

He said, "You shouldn't have come out to see who was here. Remember that. And I'd still lock my door at night."

"I do. And there's Clarissa."

Thinking about the ferocious dog that Burrows had borrowed to help him keep watch, Rutledge smiled.

They turned and walked back to the cottage.

"How much longer will you be here in Wriston?" she asked, looking up at him.

"Until I find a killer. Do you know a man called Thornton in Isleham?"

"I've met him a time or two. Very quiet, but nice enough."

"Someone named Adam Lindsay in Soham?"

"Sorry, no. I don't go to Soham very often. If I have marketing to do, I'll go to Burwell. Or Ely."

"Ruskin, the cooper there?"

"I know his work. People complained during the war—he was in France but he was needed here, they said. Is there any reason you're asking me about these men?"

"Just filling out my knowledge of the Fen country. It helps to have different perspectives on the local people. Know anyone who was a sniper during the war?"

"Snipers? No." Her tone of voice was enough. No one she might know could stoop so low.

He stood by the gate until she had gone in her door and closed it behind her. He waited and heard the latch turn, then went on his way.

I shouldn't have stopped and talked to her, he thought. I should have driven on to Isleham, to see if Thornton came home on a bicycle. It would be a long ride, tiring for him. A man could sleep after that, if he tried.

Chapter 17

The next morning after his breakfast, Rutledge asked Priscilla Bartram if she would accompany him to Burwell and show him precisely where she had seen Mr. Thornton standing.

"Is it necessary?" she asked reluctantly. "I can't be sure of the exact spot, I wasn't really there to watch Mr. Thornton."

"It doesn't have to be precise," he said easily. "Just the general idea." He glanced at the window. "It's a lovely day for an outing."

"Yes, of course. Well, I'll get my shawl, shall I? And my hat."

It was nearly a quarter of an hour before she came back down the stairs wearing an attractive hat, carrying her gloves and a shawl. She was anxious as he followed her out to the motorcar and helped her into the seat. But once settled and on her way, she was a little more at her ease.

She said as they went over the bridge by the mill, "The butcher's boy, when he delivered the sausages this morning, told me that Mr.

Banner—the butcher—told *him* that his knee was throbbing at dawn. It means a change in the weather. Mr. Banner's knee is as good as a barometer."

Looking up at the sky, Rutledge said, "It appears to be clear enough now."

"We're due a little cooler weather soon."

And that could mean fog.

When they reached Burwell, he left the car below St. Mary's and they walked around to the west door.

"Were people gathering here before the service?"

"A few, greeting each other."

"The door was open?"

"Oh, yes, the church was half full by the time I arrived."

"And you went directly inside?"

"No, there were several people before me, standing just beyond the doorway, where their voices didn't carry. But they had made it difficult for me to pass by. And so I stopped and looked around. That's when I saw him. There." She pointed to her left.

"Not under the trees by the churchyard."

"No. That tree, the large one, just below that house. He was standing in its shadow."

"And yet you recognized him." There was doubt in his voice.

"Would you remember a pretty girl you'd seen one Sunday going into your church and sitting just ahead of you?" she asked tartly.

Rutledge laughed. "Very likely."

"He'd changed, of course. After all, it's been six years. But I knew him."

"Was Captain Hutchinson standing outside the church at that time?"

"You know, I do believe he was. Yes, that's right. He was one of the group of men waiting for the coffin. I'd forgot that. I didn't know who he was, at that time, you see. Not until the luncheon."

"This is why I wanted to bring you here. To help you remember. What did you do then?"

"The knot of people ahead of me turned and went inside, and I followed. It was getting on to time for the service. I didn't wish to be late."

"Did you expect Thornton to come in and sit down?"

"Yes, of course. There was a vacant place beside me. I'd moved over a little to make room."

"But he didn't come in?"

"No, at the first hymn I looked to see if he'd taken a place behind me. And then the service was beginning, and I didn't think about him again."

Rutledge felt that part not quite true, but he said, "And when the service ended?"

"The coffin was taken out, and Miss Clayton followed, with Captain Hutchinson supporting her, and the Colonel on her other side. I was not that far behind, the coffin was just being carried into the churchyard over there. The path. And I looked up. He was still there. Mr. Thornton. As far as I could tell, he'd been there all along."

"Could you see what he was looking at?"

"Not really. I expect he was watching the coffin being carried out, and Miss Clayton with the Colonel on one side, the Captain on the other. You couldn't have missed their uniforms, could you?"

"And then?"

"We went into the churchyard to the family's graveside. I couldn't see Mr. Thornton then. And when the committal was over we spoke to Miss Clayton. She was very cut up, losing her brother. After that we went in twos and threes to the luncheon. Mr. Thornton was gone. I didn't know which direction he'd taken, and I thought perhaps the service was too—emotional, and he would join the mourners for lunch. But he didn't. I didn't see him again."

Rutledge said, "Stay here, if you will. I'll walk over to the tree where Thornton was standing. It will help me to see what he must have seen."

He moved toward the tree, taking his time, and when he got there, just under the overhang of branches heavy with dark green leaves, he turned.

Lifting his voice a little, he said, "Is this about right?"

She could hear him, but barely. He thought that with the organ still playing as people left the church, Thornton could see but not hear what was happening. Even during the funeral service, he probably heard only the music and perhaps the responses.

"Yes, that's it," she answered.

Rutledge stood there, looking toward the church and the leafy, shaded churchyard. Could he pick out a face? Certainly he could recognize Priscilla Bartram. But someone else? Someone he hadn't expected to see? A sniper was chosen for his superb eyesight.

Surely if Thornton had come this far, into Burwell, he would have joined the others in the church. And yet he hadn't.

Why?

At that moment the door of the church, just behind Miss Bartram, opened and the Rector stepped out. Even at this distance, Rutledge recognized him at once. The Rector paused to speak to Miss Bartram, and Rutledge could just hear the murmur of voices. But reading her reaction to the Rector finding her there, he could see that Miss Bartram was at a loss for what to say.

Then, in desperation, she turned and gestured in his direction. The Rector, following her pointing hand, seemed surprised. He collected Miss Bartram with a casual hand on her elbow, and the pair walked toward Rutledge.

He left his vantage point, having seen what he needed to see, and went to meet them.

"Good morning," the Rector said. "A bit early for police work."

"Miss Bartram was helping me understand what was happening during the funeral for Major Clayton," Rutledge said easily.

"Yes, I see. But surely you aren't suggesting that you now have evidence that involves St. Mary's?"

"Not at all," he responded. "But I did wonder at what vantage point someone might have been standing when Captain Hutchinson arrived. I'm not satisfied that the killing in Ely was the first that someone had seen of the victim. Perhaps it was here that the idea for killing him began."

"Oh, I think not," the Rector said. "That would mean someone in Burwell was the guilty man."

"If not this village, then another one," Rutledge reminded him. "Our killer must come from somewhere."

"Well, I shan't keep you," the Rector said. "I have a betrothed couple to counsel. Good day, Inspector. Good day, Miss Bartram. I shall pray for our killer as you call him. And for you as well, as you close the circle on this man."

With a nod he was gone.

Miss Bartram said, "I couldn't think what to say when he asked what brought me to Burwell. It was such a shock to meet him again."

"It doesn't matter," Rutledge said. "You've been quite splendid," he added with a smile. "It couldn't have been easy for you."

"No. Not when I realized that the Captain was there, not a foot from me. What if someone had decided to shoot him then?"

"I should think there wasn't time to plan his death. But later, when he came to Ely, it was the best chance anyone could have asked for."

He led her back to the motorcar, and as they walked, she said, "I shouldn't like to be a policeman, always suspicious of everything and everyone."

"It's not as bad as it sounds. Not everyone has a secret to hide."

At that she looked quickly up at him. Then she changed her mind, in the end saying nothing until they were in the motorcar, driving out of the village toward the road to Wriston. "Why are you so interested in Mr. Thornton? You're thinking he must be this murderer. But why? I don't see that he could be that sort of man."

"He was there on the one day Captain Hutchinson came north to the Fens. How many people do you think knew he was coming then? And Thornton, of all the mourners, stayed outside. It's a question that must be answered."

"Well, I hope you're wrong. I must tell you that."

He didn't reply. A murder inquiry was inexorable, and there was nothing to be done if the killer was a neighbor or a cousin or a father. When the facts fell into place, nothing could change them. Not even pity.

When he had taken her back to the inn, leaving the motor running as he helped her down, she said, "You're going to ask him about Burwell, aren't you?"

"I have to do that."

"Don't tell him I was the one who gave him away. Will you promise? I don't think I could bear it if you did."

"I shan't tell him. But if he's taken into custody, you'll have to testify that you saw him that day in Burwell. There's nothing I can do about that."

"But only if you're sure," she pleaded. "Only if he's taken into custody. When that happens, it won't matter, will it?"

"I promise." But he thought he had very little hope of living up to that promise.

When Rutledge reached Isleham, he found that Thornton was in.

There were circles beneath his eyes, as if he'd spent a restless night. Rutledge's first question was "Do you own a bicycle?"

Thornton regarded him warily. "Why are you asking about bicycles?"

"It's a quiet and simple means of travel. The roads are flat, if long, and the distances are not too great." He smiled. "No hedgerows with blind corners."

"Yes. I do, as a matter of fact," Thornton said. "I prefer the motorcar these days, but I used to enjoy riding."

"Were you riding it last evening?"

Thornton was alert now. "No. I was not."

"Yet your housekeeper told me you'd gone for a walk. I also walked around this village. And if you were here, where were you?"

"We probably just missed each other."

"How long was your walk?"

Thornton shrugged. "I wasn't concerned about time. I was trying to rid myself of cobwebs. You don't do that by looking at your watch every few minutes."

"You lied to me again, you know," Rutledge said pleasantly.

"Lied? I assure you I did not."

"I remember asking if you'd attended the funeral services in Burwell for Major Clayton. You told me you hadn't. That you avoid funerals and memorial services."

"That was the truth."

"Was it? Then how do you explain the fact that someone saw you there, at St. Mary's Church, and recognized you?"

That was a shock. Thornton couldn't quite conceal it. "I told you the truth. I did not attend the funeral. Nor did I go to the luncheon afterward."

"What you didn't tell me was that you were in Burwell at the time. And standing within sight of St. Mary's. Where you could watch mourners enter and leave the church."

"I've told you I don't do well with funerals. I paid my respects in my own fashion. And that as far as I know is not a crime."

"You also saw Captain Hutchinson there."

"What of it? Do you think if I'd wanted to kill him, I'd have waited until he happened to come to the Fen country? It doesn't say much for the depth of my desire for revenge. Still, it does rather point a finger in my direction. Do you think I'd be so foolish?"

Rutledge judged he was lying again. "But you didn't have to wait very long. He came to Ely for the wedding."

"How could I have known that? I wasn't invited to the wedding, if you remember."

"You didn't need an invitation. The wedding guests were mentioned in the Ely paper."

"I'm sure they were. But I don't take the Ely newspaper. The *Times* is delivered to me. A day late, of course, but it's my choice in newspapers."

Pinning this man down was nearly impossible. Rutledge was annoyed with him.

He said, "There are several things recommending you as a candidate for villain. You've lied to me several times. You served under Major Clayton. You were in Burwell on the day he was buried, and you knew Swift far better than you'd led me to believe. If this is coincidence, then it's leaning heavily in the favor of suspicion."

"All right. Answer me this. Why should I kill Captain Hutchinson, a man I didn't know and had no reason to hate."

Rutledge took the gamble.

"Because," he said slowly, "you were the man Mary Whiting was engaged to when she met Hutchinson and was swept off her feet."

Thornton's face flamed, anger almost a visible thing in the room.

"Who the hell has filled your head with such nonsense?" he said finally, getting himself back in hand.

"Is it nonsense? I think not. I haven't been able to learn that man's name, but Alice Worth knows it. It's only a matter of time before I'll have it from her. She was Mary's friend, you know. In fact, she would prefer to see Hutchinson's killer go free, because she knows why he wanted to kill the Captain."

"Alice who? Did you say Worth? I don't know anyone by that name. Are you quite sure she'll point to me?"

"She lives in London. She knew all about Mary's visit to Newmarket with her uncle Thaddeus. And that Mary fell in love there. She knows too that Mary changed her mind about marrying the man she met there. Mary lived to regret it. That's why she slit her wrists, she had nothing to live for and much to regret. Not even the child she'd been carrying lived to comfort her."

When Thornton said nothing, his face like stone, Rutledge asked, "Have you no defense to offer?"

Instead Thornton walked to the door of the room. "You can leave now. I have nothing more to say to you."

"Was the child yours, not Hutchinson's?"

Thornton wheeled. *"Damn you, she wasn't that sort of woman."*

"Then you knew her."

"Yes, I knew her. I was in France when she died. She wrote to me. A farewell letter. She said she had no reason to live. She told me how much she regretted leaving me. She told me she'd made the wrong choice and had suffered for what she'd done. She thought the child's death was her punishment. I could tell—I knew her that well—that she was going to do something silly. I went to my sergeant and begged for leave. He knew I wasn't married and so I told him my mother was dying. But things were going badly, we were being pushed back, pushed hard in those early days of the fighting. He refused permission, and so did the Lieutenant. I was frantic, I wrote to her and told her that life was worth living, that we would find a way to be happy. But she was dead before the letter reached her."

"How do you know?"

"The letter was returned with DECEASED printed across the address. I wanted to kill Hutchinson. Our paths never crossed. He spent more time at HQ than in the trenches, or so I was told. I looked for him in London when I came back. He was still in France, something to do with the treaty. And then he came to Burwell, and I could have killed him with my bare hands. But it was Major Clayton's funeral. I couldn't do it."

"Then Ely was your next chance."

"I thought it was. Instead someone else killed him before I could."

"You expect me to believe that?"

"I don't care if you do or you don't. I didn't kill the man."

"What I don't understand is why you killed Swift."

"I didn't. Why should I? He had nothing to do with Mary's death."

"To confound the police? Unfortunately, instead it brought in Scotland Yard."

"I can't think of anyone else who hated Hutchinson as much as I did. As much as I still do. But someone must have had a reason. Whoever he is, he's cheated me of the satisfaction. And you must ask *him* why Swift died."

"Nevertheless."

"I'm not a solicitor, but I'm sure you can't charge me with one death when there's no evidence of my involvement in the other one. And if I protest my innocence of Hutchinson's killing, then I must protest my innocence in Swift's. I shall hire the best attorney in Ely or even Cambridge if it comes to that. And when it's finished, you'll look a fool." He was still very angry.

"I very much doubt that. The Chief Constable is pressing Inspector Warren in Ely for a swift closure of this case. He'll be very pleased that we've finally done just that."

The two men considered each other.

"I expect we've reached an impasse," Thornton said after a moment.

"Hardly an impasse," Rutledge said. "I have the authority to take you into custody and let the courts sort out the question of guilt."

"Yes, that's true." Thornton was standing by the globe. He twirled it with his fingertips, watching it spin, and then turned to Rutledge. "Are you a betting man?"

"I'm not. I haven't been lucky."

"In life? In love? Very well, don't answer that. But I'll make you a sporting proposition. One that I think will appeal to you."

Rutledge smiled. "Indeed? What do you have to barter with?"

"For starters, my life," Thornton said, quite serious. "And my own need for answers. Someone killed Hutchinson for me, but I don't find that acceptable. And so I don't owe his killer anything. I didn't have the pleasure of watching the man die at my hands."

"Only through the sights of a rifle."

"You were in France. Did killing men with your rifle or your revolver give you any satisfaction?"

"No. They had to die or my men would."

"Precisely."

"We can search this house and the outbuildings. Is the rifle here?"

Thornton took a deep breath. "You *are* a determined man. Let me finish. I will help you with this search for Hutchinson's murderer—and Swift's. In return you'll leave me free to do just that. Rest assured, I won't kill the bastard when I find him. The hangman can do it for me."

"I don't consider that much of a bargain, when I can stop this nonsense now and be on my way to London tomorrow."

"Is it nonsense? I know these Fens. Far more intimately than you ever will. Did you find your valise intact after my rather cursory search?"

It was Rutledge's turn to stare. He hadn't expected Thornton to confess to that.

"Yes, I was there in the mist. Searching. When I stumbled on you, I did wonder if you were the person I was after. I could have let you wander about until you'd broken your neck falling into a ditch or off the bridge. Instead, I made sure you weren't stalking a new victim and then I got you to safety. I've walked these villages, ridden my bicycle through them, driven along every mile of road. He's out there, I tell you. Elusive, a shadow. But together we just might find him."

It was a persuasive argument. Yet Hamish was urging Rutledge to decline the bargain.

But Rutledge was an experienced policeman. And he wanted proof. Not promises.

"I could claim the same thing. That you were walking into Wriston to search out a fresh target. Which of course you did. Burrows."

"Burrows was surely a decoy. I can't think of any reason for wanting him dead, short of madness. And this killer isn't mad. He knows what he wants, and I have a very strong feeling he's finished his work here. We can still lose him, you know. Both of us."

"An interesting theory. But you can't prove it. It won't be proven until we have our man. At the moment, you're the one I want. You're too clever by half. And I have no reason to trust you."

"Then I'll give you what I know. He uses a bicycle to get around the Fens. He moves at night."

"But you were on a bicycle. Last night."

"Where?" he asked sharply.

"On the High Street in Wriston. Pedaling in the direction of the windmill."

"But I wasn't in Wriston. I was in Wicken. Don't you see, that was *him*."

"Prove it."

"Actually I can. Tom Hendricks's little dog got out and was barking at me. Tom came out to see what the fuss was all about, and he called off his dog when he recognized me. I told him I'd been visiting friends and was on my way home. He thought at first it must be the murderer. Everyone is worried he might be a neighbor or the ironmonger or the man who keeps bees."

"When was this?"

"Close on ten, I should think."

If it was true, then Thornton couldn't have been in Wriston.

"I'll find this Hendricks and ask him."

"Even better, I'll accompany you, shall I? It will save time." Thornton walked to the door. "After you, Inspector."

When they had arrived in Wicken, Rutledge said, "It will do no good if you are standing there, coaching the man to give the right answers. I'll interview him alone." Thornton was about to argue, but

Rutledge said, "If you prefer, I can take you to Ely and leave it to Inspector Warren to speak to Hendricks."

"Yes, all right," Thornton retorted impatiently.

He pointed out the Wicken village store, which Hendricks owned, and Rutledge left the motorcar down the lane just beyond where it stood on the main street. He walked around the corner to the door just as Hendricks himself stepped out to watch workmen repairing a roof across the way. Rutledge quickly discovered that it wasn't going to be as simple to question him as Thornton had promised.

Scratching his ear, the man said, "Yes, Mr. Thornton was in Wicken. My dog took out after him something fierce. Teddy doesn't care for bicycles."

"Can you tell me what time it was when you saw him?" Rutledge asked.

"As to that, now, I'm not sure. I didn't take any notice. Late, I'd say."

"Closer to nine o'clock? Or after eleven," Rutledge asked.

"I'd fallen asleep in my chair, you see. Teddy's barking woke me up. Given all that trouble in Wriston and Ely, I got up to find out what the matter was. But I never looked at the time. I went back inside and went to bed."

"It's rather important, Mr. Hendricks."

"I'm sorry. I've no idea. My guess is closer to ten, but it could have been as early as nine. Why does it matter?"

"We're trying to sort out a problem. Thank you, Mr. Hendricks. I'm staying in Wriston just now. If you remember anything that would be helpful, you can send word to the constable there."

"That will be McBride, would it?" He moved aside so that two women, their market baskets over their arms, could enter the shop. "I must go. They'll be wanting help," he said, and turned away, stepping back inside.

He'd verified that Thornton had indeed been in the village. But it was the time that was critical, and that the shopkeeper had failed to supply.

Rutledge walked back to the motorcar, debating with himself whether this had been a wild-goose chase or if Hendricks would conveniently remember the time when the local constable took down his statement.

The motorcar was where he'd left it, just past the corner.

And it was empty.

Swearing, Rutledge looked up and down the lane in both directions, but there was no sign of Thornton.

Chapter 18

I should have kept my eye on him, he thought. *Damn the man!*

He got into the motorcar and quartered the village, following first one lane to its end and then the next. He was just coming up the last one when he saw Thornton leaving a house.

He hailed Rutledge and said, "The Petersons live here. Next door to Hendricks. But he swears he never heard the little dog."

Rutledge didn't answer. He was too angry with Thornton.

After a moment's hesitation, the man got into the motorcar and said, "For its size the blasted little dog made enough racket to wake the dead. But neither Peterson nor the man on the other side of the Hendricks admit to hearing anything."

"So much for proof."

"Look, I was *here*."

Rutledge said nothing. He drove out of Wicken and toward

Wriston, intending to continue on to Ely while Thornton was in the motorcar.

They were not far from Wriston when Thornton said, "Have you considered? I'm talking about the way Hutchinson treated Mary. Was there another woman? I could never understand why he treated her so shabbily."

"It was very likely her money he was after. His sister is still living in the house in London that had belonged to Mary."

"Then why hadn't he remarried? There must be other wealthy women he could charm."

Rutledge remembered what he'd been told about Hutchinson's attentions to Major Clayton's sister. And then he'd gone back to London with the Colonel because she was staying on in Burwell for a few days. Because he discovered she was already engaged?

"There's a missing servant girl," he suggested, testing the waters.

Thornton shook his head. "He wouldn't be such a fool. She'd be poor as a church mouse. And Hutchinson falling in love boggles the mind. What did you learn in Ely? There must have been something useful—there must have been what? Half a hundred people there, if not more."

"They saw nothing."

"Ah. That explains why you moved on to Wriston. I'd wondered."

"I thought Swift's murder would be easier to solve. As it has turned out, I was right from the beginning. Hutchinson's death was the one that mattered."

"You won't know that until you've found out who killed Swift." Thornton put a hand to his forehead, massaging it as if it ached. "Did Swift and Hutchinson ever cross paths?"

"If they did, we haven't found the link."

"It's there. Have you talked to the police in Glasgow or wherever it was Swift spent his war?"

"Not yet."

"Well, then, how can you tell me that you've concluded I'm the killer? I've never been to Scotland. The question is, had Hutchinson?"

"There's Susan," Rutledge said, remembering. "She used to keep house for Swift before his wife died."

"Did she go to Scotland with him?"

"She didn't. In fact she became the Rector's housekeeper after Swift left. Still, he wrote to her once or twice after he was settled in Glasgow." She had read them over and over again, until she committed them to memory. Or to be precise, those sections that meant the most to her, those referring to her relationship with her employer. He'd had no reason until now to wonder what else had been in the letters that hadn't been important enough to her to remember.

It was unlikely that Swift would have mentioned a casual acquaintance with a young officer or anything that had come of that meeting. Not to his late wife's former lady's maid. But it had to be looked into.

Rutledge was relieved to find that the Rector wasn't in when he knocked at the Rectory door and Susan herself answered.

He'd brought Thornton with him. Susan seemed to be taken aback to find the man from Scotland Yard with a stranger in tow, asking to speak to her.

"I've the Rector's tea to make. He'll be home again in a few minutes."

"It won't take long. If it does, I'll explain to the Rector myself."

Still uncertain she asked them in, took them to the sitting room, and stood there before them, awaiting their questions.

Rutledge said, "When I spoke to you earlier, you told me about letters from Swift while he was in Scotland. Do you still have them?"

"Yes, sir. I saw no harm in keeping them."

"And there is none. I'd like to read them, if I could. There might be something in them that seemed unimportant to you, but in hindsight might lead us to Mr. Swift's killer."

"I'm sure there isn't anything, sir. It was just a kindness to let me know all was well with the poor man."

With an apology, she left them to go up to her room. A few minutes later she had returned and handed the letters to Rutledge.

They were worn almost to the point of illegibility, folded and re-folded countless times. He gently removed the first letter from its envelope and spread the pages across his knee.

They seemed immediately familiar, and he realized that she had memorized the opening, thanking her once more for her care of his late wife and asking if she was comfortable in her new position.

Rutledge read on.

I have begun to settle in. It's so unlike the Fens that I'm at a loss to know what to think. A large river, a different pattern of farming, terrain that rolls, so that when I look to the horizon, there are trees and rising land in the way. The weather is cooler, but then it's moving toward late fall. And the accents of the people I meet are almost impenetrable sometimes. It will be some weeks before I am comfortable with it. The people here are different as well. There are tenements in Glasgow as well as handsome streets of handsome houses. The Cathedral is large but not so fine as Ely. I try to tell myself that I am here to look forward and not backward, but my heart is in the churchyard in Wriston. Still. I have made some changes. I have moved from the hotel where I stayed after my arrival. It was very dear, as rooms are difficult to find, given the influx of people. The house is tall, three stories, but quite narrow. The furnishings are not the best, but comfortable enough. I tell myself that I know ancient Rome better than I know my own country. I could find my way to the Forum with the ease of someone born there. Finding my way through the twisting streets here is a lesson in humility. But I am satisfied, and much of that satisfaction is due to the maid I have hired to keep me in order.

There was no mention of friends or acquaintances. Or those Swift must have met during his day. It appeared that he was more homesick than he chose to admit.

Turning to the second letter, he found only two references to Swift's work for the Navy.

It's time-consuming and that shortens my day, no leisure in which to look back.

And again, *I like those I work with well enough. They come from all over the country, uprooted as I have been, missing families and friends as I have done. But we have high hopes that the war will end soon. While I am in agreement with them, when it does end, I shall have to find another exile.*

It was on the last page that Rutledge stopped skimming. A name seemed to leap off the page.

Catriona has kept my house in order, as you once did. She came well recommended, although she is hardly more than a child and had not been in service before this. She tells me she too is an exile, a long way from her home in the Highlands. She wants a very different life from that of her friends growing up in the small glen where she was born. Her grandfather didn't approve, but she is a determined young woman and won his permission to spend six months in Glasgow. But I expect she will have something to say about returning to a narrower life. Her grandfather had lived in England, and it's possible that she had heard his tales of his time there. She was very disappointed to learn that I'd never been to London. She seems to think that we must all have been there often, drawn by its wonders. That and the fact that Ely isn't a large and bustling city has diminished me in her eyes. But she's a good worker, cheerful and pleasant, and I am growing fond of her lighthearted presence in the house.

Was this the elusive connection he'd searched for and not found? Was this the same Catriona who had worked in the London house that belonged to Mary Hutchinson?

If it was, how had she gone from Glasgow and Swift's house, to London and the home of Captain Hutchinson? Catriona was not an uncommon name.

There was nothing more about her until Rutledge reached the last of the letters, this one written after the war, a month before Swift was scheduled to return to England.

I am no longer the man I was when first I came here. I have had to learn to put the past away, and it was a hard lesson. Return- ing to the house in Wriston where we lived so happily, my wife and I, will be difficult at best. But I must try for my own sake as well as for hers. If there was another choice open to me, I think I would leap at the chance to take it. But there is not. Perhaps God wishes me to find that courage, before He shows me His grace again as He did when I was offered this post in Glasgow.

Hamish said, "Ye ken, it's why he stood for yon seat in Parliament. London was a long way fra' here."

And it was the explanation—perhaps not what he told the men who approached him about serving, but what led to his personal decision to stand.

The final lines returned to Catriona.

She's grown into a young woman, our Catriona. If I had had a daughter, I couldn't have been more proud of her. She reminds me of someone I once knew, that same thirst for life. I cannot bring her with me to Wriston—she will not come. And so you will not meet her. She has been searching for a position in London, and there is one that she likes very much. Her cousins, who have the care of her, are not best pleased, nor is her grandfather. They blame me for opening her eyes to this other world, but she's too intelligent and too well read to go back to the glen. It would be a tragic waste. And they must see that. Still, I am writing to the woman in London to find out for myself if this is a suitable household.

Tomorrow I begin to pack up this new life and say goodbye. . . .

Thornton was standing by the window, restless and still angry. Rutledge ignored him.

Instead he returned the letters to Susan, saying, "I'm glad you kept these. They do more to explain Swift to me than all the statements Constable McBride collected. Thank you for allowing me to see them."

Susan flushed a little with pride. "I do treasure them, sir. Rector has been good to me, but I miss my mistress as much as *he* did. Mr. Swift. It was a comfort, his writing to me. And I understood why he couldn't have me back when he came home again. It would have been hard for both of us without Mrs. Swift there."

Rutledge thought that Swift had been more than a little selfish in his grief. But he said, "Thornton, we must go. I don't think we need to wait for the Rector."

Thornton followed him out to the motorcar, saying, "What was that all about? Those letters from Swift? What did they tell you?"

"I must go to London. The question is, what am I to do with you?"

"You *were* taking me to Ely," Thornton said dryly. "If you've forgot why, I'll be happy to find my own way home."

But Rutledge stood there, his hand on the crank, thinking.

If he took Thornton to Ely, Inspector Warren would hold him until the man's solicitor and a local barrister came to post bail. That could happen long before Rutledge got back from London.

He said, "Fancy a drive south? It won't be comfortable, but it's the best I can offer."

"Why?" Thornton demanded suspiciously. "Are you taking me to the Yard rather than to Ely?"

"Not precisely. I believe I've found a connection between Swift and Hutchinson. The question is, does that connection in any way change the likelihood that you killed both men? I think not. Still, it's a distraction. And I don't care for distractions."

"Are you accustomed to traveling around the countryside with an alleged murderer in your motorcar?"

"Not as a rule," Rutledge answered, turning the crank and ushering Thornton into the nearside door. "The thing is, if you escape, it will only serve to prove your guilt. And that will please the Chief Constable here in Cambridgeshire, as well as the Acting Chief Superintendent at the Yard. They are looking for a scapegoat, you see. And you'll do as well as the next man. The courts will sort it out, and I won't have to face my superior with the news that I haven't a clue who killed Hutchinson and Swift."

Thornton stared at him. "Are you quite serious?"

"That's for you to decide. Shall I take you to Ely, or would you prefer a few more days of freedom? Such, of course, as it is?"

"Put that way, how can I refuse?"

Rutledge reversed and turned the bonnet toward the London road. As he passed the police station on the far side of the pond, he saw McBride staring at him. But he was not ready to talk to the constable about Thornton. At the turn, Miss Trowbridge was just walking up to her door with her hands full of freshly cut flowers, Clarissa winding sinuously around her ankles, looking for an invitation to go in.

She turned as she heard the motorcar coming toward her, and she too saw Thornton in the seat next to Rutledge.

Frowning, she watched them out of sight.

Thornton said pensively, "She's a very attractive woman. I would give much for a proper introduction. We've met only a few times in very public circumstances. Not the sort of thing one can pursue."

"I thought your heart belonged to Mary Hutchinson."

"It does. I was hoping that by killing Hutchinson I could lay her soul to rest finally. It has been a long road. But I wasn't the one to send him to hell, where he belonged."

Rutledge was reminded of the letter Swift had written. The contrast of his devotion to his wife and Hutchinson's callous treatment of his.

"Are you sure that's what Mary would have wanted?"

Thornton turned to stare at him. "I—never considered that."

"She thought she loved him enough to marry him. Perhaps she forgave him even as she died."

"Dear God. *No, don't even suggest that.*"

He turned away, and Rutledge let a silence fall between them. It was not until they stopped for petrol and a late dinner that Thornton said, "Did you mean what you said as we were leaving Wriston? Or were you hoping to make me angry enough to force a confession?"

Rutledge waited until they had given their order to the man who was serving them, and then he answered.

"Perhaps I can be more objective. You have Mary Hutchinson's letter. Still, you don't know what was in her mind at the end, when she was dying. It's also possible that the last thing she expected of you was to waste your own life in avenging her death."

Thornton pressed his hands against his face, then dropped them. His eyes were haunted. "Is that why I never acted until Hutchinson came north? Because I was afraid it wasn't what she wanted?"

"Only you can answer that."

But Thornton said no more. He changed the subject by asking about Rutledge's war, and they spoke of other things until the outskirts of London.

Dawn was rising in the east when they turned into the street where Rutledge lived.

"You'll need a shave and a fresh shirt," he said. "I can offer both."

Thornton's hand rasped as it brushed across his chin. "My God, aren't you tired?"

"I can't afford to be tired." He pulled up in front of the flat and got out.

Thornton followed him, and twenty minutes later, they were leaving again, this time for the house where Hutchinson had lived.

Thornton stared up at it with interest. "This was Mary's. This house. I never came here, although she spoke of it often. She liked London. Her uncle preferred the country, but he brought her out in London. I didn't know her then. I'd have lived anywhere that made her happy."

"I'd rather not let the occupants know that you had anything to do with Mary Hutchinson. Can you keep your head—and your temper—or must I handcuff you to the motorcar?"

"I'd like to go inside."

It was early to make a call. The household was awake and already about its duties, but Miss Hutchinson, they were told, had not yet come down for breakfast.

They cooled their heels for half an hour in the drawing room. And still Miss Hutchinson hadn't come down to speak with them.

Angry, Rutledge went out to the stairs. Short of bearding her in her bedchamber, the next possibility was to find the Hutchinson housekeeper on his own.

He and Thornton walked unhindered to the door to the kitchen and made their way down the twisting steps.

A scullery maid looked up from cleaning carrots for the midday meal. Startled to find two strange men coming toward her, she dropped her knife and fled to find the cook, or failing the cook, anyone else of sufficient authority to deal with the interlopers.

The housekeeper, frowning in disapproval, came hurrying down the passage toward them.

It was on the tip of her tongue, Rutledge could see, to tell them the tradesmen's entrance was outside. Then, realizing that Rutledge had been here before, asking questions, she wiped the frown from her face and asked coolly, "How may I help you?"

Rutledge said pleasantly, "I see you remember me, Mrs. Cookson. Could we speak to you in your parlor, please?"

His expression, belying his voice, brooked no objections. She said, "This way, if you please," and led them to the small room where he'd interviewed her before.

"Is this about the late Mrs. Hutchinson?" she asked, offering them chairs.

"In a way. I've come to ask about the young woman Catriona Beaton. Can you tell me what her references were, when she came to you?"

"I don't know that Miss Hutchinson would ap—" she began, but Rutledge cut her short.

"I'm sure she would approve of your helping Scotland Yard. To be sure, I can ask for a search warrant, but she might not care for that added unpleasantness."

Mrs. Cookson, still standing, said, "I have the box just there."

She indicated a large flat box on a shelf behind him, and he passed it to her. Inside were packets of envelopes, each packet tied with a ribbon and each one including a small card indicating the name of the servant in question. She thumbed through them quickly, finding the one he'd asked for. Taking it out, she untied the ribbon and began to look at each of the envelopes.

"Here is the recommendation."

Rutledge took it from her and withdrew the sheets of paper inside. He scanned them quickly, then went back to read the pertinent parts.

I cannot recommend her highly enough. She's intelligent, quick, willing, and eager to serve in a larger household than mine. I believe you'll find her a very fine addition to your staff.

The second page of the letter was more to the point.

*She has grown up in my house, and I feel responsible for finding
her a suitable position. You will understand that I should like
reassurances that she will be cared for with diligence and that
the distance from her home to London will not be viewed as relin-
quishing our duty. Her family will expect no less.*

It was most certainly to the point. And the signature was what Rutledge had expected to find there.

Herbert G. R. Swift

Swift had written the recommendation and the Hutchinsons had
accepted Catriona Beaton into their household on the burden of that
recommendation.

But who the devil had set out to avenge Catriona Beaton?

Chapter 19

Turning to Thornton, Rutledge said, "What do you know about a Catriona Beaton?"

"Catriona Beaton?" he repeated, frowning. "I don't think I know anyone by that name."

Rutledge was returning the sheets to their envelope and handing it back to Mrs. Cookson, but his eyes were on Thornton's face.

"There's another letter here. From her grandfather," the housekeeper said. "It came after she had left us." Taking it out of the packet, she handed it to Rutledge.

He opened it and found a very brief message inside.

We have heard nothing from you for the past two months. Whatever is wrong, we will help you, you must know that. Just write. For the love of God, write.

It was signed, *Your loving grandfather.*

"Did no one answer this man, when the letter came?"

"She'd left of her own accord," the housekeeper protested. "We didn't like to write and tell him so."

"Did he ever come to the house?"

"If he did, he never identified himself as a relative of hers."

Then had the grandfather found his missing granddaughter?

If he had, there was surely no reason to hate either Herbert Swift or Captain Hutchinson.

Or was there?

He looked at the envelope in his hand. The return address was MacLaren, Trahir House, followed by an address that Rutledge thought must be north of Stirling, in Scotland. A man of substance, this grandfather, not a simple clansman.

Thanking Mrs. Cookson, he left, and Thornton said, as they went out the door and down the steps to the motorcar, "What the hell was that all about?"

"I don't know," Rutledge said. "But I intend to find out."

He sat for several minutes in the motorcar, staring across the road at the grassy expanses and tall trees of the square, enclosed by its iron fencing. That reminded him of Marcella Trowbridge's cottage. Setting the memory aside, he considered his position.

No doubt Sergeant Gibson could find the information, given time. But that would mean going to the Yard. And explaining Thornton. It had perhaps been a mistake to bring him, but by the same token, keeping an eye on him was paramount until a proper search of the man's house could be made. So far there had been no time for Thornton to dispose of anything incriminating. Including a rifle . . .

Who else, then?

Mr. Belford came to mind.

But did he, Rutledge, wish to be beholden to the man?

They had worked together—in a manner of speaking—on another

case. And neither man had quite trusted the other. Rutledge had looked into Belford's past while Belford had explored Rutledge's. An uneasy truce had been declared.

But there was the fact that Belford had probably worked for Military Intelligence, even though his curriculum vitae showed he'd spent the war in the Military Foot Police. It was as good a cover as any. His contacts went beyond any information that Gibson had access to, and time at the moment was important. Something had to be done with Thornton, and soon.

Hamish said, "It's haste driving ye. And you'll find yoursel' owing the Devil his due."

It was a risk. He knew that. But what choice did he have?

Taking a deep breath, Rutledge turned the motorcar toward Chelsea.

It was very likely, he thought, that Belford wouldn't be at home. But as luck would have it, when he knocked at the door, a footman told Rutledge that he was in.

A few minutes later, Rutledge and Thornton walked into Belford's study.

Nothing on the desk would indicate what the man had been working on before Rutledge came to the door. It had been cleared away with swift precision, and somewhere in this room, he thought, would be a drawer designed to hold whatever had been there.

"Mr. Rutledge," Belford said, rising from his desk. A tall, trim man, he seemed to be a gentleman of leisure, not a master of information. "What brings you here? And who, may I ask, is your guest?"

"This is Mr. Thornton, a suspect in a double murder. If you don't mind, I should very much like to lock him in a room while we talk."

Thornton said, "Here—!" and stepped back as if expecting to be taken away.

Belford said, "If we are circumspect, no harm done. Let him stay."

Rutledge smiled. Did nothing catch this man off his guard? Taking one of the chairs pointed out by their host, he said, "There were two

deaths recently, one in Ely and another in the nearby village of Wriston. A Captain Hutchinson and a Mr. Herbert Swift were shot by someone using a rifle. Suspects had a good reason to kill one or the other,
but not both. Unless of course the second man was a—er—distraction
from the real target. Until yesterday I could find no connection between these two men. Now it appears that one of them, Swift, employed
a young girl, Catriona Beaton, as housekeeper while he was working for
the Admiralty in Glasgow. When the war ended, the young woman, as
she was then, decided she preferred to seek employment in London. In
due course, she went to work in the house of Captain Hutchinson. And
in due course, she went missing from this house, and no one seems to
know where she went. Or indeed if she is still alive. A body was found
later, the identification uncertain. The only connection we have with
her past is her grandfather, a man by the name of MacLaren, who lived
at Trahir House in Scotland, somewhere north of Stirling, if I remember my geography. He could well be dead. If he isn't, he could possibly
tell me what became of his granddaughter. And whether the police ever
told him about locating her remains. And whether or not she could
have been the reason these two men were killed."

"You think someone in her family could have been out for revenge."

"It's a long way from Scotland to Ely."

"And Mr. Thornton here?"

Thornton spoke before Rutledge could answer. "I knew Hutchinson's wife. I was to marry her. She chose Hutchinson instead. It was
not a successful match, and she killed herself." It was bald, emotion-
less, and yet there were brackets of pain—or anger?—around his
mouth. "I would have enjoyed being the one to kill Hutchinson."

"In short, you're the first string to Rutledge's bow?"

"I believe I am."

Belford turned back to Rutledge. "Is there a good reason why Mr.
Thornton is here and not in gaol in Ely?"

"There hasn't been time to search his house for the murder weapon."

"And so he's here, meanwhile? Rather unorthodox, but effective." Belford toyed with the inkwell on his desk. It was surmounted by a rather handsome eagle, and Rutledge wouldn't have been surprised to hear that it had once belonged to the Kaiser. "I do happen to know of a MacLaren. I expect he isn't your man. He was in the Lovat Scouts— the Boer War. One of their finest shots. My uncle delighted in telling us tales of his prowess. But he resigned when the war was over. And was never heard of again. It was generally thought he'd gone back to Scotland."

Thornton said, "His children would have been MacLarens. But his grandchildren could have borne any name."

"I don't believe he ever married," Belford responded. "That was said to be the reason why he took on the most dangerous assignments."

"Nevertheless," Rutledge returned.

"I'll look into this matter. He shouldn't be difficult to find." Belford glanced at Rutledge. "Are the resources of the Yard no longer available?"

"They are—if one wishes to be found out by a superior who is anxious to see this inquiry closed," Rutledge retorted.

"Ah. Markham, is it? He had something of a reputation in Yorkshire. But then he knew his turf, and he was seldom wrong. London is a very different matter, I should think."

They rose, and as Rutledge moved toward the door, Belford added, "Where can I reach you?"

"My flat. I'm sure you know where that is."

"Quite."

As the door was closed behind them, Thornton said, "Remind me never to cross that man."

Rutledge grinned sardonically. "One sups with the Devil when one turns to him."

"I shouldn't think the Yard would approve."

Rutledge didn't answer him.

They spent the rest of the morning and half the afternoon in Rutledge's flat. Thornton paced the floor like a caged lion, back and forth, back and forth, while Rutledge sat by the door and waited, fighting sleep, which kept threatening to overwhelm him.

It was nearly three o'clock in the afternoon when a messenger arrived with an envelope.

"Rutledge?"

"Yes."

The man handed him the envelope, turned back to his motorcycle, and was gone in a roar.

Rutledge sat down again, hesitating before he broke the seal.

I was right. MacLaren was in the Lovat Scouts. And quite a dangerous man with a rifle. He acted as a sharpshooter in several matters where it was deemed necessary to—er—take certain measures. He never married.

However, it is reported that he had one child out of wedlock, and she in turn had one daughter. The mother of that child was killed in an accident when the girl was five. Her father died in France during the war. Her name was Catriona Beaton. MacLaren has not been seen at Trahir House for some years. It's thought that he is dead. The house is now occupied by his brother's family. I did not speak to them, leaving that to you.

I shall collect my fee for this information at some future date.

It was signed with a *B*.

Hamish said, "Aye, you've made your bargain. It willna' sit well at the Yard."

Making an effort to ignore the voice, Rutledge considered the problem of this man MacLaren. He could worry about Belford later. Where, he asked himself, was this Lovat Scout? And how much did he love his granddaughter? He was alive when she vanished. But a

Scot in Cambridgeshire would draw attention the instant he opened his mouth. And someone would remember . . .

And what was he to do with Thornton while finding out?

As if he'd heard Rutledge's thoughts, Thornton said, "Don't mind me. I'm enjoying this quest of yours. It's likely to clear me."

Rutledge turned to him. "Were you a sniper in the war?"

The question came out of nowhere, and Thornton wasn't prepared. His face betrayed him before he could school it to show no reaction.

He didn't need the War Office now to tell him the truth. But verification would serve the K.C. to prepare his case.

"A battlefield promotion. You must have done something extraordinary to deserve that. What was it?"

"That's none of your damned business."

"But it is. Anything to do with you is my business. Did you bring your rifle home with you? Against all orders?"

Thornton was prepared this time. He said blandly, "What use would I have for a rifle in waterfowl country?"

"It was your closest companion—no one else except your commanding officer accepted what you did as brave. Shooting from cover? And there was Hutchinson. Did you think it might be useful one day to kill him? It was your weapon of choice. Not the Gurkha knife. Nor the thuggee garrote."

"I wasn't ashamed of what I did. It saved lives, my skill."

As it had done. Rutledge took a deep breath. "All right. Let it go. But if I find you've armed that old man and sent him out to do your dirty work for you, I'll have you up as an accessory, to hang beside him."

"Did you know that the windmill keeper was a Scot?"

"The windmill—the one in Wriston?" And he remembered. Discussing Hogmanay with Marcella Trowbridge, who knew the man as a child. Who had told him that Angus was likely to be dead. McBride had suggested he'd drunk himself to death after the fire in the windmill cottage. But had he? And if he had, where was he buried? More urgently, was he a MacLaren?

Rutledge sprang to his feet, weariness forgotten. "We're going back to Cambridgeshire. Now."

He was on the road before he thought of something. He'd been mulling over all the evidence as he threaded his way through the London traffic, and he turned around, heading back into the city.

It was Miss Hutchinson who knew the answer, and he would see her this time if he had to break down her bedroom door.

Thornton, alarmed, said, "What the hell? I thought we were going to Wriston."

"Not yet. I want to speak to Miss Hutchinson again."

This time he found her at a late lunch, sitting at the head of the long table in the splendidly proportioned dining room. The table, he thought as he was ushered in by the housekeeper, would easily seat twenty-four.

She looked up in annoyance at the interruption, recognized Rutledge, and said, "I thought you'd left."

"I had. Another question occurred to me. Where was your brother when Catriona Beaton left this house?"

"Where he always was. He'd just returned from France, where the ministries were meeting to discuss the treaty. Where power was, there my brother could be found." There was pride mixed with bitterness in her voice. "That week, he'd gone to Gloucester with some Colonel or other. I think that's why Beaton chose to leave then."

"Because she knew he would follow her and possibly find her?"

"Don't be ridiculous. I daresay she found this household too restrictive for her—er—tastes. London had changed her. Once she had left, she was no longer our responsibility."

"Who did she know in London? Where could she have turned until she had found a new position?"

"Without a reference, she wouldn't have found a new place. No, she was most likely on her way to Scotland, where she came from. If she'd saved her wages, she could have taken the train. There was no certainty that the body the police found was Beaton's. We made the assumption, of course, but there you are."

The housekeeper had said she hadn't collected her last month's wages.

"Yet two months later her family had had no word of her. Or from her."

"I'm not aware of any correspondence from her family. Or that she had any family living."

"Mrs. Cookson received such a letter."

"Did she? She's responsible for the staff, of course. I leave such matters to her."

"Which tells me that her family was left to wonder what had become of Catriona."

"I remind you again that *she* chose to leave. Ending our duty to her as a member of this household."

"She was young, Miss Hutchinson. Surely you felt a personal responsibility."

"I was young once, Inspector, with only my brother to take care of me. Our parents left us very little. I'm well aware of the pitfalls and dangers of being a woman without protection. We lived in lodgings, we were dependent on his officer's pay. We were shunned by people who now respect us. I wore gowns I'd refurbished myself because I couldn't afford new ones. If I survived, I believe she was clever enough and determined enough to survive as well. If she didn't, if the body was hers after all, you must look elsewhere for her murderer."

And yet Fallowfield, in Ely, had believed Hutchinson had been left comfortably fixed by his parents. A claim to wealth and position to conceal his struggle to keep up appearances? Judging by the bitterness in Miss Hutchinson's voice, he thought her version of their past was very likely the truth.

"Now," she was saying, "I should like to finish my lunch in peace. Good day, Mr. Rutledge. Good day, sir."

She turned back to her plate, ignoring them. But Rutledge had got what he wanted.

Leaving her with a curt nod, he walked out of the dining room and said to Thornton, "All right, now we can go north."

"I don't see what you learned here."

Outside, cranking the motorcar, Rutledge said, "The Hutchinsons were rather cavalier about the disappearance of Miss Beaton. Her grandfather would have considered that unconscionable. But would it have driven him to kill Hutchinson? Quite possibly. On the other hand, Swift did everything that was in his power to see that this position was safe and responsible."

"Did MacLaren know that?"

It was a very good question. The young girl he had allowed to live in Glasgow had matured and decided to test her mettle in London. And something had gone wrong. Had she turned to Swift? Or tried to reach Scotland? Or had she died, an anonymous death in a city where life was cheaper than she knew? The London police had closed that case.

And where did Thornton fit in? He'd asked that before, and was still undecided. It was time to take him to Ely and arrange for a search warrant before the man could destroy any evidence. Inspector Warren could see to that.

Again Thornton seemed to know what he was thinking.

"You won't cut me out of this inquiry. Good God, it's my life that's on the line. I'm your only suspect. And I'll be damned if I won't see this through to the finish."

Rutledge remembered what Belford had said about Thornton's presence: *Unorthodox—but effective.*

Tired as he was, Rutledge knew he dared not sleep in this man's company. To sleep would mean to dream, and to dream would mean betrayal. Of himself, of Hamish.

The sooner he reached Ely, the sooner he could rest.

They were on the outskirts of Cambridge when Rutledge heard, as if from a great distance, Thornton swearing and grabbing his arm, then the wheel.

Rutledge came awake with a start to find the motorcar running down the low embankment that led to a shallow farm pond. He pulled on the brake almost reflexively, and the motorcar juddered to a stop on the brink of the water's edge, sending ducks and drakes scattering in a loud cacophony of angry quacks.

Thornton said, "If you have a death wish, I don't. Let me drive. I slept for three hours out of London, remember?"

But the shock was enough to wipe away that leaden need for sleep. Rutledge backed up with great care until the tires were on the high road once more. What had he been dreaming? Something about ambulances—avoiding ambulances as he and his men marched along the rutted stretch of muddy track toward the front lines.

They drove on, Thornton finally asleep again at his side. But it was impossible to reach Ely. They ran into a heavy storm just beyond Newmarket, black clouds pushing toward the coast. He could hear the steam pumps clattering away, straining to keep up with the incessant downpour, and ditches were running strong with rainwater, threatening to overflow.

He pulled into Wriston, still well short of Ely, noticed that there had been hail here as well as rain, and drove on to the police station. McBride wasn't there, but he took Thornton, arguing angrily, back to the single little cell, leaving him there. By the time he'd reached The Dutchman Inn, he was wet to the skin. Priscilla Bartram opened the door to him, and with apologies, he barely made it up to the room set aside for him. Stripping off his wet clothes, he fell across the bed and slept for nine hours.

When he woke, he knew what it was he had to do. Dressing, he went down to find tea and breakfast waiting for him, although it was nearly six o'clock in the evening. He ate it to please Miss Bartram, who was eager to learn why that nice Mr. Thornton was in custody. Gossips were already busy.

He avoided the question and ten minutes later was walking up to Miss Trowbridge's cottage.

The rain had stopped, a watery sun was out, and there were standing pools in the ruts of the High Street. Most of her garden was beaten down by the force of the wind, and there were petals scattered along the walk, bruised and wet.

She came to the door, acknowledged him with a nod, and then as an afterthought, invited him inside.

Clarissa stood up in her bed by the hearth, stretched, and came to inspect his shoes and trousers.

"You've been away," Marcella Trowbridge said, gesturing to a chair.

"To London. I find that you can help me with something that has been puzzling me."

"I can?" she asked, surprised and then wary. She'd been about to sit down, then thought better of it.

"You told me once about the windmill keeper. That he was a Scot."

"Angus?"

"What was his surname?"

"Do you know, I never heard it. He was always—Angus."

"Where was he from? What part of Scotland?"

"I don't know. Does it matter? I told you, he must be dead by now."

"Let me tell you a story. When Herbert Swift was in Glasgow, he took on a young girl to keep house for him. When the war ended and he was returning to Wriston, she chose not to come to Cambridgeshire with him. She was old enough then to know her own mind, you see, and she wished to go to London. The only training she had was in service. And so Swift found her a position that he believed to be safe. But it wasn't. Months later, she left one night late, bag and baggage, without the wages due her. And she disappeared. Her grandfather tried to find her. But there was no trace. It's likely that she's dead. The police concluded she was. Still, she's the only connection I've found between Swift and Captain Hutchinson. For it was his house she left that night."

"Dear God. You don't believe Angus—but he had no granddaughter. No daughter. He never married."

"Was he in the Boer War?"

"I—yes, I believe so. Does it matter?"

"When he left here, did he return to Scotland?"

"I have no idea. I'd known him all my life. But he didn't tell me where he was going. That's odd, isn't it? I just never thought of it in that way until now."

"Your grandmother lived here before leaving the cottage to you in her will. Did she know anything about his past?"

"I can't think she would. She liked him, of course. As did I. He was an interesting man. But except to speak to him, I doubt she knew him any better than I did."

But a child couldn't have judged what an older woman knew and felt unsuitable for young ears. All the same, it couldn't have been shameful, or she would never have let the child meet the man, much less become friends with him.

Where to go from here?

"And you've heard nothing from him since he left here?"

"Nothing. Except once, when I'd just come home from visiting friends in Bury. I found Clarissa in a basket on my doorstep. She was tiny, with a blue ribbon around her neck. There was no card, no message. I asked Priscilla and the constable and everyone I could think of, but no one seemed to know anything about her. It wasn't long after Angus had left. And I wondered if perhaps he'd brought her to me. She's been such great company."

Rutledge thanked her, rising to leave. She asked, "Will you be looking for Angus? Because you think he's got something to do with these murders?"

"I have to be thorough, Miss Trowbridge."

"I refuse to believe any such thing. Still—if you should find Angus, will you ask him? About Clarissa?"

"Yes, I promise."

When he reached the police station the next morning, Rutledge found Thornton fuming and pacing his cell.

"Let me out of here before I go mad. I'd confess to killing Caesar if I thought it would buy my freedom."

Rutledge had once been shut into a cell. He remembered the claustrophobia it had brought on.

Rutledge smiled grimly. "I'm going to look at Swift's house. There was nothing of interest there earlier, but we know rather more now than we did then."

"Let me go with you. He was a classical scholar. As I am. There might be something you've overlooked."

"Or something you can destroy."

"Damn it, man, I kept my word. All the way to London and back."

"So you did. All right, I'll take you with me."

Rutledge had got the key from McBride, who had all but insisted that he come as well. But Rutledge was not ready to tell the constable or anyone else what he was searching for.

The rooms were still, musty. Thornton searched through the bookcase, an occasional comment escaping him as he found a particular volume. Rutledge concentrated on the desk. But there was no correspondence from the grandfather of Catriona Beaton. Frustrated, he went through the drawers a second time, then went to search the bedside table. Swift must have read before he went to sleep, for there were several books perched precariously between the lamp and a small carriage clock.

Rutledge had thumbed through them before and found nothing. In the drawer of that table was a well-worn Bible, and Rutledge took it out, leafing through the pages a second time. He was about to put it back where he'd found it when he spotted a small handbill in the back of the drawer.

It advertised the shoemaker in Soham. He was about to put it in the drawer once more when he saw that something had been scrawled in pencil on a blank space on the back, and he held it up to the light to read it. The words had faded, almost to the point that they were illegible.

You're no better than he is. So be it.

For some reason, Swift had shoved it out of sight rather than toss it into the dustbin or the fire.

Rutledge called, "Thornton. Do you know of a shoemaker in Soham? Someone by the name of Morton?"

"Only that he's no longer in business. He must be all of seventy."

"Who has taken over his shop?"

"I don't think anyone has."

"Then let's have a look."

They had reached the motorcar after returning the key to McBride when a motorcycle came roaring down the street, stopping in front of the police station. He handed McBride a message as they watched, and McBride hailed them.

"For you, Inspector. From Inspector Warren."

"It can wait. I'm driving to Soham."

"Sir." McBride stood watching as they drove away.

"You could have asked him, you know. About the shoemaker."

"I'd rather see for myself."

When they arrived in Soham, Thornton directed Rutledge to the shoemaker's shop. It was on the outskirts, not far from the cooper, Ruskin. The sign above the door was faded, and peering in the single dusty window, Rutledge could see bundles of reeds stacked in a corner or lying spread across the floor to dry. Certainly not the tools of a shoemaker.

"He's the hurdle maker," Thornton said in surprise. "Try in the back of the shop."

They walked around to the rear of the shop, where they could see stacks of hurdles in the open shed. Wooden frames where reeds or withies had been woven to form a barrier for a gate or a garden or a pen for animals. Rutledge remembered hearing Priscilla Bartram describing such a one in the prow of the flat fowling boat her father and grandfather had used.

No one was there. A bicycle stood propped against the back wall of the shop. That was the only sign of life.

"He cuts the osiers and the reeds and the withies in the spring, prepares them, and then makes the hurdles as needed. People come and buy what they want."

"Then where is he today?"

Thornton said with some surprise, "It's Sunday. The shop would be closed."

"So it is. Where does he live, this hurdle maker?" He remembered something McBride had said about the hurdle maker. What was it?

He couldn't bring it back.

"I have no idea. I leave such matters to the man who keeps my gardens."

"Ruskin's shop is just up the street. The cooper. He may know." He'd hardly said the words when he remembered. It hadn't been McBride, it had been Ruskin, giving an account of the night he'd been drunk enough to run riot with the side ax. It had been the hurdle maker he'd been chasing, unaware of what he was doing.

But Ruskin's shop was closed as well. He lived with his wife somewhere else. That too Rutledge remembered. They walked on, leaving the motorcar, looking for someone to question. This was a street of craftsmen. The cooper, the hurdle maker on this side, there the brick maker, and then just beyond, the wheelwright. A cabinetmaker had his shop where the lane met the street, and Rutledge could smell aged wood as he passed. It wasn't until they had reached the street that they met a young couple walking out together.

"Hallo," Rutledge said, smiling. "I'm trying to locate the hurdle maker. Or failing that, Mr. Ruskin. Can you tell me where to find them?"

They directed him to the cottage where Ruskin lived with his wife, and there Ruskin told them how to find the hurdle maker.

"Do you know his name?" Rutledge asked.

"He's generally called Lovat. He came here about the time the shoemaker died. The family let him have the shop for less than what it was worth. It 'ud been closed for several years as it was. No one else wanted it. The carriage trade seldom comes as far as the lane these days."

"Where can I find him?"

"There's a stream on the far side of Soham, where he finds his materials. Sometimes he makes baskets with the reeds. The greengrocer sells them for him."

Rutledge finally found the place Ruskin had described. The hut as he'd called it was actually a small house set by the water's edge, half hidden by a stand of reeds and other tall grasses. It was sturdier than it first appeared.

Turning to Thornton, he said, "Wait here."

Thornton was about to argue, but Rutledge said, "I want to speak to him alone."

He walked around the house to find the man he was after sitting cross-legged on a square of canvas, weaving the circle that would become the bottom of a basket. He looked up, greeted Rutledge, and returned to his work.

Rutledge studied him. Tall, slender, but very strong, his short cropped hair an iron gray. His hands, long-fingered and deft, worked with the reeds with the skill of long practice.

"Mr. Lovat?"

The man nodded.

"My name is Rutledge. Scotland Yard. I've come to ask you about your granddaughter."

Lovat looked up, his gaze alert and focused on Rutledge's face. His eyes were a startling blue.

"My granddaughter?"

His voice was as strong as his body, and Rutledge could hear only the very slightest trace of the Highlands there. Was he being careful, or had time lessened his accent?

"She went missing some time ago. Nearly a year, in fact. While she was a maid in a house in London."

"I was never married," the man said. He set the work aside, letting his hands dangle as his wrists rested on his knees.

"Perhaps not. But you had a child, nevertheless. A daughter. And she in turn had a daughter. *Her* name was Catriona Beaton."

"If you've come to tell me you've found this girl, I'll be glad to hear of it. But my name is Lovat."

"I think not. You were in the Lovat Scouts at one time. But your name is MacLaren. Angus MacLaren. If I found you, I was to tell you that Marcella Trowbridge is grateful for the cat you left at her door."

The man smiled. "I won't take credit for what someone else has done."

"I have only to take you in custody and we will soon discover whether you are a Lovat or a MacLaren. It might be more satisfactory to answer my questions now."

"I've nothing to say to you."

"Where do you keep the rifle? And the mask? And the straw disguise you used to shoot a farmer by the name of Burrows?"

Lovat gestured to his house. "You may search, if you like. I'm a poor man. It won't take you long."

"I'm sure that's true." He studied the man's face. It had aged well, the features still firm, the jawline taut. He'd been handsome in his youth. He was handsome still.

Hamish said, "Ye've been verra' blind."

"You say you've never married?"

"That's true."

"But a man can have a child out of wedlock. Who was the mother?"

He saw the flick of anger touch Lovat's eyes. Instantly it was gone.

Priscilla Bartram and Marcella Trowbridge were too young. Swift's housekeeper, Susan, wasn't old enough. Who else, then? Burrows's daughter? The wrong age again. Mrs. Percy might know. But there wasn't time to consult her. Leave this man here and he could vanish before the police arrived to arrest him. He had nothing to hold him here.

But *was* he MacLaren? And was Catriona Beaton his granddaughter? There could be other secrets he didn't want the world to know.

Where did the truth lie? If this man had continued to live in Cambridgeshire, something must have held him here.

Rutledge pictured the windmill in his mind, the house that had burned to the foundations. The Trowbridge cottage close by. The Bower House.

A bower.

A retreat. A hideaway.

From what?

And then he had it. The sophisticated woman who had preferred that lonely cottage near the windmill when she might have lived a very different life in Bury. The woman who had willed it to her granddaughter, not her son.

Had she had a lover—and another child?

He remembered something Miss Trowbridge had said. About her father being the village doctor who bought this cottage for her grandmother when she was a young widow. But had he? Was it her own money? Her grandmother had very likely married well, possibly even an arranged marriage in her day, rather than a love match. Her husband had died, and for some reason she'd not wanted to go on living in Bury. Had she already met Angus MacLaren? Or was that after she came to Wriston to live? She had let her granddaughter make friends with the man . . . Marcella had liked him. Unaware that he must have been her grandmother's lover for many years.

How had she concealed a pregnancy? She could have gone away for a time, and then left the child to grow up in Scotland with MacLaren's family. She might even have visited in the summer. No one would question her wish to travel.

And after her death, Angus had stayed by Marcella as long as he could. Beside the cottage he'd known well. Until his grief for her grandmother became more than he could bear, when he'd burned down the windmill cottage and its secrets and gone away. To Scotland? But he'd been drawn back. And he'd left Clarissa to keep Marcella company. It could be checked later, all these details.

Rutledge said aloud, "Marcella couldn't be your child. There was another one, one that Mrs. Trowbridge couldn't claim. One who must have been raised in Scotland with cousins. Catriona was that child's daughter. And you killed two men for not taking proper care of her."

The man who called himself Lovat lunged to his feet.

"I'll see you dead if you drag *her* name into this business."

"You'll have to stand trial. There's blood on your hands, MacLaren. The truth will have to come out. Whether you like it or not."

"I learned to kill in the Scouts. You don't forget how to do that."

"No. You were very clever. If I hadn't discovered something you'd written, hidden in a drawer in Herbert Swift's house, I'd never have found you."

"They never found *her*. Catriona. I don't think they really looked, although they claimed they had, claimed they'd found her body in a wood. One more serving girl. But she shouldn't have been a servant. She was educated, she had prospects. Still, she was mad to go to London. After all, she had an English heritage. And that was the simplest way."

"Why did she leave the Hutchinson household? Was it Hutchinson who drove her away?"

"He drove his own wife to suicide. A servant girl would be easier."

"I can see killing Hutchinson. But Swift?"

"He did nothing. When Catriona went missing, he did *nothing*. I wrote to ask what had become of her. I asked him to act for me. As a solicitor. He told me I should find someone in London."

"What did you do?"

"I went to the police. But everything pointed to her leaving of her own accord. I knew better, and still they wouldn't listen. They told me the case was closed. I investigated on my own, but there was no trace of her. No cabbie who had helped her with her valises. No porter at the railway station who had helped her on a train. I knew then she was dead. That he must have lured her away and killed her."

But Hutchinson hadn't been in London when Catriona had left the house. And he hadn't been home when his wife killed herself.

A scrap of conversation came back to him.

What had Miss Hutchinson said?

I'm well aware of the pitfalls and dangers of being a woman without protection. We lived in lodgings, we were dependent on his officer's pay. We were shunned by people who now respect us. I wore gowns I'd refurbished myself because I couldn't afford new ones. If I survived, I believe she was clever enough and determined enough to survive as well.

What if Hutchinson hadn't tried to seduce Catriona? What if he'd fallen in love with her? And she with him? Even a man out for the main chance might fall in love with a poor girl. Only he hadn't known, had he, that she came from very different stock.

His wife had died while he was in France. Catriona had disappeared while he was away in Gloucestershire.

Miss Hutchinson hadn't come north when her brother was murdered . . .

That handsome house on a handsome square.

Rutledge said, "Dear God. I'm not sure that he did."

"Did what? What are you talking about, man?"

"I don't know that Hutchinson had anything to do with your granddaughter's death. It was his sister. And that house. It had belonged to Mary Hutchinson. She was pregnant. The child had died, but there was every likelihood she would have another. An heir. The question is, was she driven to kill herself, or was she murdered?"

"What are you saying?"

"I'm not sure. But I think both of us got it wrong. It wasn't Hutchinson who was responsible for her death, although he was self-absorbed enough not to realize his role in it. It was his sister. Any woman Hutchinson married would be mistress of that house. And now Miss Hutchinson is. Because everyone else is dead. Her brother's wife. Catriona. And the Captain."

He was still trying to work it out, his mind rapidly sorting through what he knew. But MacLaren was there before him. He picked up one of the lengths of wood that framed the hurdles and swung it with all the strength of his lean body.

Rutledge dropped like a stone, in spite of Hamish's warning. His guard down, it had taken precious seconds to realize what was happening.

Dazed, his wits scattered, he lay there, fighting to hold on to consciousness. And then Thornton was bending over him.

Even as he did so, he straightened, whirled around, and said, *"He's taken the motorcar."*

Rutledge struggled to his feet. "It's MacLaren. He's on the way to London."

"There's my motorcar. But it's in Isleham."

Shaking his head, desperate to clear it, Rutledge said, "We don't have time. Find someone with a motorcar. Quickly." He put up a hand and touched the wetness on the side of his head. His fingers came away dark with blood.

"You're in no condition to drive. You need a doctor. Let Warren deal with it. They'll find him soon enough."

"Damn it, I'm ordering you. Find a motorcar. You can drive it, can't you? We can't let him reach London or there will be another murder. I'll explain on the road."

Thornton turned on his heel and ran out toward the street. It was nearly a quarter of an hour later when he came back, driving a well-polished Rolls with a dark green body. Rutledge was standing by the road, waiting.

"I had to twist some arms. Get in."

Rutledge did. It was a chauffeur-driven car, and they sat up front. Rutledge could smell something but dared not look over his shoulder. Later he discovered a bouquet of wilting heliotrope in the crystal vase on the lady's side of the passenger compartment. For hours its heavy sweetness made him feel slightly ill.

Gingerly leaning his head back, he closed his eyes and let Thornton drive. After they had passed Newmarket, Thornton said, "Are you going to tell me what happened?"

"All right." He told the story slowly, putting it together in his own mind as he did.

Thornton swore. "It wasn't Hutchinson who killed Mary?"

"I've no doubt he neglected her. He was a selfish man, looking out for himself. Still, I wouldn't be surprised if the sister had done all she could to make her sister-in-law wretched enough to believe he didn't care for her, only for the house and the money."

"I was there at your last meeting with her. A cold woman. She was sitting at the head of the table, did you notice? Her brother's chair. Not at what must have been her usual place. What do you think MacLaren will do?"

"I don't think he has a weapon." But what about that sharp knife used to cut the osiers and withies, the stiff stalks of reeds and young trees? Easier to carry inside a London house than a rifle.

Thornton was making good time, but they were still nearly half an hour behind MacLaren, and Rutledge's touring car was probably faster. As it was, they were thundering down the long straight roads. It would be different once they had left the Fens behind. Their speed would have to drop considerably. And so would MacLaren's.

It was some time after Cambridge that Thornton said, "He killed two people. MacLaren. The wrong two people, as it transpired. He'll kill her as well. I don't know that I wouldn't much prefer arriving too late to stop him. I loved Mary, you know. Very deeply. And there was nothing I could do."

"Just as well. You'd hang instead of MacLaren. Pull over, I'll drive now."

"You've a lump the size of a goose egg on the side of your head. I don't want to find myself in a ditch."

On the outskirts of London, late into the night, Rutledge said, "I'll drop you at Scotland Yard. Ask for Sergeant Gibson. If he isn't there, tell someone where to find us."

"I told you," Thornton said grimly, "I'll see this through."

"And if he's there? If he hasn't killed her by the time we reach the house? Will you stop him—or stop me?"

Thornton considered the question. "I'd rather not hang. That's the only reason I'd act. But if God is good, she'll be dead when we get there."

There was no time to argue, although Hamish was warning Rutledge that he was taking a grave risk. But Miss Hutchinson's life hung in the balance, and he would have to take his chances with Thornton.

The late traffic was heavy, laden wagons and lorries and vans bringing foodstuffs and flowers and everything else London lacked to stock the markets and the shops for the coming day. They followed a butcher's van, the back open, great carcasses of beef and pork swaying as it made its way over the uneven cobbles. And then they were in the clear, only a mile or less from the square where Miss Hutchinson lived. As they turned into the street, even in the gray light of a cloudy dawn, they could see Rutledge's motorcar standing before the house door.

"He's here."

Thornton sped down the street, braking sharply as they reached the house. The front door stood open, and they could see a lamp lit on a table by the stairs.

Thornton didn't waste time pulling in behind Rutledge's motorcar. He left the borrowed vehicle in the middle of the street and was close on Rutledge's heels as they raced to the door and up the stairs. Rutledge had no way of knowing which room belonged to Miss Hutchinson. He stopped at the top of the steps, and Thornton nearly plowed into him.

Somewhere they could hear a woman crying, soft mewing cries.

"This way, I think." Rutledge moved swiftly down the passage, found an open door, and stepped into the room.

It appeared to be the master bedroom, very masculine, with dark woods and heavy drapes over the windows. There were no lamps lit. Rutledge stepped forward and flung open the drapes. In the pale light coming through the glass, he could see Miss Hutchinson lying across her bed. A pool of dark blood had soaked the sheets and the coverlet, and her hair was black with it.

Cowering by the washstand, he saw Mrs. Cookson, the housekeeper. Looking up with tears running down her cheeks, she said, "I tried to stop him. I thought he would kill me too, when he was done."

"Where is he?"

"There." Thornton pointed to the shadows beside the bed. The hurdle maker was lying there, blood blackening the front of his shirt, his head bowed. Rutledge went across to him and knelt by his side while Thornton bent over Miss Hutchinson.

MacLaren was still alive. Just.

He glanced up at Rutledge, his eyes a fierce blue. "It's better this way. She told me. She took Catriona to the country and stabbed her. In a wood. Hers was the body the police had found, after all. My darling girl buried in a pauper's grave. She feared her brother was going to marry Catriona. He loved her, she said. And it wouldn't be like before, when he was away in France. I killed that woman in spite of her confession. She had no room for mercy. Nor did I." The Highland accent was more pronounced now, as if he were too tired to care.

Thornton said, from where he was standing by the bed, "Too late. She's gone."

The blue eyes were dulling, his breathing more difficult. "Don't tell Marcella it was the windmill keeper. He died long ago, anyway. He had nothing to live for."

"But you continued to live as Lovat."

MacLaren smiled faintly. "The Boers always said I couldn't be killed. I tried drink. It didn't dull the pain of losing Ellen Trowbridge. I tried to starve myself, and my body refused to quit. In the end, I came back to the Fens and simply existed. To tell truth, I'm glad it's finally over. There will be no trial. No need to sully *her* name."

He meant the woman he'd loved.

His body shuddered and the knife slipped out of his hand, falling down beside his hip. He paid it no heed. "I'm sorry for nothing. Except perhaps for the farmer, Burrows. He was merely a diversion. Still. It was his own stubbornness that nearly killed him. The wound was slight enough. I made sure of that."

And then he reached out, his fingers fastening over Rutledge's wrist. "Please. Tell them I killed for Catriona. A servant girl. But don't tell them who Catriona really was. Don't shame the memory . . ." His voice caught. Then it strengthened again. "I was always a killer. It was my skill, and they'd taught me well. *She* taught me love."

The grip tightened, almost as a death grip, and then MacLaren's hand fell away. The blue eyes were empty, the strong face now slack.

After a moment Rutledge reached out and touched the man's throat. Rising to his feet, he said, "He's dead."

"I'm glad he won't hang." Thornton walked away to the window. After a moment, he added in a very different voice, "How do you cope with this sort of thing? God, it brings back the war!"

But Rutledge was bending over Mrs. Cookson, helping her to her feet and drawing her out the door. "Go down to the servants' hall and send someone for the constable. Tell him to go for Sergeant Gibson at Scotland Yard. At once."

She clung to his arm, still weeping. "I couldn't stop him. He was too strong."

"You did your best," he told her. "Now you must go for the police."

"But you *are* the police."

He had to help her down the stairs, but when she saw the door standing wide, she seemed to come to her senses. She hurried to close it, and then turned toward the servants' hall. He watched until she had shut that door behind her, then went back up the stairs.

Thornton was still by the window. "Am I a suspect?"

"Until this is settled. So far we have no rifle. And until we do, you're under suspicion."

He cleared his throat. "Are you going to keep Miss Trowbridge's grandmother out of this?"

"Yes. And I'd advise you to do the same. All that matters right now is the hurdle maker Lovat whose granddaughter went missing in London."

Turning, Thornton nodded, then added, "I feel like a fifth thumb. How will you explain my presence to the Yard?"

Rutledge looked toward MacLaren's body, half hidden in the shadows by the bed. "I'll think of something," he said. "You're a witness, after all."

"I wish I hadn't been," Thornton said under his breath. Then aloud he said, "It's different from the war, isn't it? Murder."

Listening to Hamish in the back of his mind, Rutledge said curtly, "Very."

"Mary is avenged. Why don't I feel happier about that?"

But it was a rhetorical question, and Rutledge let it go. He went to another room and found two chairs, setting them out in the passage for himself and Thornton.

And there he waited for Sergeant Gibson and the machinery of the Yard.

Chapter 20

When the bodies had been removed and the master bedroom shut off, when Rutledge and Thornton and Mrs. Cookson had given their statements, it was finished.

Acting Chief Superintendent Markham made an appearance, striding into the house with the air of a man who was pleased to see an inquiry closed.

But Rutledge told him quite frankly that it was necessary to return to Wriston and Ely. "We don't have the rifle, you see. Or the helmet. We need them to connect the dead man with the shootings there. Otherwise, that inquiry is still open."

"See that you're quick about it, then." Markham rubbed his hands together in a gesture of satisfaction. "Took you long enough, Rutledge. But well done. Well done, I say." He seemed to notice Thornton. "Who is this?"

"His name is Thornton. He's been helping us with our inquiries."

Markham looked the other man up and down. "He has the look of a soldier." There was speculation in his gaze. "Certain he's no more than that?"

"Not unless the rifle turns up in his house."

Thornton threw Rutledge an angry look, but Markham said, "See it doesn't." And then he was gone, followed by one of his people.

"Who the hell was that?" Thornton asked. "I can't say I like him."

"He's my superior," Rutledge said mildly.

"More's the pity," Thornton retorted and walked out to the motor-car to wait.

Rutledge took two rooms in a hotel in Cambridge where they slept most of what was left of the day and started early the next morning for Soham. They had brought both motorcars in tandem, Rutledge's and the one Thornton had commandeered.

Rutledge had remembered the message from Inspector Warren that he'd neglected to answer, but it could wait another day. In Soham, after restoring the motorcar to its still irate owner, they searched both the small house where the man who called himself Lovat had lived and the shop where he dried the reeds and made his hurdles.

All they found were the belongings of a man who lived quietly and frugally. Rutledge even emptied the dustbins, and there he found several bloody bandages. Had MacLaren been wounded by Burrows's shotgun? It hadn't been visible. And it hadn't slowed the man. But here was proof.

Where then was the rifle?

Standing where Lovat was sitting when he first saw him, Rutledge looked down at the bottom of the unfinished basket the man had been making. A rain had fallen, and the reeds had begun to curl.

MacLaren had been a tormented man, and Rutledge knew a little about torment. But it was Thornton who said, "I think he was glad of a reason to die. Finally. Better than the hangman."

The tone of his voice conveyed what he'd left unsaid, that he also knew what torment was.

After a moment Thornton added, looking up and down the stream that flowed quietly just beyond where they were standing, "He must have known all these waterways. He went out to find his materials for the hurdles. He could have stowed anything anywhere. It would take weeks to search." Turning back to Rutledge, he went on. "Are you going to keep me here until you find the rifle?"

"If I must." He walked back into the house. "He was a tidy man. I don't think he would leave the rifle to be caught in a storm and ruined." Stepping outside again, he said, "But there is one place he could be sure to leave something. Back to the motorcar, Thornton."

They drove on to Wriston but didn't stop until they'd reached the windmill and the ruins of the keeper's house.

"Why here?"

"Because no one would connect anything found here with the hurdle maker in Soham."

He got out of the motorcar and moved carefully into the foundations. Anything salvageable had been taken away long since. The rough stones of the foundation itself were still in place. The ground here was too low to dig a proper cellar, but there were steps leading up to what once had been the main door, and opposite them on the far side, a second pair of steps going to the small back garden and the path to the windmill.

Was this the reason why the ruins were said to be haunted? Because MacLaren had come here, like a shadow in the night, to retrieve what he needed?

Rutledge searched carefully, testing every crack and crevice, to see if it yielded anything that might be a hiding place. It would make sense, if Rutledge found what he was looking for here.

But there was nothing, not so much as a hollow behind those steps, no receptacle large enough for a rifle and the other things the man would wish to hide. Still—it couldn't have been left where someone might stumble over it—a curious child or a scavenging Traveler.

Rutledge refused to give up, probing every inch of the ruins.

Nothing.

Where, then?

Thornton swore as he tripped on rubble. "He'd have broken his neck, coming here in the dark. He must have been more clever than that."

"What are you looking for?"

The two men turned in unison. Marcella Trowbridge was standing in the road, watching them.

Rutledge said, "There has been a suggestion that the shooter might have left his rifle here."

"But that's impossible. Who would do such a thing?"

Rutledge's gaze met Thornton, then he said, "Someone from Soham."

"Oh. No one I know. That's all right, then."

He went on searching, to no avail, and then walked to the windmill. But that was now managed by the ironmonger, he remembered as he looked up at the weather-stained sails. It would not serve MacLaren to have the ironmonger pawing through his things, out of simple curiosity.

Miss Trowbridge was still there on the road watching. Rutledge said to Thornton, "For the love of God, go and distract her."

Reluctantly Thornton did as he was told.

Rutledge moved on to the humpback bridge, scrambling down the embankment to look under the arch for a hiding place.

But there was nothing here either. And in a storm the high water would brush against anything hidden here and possibly dislodge it.

He clambered back up to the road again and stood there, wiping his muddy hands on his handkerchief.

Had MacLaren lied to him?

Or had he hidden his proof where no one would ever expect to find it?

Think, he ordered himself. If it wasn't the windmill house, if it wasn't the bridge or the mill, where then? Miss Trowbridge's house?

Hamish said, "He wouldna' put the lass at risk."

That was true. What's more, she believed MacLaren to be dead.

What do I know about the man?

Rutledge stood there, searching through every fact he'd learned about the hurdle maker, and still he came up with nothing.

Was Thornton his killer after all? At the very least, of the two men, Thornton had easier access to the new army rifles than MacLaren did. After all, MacLaren had used a knife, not a rifle, to kill Miss Hutchinson.

He refused to believe it. It was Catriona who connected the two dead men. Not Mary Hutchinson.

Then where was the proof he needed?

A memory came back to him. The Green Man. The church and the feel of those cold, worn steps leading up into the pulpit, pressing hard into his back. The Rector, Mr. March, finding him there.

No, before that. *What had he seen in the churchyard?*

And then he remembered.

The mausoleum. But Miss Trowbridge's parents had not liked Wriston. They would surely have been interred in Bury.

He hurried back to where Miss Trowbridge was standing with Thornton. "Where was your grandmother buried, do you know?"

"She had a horror of being in the ground. There's a mausoleum in the churchyard here in the village."

"It must be locked. Most such tombs are. Do you have the key?"

"Do I—I never thought about it. I expect it's in my grandmother's things. My father was not happy about her choice. He wanted her to be laid to rest in Bury, beside her husband. But she insisted, and it was her money, after all. So she built it. I wondered if she hadn't loved my grandfather very much. She'd married him to please her own father.

He died quite young. She went away for a time, to mourn properly, she said. And when she came back, she wanted to live here. In this cottage bought for her. She told me several times that her heart was here, not in Bury."

Rutledge said earnestly, "If there is a key, I must open the mausoleum. No," he added as she started to interrupt him. "Only the outer door. It's unlikely, of course. But someone could have found a way in."

"That's horrible."

She turned, was leading the way toward her cottage, and inside, she left them standing in the small parlor while she went on into her bedroom. In a few minutes she came back with a lovely carved box in her hands.

"It's from Africa, this box. She never told me how she'd come by it, but it held her most treasured things. I never felt like opening it. I still don't. It's—very personal."

She held the box out to Rutledge, and he took it over to one of the chairs by the cold hearth. Clarissa stirred from her bed on the far side, then subsided into sleep once more.

"It's locked," Rutledge said, looking up from his examination of the top.

Miss Trowbridge, frowning, said, "I believe the key is there. On the side."

And she was right. He found the key set into a small opening in the side of the box, invisible if you didn't know where to look for it. Carefully removing it, he inserted it into the lock and turned it. Lifting the lid, he looked inside. Thornton came to stand beside him. Miss Trowbridge made a movement to stop him, and then stayed where she was.

There were papers inside. One of them caught Rutledge's eye. In an elegant copperplate it said:

My Last Wishes. To be opened by my granddaughter after my death.

Rutledge glanced up at Miss Trowbridge. It was not his place to look at these papers. But Marcella Trowbridge had told him she had not wished to pry.

And so he broke the seal and took a sheet of paper out of the envelope.

Miss Trowbridge cried, "Stop. You were looking for a *key*!"

He had already seen a name. He said, "You must read this, I think."

"No, I told you. She was a very private person, my grandmother. I won't pry into her secrets now. It would be wrong."

"You have no choice. Look." He passed the sheet to her.

She gazed at him for a moment, then against her will, unfolded the sheet.

"Oh!" she gasped, reading it once, then going back to the beginning. "She wants—she wanted Angus MacLaren to be buried beside her. *Angus?* The windmill keeper? But why?"

"I believe it must be the same man," he said carefully. "Perhaps he was a friend when she needed one."

"But I thought he was long since dead. I don't know what to do."

Thornton spoke then. "He died in London this past week. I—happened to come across the obituary. Would you like for me to see to it for you?"

She stared at him. "In the normal course of events, I'd have asked Mr. Swift."

"I owe Mr. MacLaren a debt," Thornton answered her. "This will be my opportunity to repay it."

Unconvinced, she turned to Rutledge. "I don't know what to think."

He said gently, "It would appear that she cared for him. You must do as she asked."

"She liked him—she—I was so young, you see." Frowning, she added, "I liked him too. I've told you that. But to bury him beside her? I don't think that would be right."

Rutledge handed her the envelope. "It's what she wanted. You can see for yourself. She expected you to do as she asked."

"But what will people *think*?"

"Does it really matter?"

"No," she said slowly. "Not really."

He went back to the box, and in it he found a record of the marriage of Ellen Trowbridge and Angus MacLaren. Next to it, he found the record of a child's birth. Catriona's mother, who had married a Beaton.

She hadn't been able to keep the child. But she had kept this piece of paper, if any question had ever come up about its heritage.

Society wouldn't have approved of what she had done. Not her family nor her friends in Wriston or Bury. It would appear that there was too vast a difference between the man and the woman in station and in everything else, in spite of his standing in his own glen. What's more, according to the marriage record, he'd been two years younger. But they had found a way. And no one had ever guessed.

He felt a great sadness for Ellen Trowbridge and Angus MacLaren. The Bower House . . .

Rutledge set these back into the box. He didn't think Marcella Trowbridge was ready to learn the truth about the grandmother she'd adored.

At the bottom of the box, under the papers, lay the photograph of a small child sitting on the back of a pony. The background wasn't the landscape of the Fens. A baronial hall and mountains instead. Catriona's mother as a little girl? And beneath that lay the heavy iron key to the mausoleum. Someone had put it there. Had Angus been given another?

Closing the box, Rutledge gave it to Thornton, who handed it to Miss Trowbridge.

"What do you want with the mausoleum key?" she asked again, worried. "I don't understand. Why would someone desecrate a tomb?"

"I'm only being thorough," he said with a smile. "We were looking for something and thought perhaps it had been left here. By the ruins—er—where no one would think to look for it. Or in a mausoleum where no one would think to search. I shan't disturb your grandmother. It will be all right."

"I'll come with you," she said resolutely.

He glanced at Thornton. "I think it would be best if both of you stayed here. This is police business, after all. I'll bring the key back shortly."

Still she protested, and it was several minutes before Rutledge could persuade her that it would attract unwanted attention if all three went to the churchyard.

"It won't be in her coffin, what I'm looking for. Just inside the door." He hoped he was telling the truth. It was what he believed MacLaren had done. Which meant that there was another key to the mausoleum and MacLaren must have kept it on his person. He hadn't searched the dead man's pockets, he'd left that to Sergeant Gibson. The list of items would be on file at the Yard . . .

"Is it something—awful?"

"Nothing so important. That's why I haven't asked for a search warrant."

Finally she agreed to allow him to take the key. He could see that Thornton was eager to accompany him, but he didn't want the man there, any more than he wanted Miss Trowbridge to come.

Walking out to his motorcar, the key heavy in the palm of his hand, he wondered if he was right. If he would find what he wanted.

It took no more than five minutes to drive down to the church. He left the motorcar behind some trees, out of sight, and then crossed the grassy churchyard to the mausoleum.

It was built more like a Greek temple than the usual edifice of this kind, he thought, and perhaps that was what Ellen Trowbridge had wished to have. He stood for a moment, looking up at the inscription above the door. She had been buried under the name of the husband who had died. Had that rankled?

And then he set the key into the lock.

He expected the key to turn with some difficulty. Instead it clicked open without a sound, and he swung the gate wide. It moved smoothly on its hinges. The second lock yielded just as easily. And he knew then what he would find inside.

There was an opaque glass window in the back of the mausoleum. It gave a little light, enough to see the coffin of Mrs. Trowbridge to the right, and an empty ledge to the left.

And against the back wall in the space between the ledges was a small altar with a photograph and a candle and, of all things, a Celtic cross, not an Anglican one.

On the floor just inside the door was a large canvas sack.

So it was here after all. Almost a sacrilege, to leave evidence of murder in the tomb of the woman MacLaren had loved so deeply.

Or perhaps it was not. Catriona was her granddaughter too. And if she loved Angus MacLaren, then she knew the depths he was capable of. It was possible that she herself would have wanted to see Catriona's persecutor dead.

Only MacLaren's revenge had gone wrong. Was that why he'd killed himself? Or had it been to spare Marcella Trowbridge the truth about her grandmother's other life? Or for Ellen MacLaren?

There was no way of knowing now.

Rutledge knelt on the smooth cool stone, his hands on the length of rope that tied the top of the sack. Then, remembering that he was in the churchyard where anyone might pass by, he decided against opening the sack here. Instead he picked it up to carry back to his motorcar. It didn't clank or rattle, he noticed. Giving nothing away.

There was no one about when he locked the door and the gate again. He shouldered the heavy sack, pocketed the key, and started for the motorcar.

Halfway there, a voice called to him.

Rutledge turned to see Andrew March striding across the church-yard toward him.

Tensing in every muscle, he stopped.

"What have you got there?" March asked, coming up to him.

"Evidence, I'm afraid," he said. "It's a police matter."

March looked around. "Did you collect it *here,* in the churchyard?"

"It was hidden here. It belongs—belonged to someone in Soham."

"Ah. Not a Wriston man, then. Well. I'll pray for his soul all the same. And how are you? Have you considered my offer of a little talk?"

"I—don't believe I'm ready. But I'm grateful, all the same."

March nodded. "I understand. But I will tell you that the longer you keep your fears trapped in your head, the harder it will be to free yourself from them. Remember that. And if you don't come to me, find someone else to trust."

Rutledge said, before he could stop himself, before Hamish could warn him to beware, "It was a letter, Rector. I received it just before I came north. It was from someone I cared for. Rather deeply." He stopped, and then added, "It closed a door."

It was offered as an explanation for Hamish's presence, vigorously pursuing him from the time he left London. He wasn't certain the Rector would understand. But it was the best he could do.

The letter had come from Meredith Channing. It had told him she wouldn't be returning to England, that she was staying in Belgium with the man she believed was her missing husband.

I must do this, she had written. *For my sake as well as yours. We would have nothing if we tried to build on a broken past. But I have given my heart in your keeping. And if you find someone else to love, then you must promise to send it back, so that I will know.*

And enclosed in the letter was a gold locket on a chain. The initials engraved on the front were those of her maiden name, not Channing.

He'd thought it must have belonged to her as a young girl, for it was small and delicate, the sort of thing a child might have been given on her birthday. His parents had given his sister Frances a similar gift when she was twelve. Not a heart but a book that opened to show the photographs of her parents.

He hadn't opened Meredith Channing's locket. He didn't want to see what was inside.

March, watching him, said, "And so the nightmares have been worse. Yes, it explains so much. Well, I'm here. You can always find me here."

And he turned to walk away, not looking back.

Rutledge carried the canvas sack the rest of the way to his motorcar, and there he opened it.

Inside, well wrapped in wool, he found the steel helmet that a German sniper had worn, a Lee-Enfield rifle, with the name H. R. I. BEATON roughly carved into the stock, a medal with the same name on the back. Catriona's father, who had died in the war? Brought home on leave, a gift from a present-day sniper to a man who had served in the Lovat Scouts? There was also a German sniper scope. Under them lay a smaller holdall with what appeared to be the tools of a scissors sharpener, a long-haired wig made of silk threads, and a gray cloth.

Rutledge stared at the last item and then reached into his pocket for the handkerchief he'd kept there, folded over a gray thread. He gently put the two together.

The thread and the cloth matched perfectly.

Rutledge stowed the items in the boot of his motorcar, all except the medal. He saw no reason why that should become the property of the police. It belonged in the African box.

Driving back to the Bower House cottage, he found Miss Trowbridge and Thornton waiting for him in the parlor.

She rose at once as he came in the door, saying, "What did you find?"

He handed her the medal. "I was mistaken. There was nothing to find. Except this, caught in the doorway. Someone must have wanted your grandmother to have it."

She looked at it, then turned it over. "Beaton? But I don't know anyone by that name."

"Perhaps your grandmother did. I shouldn't worry about it, if I were you. I'd put it in her box. After all, she'd have explained if she'd wanted you to know."

Nodding, she said, "Yes, of course," and then took the key from him as well.

Rutledge turned to leave. Thornton hesitated. "I'll be in touch," he said finally to Marcella before they walked to the door.

Miss Trowbridge, smiling, thanked him for offering to see to the windmill keeper's remains, and then she stood in her doorway, watching as the two men went out to the motorcar.

After they were well away, Thornton said, "What did you discover? Surely it wasn't just that medal?"

Rutledge pulled to the side of the road. It was empty in both directions, the day quiet, the land basking in the sun. He went to the boot, retrieved the sack, and showed Thornton the contents.

He whistled. "Good God. Is that what he was wearing when he shot Swift?"

"Very likely."

"Where's the straw suit he wore when he shot Burrows?"

"If he was as clever as I think he was, he's burned it long since."

Rutledge showed him the thread and how it matched the gray cloth, explaining the connection with Ely Cathedral.

Thornton shook his head. "Remarkable. His planning—I couldn't have—I'd have been caught straightaway."

Rutledge put everything back in the boot, got back behind the wheel, then turned to stare at Thornton.

"If I had obtained a search warrant, what would I have found in your house?"

Thornton blinked. Then he said, "Only a few unimportant souvenirs."

Rutledge nodded. "I thought as much," he replied dryly.

I nspector Warren was not happy to have missed the conclusion of the inquiry. He looked at the items that Rutledge had spread across his desk, and said, "You're sure of your information? You're satisfied with it?" His glance strayed to Thornton, standing in the doorway. "It will all be in your report?"

Rutledge said, "Everything you will need to know will be in my report. I'll finish it tonight." It was not quite what Warren had asked for.

But the Inspector was moving on to what had happened in London. "And you say this man Lovat is dead?"

"Ruskin and others in Soham can show you his place of business and where he lived. They should be searched."

"Then why were these items found in Wriston?"

"Would you keep evidence that would send you to the hangman in your house?"

"No, I expect I wouldn't."

They went over the details a second and a third time before Warren was satisfied. And then he remembered.

"That washerwoman. The one you questioned. She sent me an urgent message. I passed it on to you. What did she want?"

Rutledge had all but forgot about the messenger and his urgent summons.

"I haven't spoken to her yet."

"Then I'll go with you."

Hamish was in the rear of the motorcar as Inspector Warren stepped in. Rutledge tried to shut the thought out of his mind as Thornton turned the crank and they went to find Mrs. Boggs.

They were forced to wait for more than an hour until she came home from her work in the households of the well-to-do.

Her face was flushed, her eyes tired, but she smiled when she saw the three men on her doorstep.

"Well, then," she said, "I thought perhaps it wasn't important. What I've got to say. No one came to ask."

"I was in London," Rutledge told her. "Mr. Thornton here has also been helping us with our inquiries, and you know Inspector Warren, I think."

"Indeed," she said, nodding to him. She insisted that they come inside and have a cup of tea, and Warren, trying to quell his impatience, reminded her that he was expected back at the police station sooner rather than later.

Disappointed, she offered them the chairs in her tiny front room and sat on the end of her own as she faced them.

"You'd said, Mr. Rutledge, that if I remembered anything I thought might be important I ought to speak to Mr. Warren, here. And I did. I don't quite know what brought it back to mind. I was doing some mending at the time, so I expect it was looking for my scissors."

"What did you see?"

"I did tell you that I came quickly to see what the fuss was about. There were all these ladies and gentlemen come rushing out of the church, staring up where that poor man, Captain Hutchinson, was lying. It was then I saw him. The scissors grinder. He came out of the Cathedral behind them and walked away down the street there, toward the school or perhaps the shops. He had his canvas holdall, and I wondered what he was doing in the wedding, if someone putting up the ribbons and the flowers had sent for him. And then the police came, and he went clear out of my head."

"Did you know him?"

"I'd seen him there and about. But he seemed a little taller than I remembered. I expect that was just because he was standing a little straighter in that company. I mean to say, he was the *scissors grinder*. The old man. As ordinary as can be. Still, I thought perhaps he might have seen something, and you'd want to question him if you hadn't already."

"Yes, that's very true, Mrs. Boggs. We appreciate your help," Rutledge said. "No one else reported seeing this man." But he was thinking that even if he'd known about the scissors grinder, it wouldn't have led to Lovat. Now, however, it reinforced what he knew.

They rose to leave, and Mrs. Boggs, basking in their gratitude, thanked them for coming, as if they had been valued guests.

In the motorcar, Rutledge said to Inspector Warren, "This scissors grinder. Who is he?"

"Old as he is, he gets about on his bicycle, going door to door, or wherever anyone stops him and asks for his services. He was at our kitchen door only last week. My wife was complaining that her scissors and some of the knives needed a new edge. My God, it never occurred to me to ask if he'd been in the Cathedral that day."

"I doubt he was. But someone had a bicycle and tools. And he went unnoticed because everyone was accustomed to seeing him—or someone like him—around the countryside."

"He's a religious man," Warren said. "He's often coming in or out of a church."

And MacLaren had somehow discovered that. It had been useful.

Thornton, listening, said, "Dear God."

Rutledge knew what he was thinking. That whatever he himself had considered doing to Captain Hutchinson, it was MacLaren's clever plan that had made it possible to kill the man.

They left Inspector Warren at the police station, still fingering the items from the canvas sack, as if still only half convinced that Rutledge was right.

From there, Rutledge drove to Isleham and set Thornton down at his house.

"It was a near-run thing," Thornton said. "I could be facing trial right now."

"Is that why you were searching for the killer on your own?"

"I wanted to know who held a grudge stronger than mine. I wanted to know who had killed the man I hated so much. I didn't know what hate was."

"Do something about your own rifle," Rutledge warned him. "Don't leave it for someone else to find."

"I told you, I have nothing more than a few souvenirs."

Rutledge said nothing, his gaze never leaving Thornton's face.

"Damn it, you're as sharp as that man Belford," Thornton said finally. Then, "You must have kept your service revolver."

Rutledge had. It lay in his trunk beneath the bed. Waiting until Hamish became unbearable. Cleaned, oiled, and ready to use.

Thornton must have read something in his face, in spite of his effort to school his expression.

"Most of us need a way out," he said with a nod, and walked to his front door. Opening it, he went inside, without looking back.

Rutledge, trying to ignore Hamish's voice from the empty rear seat, turned the motorcar toward Wriston.

There was Constable McBride to see, and then one last night at Miss Bartram's while he wrote his report for Inspector Warren and another for Acting Chief Superintendent Markham. A cleverly expurgated version, both of them. The MacLaren laid to rest in the mausoleum would have no connection with the man Lovat in Soham. It was not necessary to ruin more lives. Justice had been served.

He was nearly to Wriston when he noticed a bicycle approaching. As it got closer, he saw the lined face and long white hair of the scissors grinder, his satchel over his handlebars, his eyes tired.

Rutledge stopped and offered him a lift to wherever he was going.

Insights,
Interviews
& More . . .

Meet Charles Todd

CHARLES TODD is the *New York Times* bestselling author of the Inspector Ian Rutledge mysteries, the Bess Crawford mysteries, and two stand-alone novels. A mother-and-son writing team, they live in Delaware and North Carolina. ᴄᴧ

How Rutledge Finally Got to the Fen Country

An Essay from the Authors

WE LIKE TO SET OUR MYSTERIES in different parts of England, mainly because a new place is always exciting to explore, but also because each setting brings something special to the books. Small as it is, England is quite varied—a few miles this way or that can change what you see and what you feel, and offer a very different history to enrich the story and the characters.

We'd always skipped over the English Fen Country, where *Hunting Shadows* is set. Dorothy L. Sayers's marvelous Lord Peter Wimsey mystery, *Nine Tailors*, was such a favorite we didn't think we could possibly write a finer one for that part of England. And yet there the Fen Country was, tempting us every time we passed through it and saw its potential as a backdrop for murder. And we wondered if we dared to use it. Finally, two years ago we had an unusual opportunity to spend some time in a slightly different part of the countryside from where the Wimsey had been set. And while there, exploring Ely and its amazing cathedral, wandering through the outlying villages where the secretive, marshy fens had been before the drainage began, we could feel an idea stirring. Before we left, it had grown so strong we knew we couldn't put it off any longer: ▶

3

How Rutledge Finally Got to the Fen Country *(continued)*

Rutledge had to visit the strange, flat, watery landscape that had so attracted us.

Looking down from the tower of Ely Cathedral gave us the first step of our plot, and it was so exciting that we couldn't wait to get back to the computer. We could see how war and love and hate could end in an implacable will to murder. The hardest part was saying goodbye to the local characters at the end of the book. We'd come to know them so well; we'd followed Rutledge as he interviewed them and questioned them and suspected them. And yet he also saw the human side of all of them. It brings home the fact that a good detective, whether Wimsey or Rutledge, always shares his insights with the reader standing at his shoulder. To let them see his world for themselves. ❧

Reading Group Guide

1. How does the strange flat world of the Fens add to this story? Does their past still shape their present in 1920?

2. The only witness to either murder describes the killer as a monster. What was your own reaction to this description?

3. Women play a subtle role in this story, although the victims and suspects are men. What struck you most about each of them?

4. Rutledge digs deep into the crime he's investigating, determined to reach the truth. How does this reveal his character and his qualities as a policeman?

5. If Rutledge had failed to find the link between victims and killer, could this have been the perfect crime?

6. How has war affected not only the Fen Country, but many of the people in this story? How have they coped with those changes? For better or worse?

7. Rutledge can't bring himself to speak of Hamish to the kindly vicar who offers to help him. Do you think he will ever be able to talk about his war? Why? Or why not?

8. Why does Rutledge prefer to keep a suspect with him, instead of putting him in jail? How did their relationship change on the return journey? ▶

Reading Group Guide *(continued)*

9. Rutledge makes the decision not to tell Miss Trowbridge the truth about her family's past. Do you think he did the right thing? Why?

10. Why is the title of this novel *Hunting Shadows*? ⌒

The History of Inspector Ian Rutledge:
A Complete Timeline of Major Events Leading Up to *Hunting Shadows*

June 1919—*A Test of Wills*

Ian Rutledge, returning home from the trenches of the Great War, loses his fiancée, Jean, after long months in the hospital with what is now called PTSD and faces a bleak future. Fighting back from the edge of madness, he returns to his career at Scotland Yard. But Chief Superintendent Bowles is determined to break him. And so Rutledge finds himself in Warwickshire, where the only witness to the murder of Colonel Harris is a drunken ex-soldier suffering from shell shock. Rutledge is fighting his own battles with the voice of Corporal Hamish MacLeod in his head, survivor's guilt after the bloody 1916 Battle of the Somme. The question is, will he win this test of wills with Hamish—or is the shell-shocked witness a mirror of what he'll become if he fails to keep his madness at bay?

July 1919—*Wings of Fire*

Rutledge is sent to Cornwall because the Home Office wants to be reassured that Nicholas Cheney wasn't murdered. But Nicholas committed suicide with his half sister Olivia. And she's written a body of war poetry under the name O. A. Manning. Rutledge, who had ▶

The History of Inspector Ian Rutledge
(continued)

used her poetry in the trenches to keep his mind functioning, is shocked to discover she never saw France and may well be a cold-blooded killer. And yet even dead, she makes a lasting impression that he can't shake.

August 1919—*Search the Dark*

An out-of-work ex-soldier, sitting on a train in a Dorset station, suddenly sees his dead wife and two small children standing on the platform. He fights to get off the train, and soon thereafter the woman is found murdered and the children are missing. Rutledge is sent to coordinate a search and finds himself attracted to Aurore, a French war bride who will lie to protect her husband and may have killed because she was jealous of the murder victim's place in her husband's life.

September 1919—*Legacy of the Dead*

Just as Rutledge thinks he has come to terms—of a sort—with the voice that haunts him, he's sent to northern England to find the missing daughter of a woman who once slept with a king. Little does he know that his search will take him to Scotland, and to the woman Hamish would have married if he'd lived. But Fiona is certain to hang for murdering a mother to steal her child, and when she turns to him for help she doesn't know that Rutledge killed Hamish on the battlefield. He couldn't save Hamish—but Rutledge is honor bound to protect Fiona and the small child named for him.

October 1919—*Watchers of Time*

Still recovering from the nearly fatal wound he received in Scotland, Rutledge is sent to East Anglia to discover who murdered a priest and what the priest's death had to do with a dying man who knew secrets about the family that owns the village. But there's more to the murder than hearing a deathbed confession. And the key might well be a young woman as haunted as Rutledge is, because she survived the sinking of the *Titanic* and carries her own guilt for failure to save a companion.

November 1919—*A Fearsome Doubt*

A case from 1912 comes back to haunt Rutledge. Did he send an innocent man to the gallows? Meanwhile, he's trying to discover who has poisoned three ex-soldiers, all of them amputees in a small village in Kent. Mercy killings or murder? And he sees a face across the Guy Fawkes Day bonfire that is a terrifying reminder of what happened to him at the end of the war . . . something he is ashamed of, even though he can't remember why. What happened in the missing six months of his life?

December 1919—*A Cold Treachery*

Rutledge is already in the north and the closest man to Westmorland, where at the height of a blizzard there has been ▶

The History of Inspector Ian Rutledge
(continued)

a cold-blooded killing of an entire family, save one child, who is missing in the snow. But as the facts unfold, it's possible that the boy killed his own family. And where is he? Dead in the snow or hiding? And there are secrets in this isolated village of Urskdale that can lead to more deaths.

January 1920—*A Long Shadow*

A party that begins innocently enough ends with Rutledge finding machine gun casings engraved with death's-heads—a warning. But he's sent to Northamptonshire to discover why someone shot Constable Ward with an arrow in what the locals call a haunted wood. He discovers there are other deaths unaccounted for, and there's also a woman who knows too much about Rutledge for his own comfort. Then whoever has been stalking him comes north after him, and Rutledge knows that if he doesn't find the man, he'll die. Hamish, pushing him hard, is all too aware that Rutledge's death will mean his own.

March 1920—*A False Mirror*

A man is nearly beaten to death, his wife is taken hostage by his assailant, and Rutledge is sent posthaste to Hampton Regis to find out who wanted Matthew Hamilton dead. But the man who may be guilty is someone Rutledge knew in the war, a reminder that some were lucky enough to be saved while

Hamish was left to die. But this is a story of love gone wrong, and the next two deaths reek of madness. Is it madness? Or were the women mistaken for the intended victim?

April 1920—*A Pale Horse*

In the ruins of Yorkshire's Fountains Abbey lies the body of a man wrapped in a cloak, the face covered by a gas mask. Next to him is a book on alchemy, which belongs to the schoolmaster, a conscientious objector in the Great War. Who is this man, and is the investigation into his death being manipulated by a thirst for revenge? Meanwhile, the British War Office is searching for a missing man of their own, someone whose war work was so secret that even Rutledge isn't told what that was or even his real name. Here is a puzzle requiring all of Rutledge's daring and skill, for there are layers of lies and deception, while a ruthless killer is determined to hold on to freedom at any cost.

May 1920—*A Matter of Justice*

At the turn of the century, during a war taking place far from England, two soldiers chance upon an opportunity that will change their lives forever. To take advantage of it, they will do the unthinkable and then put the past behind them. Twenty years later, a successful London businessman is found savagely and bizarrely murdered in a medieval tithe barn on his estate ▶

The History of Inspector Ian Rutledge
(continued)

in Somerset. Called upon to investigate, Rutledge soon discovers that the victim was universally despised. Even the man's wife—who appears to be his wife in name only—and the town's police inspector are suspect. But who among the many hated enough to kill?

June 1920—*The Red Door*

In a house with a red door lies the body of a woman who has been bludgeoned to death. Rumor has it that two years earlier, she'd painted that door red to welcome her husband back from the Front. Only he never came home. Meanwhile, in London, a man suffering from a mysterious illness goes missing and then just as suddenly reappears. Rutledge must solve two mysteries before he can bring a ruthless killer to justice: Who was the woman who lived and died behind the red door? Who was the man who never came home from the Great War, for the simple reason that he might never have gone? And what have they to do with a man who cannot break the seal of his own guilt without damning those he loves most?

July 1920—*A Lonely Death*

Three men have been murdered in a Sussex village, and Scotland Yard has been called in. The victims are soldiers, each surviving the nightmare of World War I only to meet a ghastly end in the quiet English countryside. Each man has been garroted, with small ID discs left in their mouths, yet no other clue suggests a motive or a killer. Rutledge understands all too well the darkness that resides within men's souls. Yet his presence on the scene cannot deter a vicious and clever killer, and a fourth dead soldier is discovered shortly after Rutledge's arrival. Now a horror that strikes painfully close to home threatens to engulf the investigator, and he will have to risk his career, his good name, even his shattered life itself, to bring an elusive fiend to justice.

August 1920—*The Confession*

A man walks into Scotland Yard and confesses that he killed his cousin five years earlier during the Great War. When Rutledge presses for details, the man evades his questions, revealing only that he hails from a village east of London. Less than two weeks later, the alleged killer's body is found floating in the Thames, a bullet in the back of his head. Rutledge discovers that the dead man was not who he claimed to be. The only clue is a gold locket, found around the victim's neck, that leads back to Essex and an insular village that will do anything to protect itself from notoriety.

Summer 1920—*Proof of Guilt*

An unidentified man appears to have been run down by a motorcar; a clue leads Rutledge to a firm, built by two families, famous for producing and ▶

The History of Inspector Ian Rutledge
(continued)

selling the world's best Madeira wine.
There he discovers that the current
head of the English enterprise is
missing. But is he the dead man?
And do either his fiancée or his jilted
former lover have anything to do with
his disappearance? With a growing
list of suspects, Rutledge knows that
suspicion and circumstantial evidence
are nothing without proof of guilt.
But his new acting chief superintendent
doesn't agree and wants Rutledge to stop
digging and settle for the easy answer.
Rutledge must tread very carefully, for it
seems that someone has decided that he,
too, must die so that justice can take its
course. ∾